D1522529

TO WHOM IT MAY CONCERN

PRISCILA UPPAL

A Novel

DOUBLEDAY CANADA

Doubleday Canada and colophon are trademarks

Library and Archives of Canada Cataloguing in Publication has been applied for

ISBN: 978-0-385-65993-2

Printed and bound in the USA

Published in Canada by Doubleday Canada,
a division of Random House of Canada Limited

Visit Random House of Canada Limited's website: www.randomhouse.ca

BVG 10 9 8 7 6 5 4 3 2 1

For my father,
Avtar

Lear: So young, and so untender?
Cordelia: So young, my lord, and true.

King Lear, William Shakespeare

PART ONE

BASIC STEPS IN A FORECLOSURE PROCEDURE

CLAIM FILED BY MORTGAGEE
Normally for foreclosure, immediate payment and possession.

↓

**NOTIFICATION PROVIDED TO
ALL SUBSEQUENT ENCUMBRANCERS**

↓

REQUEST TO REDEEM
Mortgagor provided with a 7-day accounting period followed by a 60-day grace period if Request to Redeem filed within 20 days of claim.

If no Request to Redeem, final order of foreclosure will be granted mortgagee.

If notice filed, mortgagee can still get order for payment and possession (but not foreclosure).

↓

IF PAYMENT NOT RECEIVED, FINAL ORDER OF FORECLOSURE IS ISSUED AT END OF GRACE PERIOD.

Thanksgiving

My kids have the manners of savages, he thinks, as his son lifts a slice of pepperoni pizza from the box to his open mouth, grasping the cheese with loose fingers, forcing separation from its neighbour. It's Monday October 13, 2003, Thanksgiving, and Hardev Dange hasn't enjoyed a traditional turkey dinner since his wife, Isobel, left. That first year, 1988, he tried preparing the meal himself— or, to be more exact, monitoring the meal once the homecare worker left. Manoeuvring around the stove was difficult, the door troublesome to control with only one good hand, and the pots of potatoes and carrots were nearly impossible to stir from his wheelchair. The bird burned. Meat dry, skin tough—the children didn't hide their distaste; the girl, twelve at the time, called it "disgusting" as she removed it from the oven, ribcage split, stuffing black. Hardev had forgotten the gravy. The mashed potatoes dripped. The only thing not spoiled was the canned cranberry sauce from Dominion's. Since then he'd given up on traditional trimmings for family gatherings—since then the Dominion's had become a Loblaws, then a No Frills—and opted to let the children choose takeout instead. Pizza won every time. A good choice, he admits. There's a pizza place on every block in the city, and it can be delivered every single day of the year, right to your home.

But Hardev still yearns for his family to be like other families on Ashbrook Crescent; now more than ever, with Mr. Karkiev signing notices in the back of his mind. He wishes they were settling into an afternoon of Thanksgiving Monday football (though he doesn't follow football, only hockey, as any good Canadian should), or card games around the dining-room table after the dishes are washed (though they have a dishwasher, and no one's played cards in the house since childhood Go Fish days). He doesn't want his girls, or even the boy, to mind the time, worrying whether they should scoot off to their mother's place to wish her a happy holiday too. Hardev Dange wants a white linen tablecloth (preferably handed down through the generations), pewter or brass candleholders, a horn filled with corn and gourds, and pumpkin pie. Yes, pumpkin pie, that glorious solid yet mushy mixture he tasted with delight shortly after immigrating from India. To add insult to injury, this year Isobel has insisted on keeping Dorothy because of the flu. "Dorothy wants to come, but she has the flu." That's what Isobel said. How can Hardev argue, when he has kept them all in the dark about the impending changes to his living arrangements, the legal papers, the telephone calls, and when it's common sense and general practice that he should be exposed to as little sickness as possible, even when it's his year to host Thanksgiving?

None of them bothers with utensils. Earlier, when the girl's new boyfriend, Victor, opened the cutlery drawer in the kitchen and began counting the nickel-plated knives and forks, she stopped him. "We use plastic. The less hassle the better." Tearing open a package of paper plates from the supply in the bottom cupboards under the microwave, she gleefully presented them as "The Family China."

At least Victor is dressed well, Hardev notes, and is wearing a pleasant sea-breeze cologne. No tie, but decent navy blue dress slacks and a creaseless beige Polo shirt. Tidy brownish-blond hair cut close to the scalp, clear coconut-white skin except for a few tiny pimples on his forehead, a thin nose, eyes slightly squinty and blue, he reminds Hardev of his old classmates at the London School of Economics.

The girl, Birendra, tries to catch a straying slice of pepperoni before it hits her maroon blouse. Too late. Rolling her eyes, she dabs at the sauce, smushing it into the clown-face napkin on her chest. "Was there a sale on?" she asks Hardev, nudging Victor and extracting another napkin from the small pile. "Did your home-care worker pick these out? The one who wears women's clothes?"

"I bought them for Dorothy. Dorothy likes clowns. And Ludwig, that's his name. He was fired four years ago, after he stole your mother's old skirts and high heels—the ones from her university days she left behind because they didn't fit—from the basement. I reported it when they went missing. You know that."

Bending over the cherrywood dining-room table he purchased from the Bay the year they moved into the house, a six-seater with a leaf that can add two more—although not comfortably, in this room lined with cabinets full of unused china and cassette tapes, boxes and boxes of newspapers, and a broken electric wheelchair that sits like a shamed sentinel in the corner—Hardev sips ginger ale from a bendable straw and tries to concentrate on the dinner, on his children around him, to keep his mind free of other thoughts. He doesn't want to be annoyed with the girl, but he is. And the boy, already on his third slice, will probably end the evening with a stomach ache.

"Dorothy's seventeen, Dad."

"That doesn't mean she doesn't like clowns anymore." He tries to catch his son's eye, send a signal to back him up, as family should, but Emile continues to munch on crust while Hardev stares futilely at his bushy black eyebrows—a Dange trait they all have in common, except Dorothy. "I thought for sure he'd stop fiddling around with magic books and hocus-pocus once he grew up. But look, that's what he studies at university. At a recognized university my boy studies superstitions and curses!"

Securing a fourth slice, Emile hands another to Victor. The two large pizzas are vanishing quickly, even though Hardev does not join in. Pizza isn't part of his diet, though he might be able to get away with a slice as a treat. Such things are permitted. But he sticks to his daily regimen of frozen Green Giant mixed vegetables, thawed in the microwave, and a single drumstick of Shake'n Bake original or barbecue chicken, cooked in bulk at the start of each month by Rodriguez, his main homecare worker for the last two years, and stored in dozens of plastic microwavable trays. A glass of ginger ale and a coffee pot of watered-down cranberry juice to aid digestion complete his meals. No dessert. Ever. The sugar balloons his stomach into a giant mixing bowl, and since he can't exercise, he always gains weight when he eats sweets—unlike his children, who are all, as he was before the accident, uniformly thin.

"Let's not argue," Birendra sighs, raising her deep brown eyes from her plate and correcting her hunched posture. "Today is a special day."

Yes, it is, Hardev agrees. Holidays are family days, special days, days the house is once again filled with his children. But he can see that the girl has slipped her hand underneath the table to grasp her boyfriend's. She always brings a boyfriend to each occasion. Even if they've only been dating a few weeks, she never arrives alone. With her mahogany skin, long black lashes, sleek legs, lean face (though she has always hated the tiny bump at the bridge of her nose), and very small breasts, she is assuredly pretty and has attracted all kinds of boys over the years, most of them white and preppy, donning each like a new bracelet or necklace, something to show off at the beginning of dinner, something easily forgotten. Victor, who has been admiring her hand in his, meets Hardev's gaze and, smiling awkwardly, lets go. Hardev does not want to upset the girl. It saddens him how often their short time together as a family is spent in uneasiness or outright discomfort, and now, more than ever, he wishes everyone would get along.

Though the dining room might be considered to be in disarray, in need of dusting, wiping, and proper sorting, with stacks of *Ottawa Citizens* along the wall, a broken record player and finicky sewing machine awaiting a new pedal, the table without a proper cloth, plates, or cutlery laid out, it is all still *theirs*, and he wishes he could stop time so they could all take a moment, as other families do for grace, to appreciate the house: the frayed but resilient light brown carpet, the chipped but bright white paint on the walls and ceiling, the sturdy nails that for fifteen years have held up school photographs of Emile and Birendra and the baby photograph of Dorothy taken hours after her birth, even the maudlin red-tinted glass chandelier with the dangling red beads, its cobwebbed red bulbs like jilted hearts. All this moves Hardev; it's not perfect, not expensive, their dining room, but it's *theirs*: loyal, reliable, worthy of some attention, like family. Or like family should be.

"Thank you for inviting me, Mr. Dange," Victor says, closing the lid of the second pizza box and rolling his sleeves back down.

"I didn't invite you. But you're welcome. My daughter's friends come and go. Come and go. My son's never come here. Call me Harry, like everyone else."

"They have their own families to visit," Emile mumbles absently, wiping a slice of green olive off his chin.

"Victor will be sticking around," Birendra states firmly, her straight black hair adding severity to her face. Smiling with the same awkwardness as when he released her hand, Victor now produces a bottle of white wine from the green shoulder bag tucked underneath her chair, then gestures silently at the open package of Styrofoam cups to Emile's left. Without hesitation, Birendra nods.

"It's nice wine," she offers, as Victor lines up four of the cups and uncorks the bottle with an opener also procured from her bag, "if a little on the warm side by now." Hardev stares at his plate. A few peas and carrots and a piece of broccoli remain. The drumstick was cold in the middle. The girl didn't pay attention when he instructed her on how long to heat it, and to turn the leg after a minute and then heat it a little longer, and now he guesses why. She's never brought wine to dinner before.

"I don't drink," Hardev informs Victor before he pours out a glass for him. "My medications prevent it. Besides, as my father used to say, *Nothing ever gets solved when drinking's involved.* You must know that the statistics—"

"Please, Dad. This once?" the girl pleads, pushing a Styrofoam cup across the table. "You can just have a little sip." But Victor fills it with ginger ale.

The couple stand and Hardev notices that Victor is as tall as he used to be, six foot one or two, head less than two feet from the flaking moulded ceiling. A good five-eight, the girl rests just underneath his chin as she leans backwards into his chest, like a shingle to a roof, their stance blocking the sight of his outmoded electric wheelchair, a tin snow shovel the boy bought at one of the many garage sales held by their old neighbours over the last year, and a box of tangerines. Birendra lifts her left hand and something twinkles in the red chandelier glow. "A toast! Victor wanted to make the announcement, but I wouldn't let him. Dad, Victor has asked me to marry him! Or I asked him, or we asked each other, really . . . Anyway, I can't remember how it went exactly, but we both said *Yes, Yes!* The wedding will be in May!"

Hand shaking—Hardev now sees that it is adorned with a diamond ring on a white gold or platinum band—Birendra edges back down to her seat and rests her cup of wine on the table. Victor lifts her hand again, kissing it warmly. Emile does nothing and says nothing, his face wide and expressionless, shoulders hunched. Hardev tries to shake off the desire to be back in his bedroom watching television, waiting for Rodriguez to put him on his side—tries to undo a wish for it to be the day before yesterday, the day of preparations, always full of hope about what one will do, what one will say; not today, the actual holiday, when things are always beyond his control. Why are holidays never as you imagine them? He knows this should be a happy moment, a proud moment, the kind of moment fathers live for, have speeches prepared for, dream about for decades, but the last few minutes have nothing in common with what he pictured yesterday in his mind. Nor do they correspond to any imaginings he's ever had about his children's engagement announcements. Naturally, he's assumed that one day the children will marry, but in his head he spends time with these suitors first, gets to know them, the child asks his permission, for his opinion and blessing—in the case of the boy, asks if his father approves of his choice—before anything moves further, certainly before a date is set. He never imagined his daughter would ask a young man to marry *her*, without her father's permission, without her father's advice. Yet here is this man, this Victor, whom he's met for the first time—the first time!—today, this stranger standing in the middle of his dining room in dress slacks and a Polo shirt, blue eyes twinkling like the girl's diamond, towering over them all as if he owns the place.

Impaling two peas on the plastic teeth of his fork, Hardev points them at Emile. "Did you know about this? Did you know and not tell me?"

The boy shrugs, stares blankly at his paper plate littered with abandoned crusts.

"What do you mean, *you* asked *him* or *he* asked *you*? Why did no one ask *me*? Victor? I don't even know your last name! Where did you come from? You have no right to intrude on my family occasion and . . . and . . . *who are you?*" Hardev can't bear to continue. It's late; he's too tired. He wants to escape from the table, but he doesn't have the strength to back out with his good hand, as it's sore from cutting up the chicken, and he's embarrassed that his bib has slipped into his lap, exposing his stomach. Racking his brain, he tries to remember what the girl said when she rattled off some information about this man named Victor over the phone, when she relayed she was bringing him to dinner. Now this Victor is his daughter's fiancé? This intruder? Did she say he specialized in political science when he was at Ottawa U? That he works for the government? Hardev thinks so, yes, he was pleased that he worked for the government, but what branch? What department? How did they meet? She didn't tell him. He remembers her saying that a large business is connected to his family. The Dairy Lane family fortune? He didn't expect these details to matter, so he didn't take them all in, either as points against the man or as things to be impressed by—she'd bring a new one at Christmas and he would sit in that same seat and eat pizza, as others had before him, but he wouldn't intrude or interfere with their holiday. Yes, she did, she did mention the Dairy Lane family fortune. He comes from money; that's why he's so well-dressed. That's why she has a sizable diamond on her finger. Dairy Lane money.

"No, no, Dad, please. Let's keep this a happy occasion. Victor, let's have a toast!"

Unable to respond, Hardev focuses on the china cabinet with the brass handles—twenty-four wine goblets of Italian crystal kept behind the glass, a wedding gift, anticipating the large dinner parties the happy couple would host throughout the years. When was the last time they were used? Yet he doesn't think it's fair to discount a thing's importance even if—like his legs—it hasn't been used in over a decade. And the Thanksgiving-themed tin plates of pumpkins and corn. When did anyone last look at them? Ten years ago? Earlier? Earlier, yes—earlier, when Isobel still lived with him, when *all* the children lived with him, and they crowded around this very table the nights when he was home for dinner and not in Africa or Asia or South America to survey hydroelectric plants. The Water King, his co-workers nicknamed him, when he took over the major hydro projects at the Canadian International Development Agency. *The Water King.*

"No disrespect was intended," Victor assures, squeezing the girl's arm to calm her. "I wish we had met before now, but—"

"Dad, you've had so many bladder infections lately. I didn't want to bother you . . ."

"I have only the best . . . the very best of intentions, sir."

Hardev recognizes in Victor's voice and composure training as a public speaker. Although Birendra beams, he suspects that Victor's declaration is a little old-fashioned for her taste. From earliest childhood Birendra has voiced dislike for anything old-fashioned. She was the one most in favour of the pizza dinners. Yet he knows Birendra has always dreamed of getting married, or at least of her wedding day. As a girl she cut out pictures from the Eaton's and Hudson's Bay catalogues and the Sears Christmas Wish Book, stylish modern pieces of furniture and jewellery so unlike the traditional and ornate styles he and Isobel favoured, and large, puffy white wedding dresses. A common enough childish pastime, but now Hardev shudders at the memory. Puffy white wedding dresses. Dozens of them. Not one sari. Not one gold bracelet or foot bangle. And if he offered her the Dange china cabinet as a wedding gift, would she take it, or would it not fit in with her desired decor? Would it only remind her of the faded walls, deteriorating shingles, or fraying carpet of her father's house?

"I too had the best of intentions," Hardev says, pushing his paper plate off his lap tray. "You are going to need a lot more than that to keep a marriage together."

"Of course, sir, I understand that," Victor adds, refraining from sipping his wine. "I've just been offered a promotion to Foreign Affairs, an area I know you know a lot about, and . . ."

"I guess your mother has approved this already?" Hardev asks, looking once more to Emile, whose head is still bent; then he gives up. What could the boy do? He was probably let in on the secret as Birendra was heating up Hardev's chicken leg in the microwave. A toast! Shouldn't Hardev give the toast? Is this not still his house? Is he not still the head of this family? If not the head, what else could he possibly be? Certainly not the legs. What does it matter if the dining room is not in perfect order, if they eat on paper plates? It doesn't give anyone the right to take away what's his.

Securing the straw in his ginger ale between his lips, Hardev hopes he can make it through the rest of the evening, regardless of his discomfort, his rising headache, and the upset stomach he knows he will share with his son even though he didn't partake of the pizza or the wine. Emile stands, while he cannot, to congratulate his sister and future brother-in-law—The Milk King, Hardev thinks, then berates himself to stop all this disappointment and enjoy, enjoy it, the boy and the girl and even this Victor, enjoy it, even without Dorothy, his little Dorothy, taken from this home too young, enjoy it, because tomorrow Mr. Karkiev from Crown Bank will be calling again about the notice of foreclosure on the house, the house Hardev has lived in for twenty-five years, with his wife and family, and then with his boy, before and after the accident, and it's now only a matter of time before he and the boy will have to find themselves another place to live. So, yes, one must enjoy it as long as one can, as long as the house is still in his name and his children can still meet here, even if they don't understand what it means to be a father, or appreciate that a father's advice and blessing are important in life. Scanning his dining-room table, he imagines a single newspaper, a paper cup, being removed from its place, and a hot pain swims through his shoulders and neck to his forehead. He unlocks, then securely locks, the brakes on his wheelchair. *This may be the last Thanksgiving we have in this house after all,* he realizes, and wishes that the children, or at least the girl, had just this once demanded a turkey.

The suicide bombings are not going to stop. Hardev pushes the lever on his electric bed, and the upper half of his body forms an L and greets the morning news, Rodriguez ready and waiting with a fresh dishtowel, a bowl of porridge, and the remote. Eight o'clock: on schedule. Rodriguez is late sometimes because of the bus service, and sometimes because he works extra shifts at Riverside Hospital, leaving him little time to rush to Ashbrook Crescent.

"Sleep well, Harry?"

Even though he doesn't yet know which city has been targeted now, Hardev mutes the bulky colour television on the far side of his dresser. Footage of a distressed Middle Eastern mother with two young children beside rubble that must have once been their apartment complex flashes by. A boy with mud on his face holds a doll's head covered with soot. Back to the woman. Hardev wonders if she is speaking English, as it's always surprising to him how many people speak English in countries that were never colonized by the British, as if it were some airborne disease. If Dorothy were here, she'd be able to tell him. Unlike his deaf daughter, Hardev can't read lips, despite all the books he has acquired about the practice over the years; beyond finger-spelling, he can sign little with one hand. Dr. Southgate said it was due to misfires in his motor skills, but Dr. Pittu thought that at his advanced age Hardev had simply reached his language-learning limit. "The girl will find alternative methods to communicate with you, as she will with the world around her," he told him. "My wife learned with little difficulty," Hardev countered. "Your wife is a dancer," was the doctor's reply. Funny, Hardev noted at the time, that Dr. Pittu did not add that his wife was also a speech therapist.

"The rain kept me up," he answers as Rodriguez shuffles back downstairs, though it has been years since he's slept what you might call well, falling into a heaviness, wiped out from travel and work or in an after-sex haze with his wife. Turning to one side of their queen-size oak-framed bed, he would rest his hand between her thighs and drift off to sleep. But now here he is, every morning and night, unequivocally alone, the queen-size bed replaced by a steel-frame with removable guardrails and plastic sheets, a contraption rather than a bed, really, taking up the majority of what used to be a warm, inviting bedroom. Plopped onto his bed at night, he recognizes every syllable of rain that warbles against his white windowpane, can identify every moan of his double mattress, every cough of his bungalow house, from the furnace ducts clanking and toilet tanks leaking to eavestroughs cracking, refrigerator humming, floorboards creaking, telephone wires murmuring, the boy dropping a textbook or kicking over a glass of water in his sleep, sleep as bad as his father's. Doctors have prescribed various sleeping pills over the years: lorazepam, diazepam, alprazolam, triazolam; but Hardev refuses to take them. After the accident, Isobel pleaded, "Harry, you need your sleep. For strength." "For what?" he wanted to say. "So *you* can go out and work?" But there are still many awful mornings when he forgets and thinks he will be getting up for work, and tries to swing his legs over the side, and can't. The house they purchased right after marrying, that he barely paid attention to, leaving the day-to-day running, decorating, and arranging to Isobel, became his new wife. Trapped in the house, Hardev couldn't help but take note of the wallpaper and tiles, wastepaper baskets, drawers, cupboards, banisters, rugs, window shutters, curtains, upholstery. They were now his co-workers, his colleagues; he had to make sure things were in their place, performing their proper tasks. After the visible features of the home, he became acquainted with the wear and tear of the house's unseen elements, its internal organs: plumbing and wiring, foundational shifts in the roof or walls, furnace ducts. Now he detects even the subtlest complaints and, like a caring nurse, tries to offer comfort: *These are just ordinary aches and pains. Oh, sure, we can call in the doctor now and then, but it's certainly not time for the priest!* He astonished a plumber once by figuring out where the pipes were cracking before the plumber could. "I know when something's wrong with my house," he stated proudly.

Cupboard hinges creak. Crinkling plastic bags. Front door swings open. "Rodriguez, have the workers arrived?"

"Not yet. Day after a holiday, they come late, I bet. I go take out the garbage." Heel taps door shut.

Last night Hardev could hear the unmistakable patter stuttering on the blue and orange tarps of the construction sites, protecting the hardware and tools left overnight on his neighbours' properties. Correction: Gateway Land Developers' properties. His neighbours moved out months ago in a parade of garage sales and moving trucks, their modest bungalows and split-levels already demolished, no trace left of their former post-war selves, as if the earth had swallowed them and all their memories whole. Now steel machines and young builders have sprouted in their place, and Hardev wakes with a start every morning, rushes through his breakfast so he can be turned on his left side to face his bedroom window, observe how quickly the new two-storey and three-storey skeletons are drying and what, if any, changes can be spotted since the previous day's work. Having supervised all those hydro plants, Hardev is no stranger to the frustrations of inevitable worksite delays, nor to the delights of progress. Notwithstanding his fight to keep 90 Ashbrook Crescent off the Gateway Land Developers' destruction block, he genuinely appreciates the ingenuity and discipline required to set designs into action, the many hands that must work harmoniously in order to accomplish them; he truly loves how such otherwise solitary and disparate actions can eventually intersect to produce a single beautiful structure.

Taking out the yellow foolscap pad from the wheeled trolley straddling his bed, Hardev flips to a free page. With an HB pencil, he writes:

> Tuesday:
> Suicide bombings continue in Iraq.
> Protestors die in Bolivia.
> Pregnancy created using egg nucleus of infertile woman (China).
> Crown Bank is taking my house.

He underlines *Tuesday* three times. Hardev believes it is his duty as a citizen to keep track of the news, and does so through hundreds of foolscap notes stored away in basement filing cabinets.

Every time he presses one of his HB pencils onto paper, he has the sense that he is recording vital history, important to his family and to the global community—the fluctuations of the world observed, monitored, recorded. *Crown Bank is taking my house. Crown Bank is taking my house.* Hardev has made this notation a number of times, personal news rather than public news, but also worth recording. Distressingly, over the last few months this piece of personal news, like the suicide bombings and like the spasms that run though his arms and legs, has yet to cease its attack. Sometimes Hardev believes that, between his body and his house, he's fighting his own internal war on terror.

Eating hot porridge straight from the microwavable container, Hardev holds his breath that the phone won't ring. Mr. Karkiev of Crown Bank likes to call at the beginning of the week to give updates on the status of the legal proceedings. Early is his style, as if the worms are just itching for the birds to nab them. Consistently, he asks whether in the span of the last week Hardev has miraculously been contacted by a long-lost family member who is only too willing to give him ten, twenty, thirty thousand dollars, or if he's discovered a suitcase full of money under the kitchen tiles, banknotes or IBM stocks in the freezer ice trays. *We'd be only too happy to reverse the process should you come up with the funds, Mr. Dange,* he promises, pronouncing his name Don-gee. *Are you sure you've covered all the possibilities?* Today Hardev imagines himself retorting, *How did you spend your holiday? Thinking up ways to evict quadriplegics?*

Hardev reaches for the blue Thermos of water beside the bed, and Tuesday's pillboxes. The water is lukewarm and he holds a sip in the gully of his throat, lowers each pill onto his tongue, and flips a cluster backwards. Maybe because it's Tuesday and not

Monday, he will be spared. Now, wouldn't that be something to give thanks for? he thinks, palming more pills into his mouth. Upon first contact, Hardev trusted Mr. Karkiev, who said he wanted "to talk about how the bank might help him meet his financial responsibilities in light of the rising property taxes in the area and the vast decline in disability benefits." *Yes, yes,* Hardev thought, *please help me, I need your help, I've just been informed that my bathing apparatus is now a "luxury" and I will need several thousands of dollars to rent it, as it's no longer covered, added to the list of other medical supplies and access aids "no longer covered," and soon I will no longer be covered either, no roof, no home, unless someone helps;* and so he trusted, the same way he's trusted and accepted the help of the doctors who revolve in and out of his life, prescribing medications to eradicate infections which certainly exist, but which due to his paralysis he cannot feel destroying his body. But Mr. Karkiev did not offer Hardev help; he offered ultimatums. *If you cannot come up with the funds, we are within our legal rights to . . .*

Door swings, bangs the left kitchen wall. Garbage bin squeezed into stall underneath sink. Faucet on. Sink drains. Down stairs. Freezer. Suction. Open. Suction. Shut. Up stairs. Countertop business, pans laid out.

Hardev refrains from turning the sound back up on the television in hopes of catching the construction workers arriving. Sometimes all the crews on each property work at the same time, and on those days, if he closes his eyes, the medley of digging and sawing and drilling and cutting and banging and laughing and yelling and crashing can almost transport him, like the birds outside, south of the equator, where he was in charge of projects ten times, no, one hundred times larger than this piddle of a housing development. He helped hundreds, in some cases thousands of families, providing them with fresh water and electricity and jobs. *The Third World meets the First World,* he would say. Not like these Gateway Land Developers, who build for the few, realizing dreams for those who can afford them by pushing others to sell out their own.

Impatient, Hardev has the urge to rip down the white blinds, to strip the window of obstructions, although it wouldn't give him a significantly better view. "Do you think they're not going to work today? I want to speak to the head one about the schedule. I think they're behind. What's his name? Mr. . . . Mr. . . . ?"

"Mr. Karkiev?"

"No! No! Not him. Please don't say that man's name today!"

Hardev dislikes raising his voice, but sometimes it is the only way to talk to Rodriguez, now in the kitchen defrosting frozen drumsticks and chicken breasts and another bag of mixed vegetables. And he also dislikes sounding too much like his son, as if uttering a name could bring about worse luck than what has been dished out already, but the boy isn't here, he's at the university and won't be back until dinnertime, if then. Many nights he only returns right before bed, heading straight to the other end of the hallway in silence, past the washroom and a storage room, what used to be the girl's bedroom, to a doorway too narrow for Hardev's wheelchair to pass through. Last March, they went two weeks without seeing each other. Hardev only detected his presence by the give in the floorboards, and the shower water rushing through the pipes. When the phone calls and letters from Gateway Land Developers and then from Crown Bank first began, he worried the boy would find out. But there was no need to worry; the boy paid little attention to anything these days but his studies.

"I can't believe these workers! The holiday was one day, not two!"
Hardev writes:

Things to Consider:
My eldest daughter is twenty-seven years old.
Same age as when I got married.
How much is this going to cost?

He adds three more question marks—*???*—and puts down his
pencil, pinching it between his Thermos and the pastel green spitting dish for his toothpaste waste, his left fingers twitching already
from soreness. Although he has managed to rehabilitate his left
hand and retain some use of it—unlike his useless right hand—
his range of movement is drastically limited. Though his scrawl
is tight and economical by nature, he tires easily. And felt-tip pens,
certainly much easier on his writing hand, bleed onto the other
pages and lack the physical satisfaction of the HB pencils. He uses
the pens only in an emergency or when his signature is required
in ink. *Just sign, Mr. Dange, and you can make money off this old place.*
Your neighbours saw the sense of this proposal, how is it that you … ? And
the boy's old computer, with microphone and voice-processor
software, is kept in the alcove attached to Hardev's bedroom, the
old baby room now a makeshift medical supplies and study area.
Still, he finds his letters get typed much more quickly and accurately with Rodriguez's help. Hardev's South Asian accent
confuses the system, and the technological merry-go-round
involved in correcting the mistake is more trouble than it's worth.

The girl said May. A May wedding. She doesn't know about the
house, that Mr. Karkiev has his own May ceremonies planned. *The*
final deadline is May, Mr. Dange. You will need to vacate the premises if

you cannot come up with the funds. The paperwork might stretch out to June, but don't count on it. Calculation: seven months, possibly eight. In Hardev's letter to his MP he quoted Mr. Karkiev directly. He told the MP that he had little time left. May. Can't count on June. At Rodriguez's insistence, he copied the letter to the Premier of Ontario as well as to the Prime Minister of Canada. Originally, Hardev was ashamed to write even to his MP to explain how hard it had been to keep his family afloat since the 1985 accident. *I am a fifty-eight-year-old man and a pensioner of the government. I worked at CIDA and five times over ten years received promotion. To detail all the costs associated with my physical condition plus the costs of keeping this modest house in order would take pages and pages and, I'm afraid, would exhaust your patience. Although my two daughters have lived with their mother following our separation, they return regularly for family occasions and visits, and my boy has never left my side.* Hardev argued that these men were too busy to be bothered with his problems; you couldn't just ask the Prime Minister of Canada to help you with your family affairs. But Rodriguez disagreed: "Why not? He's supposed to be there for the people. Like God. We ask God to help our family all the time." Desperation won out over pride. Anything at this point was better than nothing, so they sent off dozens of letters to every official they could name or imagine. They even included a photograph, on the back of which Hardev wrote: *1987, my then young wife and three children, our home in the background.*

> *Reminders:*
> *Ask R. to make a list of the current contents of the basement*
>   *pantry.*
> *Schedule yearly physical appointment with Dr. Pittu.*
> *Find ways to stop time.*

"We must do something! We must . . . Rodriguez?" Hardev has lost track of Rodriguez, as the shuffling in the kitchen area has stopped. *May. I have until May,* he assures himself. *Until my daughter's wedding. Oh, my daughter is lucky to be marrying rich, into a stable, rich family.* They won't have to scrounge for every dollar, plan ahead for every bill and expense, as he has had to do since the accident. They will have more money than they know what to do with. More money than . . . *Could I?* No. No, he couldn't. He would never ask the children or Isobel for money, so he won't ask his future son-in-law either, no matter how much he has. When Hardev figures out where Rodriguez has got to, he will ask for his red-and-white striped sweater with the circular collar that looks absolutely British on him and reminds him of his tennis-playing days, the kind of sweater Victor might wear, the kind he'd wear if he had an appointment with the Prime Minister or, for that matter, with Mr. Karkiev. But Hardev hasn't heard from the Prime Minister, or from his MP, or from anyone else's office except Mr. Karkiev's; nevertheless, the sweater will keep him warm and comfortable as he stares out his window waiting for the construction workers to arrive, and if they do come, and if they spot him in his good sweater, they will know that he respects them too. And suddenly Hardev wishes that Mr. Karkiev would call so that he could explain a few basic things about his life; it's important one man understands where another man is coming from before he takes his house from underneath him.

"They're here! They're here!"

Rodriguez re-enters the bedroom, swerves around the trolley, and presses his face against the bedroom window. "They've brought truckloads of drywall again!"

"Excellent! It's good to know they're on track. Now come, sit for a minute." Hardev flips to another page on his yellow foolscap pad. "There's so much news."

"They went to Tim Hortons," Rodriguez blurts, gesturing again at the window as he seats himself on the stool at the foot of Hardev's bed, and Hardev can practically smell the dozens of cups of coffee and the blueberry and oatmeal muffins the workers must have enjoyed. "Good news or bad news?"

Spoon dropped into his empty porridge bowl, Hardev's balding scalp and wide forehead reflect grotesquely back at him. "An apartment complex in the Middle East has been bombed, and my daughter is getting married."

"Dear God!" Rodriguez exclaims, collecting the dishes over the guardrail onto his lap. "Where will they live?"

Before Hardev can answer, the telephone rings.

Dear Dor,

I hope you have recovered one hundred percent from the flu and are back at school. Your latest report card made me very proud. Thank you for making a photocopy of it for my files. Soon you must visit and reread all your report cards with me, from kindergarten through high school. What will you spell with all those As and Bs?

But enough of your father's irrelevant musings. I've decided to write because now that Birendra is getting married, I can't ignore the truth: my children are adults. While I hope it will be several years before you follow in your sister's footsteps, I feel more pronouncedly than ever the difficulties we face communicating with each other. Technology, however, seems on our side. The keyboards manufactured now are much easier on a one-hand, two-finger typist like me; there is also voice-recognition technology, and when I am tired or the machines malfunction, I can ask your brother or my homecare worker for help. I spend a lot of my time writing letters, official letters, To Whom It May Concern letters, to all kinds of government organizations and corporations, and, as you know, they drain a lot of my energy. I wrote a very long one the other day, and while I was working out the right phrasings, it occurred to me that I've never written you a letter, not a single letter, and that isn't right. I would like to tell you some important things that I have learned before, well, before it's too late. I want to tell you about my life. These tidbits may be of interest to you someday, or you may look upon them as misguided forms of affection, but regardless, I am writing them to you and here's your first.

Dor, you were taken from me when you were so young. Barely two years old when you left with your mother and sister, out of the basement suite you and your mother shared and into a townhouse at the other end of the city, and not only is that too young for a child to be separated from a parent, but because of it I have very few memories of you in this house. The alcove where you slept as a baby no longer has a crib or a Sesame Street mobile or daisy wallpaper. But I do remember that you loved to sit at the top of the second-floor stairs, curled up like a cat. We used to joke that the dust bunnies would nab you. Your mother would place you near my arms on the bed, and you would try to reach the triangular hoist device with your small determined hands. Over and over, with all your strength, you'd reach for it, thinking it was a toy, a magical trapeze in some circus act, not a tool for getting me in and out of bed, another one of the gadgets forced into our lives, and you made me feel a little less sad and hopeless. Happy memories, but few. I wish we had spent more time together. I frequently wonder: *What is Dor thinking right now? Who is she thinking about?*

I've tried to keep anything you might be interested in one day. The basement boxes are all for you kids. Anything you want from them, you can have. The Sesame Street mobile is among your brother's old toys, although your crib left with your mother. Does she store blankets in it now, or did she give it away? As for these letters, they are addressed to you; and I can send them by mail or by e-mail if your brother helps me. Better yet, I can wait for you to visit and hand them all over at once.

Your father,

Hardev

"If you don't have a clear idea of your wedding, and I mean from the design on the invitations down to the favours for your guests, Victor's family will walk all over you. They'll take over completely."

Isobel, in a red and white yoga outfit, brown hair pulled back in a ponytail, is seated across from Birendra, in old jeans and pink cotton zippered sweater, at the round four-seat kitchen table, a pad of lined white paper in front of them, two pencils, two mugs of hot coffee, and an open box of Oreo cookies. On the top of the page is written:

Birendra Dange's Wedding
May 17th, 2004

"Mom, you can't say that. You don't know them," Birendra protests, blowing on her coffee.

"Neither do you."

"They don't live in Canada. His mother and father don't even live in the same hemisphere as each other. How are they going to organize the wedding from afar?"

"They have money. People with money think they can run everything," Isobel replies, pointing an Oreo at her daughter for emphasis. "You'll want to make sure his family knows that you have your own ideas, that you have a family of your own to consider."

Birendra doesn't want to argue; it's going to be a long enough day as it is. Excited by the prospect of planning the wedding, her mother couldn't be convinced to shower after her morning workout, and the bright blue Exerball wobbles underneath the table between their feet. Birendra has already bought herself a bridal planner—it's on top of a pile of sweaters in her closet—but she hasn't bothered to mention it. At this point she's only written in the date, and since her mother has her own ideas, Birendra is happy to let her do most of the work, as long as she's married and out of the house in May. Besides, she is finding it hard to concentrate, as she dreamt about that damn baby again.

In this version of the dream she's on the telephone—the cordless one that charges beside the living-room television—lounging on the uncomfortably hard couch, when the police-siren-like noise sounds. *Hold on, something's happening,* she says to the nameless person, and then lays the phone down on the *TV Guide.* Every one of the dreams starts similarly innocuously, but she's begun to detect the feel of this particular dream in her sleep, like a faint but persistent odour. She's tried reasoning with herself that these dreams don't matter, and she's attempted pre-sleep cures like hot milk, abdominal crunches, reading a book, listening to Water Music, and even making use of the Guatemalan worry dolls that Victor's mother brought back from vacation, but the dreams don't disappear, and they do matter, and Birendra can't shake the sensation that the stupid baby is trying to communicate something important to her.

"I'm sure you've thought about the flowers. We should all leave that up to you, considering it's your occupation. I can't see how the Lanes can object."

Light falls from the kitchen window onto the paperwork. Squinting, Birendra can see the neighbour across the road struggling with too many bags of groceries, her golden retriever jumping up and down, nipping at her coat sleeves. In the dream it's evening, and Birendra flips open the blinds but she can spot only a few streetlights and the outlines of cars in driveways. No one seems to be out. No dogs bark. The bleating suddenly softens, as if smothered. *It's in the house,* she realizes, as if it came in with the groceries, like the woman across the road, and in the dream she stares up the narrow staircase of the townhouse, a staircase exactly like every other one on the block. As she grasps the banister, a sharp pain shoots up her arm. *Is this what it means to be paralyzed with fear?* she thinks. *This must be how my father feels.* The noise gets louder. Not a police siren. Not a fire alarm. What is it?

Birendra sighs, resting her chin in her hands as if she's already worked a full day. "Victor says we are pretty much free to design the wedding the way we want, and his parents will pay for it. They know I don't come from money. They know about Dad. They would like the Château Laurier for the reception, but they're open to other options. Just no more than two hundred people. They don't want a stadium-sized wedding." She dips another Oreo into her coffee. Her mother makes delicious coffee. Delicious pasta and hamburgers, too. *I'll miss her cooking,* she realizes, *but it will be a small sacrifice.* Overall, she can't wait to be free of the cramped bedroom she's shared with Dorothy since they moved to Augusta, the finicky bathroom with the simultaneous cold-hot showers, the living room with those awful Quebec landscape paintings, and that neon blue Exerball her mother's always trying to get her to use. She gives it a little kick. *So long to you too,* she thinks, with a smile.

Frowning, Isobel gazes up at the yellow sphere of the kitchen light. "Do we know two hundred people? A wedding should just be family and close friends."

"Wasn't your wedding full of Dad's co-workers? And you both designed it the way you wanted, didn't you? Victor's family isn't close," Birendra admits, dusting cookie crumbs off her pink sweater, "but there are a lot of them, and they might make the trip here for the wedding. It'll be strange meeting them all at once like that. My *in-laws*," she says, for the first time out loud. "We'll be family by law, even if we meet only once. That's sort of intimidating."

"That's why you need to know what you want. Who you are. Then they can't force you to be something you're not. Your father and I, we went too far the other way raising you, letting you kids all invent yourselves, not giving you enough sense of what it means to be French or South Asian, teaching you nothing about religion or geography or politics, nothing about your roots. *What's so great about Canada is that you can shape it to your imagination,* your father would say when he was working. He was such a Trudeau man. But there's only so much you can invent, Birendra, and then there's reality. Your father and I had to learn hard and fast about reality. Sometimes inventing things works against you. You should care about your roots more, before you lose them. Those Lanes, they know what it means to be a Lane, I bet you. Do you know what it means to be a Dange?"

In the left margin of the pad, Isobel writes:

Locations
Guest List & Invitations
Bridal Party
Wedding Dress
Flowers
Menu

Weddings bring out the most preposterous territorial rights, Birendra thinks, working on a fourth cookie, licking out the white centre. That her mother wants her to stake a claim, as a Dange of all things, for pink-bordered invitations rather than silver, asparagus over leek soup, a chocolate fountain instead of a dessert cart, as if these minor accoutrements are essential stamps of one's familial makeup, is almost too ridiculous to discuss. Yet here they are. And Birendra's supposed to know who she is. *That's a good one. I guess,* she muses, *I should just print on the wedding invitations: "Birendra Dange is a French-Canadian, South-Asian mix, which means not much to her except that it accounts for her black hair and brown skin and her perfect French scores in high school. She's wanted her whole life to be someone else, somewhere else. She's always wanted to be part of someone else's family, just to see what it might be like . . ."*

"Victor's family might change their minds," Isobel insists, tapping her nails on the coffee pot. "Victor is their only son. Only child, right? They'll have expectations, even if they're not voicing

them. Everybody does. You'll need to be very orderly. Are you listening, Birendra? You need to be very orderly. You can't put these
decisions off or they'll be made for you, and then you'll be sorry."

In the dream, Birendra follows the sound to her bedroom, but
it's not the shared bedroom of her townhouse; it's the bedroom
she had all those years ago in her father's house, that's now stacked
with files, files, and more files, but then housed her adored old
bed with the pastel green headboard and matching dresser, and
dozens of Top Ten music charts taped to the walls. On the bed,
there's something lumpy. When she first notices the bunched green
comforter, she thinks it might be a cat, or a small dog like a pug
or Pomeranian, but then, as she inches closer, she discovers that
the mound is not a fuzzy animal at all; it's a baby, a baby, and the
baby's body and limbs aren't moving. Only every so often its
mouth opens, making that awful noise.

"I suppose Victor should be here when we compile the guest
list, so we should settle the other details as soon as possible, figure out the theme, the decor, the aura you want to create for your
wedding. We have to ask ourselves—or *you* have to ask
yourself—excuse me, I'm getting a little carried away—my
daughter's first wedding. Not that you will have more. I meant
the first wedding for one of my children. And if Victor's parents
are really giving you free rein and will pick up the cheque, then
you have a rare opportunity, something your father and I certainly didn't have. You have to ask yourself: *What do I want this
wedding to say?*"

What does Birendra want her wedding to *say*? Even as a child
cutting pictures of china and wedding dresses, hutches and lamp
fixtures out of catalogues, she never considered that as a group
all these objects should *say* something. Did the blinds on the

window say something? Did the white refrigerator with the finicky ice-cube dispenser say anything? The lily wallpaper? The Van Gogh calendar near the light switch, marked with her mother's speech therapy appointments? Dorothy must be her maid of honour. No question; her mother would be very disappointed otherwise. Emile will also have to be in the wedding party, a groomsman most likely, if not the best man, since Victor has no siblings to accommodate. But other than these two obvious role assignments, Birendra feels tricked somehow, every decision like a multiple-choice question on a test that she didn't plan on taking, that she didn't study for; just as she feels tricked by her dream when she rushes back into the hallway, hoping to enlist her brother or father, even her mother or sister for help, but knows deep down that the house is empty, from the sagging roof to the cold basement (once a storage space for decorations and canned goods, then a bedroom for Dorothy and her mother, then back to a storage space with added files and medical supplies), that she has no one to turn to, no one to take care of things for her. "Please, no," she begs the empty hallway, "I don't want you."

"Birendra, are you listening?"

She nods, but it's a lie; she isn't listening to her mother. She's still listening to the no-name baby that intrudes in the sunny kitchen as if perched on the microwave oven, or on the shelves of jars of sugar and flour and pasta.

"Are you feeling sick? Are you worried? Tell me."

"No. It's nothing."

Leaning in, Isobel wraps her hands around Birendra's mug. "I can't make all the decisions for you. What's bothering you? Tell your mother. Are you worried you're making a mistake? That you're moving too fast?"

Unable to stomach any more cookies, Birendra plops her chin back into her hands and shakes her head. Victor was an easy choice to make. Handsome and conscientious, friendly but not aggressive, secure, reliable, independent, and most of all a man with the right career to offer the kind of life Birendra's always dreamed of, travelling the world, not tied to one city or one country, not bogged down by family obligations. How can she explain to her mother that she wants her wedding to say: *Goodbye old family, hello . . . no family?* That she wants the occasion to be fun and happy, but that it should also mark the beginning of her leaving them behind? Mother, father, sister, brother; all of them. Wrong. Her mother is wrong. She has too many roots as it is, and they've never helped her know who she is. In fact, she barely knows that she exists. Is it wrong to want to be someone else? Somewhere else? The wedding details don't matter to her in the least as long as the end is achieved, as long as she and Victor are soon living in another house or apartment in another country. Looking over the mug at her mother's eager green eyes full of concern for her future, her thin lips pursed and her freckled hands ready to catch Birendra if she says she wants her to, how can she tell her this?

"There are so many details. It's just a bit overwhelming, that's all."

Reclining in her chair, throwing up her hands in a gesture of mock exasperation, Isobel laughs. "The wedding is the easiest part. After the wedding you'll have to make all kinds of decisions, sacrifices, compromises. It doesn't end once you start, you know, and one day you'll look at your kids all grown up and beautiful and on the verge of moving out, and you'll wonder where all the time has gone."

Bloated and dizzy; that's how time seems in the dream. Birendra doesn't know what to do. The baby willfully opposes her,

her very nature, she thinks, and there's no end she can envision. Not in the dream and not beyond. This bulbous thing with hands and feet and eyes, tufts of dark hair, a mouth, a loud wet mouth that screams and that she can't understand, already making demands Birendra doesn't want to fulfill, is all too much for her. No, no, this won't be part of *my* marriage, she vows.

"Then you'll be planning your own daughter's, my grand-daughter's wedding." Isobel rises and plugs in the kettle again. The bright blue Exerball rolls across the room, bouncing off the cup-boards, as the lined pad waits for Birendra's input. *It's not healthy,* she thinks, when the baby's wailing won't stop. Then it does and she feels worse—the baby looking up at her like her mother moments before, waiting for her to speak, to say something important, reveal something essential, willing to listen, listen to her deepest thoughts, and yet she can't speak, has nothing to say, is left to wonder if *she's* the one who's not healthy. And then—and she does not like to admit this—the end of the dream is always the same. Inevitably, her hands clench, her legs tighten, and a vio-lent urge ripples across her whole body, but she can't move, and the baby remains as silent as a judge who has passed sentence.

Dorothy tries not to judge people by their mouths, but she can't help it. This one's deep red, nearly purple, and the left upper lip, larger than the bottom, lifts when he laughs. Ts stressed, lets Gs drop; it reminds her of her father, who also stresses his Ts, and whose lips—unlike hers, inherited from her mother's side—are equally full and purplish. But her father never lets his Gs drop, firmly pronounces all suffixes, and his lips stick to his gums when he's in discomfort. This one's name is Anton and when she approached he had his head in his hands, his nearly purple lips trapped behind finger bars. Something snail-like in his posture is also like her father—she can't stop thinking about him—the way he slinks into his wheelchair when he's tired, as if it's too large for him—this one too seems to disappear, into the broadness of the table, and she feels guilty that she wasn't up to visiting her father for Thanksgiving. No flu. Her mother knew she didn't have the flu, but didn't argue. It isn't that Dorothy didn't want to see her father; it was just that right now she didn't want her father to see her.

Dorothy does not particularly like this one's mouth, with its dimple at the chin, even though his speech is not difficult to decipher—the opposite, in fact, its movements clear and direct—but it's becoming evident that he may just talk her ear off and never say a damn thing that's important. The expression *talk her ear off* is amusing, even if she hears with her eyes and the back of her head, because her ears have names. The right one is Roof, the left one Key. Dorothy knows when people are speaking even when she can't see them, and she's come to think of her eyes as convex mirrors, like the lens diagrams she sketches in physics class. *My eye nearly orbits my head if I let it,* she thinks, sitting at the bar, staring at people's lips and sorting out other sensations—bar tap flow, waitress call, cocktail shake, flushed toilet, cork pop, woman in tears—with the edges of her eyes. This one called Anton is closer to Roof than to Key and is explaining that the lead singer of the band got her hand crushed under a car wheel—the doctors say it's a miracle how quickly she's been able to get back to playing the bass. Turning toward the stage, Dorothy scans the singer's red dreadlocks and gold bell-bottoms, left wrist wrapped in silk like a boxer's, and wonders if the story of her accident has been exaggerated for publicity purposes.

Crushed bones as fashion statements. Or rather, the illusion of crushed bones.

It's hot in the SoundScape tonight. Dorothy wears a blonde bob wig and orange glitter lipstick, both bright contrasts to her light brown skin and grey eyes, and a black top with the words *Out of Order* on her chest. Her mother dislikes this T-shirt and thinks Dorothy gave it to the Salvation Army a month ago, but she stores it in her school locker, along with a silver handbag with *Bite Me* written along the handle and a picture of her father in his teens in his tennis uniform which she stole out of one of the basement boxes last summer. Lean and happy, tennis racquet held proudly, hair so thick from the humidity that he seems to have an Afro—she is very fond of the photo, though she has little idea why it was taken. When her locker-neighbours ask, even though the size of the photograph and the yellowing corners and pinkish fading suggest otherwise, Dorothy tells them it's a recent picture of her brother, that her brother lives in Greece and teaches tennis for a living. She's not ashamed of her father or brother; she just doesn't want to answer questions about them. What does it matter to them in what way they are related, or if they are related at all? If she wants to put up the picture and give it a name, why shouldn't she? She's more connected to these strangers in the SoundScape than to her locker-neighbours or the other students at Rousseau Secondary. More and more over the last year she's found herself moving through the school's corridors completely removed from the people everyone else seems desperate to connect with, boys playing guitar at lunch hour or girls with gossip sprouting out of their ears, conspiring and giggling from floor to floor, class to class. At each and every assembly, the principal of Rousseau unabashedly praises what he

calls the Rousseau Family and their unequalled alumni donations, but Dorothy doesn't feel she belongs to such a family, nor
does she understand how she is supposed to benefit from the
family connection. Instead, she feels at odds with her surroundings, an ice floe in a rainforest. The SoundScape is more of a
family to her. So are the people at Signature Tattoo and Body
Piercing, where she apprentices twice a week. One of three hundred students who attend the special needs Rousseau school,
Dorothy will simply be one of forty to graduate this year, and she
will have earned the required grades to get into a regular university, even if she doesn't want to go.

"Can I get you a drink? Do you want a beer or something?"

Dorothy shrugs. She likes to listen; is constantly told by others that she's *a good listener*. Yet listening is the biggest crock of shit
she's ever heard. She knows most people don't listen to each other
at all. Roof is good at collecting men who want to talk, like this
Anton, though her patience is waning since he hasn't said anything substantial yet, just a bunch of CD liner note stuff. Key's
job is to empty them. *Everyone deserves to be listened to at least once
in a life*, she tells Key, *no matter what the story*. It doesn't even occur
to people at the SoundScape that she's deaf. An X made with the
fingers gets her an Export. Bartenders and waitresses take orders
from hand gestures even more accurately than from words, especially at a distance. And so do men. Dancing isn't a problem either,
beats deciphered through vibrations. Only Ted, the tall bouncer
with the shaved head and Japanese jazz dancer girlfriend, seems
to suspect. "You're listening to music no one else is listening to. I'd
like to know the name of the band sometime," he said to her two
Fridays ago. Anyone but Ted and she would have thought he was
either making fun of her or hitting on her, but Ted was doing nei-

ther. In fact, she knows that she makes him uncomfortable and he just can't pinpoint why.

"Are you sure?"

This one is uncomfortable too. Why do people always want to buy you something to keep your attention, she wonders, as if money is a sturdier bond than conversation? Two giddy well-dressed women stumble by, close to her mother's age, on a ladies' night out, but women don't interest Dorothy much.

"Four surgeries in a row. I bet she thought she'd never be able to use her fingers again," he adds, still roadblocked on the lead singer. "So, what's your name? I don't think you told me."

DOR, Dorothy types in her Palm Pilot.

"Is that your real name?"

She'd rather deal with older men; they care less about these things. Names are merely a system of filing, a way to differentiate the sources of words. Smiling, Dorothy passes the message to him.

DOR IS MY REAL NAME ASSHOLE

Sometimes she needs to be firm, not just with Roof and Key but with the men, establish boundaries right from the start, or else they think they can create their own.

Anton laughs good-heartedly. "Why do you use that, anyway?" Filed under "Anton."

I HATE COMPETING WITH NOISE

"That's a good idea," he replies, as have several before him, yet she's never seen Palm Pilots or cellphones used for this purpose. Nevertheless, her communication device is accepted rather easily in the SoundScape mix, where there is always music and it's always loud, whether live or recorded: industrial, techno, or rock on weekends and Thursdays; rockabilly, funk, rap, and hip hop the rest of the week; a stage the size of a six-car garage, with speakers at every corner and along the walls. If Dorothy ever needs to speak, she has a pretty firm handle on whispering (and most people expect whispering to be harder to understand, especially in a bar), plus she's been more rigorous with her speech training lately, practising pitch and pronunciation for hours in front of her mirror with her mother's therapy books.

The band finishes its set with the singer falling to her knees at the foot of the stage, whipping her red dreads over her face and across her back in a fanlike arc. This one named Anton claps enthusiastically.

Dor writes: TELL ME A STORY

Anton takes a sip of his gin and tonic, then places it in front of him on the tabletop. "What do you mean, tell you a story?"

TELL ME SOMETHING YOU NEED TO TELL SOMEONE ELSE

A school night—Dorothy will need to leave in less than an hour for her mother to pick her up at Memories, a dessert shop in the Market specializing in cheesecake, so she can't afford to waste any more time. Memories is where she tells her mother she goes after studying at the library or practising sketching at the National Gallery, and her mother doesn't question her. As long as Dorothy isn't pregnant and hasn't been caught stealing clothes or booze at the Rideau Centre, she's generally satisfied. And there's no danger of either of these things happening; Dorothy can't abide shoplifters and, unlike the majority of her ditzy classmates, has little interest in acquiring a boyfriend. It's hard enough just getting around the idea of how many people there are in the world, let alone picking one to get to know everything about you, she thinks. She doesn't want people to know everything about her. *She* doesn't know everything about her. Besides, what do these

Rousseau boys have to offer? Their stories are childhood stories. What could they teach her about life?

"Someone else? You mean you? I could tell you that you're beautiful, but you must already know that."

NOT THAT STORY

Running his hand through his oily hair, Anton looks at the empty stage as if it is somehow responsible. "I don't understand," he says more firmly. "What is it you want me to say?"

Roof and Key are now very impatient. Dorothy can only manage to visit the SoundScape once every week or two. She doesn't mind the lying, but only if the lies are a means to an end.

LET'S TRY AGAIN: TELL ME A STORY

Bottom lip puckers. "Seriously? You want me to tell you a story? A story I need to tell someone else? You can't be serious. But you're a stranger, a perfect stranger. You can't just intrude on people's lives like this."

YOU DIDN'T MEET ME BY ACCIDENT

"Look, I thought we could listen to music and relax. Have a drink. Have fun." The word "fun" puffs out like smoke in Dorothy's face. This Anton is staring at her now with something akin to anger, but not quite: consideration. Considering what to make of her and the request. Sometimes telling stories makes people uncomfortable, Dorothy realizes, but there are means and there are ends, and listening must start somewhere.

YOU THOUGHT WRONG

Dear Dor,

You were nearly two before we realized you were deaf. Your reaction to movement was so intense we thought you were *hearing* it, not just sensing it. You looked up at us so attentively when we spoke to you in your crib or highchair, while you played in the backyard sandbox, even latched into your car seat. It's true we wondered when you would start to speak, but it didn't really trouble us. Something was always in your mouth: a carrot, a soother, bits of cereal, your fingers; we joked you would have to stop eating before you could start speaking. But it was a joke. We didn't know.

We found out at Dr. Brossard's office. You had the flu. Three nights in a row you cried and cried and wouldn't keep anything down, not even apple juice, and we were all exhausted. We made an appointment. Now doctors test things like hearing early and regularly, but even just seventeen years ago they didn't so much. Funny how quickly times change. Now they check for absolutely everything, even before the baby is born, in the womb. Microrobots. Corrective surgery. Amazing. It's almost unbelievable that children are still born with disabilities or deformities at all. But I guess that's life. Fix one problem, another takes its place. Look at all the people now who can't have babies. It's all over the news. Fertility treatments. Babies sold over the Internet. Bulgaria the newest hope for Canadian adoptions. Must be something we're doing to ourselves: genetic foods, airport detectors, pesticides, acid rain, roller coasters. Who knows? Later we found out that odds are you were born with some hearing, which explains your natural ability to learn some English and French speech, but it probably deteriorated quickly. The books say you may remember the intonations of your mother's voice, but not much else. I have always been a bit jealous of that, Dor. I hope my voice is also tucked somewhere inside your mind, even if you might not know what to make of it yet. Fifteen years ago, the doctor examined your little chest, and you didn't cry or throw up the entire time we were in his office, and your mother and I were thankful for it. Then the building started testing the fire alarm. We prepared for the worst. But you didn't cry. The kids in the waiting room were wailing, but you couldn't see them. Initially, Dr. Brossard exclaimed, *What a calm girl she is*, but then, as the loud beeping continued and you still showed no indication that you were the least bit troubled or interested, he got worried. *She might have a bit of hearing loss*, he said. *It's common during infancy. Could be her ears are blocked from the flu. Let's just check.*

I must admit, I was annoyed. We'd already waited for over an hour in the office and I didn't want us to get stuck in rush hour. I remember this because I kept thinking about the headaches I get in traffic, and how I used to stay longer at the office if necessary in order to avoid it: exhaust from cars, blasts of loud music thundering out of windows, running engines, honking, stuffy car smell. Considering how much travelling I did with my job, I've never been a great traveller, much more of a destination man. When I am not the driver, I suffer motion sickness easily. And that's why I don't go out very much, Dor. I can't drive and the Para Transpo turns my stomach. But we stayed, because your mother and I never disobey doctors. Dr. Brossard left us for a few minutes and returned with a tape recorder and a small set of headphones. When the speakers were secured inside your ears, Isobel laughed. You looked adorable, a regular rock star. You laughed back and slammed your fists on the bench, which only added to the effect. Dr. Brossard bent over and pressed PLAY, his other hand on the volume knob. You never took your eyes off him. I know now it was because you were drawn to his concentration, and you held his gaze without fidgeting or trying to pull the headset off. You didn't even blink. Your mother stopped laughing. *It's a single note at a high pitch,* he said slowly, inching up the volume dial. *Like the test of the Emergency Broadcast System on your television.* I thought, how lucky the sound doesn't bother her. I didn't yet realize what it meant. *If I raise the volume any higher, I could jeopardize what hearing she might still have.*

Your mother was really tired. Aside from sleep deprivation and her speech therapy appointments that day, it had taken her longer than usual to help me into dress pants and a sweater and slide you into your jumper. There we were, two peas in a pod, both dressed by your mother and latched into the car. This wasn't the kind of life she had imagined for herself, stuck with a man in a wheelchair and three children to raise. We'd been fighting the night before. I can't remember about what. And I'm not just saying that. I really can't remember. You fight about the stupidest things when your life turns into something you can't imagine: the way the condiments are arranged in the refrigerator, lost register receipts for pills, a garden hose left out in the rain. We may even have been fighting about rush hour and the doctor's appointment the next day. I don't know. What I do remember, very clearly, is that your mother did not look surprised. I always wondered if she suspected it. Frowning, she took a deep breath with the look of a person accepting due punishment, but what she felt she was being punished for, I do not know. She probably didn't know either.

Two months later, you were both living on Augusta Street.

Downstairs Food Inventory

12 cans of Campbell's Tomato Soup 8oz 227 ml
12 cans of Campbell's Cream of Mushroom Soup
12 cans of Campbell's Cream of Broccoli Soup
16 cans of Aylmer's Whole-kernel Corn 19oz 540ml
7 cans of Aylmer's Peas and Carrots 19oz 540ml
20 tins of Ocean Breeze White Flaked Tuna
4 tins of sardines
4 boxes of Quaker Oats Honey Hot Breakfast Mix
6 boxes of Quaker Oats Hot Breakfast Mix
5 11lb bags of No Name White Rice
2 11 lb bags of No Name Brown Rice
5 Equality Southern Fried Crispy Coating Mix for Chicken
5 Equality Mesquite Coating Mix for Chicken
8 Equality Bar-B-Q Coating Mix for Chicken
9 500ml bottles of President's Choice Cranberry Juice
1 262 Tetley Tea bags box
1 10lb bag of No Name 1% Homogenized Powdered Milk
3 275ml cans of Carnation Milk
1 2lb bag of Redpath Special Fine Granulated Sugar
3 500gr. boxes of salt

Freezer:

6 loaves of Dempsey's Sliced Enriched White Bread
4 loaves of Dempsey's Sliced 6-Grain Brown Bread
10 packages of 6 Loblaws Chicken Breasts
4 packages of 10 Loblaws Chicken Legs
1 2L Dairy Lane Neopolitan Ice Cream tub

Halloween

Energized, Emile enters the graduate anthropology student lounge. His early-morning presentation on the persistence of curse beliefs in the twentieth and twenty-first centuries through an examination of the Kennedy family received a very enthusiastic response from Professor Lattimore and the class. The evidence of family misfortune undeniable, Emile explored the notion of curse not just in terms of the individual members of the Kennedy family, but in terms of how perceptions of the family as cursed have affected public feeling around them for generations. *America believes in the curse, he stated, and there is a sense in which the fate of*

the Kennedy family is inextricably linked with the fate of American poli-
tics and American families. The effects of such a correspondence have only
recently begun to be analyzed. Remember that Joe Kennedy Sr., in the most
celebrated speech of his political career, told Americans that he and his wife
had everything at stake in America and had given "nine hostages to for-
tune." "Our children and your children are more important than anything
else in the world."

Question period was handled confidently, and several students asked to photocopy his bibliography. Professor Lattimore ended the class by deeming the session particularly productive, adding that he hoped "the anthropological dilemmas at work in this case would be brought up in future discussions." The weeks of read-ing, note-taking, organizing, and preparing had been well worth the results, propelling Emile's brain higher and higher, like a hel-icopter, with new ideas. He can't wait to send off his PhD applications—which he has been working on for the last two months, ensuring that his interest in superstitions and curses in contemporary culture is properly situated within each university program's mandate—and to work out more theories on the sub-ject. How wonderful it is, he thinks, to be in rooms full of people who are all interested in debate and discussion, who all speak the same language.

It is not uncommon to find the lounge empty after the first few weeks of class and before winter research papers, vacated in favour of campus cafés and pubs. Today, however, Mohab Adnan is flopped in the yellow armchair beside the binder of course eval-uation forms, staring at the ceiling. Suddenly aware of another person, Mohab removes his glasses, places them in their case, and drops the case into his satchel. He is the only Middle Eastern graduate student in the department, and Emile thinks it must not be easy for him. Everyone has an opinion of the Middle East and the war in Iraq, and few keep it to themselves.

"Would you like some coffee?" Emile offers as he opens a sugar tin. He enjoys a mug of coffee following a presentation, savouring it in one of the lounge chairs, ensconced among copies of *Social Anthropology* and *Anthropological Journal on European Cultures*. Dorothy made him the mug at school, an imprint of her hand pressed into the clay. Other students assume it's Emile's own handprint, and he doesn't correct them, enjoying the idea that Dorothy's prints are potentially interchangeable with his, contradicting DNA, opening up the possibility that there could exist several Dorothys or Emiles, or even Mohabs out there, now and for generations. If the Kennedy curse research has taught him anything, it is that no one is unique, not even a Kennedy.

"No. No thank you. I can't stay," Mohab says, but sinks down farther into the chair.

Emile knows that at least four students have asked Mohab out over the last term, but that he has brushed them off. "I think it's a religious thing," Rachel McGovern, PhD, role of cross-dressing in initiation rituals, told him in the lounge once. Emile doesn't know if that's true, and he doesn't think it's polite to ask—they aren't close, only two courses in common over the last two years— but what is true is that Mohab has been presented with the opportunity of easy sex on a number of occasions, and Emile feels half-envious and half-pitying that he turned it down. But then, these things are complicated, particularly with graduate students. Emile's last girlfriend, Monique, just broke up with him over Thanksgiving because he wouldn't visit her mother's house for the holiday. She accused him of only caring about his work. He had to remind her that they had agreed not to get too attached;

he would be leaving at the end of the school year, after all, and she
still had two years of her BA in leisure studies. What was the
point of meeting her mother? He had never once brought her to
meet his father. *My father doesn't even know you exist,* he thought.
Why do people spend so much time meeting each other's families anyway?
Isn't it hard enough getting along with one person, let alone a whole group
of people who might have little in common other than a last name? We're
not Kennedys. A nation's fate is not in our hands. His sister was smart,
only bringing Victor to the house to meet their father once they
were already engaged. "I don't care for holidays," he told Monique.
"They don't mean anything to me. I'm not religious. I don't see
why I should celebrate something I don't believe in." Although
Emile expected to feel lonely at the loss of his girlfriend—to miss
those grey eyes of hers and her shaggy blonde hair with the dark
highlights, her perky breasts and warm thighs, the way she'd wink
at him to get his attention when his mind wandered—the truth
is that he doesn't really miss her. Or he doesn't miss her enough
to regret all the time spent with his books and his classes.

"Maybe you can help me with something."

Adrenalin still running high since his presentation, for a
moment Emile barely registers the voice. "Maybe, sure," he
responds absently, stirring his coffee, vaguely certain that Mohab
must want to talk to him about his troubles picking a dissertation
topic, as Mohab has written papers on such diverse subjects as
food rituals and the family dynamic, Aztec wedding ceremonies,
and the nomadic habits of various Central American peoples.
This kind of information circulates frequently and widely in the
program, as most of the students spend more time on campus,
talking to each other, than they do with friends and family. Who
is writing what, who is receiving funding to do it, who has secured

travel grants to conduct field research, who has requested which
supervisor and which supervisory committee, who was successful, who wasn't, who passed the field examinations, who has to sit
them again. So Emile is aware that although Mohab is a second-
year PhD, he has no thesis supervisor. "It's like not having a father
or mother," one of the upper-year PhDs said during orientation.
"You want to benefit from their guidance as early on as possible."
Time is running out for Mohab, as he could lose a year searching
for a committee and seeking approval for his topic. Apparently, he
initially proposed studying suicide rituals in tribal societies, but
ended up abandoning the subject, claiming it was probably bad
for his health to think about suicide for years on end. Professor
Blanchford, the head of the program, sympathized and told him
to pick something else. Because the information is factual, Emile
isn't sure if it qualifies as gossip; it doesn't interest him as gossip,
only as anthropology, which attempts to make all human dealings
transparent, like ripping the roofs off people's houses and observ-
ing the happenings inside.

"Do you need an ear?"

Mohab rubs his eyes. "An ear?"

"To bounce off dissertation ideas?" Emile hopes his tone of
voice sounds encouraging, not patronizing.

"No, no." Mohab shakes his head, waves his hands dismissively.
"I'm not worried about that stuff right now. It's something else.
Are you going to pub night?"

Emile hasn't made up his mind. Fridays are pub nights in the
program. Invitations are open, but there are regulars and small
cliques, and those who drop by only once in a while and rarely
stay past ten o'clock. Emile is somewhere in the middle. He's an
MA, not a PhD; his distance from some of the students in the

department is expected, as he will likely be leaving at year's end, but sometimes he thinks his choice of subject also has something to do with it. When he really gets going about how superstitions and curses persist in contemporary culture and affect the choices people make in their daily lives even without their being conscious of them, he can see the window blinds roll down in their eyes, leaving him on the outside. Though he doesn't mind standing in the cold now and then, he does hope to find a PhD program where he is more permanently welcome, as he felt today for the brief duration of his Kennedy presentation.

"I don't know. Tonight's Halloween, so I've been toying with going. It should be fun, but I've got a lot of work to do."

"Yeah, Halloween," Mohab says, straightening up. "I like pub night. It relaxes me. I don't always care so much for the people or conversation, but it is satisfying to end the week having a drink with people who do the same kind of work as you."

"Yes. I think there's something to that," Emile agrees, wondering if this is why he didn't invite Monique to any of them, another complaint on her lengthening list. And he had only one: she is French, like his mother; this reminded him of the years of torturous sessions he had endured to learn the language. Thankfully, his father had never attempted to teach him or his siblings Hindi. *English is difficult enough,* he thinks. *We can't agree in English so why would we agree in other languages?* And French is too lyrical for his tastes; he prefers the harsher sounds of English, how they seem precise, accurate, not exaggerated or ornamental.

"Well," Mohab adds, leaning in across the cheap, ring-stained coffee table, "the problem is that lately the pub nights have been kind of . . . uncomfortable for me."

"What seems to be the problem?" Emile asks.

"My problem has a name," Mohab chuckles, rolling his eyes. "Tiffany Berdichevski. You know her, right?"

"Sure."

"She's nice, fine," he continues, the qualities seemingly uninteresting to him, "but she's been kind of, well, cornering me."

"Cornering you?" Emile immediately recognized the name; now his mental Rolodex locates a face and body. Tiffany Berdichevski: Russian accent, tight sweaters; male professors' thoughts wander over her chest.

"Yeah, she's in my Ethics and Research Methodology seminar, and she's kind of getting aggressive."

"Aggressive?"

"Yes, I think that would be a fair word. Aggressive."

Genuinely stumped, Emile passes his hands over two books he's placed on the table, *Curse Tablets and Binding Spells from the Ancient World* and *Magic Bowls: Aramaic Incantations of Late Antiquity*, as if they might contain an answer, then rolls an HB pencil in his hand. He loves the way pencils smell, the satisfaction when one breaks in his grip from intensive study, the fine point pressed upon the inside of his palm when he can't think of the right word, when it is on the tip of his tongue, and he likes to hold onto them even when he's not using one. "What can I do?"

"I'm not entirely sure," Mohab admits, rising from the yellow chair and picking up his satchel, "but it feels good to get this off my chest. Let's go talk somewhere off-campus. I can practically smell her approaching. She'll be at pub night. I don't even want to think about what costume she might be wearing."

Before picking up his books, Emile swishes water over his handprint mug and leaves it to dry in the plastic tub. Although he has no idea what they're going to do about Mohab's situation, he is somewhat flattered that he's been chosen to help. Besides, he might as well find something to do besides working in the library, tonight of all nights, when superstition is allowed free rein. If not for the breakup, he probably would have ended up with Monique at some dance bar, downing shots and trying not to look too stupid boogying down in a cowboy hat or a Frankenstein mask, trying to figure out what half the people, who always discarded the more uncomfortable parts of their costumes over the evening, were supposed to be. The evening with Mohab should be at least as interesting, likely more so. The two men leave the building joined by a common, if at the moment unknown, purpose.

The Crown Bank insignia is unmistakable, and the manila envelope is too large to be a monthly statement or an advertisement, and weighs as much as a magazine. *To: Mr. Harry Dange, 90 Ashbrook Crescent, Ottawa Ontario. K1B 3L9. Important Documents Enclosed. Confidential.* From his vantage point at the bedroom window, Hardev can see three Gateway Land Developers structures on the north and northeast sides of the street. It's amazing, he thinks, that they already look like homes, even though nothing works inside them.

"How's your wife?" Hardev asks Rodriguez, late again this morning, as he mutes the noon news. "She must be far along now."

Gripping the small of his back, Rodriguez puffs out his cheeks and shoves out his belly. "Yes, she looks like she's giving birth to a house!"

"I wish she would," Hardev sighs, the envelope resting on the tail end of his bib as Rodriguez drops his hands. Hardev waves off his concerned expression. He wants to joke about it. If he can laugh about the legal proceedings, maybe there's nothing to be afraid of.

Retrieving Hardev's toothbrush and toothpaste, and the electric razor from the trolley, Rodriguez places them on the dresser. Hardev can shave himself. The only one who ever insisted on shaving him was Lindsay, a former homecare worker, an ex-prostitute and drug addict who managed to get her act together in her late twenties, and he used to shiver when she lathered his face and neck, drawing long mini-driveways on his skin. He was a bit relieved when she left for the States, undeterred by her lack of a green card. "Where there's money, there's work," she said. Hardev was taught to be wary of knives, sharp objects, dangerous chemicals, but no one told him to be afraid of paper. Yet he knows now that paper is as dangerous as razor blades, is the way people come and go, the way objects are owned or repossessed, the way the most devastating news gets delivered.

"I hope this is the last," Rodriguez says, as he sits on the folding chair beside the television to sort laundry. The news is back on again, low enough not to be disruptive but loud enough to hear. "Four is plenty. Now five! I have teenagers! If I knew my kids would be wanting this and that videogame or pair of blue jeans in this country, I'd never have come."

Hardev is sure Rodriguez is kidding; they all are when they say such things. Had they remained in their homelands, their children would be begging for English lessons and a visa to Canada to study or work. "Children are blessings," he replies. "There's not a religion in the world that doesn't agree on that point."

"Then I must be very wealthy and you should be doing my laundry!"

It is good to laugh, and Rodriguez laughs with him. If he were close enough and strong enough, Hardev would slap Rodriguez on the shoulder. Working with so many immigrants over the years, he knows that when you can make a joke in your new language, you have finally moved from tourist to citizen. He laughs a little longer as Rodriguez folds bathroom towels, today's food segment playing behind him. Weight loss. Previously underweight immigrant populations are ballooning at a rapid pace with low-cost, high-fat, fast-food burger, pizza, and wing joints. Shaking his head at the film footage of flab, Hardev laughs again. The unopened envelope bobs up and down on his belly.

"Maybe I should invite this Mr. Karkiev for lunch, for dinner," he announces. "When you eat with someone you make a connection. If he's invited here, sees the family photographs, meets the . . . well, you understand what I'm saying, right?"

Frowning, Rodriguez clears his throat. "In Nicaragua I saw men take bread from their own children when they were hungry enough."

"What food do you think the bank likes best? Pizza, probably. Like everybody else."

"On garbage day those workers leave all kinds of pizza boxes on the curb. Every week more than the last!"

Three nutritionists advise low-calorie diets and aerobic activity; then the newscast switches to a commercial for Swiss Chalet chicken. "Want to hear something funny?" Hardev passes Rodriguez the envelope, gestures for him to open it. "I never liked pizza. When I first came to Canada the CIDA men went for pizza every Monday night. The invitation to join in was a sign I was accepted. I was so glad. Lorenzo's Pizza, every Monday night, and I ate whatever they ordered. I didn't care. Not all these gourmet toppings they have now, jerk chicken or jalapeños or goat cheese, but one night there'd be pepperoni and mushroom and green pepper, and the next ham and pineapple, or tomatoes and onion and sausage. I didn't care. Two slices and a Molson Canadian or a Coca-Cola and a coffee, every Monday, but I never caught the taste for it. I used to think there was something wrong with me. I never met anyone who didn't like pizza. Other immigrants in the department from all over the world, the Balkans, Trinidad, Argentina, China, they could cite the exact date and time of their first taste of pizza, and list the toppings. I'd smile, nod, try to look dreamy and say, *Oh yes, I hear you, it was the same with me,* but it wasn't."

"Maybe they don't like pizza too. No?" Rodriguez glances over the cover letter, but has obvious trouble reading it. "I hate chocolate," he adds. "At Christmas, I get so much chocolate from clients. Boxes and boxes of chocolates. Turtles, After Eights, if I'm lucky, Laura Secord. My wife likes Laura Secord. But me, no. I don't like chocolate. My wife and me, we don't need chocolate. We need water, electricity, good food. We need money. You invite that bank man over, I bet he brings you chocolates. Cheap ones. Toffifay. Russell Stover. Something like that. The only bank I think is good is the food bank."

Again Hardev wishes he were closer and in better shape to give Rodriguez a friendly slap on the back, though he is guilty as charged. It's difficult for him to shop for the holidays; he usually sends the boy to pick up a dozen Pot of Gold when they go on sale in early December. But Rodriguez is right. These homecare workers don't need boxes of chocolates. Hardev doesn't need boxes of chocolates. Do people give chocolates because they hope the small pleasure in the mouth will soften the burden of everyday life, or because they lack the imagination to figure out what someone might really need? If Mr. Karkiev thought long and hard about how to help Hardev, how to truly help him, most certainly he could come up with a better solution than these legal papers.

The next segment on television is Safety Tips for Halloween. Hardev is embarrassed that he can't remember the names of Rodriguez's kids, or his wife for that matter. It occurs to him that he doesn't know what year they arrived from Nicaragua, only that it was during the eighties. Until today, he had no idea Rodriguez didn't like chocolate. And look at Mr. Karkiev! What does he know about Hardev Dange? And yet he wants to take away his house. "Are your kids going out for Halloween?"

"Oh yes!" exclaims Rodriguez, careful not to smudge the ink or fold the ends of the papers. "They like this Canadian holiday best! Get so angry if someone isn't home, no porch light on. They think they've been cheated. Knock. Get a candy. Knock. Get a candy. I'm glad it's only once a year, Harry. Teaches them nothing about life."

"You said it," Hardev agrees, although he never objected to his own children going out on Halloween. In fact, he enjoyed taking the boy and girl door to door in costumes their mother made; one year the boy was a skunk—what a tail she constructed out of cotton balls and a hanger!—and the girl loved her pink princess costume best, parading around the house, up and down the few stairs for days before the holiday. He relished the time spent chatting briefly with the neighbours, trading winks and chuckles as the made-up creatures fumbled with pillowcases and plastic pumpkin carriers, fake blood and glitter on hands and faces, waiting to tear open a chocolate bar or toffee kiss. Later on, when Dorothy visited on Halloween, Hardev would get the boy to prepare a bag of candy hearts, lollipops, licorice whips, and Big League Chew gum. Now he likes to station himself in the kitchen so that, even if he can't give out the candy himself, he can still watch the children approach on the driveway and listen to the doorbell ring like the pleading voice of each child: *Trick or treat, trick or treat*; then take in the joy on their faces as the homecare worker walks out with a large plastic bowl of candy. "I wish Mr. Karkiev would go away if I gave him a bag of candy."

"Oh, Harry." Rodriguez secures Hardev's reading glasses onto the bridge of his nose and places the papers tidily in front of him.

Amounts Due. Property Taxes and Interest Rates Owing. Foreclosure Dates. Bank-speak; another language Hardev barely understands, which he assumes is the intention. "You know what I'm giving Birendra for her wedding? Water."

"Water?" Rodriguez returns to the basket of laundry.

"Not just any water. Water from the Holy River Ganges. In India. My father told me that no matter where I travelled in life, I should keep a bottle of water from this sacred river with me. It's an Indian tradition, one of the few I still practise. Five vials left India with me. I hoped for five children."

"Like me!" Rodriguez points out, snapping a white pillowcase.

"Yes, like you. I wanted a large family like many of the families back home, at least five children, but it wasn't meant to be. I've used three vials, one on each of my children, when they were born. I doused their foreheads with the water, said a little prayer for their future. My boy would call this superstition, but he'd be wrong. There is a vast difference between superstition and tradition, fear and respect. Now I have only two bottles left. Birendra is the oldest and the first to marry, so I will give one to her for her own children. The other I'm saving for when my number comes up. Though maybe it has," he adds sadly, tapping the legal papers. He feels tears forming at the corners of his eyes, but swallows hard to stop them. It will take days to get through it all. Days and days. And he can't ask the boy for help.

Leaning in closer, Rodriguez whispers, "What does it do?"

"The water protects you," Hardev eagerly explains; it's harder for him to start crying if he's busy speaking, and he doesn't want to cry in front of Rodriguez, who's been so strong bringing up his own children in hard circumstances. "People like to say here that blood is thicker than water. What a silly expression, when most family members don't even share the same blood type. Blood only separates people. Look at the news. Everyone fights about blood. But water! Water connects us. My nickname at work used to be The Water King. When I was working . . ."

"Harry—I forgot," Rodriguez interrupts, dropping one of Emile's blue sweatshirts back into the basket. "I'm supposed to call my wife. I'll be right back. Just the recap now."

The recap of the hurricane. Hardev turns his eyes back to the window, to the shells of houses waiting like those discarded by snails for other living creatures to take up, and wonders if Rodriguez was listening to him, or if he was busy contemplating his own potential disaster. Children, more unpredictable than hurricanes. They too can strike, but you never know how or when. You never know if they'll be able to stand their ground, or if they'll be swept away, destroyed. Though he's saddened by the thought that his parents never had the chance to meet their grandchildren, he's glad they did not live to see what happened to him. Swallowing hard again, he examines the first paper in the pile, his name clearly typed in bold capital letters. "Sometimes you have no idea what's coming down your path, do you?"

Already dialing the kitchen telephone, Rodriguez does not hear the question.

Bursting out of the stairwell like a horse out of a starting gate, Dorothy tears down the home economics wing to her locker. If she doesn't get to the cafeteria within five minutes of the beginning of lunch hour, the lineup will be long and the coffee will have grime at the bottom. A navy blue sweatshirted arm slows her down. She flicks her mane. Orange-red spiky hair.

"Meet me at the Landing Pad," Kite signs.

"Ten minutes," she signs back, throwing her physics binder into her locker.

Kite and Dorothy have only visual arts class in common, but have been paired up to work on the school mural together, Dorothy being the best sketch artist at Rousseau and Kite the best painter. The project still at conception stage, Mrs. Kotek (the girls all call her Mrs. Kotex) has given them until the end of the school year to finish. The quality of the mural, she says, is more important than haste.

Kite is alright, but Dorothy doesn't like group work, and wouldn't be working on the mural at all if she hadn't been absolutely forced into it. "You don't belong to anything," Mrs. Kotek said to her at the start of October, as if informing her of something she didn't already know. "I've received permission from Principal Jacobson that if you complete this project it will count as your club or team requirement so you can graduate. You know about the requirement, right? Did you think it would be waived because of your high grades in all your academic subjects? You need to get connected, Dorothy. It's important." Dorothy wanted to tell Mrs. Kotek that she was connected, that she was a transmitter, actually, and the problem wasn't in the circuits but in the receptors. The reception at Rousseau Secondary School was at fault. But she knew Mrs. Kotek wouldn't understand, and

Principal Jacobson, whom the students called Any Excuse Jacobson because he gave in to all parent demands to keep the funding coming in, wouldn't care. Hanging out in the smoking section or at the Landing Pad doesn't count for school credit, and these people aren't really Dorothy's friends either, only acquaintances, people to shoot the shit with once in a while, who offer her free joints since she has started apprenticing at Signature Tattoo and Body Piercing and has inked a dozen or so of them—mostly small tattoos on arms or the small of the back—and has pierced a few more—nose and tongue rings (tongues are a favourite, especially for the deaf). Some question her about the pros and cons of labia and cock rings, but none, as far as she knows, has gone through with one. If so, she would have heard; teenagers can't wait to tell those kinds of stories.

Kite's also deaf. Meningitis. Thin mouth, orange-pink lips, left canine chipped in a motocross mishap—he braked to avoid what he thought was a person lying in the middle of an Algonquin trail. "There's this full set of clothing: running shoes, T-shirt, Adidas track pants, a girl's underwear with a pink elastic waistband, and dollar-store sunglasses with a blue tint. I suppose it was a joke," he explained to Dorothy. But it's why he started to refer to his favourite lunch and smoking spot as the Landing Pad. "If my Mystery Girl returns from wherever she's vanished to, I want to welcome her home." The story suits Kite—so called because he's a reliable connection for weed, hash, acid, mushrooms, and ecstasy. His real name is Corey, but no one—not even the teachers, after the first rounds of attendance—call him anything but Kite. Perhaps they think it's a childhood nickname, or accept that the students' choices in life are already limited and the least they can do is let them choose their own names.

At lunch Dorothy likes to leave the school—which is divided between Rousseau Secondary and a technical high school, the building a four-storey U-shape but with Rousseau taking up more than its allotted half—walk past the General and Children's Hospitals to St. Laurent Boulevard's strip malls and fast-food restaurants; on longer breaks, when she has a spare period before or after lunch, she can walk farther, to the Museum of Science and Technology, and eat on the stairs of the old Nova Scotia lighthouse. No one is ever manning it and from the top of the stairwell, near the door, she can survey the busy street while perched upon the transplanted landmark bolted into its bed of green grass. The museum has other good lunch spots on its well-kept property: underneath a missile or satellite, on top of the steam engine (though teenagers are sometimes passed out drunk there, even at midday) or the coal carrier; but the red-and-white striped lighthouse with its revolving spotlight is her favourite. Poking her legs between the railings, she is content to spend long stretches of time concentrating on the beam, trying to read it, ascertain where danger might exist. She likes to imagine that Roof and Key are her own miniature lighthouse, whose job it is to stop people from hitting the rocks.

The cafeteria is the one area of the school shared between Rousseau and tech students—there are separate libraries and gymnasiums and even the back fields are divided by a clear yellow spray-painted line—and Dorothy notices a number of tech students in the lineup as she purchases an oatmeal-and-raisin muffin and a lukewarm coffee, and zips up her black sweater with the pink skull and crossbones on the back. The Rousseau smoking section is located at the back of the school, between the two wings, and the U-shape contributes to an unfortunate wind-tunnel effect, making it difficult for people to light their cigarettes. Some teachers say it's an incentive to get the students to quit, but several of them, including Mrs. Kotek, smoke there too, sneaking out for a few minutes during class. *You kids didn't invent rule-breaking*, Mr. Yangley, the physics and chemistry teacher, likes to say. Dorothy doesn't smoke cigarettes but she's more comfortable with the smokers, who are generally less intrusive and more casual than the non-smokers. Dorothy likes to watch, to listen, hands and fingers darting and weaving as cigarettes teeter between lips; blind with deaf, one-handed with two-handed, mild autistics, aphasics. In the smoking section, it's easy to float among the students, who are bound by a habit rather than an identity, without any claims of joining them.

The Landing Pad is off school property, past the soccer and field-hockey pitches and the award-winning rose garden which the smokers joke is there to remind them all that they're special and should be happy as pigs in shit. The inside of the school is littered with posters designed to boost self-esteem and to quickly match up any potential depressive or psychotic with a counsellor or government-funded organization. Who's heard of a public school with its own award-winning rose garden? A Sunshine Wing sporting awards for Best Classroom Friend and Greatest School Spirit? A gymnasium with a forty-foot long *Everyone's a Winner* banner? The students resent a good many of these efforts to make them feel good about themselves, which only make them feel worse, but they please the parents and, more importantly, the donors, and so all the students can do is roll their eyes, rip down a few posters, spit on the rosebuds.

Dorothy speculates that Kite is likely waiting for her at the Landing Pad to "brainstorm," to catch thousands of little brains dropping out of the sky with parachutes, or to "pick her brain," to unhinge her skull and poke tiny steel utensils into unnamed areas. The truth is, whether they want to do this mural or not, they're having trouble with it, are at a loss as to where to begin. What does Mrs. Kotek expect? That they'll paint a serene and happy landscape of deaf, blind, mute, paralyzed, and autistic teenagers holding hands (those with hands) underneath a rainbow? Does she want candy and balloons and streamers? No sketch pleases them. All the paper ends up either on the floor or in the garbage, or crossed out in the sketchbook. *What does it mean to be here? To be us? The Rousseau Family?* These are questions Mrs. Kotek said they were supposed to confront and answer. *It means shit,* Dorothy felt like signing, the teachers too eager to make them all think they are bound by more than their disabilities, by some common struggle or fierce spirit. *We wouldn't be here if we didn't have to be,* she wanted to tell her, *if we belonged in the regular world,* but instead she just exchanged e-mail addresses with Kite. Kite first proposed painting Noah's ark washed up on Parliament Hill. Suitably epic for a mural, but Dorothy found the idea upsetting and e-mailed back, *Are we to hide behind the masks of animals?* Kite saw her point and admitted that it was probably too Judeo-Christian anyway, and that the Buddhist and Muslim students might feel left out. *Plus,* Dorothy added, *in the Bible disabled people are only mentioned if they are going to be cured.* But Dorothy knows she's running out of goodwill, as she's spent the last month criticizing his ideas without proposing a single one of her own.

The beaten trail ends at Kite finishing rolling a joint and licking the paper. Two girls with boyfriends or fuck-friends are passing around a cigarette and a two-litre bottle of Pepsi. A partially eaten ham and cheese sandwich lies between the legs of a brunette in jeans and a tight purple sweater. She snorts smoke as Dorothy sits down on a stump.

"Good timing," Kite signs, passing her the joint. Dorothy smiles to show she appreciates the offer, then inhales. "You should come to Kelly's Halloween party. You don't need a costume, and I'll be bringing plenty of candy, if you understand me." Kelly, the brunette—deaf at birth—nods, as her boyfriend, Todd, a stocky guy with a goatee—brain damage, water aspiration, swimming accident—plays with her earlobe. "Her mom's out of town for the weekend and her aunt has an overnight shift at the grocery."

"Thanks, but I already have plans." Dorothy heard about the party earlier from the smoking section. She exhales and passes the joint back. "Next time."

Kite inhales. "What plans?"

"Working. Halloween's a busy night."

"Shame," he replies, still holding his breath, one advantage of speaking with one's hands. "Maybe you can cancel. Phone in sick? Or stop by afterwards?"

"No," she signs firmly.

"You'll miss all the fun!" Kite finally exhales, the stream of white smoke wafting through the air, and passes the joint along. "I'm going as George Bush. I'm going to smoke a bunch of joints and mis-sign words. And we still don't have a single decent mural idea."

Alex, mute, playing videogames with Pepper on his cellphone—black-and-white striped hair, high-functioning autistic—inhales twice, drops the roach on the ground, and rolls another. For the next twenty minutes, until Dorothy needs to return for communication studies class, Kite smokes a regular cigarette, describes his costume and who else will be at the party, while the two couples trade saliva and text messages.

Finally rising from the stump, Dorothy flicks dead pieces of grass off her pants. Kite signs, "I know you lie about working. Not tonight maybe, but in general. I've stopped by and you're not there. As Mrs. Kotek says, *Art may be the lie that tells the truth, but until your work is hanging in the Louvre, you're expected to tell the truth in here.* So why are you lying to me?"

Stunned, Dorothy doesn't know what to say. He's right, she does lie about working, and she'll only be working for a couple of hours tonight and then plans to go to the SoundScape. No one at Rousseau knows about the SoundScape. SoundScape people are not part of the Rousseau Family. She retaliates: "The mural's not really important. This school's not really important."

Kite rises, shoves his cigarettes into his back pocket and his Ziploc bag of weed into his front one. "You think spending four years in the same place with the same people isn't important? Are you just going to forget you were ever here?"

His voice isn't angry, it's baffled, which makes Dorothy even more annoyed. As flippantly as possible, she signs, "Probably. Why not? We have until the end of the year to finish this stupid mural. What's the rush?" Then, without waiting for his answer, she drops her sweater cuffs past her hands and heads briskly back down the path.

Twenty feet along, the navy blue sweatshirt pulls once again at her arm. "I might be leaving Rousseau soon," he signs in small, slow motions, as she turns around. "I don't know when. I thought we could go out, smoke, have fun. It's been fun hanging out the last few weeks. My parents want me to get the implant, even though I'm probably too old and it'll just be a huge waste of time and money. Don't tell anyone. I . . . I haven't told anyone yet. But I wanted to tell you."

At the mention of the implant, Roof and Key's lighthouse sounds an alarm, suggests dispatching a search party. Where did the Kite go who a minute ago wanted to defend all the Rousseau kids as special, worth paying attention to? If people are so happy with their disabled children, why are they always looking for technologies to fix them? It's a bunch of hypocrisy, mixed wires. Fifteen deaf kids in the last five years have left Rousseau after undergoing cochlear surgery. They even brought in a batch of professionals to talk to the parents and give assessments on the likelihood of success. Dorothy's mother attended the session. Two percent chance. What was Kite given? Fifty probably, if his parents are going for it. Maybe just thirty percent, if they're desperate. To your face Rousseau says it's fantastic to be different from "normal" society, but behind your back they all wish you were something you're not. Just like every family, Dorothy supposes.

The skunky smell of weed clings to Kite's sweatshirt and to his hands. Dizzy from a puff too many, she finds it hard to picture him, shivering now like a bird in the wind, with an implant, and so instead she pictures the day she was rummaging through boxes in her father's basement and came across a picture of her parents at Notre-Dame Basilica. The photographs from before the accident are all hidden away in boxes. No wonder she knows so little about her father, her mother, about their life together before everything changed. When she brought the picture upstairs—it must have been from their Paris honeymoon—to ask about it, her father snatched it away. *A picture isn't worth a thousand words,* he said, *it's worth a thousand questions,* and hid it in his trolley drawer. *Whoever says we choose our burdens must have been able to walk, that's all I know.* Dorothy stole this picture too, but she didn't put it up in her locker. She taped it to the inside of her SoundScape Diaries notebook.

And her father was right, she does ask the photograph questions, and the questions keep changing though the photograph remains the same. Today, for Kite's sake, she might ask it: *Where does God live? Does he live here and listen to us? Or is he a man of no fixed address? If so, what messages does he actually receive? What are our chances of success? When Adam and Eve had questions, he just evicted them.* And suddenly she wants to share this thought with her father, who seems even farther away than Paris or God, but all she can do is try to catch her balance, leave Kite hurt and unanswered in the path, and rush off to communication studies class.

Subject: What do you really want?
Hi Birendra,
Mom called and said that it would be nice if I sent you an engagement gift. You know I'm horrible at these things. Could you e-mail me back a list of stuff you actually want so I'm not left getting you a breadmaker or fondue set or some other such potentially useless device since I'm pretty sure you don't even know how to cook?
Another option: a gift card?
Emile

Dear Dor,
You and your sister moved to Augusta Street. The boy stayed with me. I don't think your mother had the heart to leave me completely alone. *A boy needs a father,* she said. And I said, *And girls, what do girls need?*
    It's better this way, Hardev. You know it is. She had started calling me Hardev, instead of Harry. I think she was trying to be respectful, give me back some dignity, but I felt worse

for it, like our marriage had never existed, like our lives were no longer intertwined. April. Springtime. Time for creatures to stretch after winter hibernations, for new families to emerge. Snow melted, it was sunny the day your mother moved out. Luggage in a rent-a-car. Dust on her face and hair. She didn't even wait for Easter. I wondered who would hide the chocolate eggs for you kids, who would go to the store and buy them. You were at her friend Molly's house, one of her teaching buddies, likely eating the sugar cubes this woman used to try and pass off as cookies. Birendra was at school, her clothes and stuffed toys packed earlier in the van. She had already picked out blue paint for the new bedroom. Blue paint and a new grown-up desk and full-length mirror. What was I supposed to do with your now empty rooms?

No, it isn't, I said. But we'd fought enough. Even I was tired of arguing, and arguing was all I had left. The space between us, between kitchen and door and driveway, was civil, but I knew your mother and I would rarely be civil to each other again. I stared at her face: her algae-green eyes set slightly inward, her square cheeks flushed by embarrassment, those light pink soft lips that used to meet mine so openly when I'd walk her down the Market streets to buy a freshly squeezed lemonade or those packets of maple fudge she adored, her hair grazing her shoulders, an old perm crinkling on the ends, a few missed strands of grey. I think she felt that day how hard I was looking at her, thinking of the past. It must have been the last time she felt my love.

I've loved her since, Dor, though I don't like to talk about it because loving her since hasn't done me any good. What's the point of this love, worse than phantom limbs, reminding me? Who do memories belong to? They don't seem to belong to me. Dor, my dear Dor, should I wish this kind of love on you? I don't know. It's the kind of love that lasts a lifetime.

Think of that.

Birendra is on hold. The new girl, Tracy, has been instructed to tape up more sale signs along the Wall Flower Florist and Gifts storefront. Unlike winter and spring, fall has few holidays to boast of, and since Halloween is not a flower holiday, business tends to dip. *Order Two Dozen Roses, Get Another Dozen for Half-Price. Free Delivery on Weekdays, for a Limited Time. Potting Soil and Clay Pots 33% Off. Selected Items.*

The walk-in clinic loops a pre-recorded phone message about free flu shots. Annoyed at the wait, Birendra pulls at the coloured-ribbon spools attached to the cash. The after-work rush will start soon, and she doesn't want anyone to overhear her. Right now, the only person in the store is a middle-aged woman, a very good customer who wears knit hats and regularly sifts through the cards and gardening books after placing large orders for office events. She never buys anything for herself—enough simply to take in the sights and perfume smells of the fresh-cut flowers for a few minutes without any pressure to care for them, likely because she already has too many relying on her. A Humane Society volunteer, after ordering her centrepieces and vase arrangements she'll now and then drop off a few flyers and posters. Today, one about rabbits: *Care for Me. Adopt a Rabbit Program.* Their eyes meet briefly and Birendra smiles; then the flu-shot reel ends abruptly.

"Yes, oh, yes. I'd like … to make an appointment," Birendra says as casually as possible, keeping her head bent, the receiver close.

"What for? Ummm, that's . . . personal . . . Huh? . . . Yes, I said *personal* . . . Oh, of course, I'm just, I'm calling from work . . ."

Returning the Scotch tape to the counter drawer, Tracy swivels around Birendra, brushing her elbow. "Sorry," she chimes. "I need to ask you a question."

Birendra raises a finger, switches the receiver to her other ear, and lowers her voice to a whisper. "I want to talk to a doctor about my . . . my periods . . . yes, that's right . . . yes, I think I am due for my yearly physical. OK . . ." Pulling on Tracy's green smock, she gestures to the sticker gun and then to the hanging baskets. "Evenings are best for me. Next week? Yes, OK. Thank you."

Two women extract carnations, a man tiger lilies, out of the pails containing prearranged bouquets, from simple carnations or daffodils to sunflowers and daisies, roses and lilacs, affordably priced between $3.99 and $19.99. On Fridays they nearly sell out. "Don't forget our delivery specials," Tracy reminds them, handing each a business card for the store. "What's this?" she adds, flipping over the Humane Society flyer as the man walks off with his briefcase in one hand, bouquet in the other. "You thinking of getting a rabbit?"

Hanging up the phone, Birendra punches her chin toward the middle-aged woman in the orange knit hat, now reading the back cover of a new book: *The Art of Zen, Healing for Your Home.* "She orders a lot for Crown Bank, brings this stuff in sometimes. Apparently they're filled to capacity with rabbits," she says matter-of-factly. "Here, take a look."

Tracy is silent for a minute as she reads the pamphlet. "Wow. I knew we had a cat problem, but rabbits? Ever visit the cats of Parliament Hill?"

"Yeah, I was a tour guide two summers in high school. The cats of Parliament Hill were on my route," Birendra replies, slightly amused by the remembrance. Her father was so proud of her those two summers, his daughter teaching visitors about Canada's history, he was sorry when she quit to make more in tips as a waitress in a sports bar. She didn't have the heart to tell him that most people on her tour couldn't care less about Canada's history; they wanted to admire the marble floors and the staircase to the clock tower, wave at Mounties, and fawn over feral cats in ramshackle multiplex wooden cat houses.

"Ahhh, Easter presents seem to be the culprit. People get rabbits at Easter but have no idea how to take care of them, don't realize they need to be fixed or they'll get aggressive. How sad. I don't know how people can do that, take something into their homes without knowing how to care for it."

"If it was a gift, maybe they didn't want the rabbit in the first place," Birendra posits as Tracy hands the flyer back. All of a sudden she wishes the woman hadn't come in today; now she'll have to put the leaflet out with the others. Good for customer relations, but bad for her conscience. Birendra doesn't want a rabbit. Neither does Tracy. Who does? And how is this her problem? "What did you want to ask me?"

"Oh, I'm sorry. I didn't mean to interrupt you talking to your doctor—"

"No. It's nothing," Birendra assures her, cutting her off, pulling a yard of gold ribbon off one of the spools to tie around a glass vase. "I'm just getting my physical. I . . . I want to make sure I'm perfectly healthy, you know, for the wedding."

"Oh, yeah." Tracy nods wholeheartedly, slapping stickers from the gun onto the counter. "It's smart to get checked out. My cousin did the same thing when she got married last year. Wanted to talk about going off the pill. Do you want to have children right away?"

Birendra's jaw hardens; her cheeks flush. Tracy's openness can be good for business, but at this moment Birendra wishes she'd hired an actual wallflower. "Right away? Oh, I don't know . . ."

"Hey, why not? If you can afford it, right, why wait? Shit, I already have names picked out, but no man prospects in sight. I was just wondering, while it's not that busy, if you want me to hand out coupons at the escalators."

"That's not a bad idea. Go ahead," Birendra replies, though with somewhat less enthusiasm than she intends.

Tracy nods again, grabs the stack of "Free Delivery" coupons beside the register, and walks out. Birendra pops the orange stickers from the countertop onto her left arm and heads for the hanging baskets, scanning the store where she has been manager for the last two years, and where she first met Victor; he was sending a *Get Well Soon* rhododendron to a secretary in the office who had broken her leg falling off a ladder while putting a box of paperwork away. "Work injury, so we all feel responsible," he said, handing her an oversized card with a dozen or so signatures on it. He forgot his credit card on the counter and had to return for it. She was just getting off work, her hair down, dressed nicely in her favourite gold hoop earrings, a short black dress, high heels, because she had a date, a second date with an insurance agent. As she gave him back his credit card, admiring his impressively dense dirty-blond hair, his deep-set blue eyes, she told him to be careful. He asked of what. "You never know. Ladders aren't the only dangerous objects in a room." He replied, "What about dinner? Is dinner dangerous?" Birendra blushed; "Oh yes, in some countries dinner is very dangerous." And she stood up the insurance agent, just like that. She is still amazed at how quickly everything progressed between them, how it took only a few months for him to decide he wanted to take care of her for the rest of his life, telling her that he needed someone just like her at just this time, that it was fate he had forgotten his credit card and had been forced to return to the dark-haired beauty with the golden skin, that he had focused so hard on his career that he had nearly forgotten *why* one worked so hard. And he wasn't afraid of all her siblings, her mother's overbearing nature, her father's condition; no, surprisingly, he welcomed it all. "I'm an only child," he said, "and my parents let money raise me. What happened to your family was tragic, what happened to mine was merely typical. So your family's a little unusual, I don't know what a usual one is like." How lucky, Birendra thought, but she kept this to herself, happy to let him romanticize her family situation if it made him more determined to take care of her. What matters is that Victor loves her and he's going to marry her. They can make a family of two, just two, no one else.

Yes, that would be bliss, she assures herself, noting that the African violets are wilting and the wreaths for McKay's Funeral Home need to be removed from the walk-in fridge so she can tie their ribbons. Flowers are so fussy, she often laments, they need constant supervision and attention; water here, trimming here, pruning here, food there, and most often the blooms barely last a few weeks. It's the part of the business that she can't stand, and she won't be sorry to leave it behind. She is content to balance accounts, file papers, count inventory, make up work schedules, organize with distributors; the actual tending of the flowers is her least favourite activity, and she often wishes she worked at a place that sold plastic or leather flowers, or more dried flowers, instead of live or cut ones. Especially on a day like today, when she doesn't want to be thinking about living things at all.

The baskets discounted, she is about to attend to the funeral wreaths when her smock pocket vibrates. "It's your mother, your mother!" the high-pitched voice on the line shouts. "Birendra, I think I have a bad connection. Damn cell. I can barely hear you. I wanted to tell you, I can't remember if I told you, the secret to a healthy marriage is you need to keep . . ."

"The lines of communication open," Birendra finishes, sighing into the phone as a customer removes a bouquet of yellow and white daisies from the first pail. The line crackles, and Birendra remembers something her father told her the other day—that all cellphone conversations are now recorded. "Never assume the only person listening to your conversation is the intended recipient," he said. *Why can't communication ever be private?* she thinks, trying to keep her voice low. E-mails can be forwarded; discs copied; phone conversations taped; video cameras installed. *The only true privacy is inside a family*, her father claims. But Birendra disagrees. The only true privacy is what you never say. She whispers into the phone, "Mom, you phoned to tell me this?"

"It's important . . . dress appointments tonight. The one you like . . . price of a small country . . . don't care . . . need to talk. Can you . . . damn . . . your father. I remembered something. Text-message Dorothy. Remind her . . . bridal shop address is. . . . OK? I have a client now. Autistic. The parents are impossible. See you tonight!"

Tracy returns empty-handed just as Birendra slips her cellphone back into her pocket. Two men in fast-food uniforms walk in and stop at a display of vases while another, in a three-piece suit much like the one Victor was wearing that day he forgot his credit card, saunters up to the cash. "Don't look so worried," Tracy offers, picking up a water jug on her way to the backroom sink. "Your mother had healthy children, right? Then you will too. I'm sure your doctor's appointment will turn out just fine."

"You sell candy?" the man asks.

"Drugstore," Birendra blurts, surprised to find she's shaking and her knees feel weak. No one will understand, she thinks. How can she explain that she doesn't want to check out fine at the doctor's? That this isn't why she made an appointment? She wants her future home to be free of children.

"No, but I can adopt a rabbit?" he snorts.

The old-fashioned cuckoo clock, a leftover from the last manager of Wall Flower Florist and Gifts, sounds five chimes. A young mother dragging two plastic Halloween costumes along the tiled floor, a Spiderman outfit and a witch's dress, stops at the counter and picks up a flyer. We must read dozens and dozens of flyers and signs per day, Birendra calculates. What is it we're looking for? Valuable information, a deal, love? Most often we don't follow up, just as this woman, so intent on the message—so saddened by the plight of the rabbits, like me and Tracy before her—won't adopt a rabbit. This man certainly won't. That woman must distribute hundreds of these flyers, if not thousands, hoping for what? Maybe fifty or sixty responses, if that? Like Wall Flower's free delivery coupons. What a pathetic method of communication, she concludes, as she reminds herself to send Dorothy a text message. What a waste of paper.

Text message from Dorothy Dange to Birendra Dange:
TONIGHT WE PICK OUT OUR COSTUMES!

Remembrance Day

Pedestrian traffic is dense on Parliament Hill and at the National War Memorial as mother and daughter rush to Sparks Street past the granite figures of Peace and Freedom searching for wedding ideas. Sunshine yellow has been agreed upon for the bridesmaid dresses; yellow daffodils, white daisies, and pale pink ribbons for the flower arrangements. They've also agreed upon the wording for the invitations, and that her mother's favourite poem, a love sonnet by Pablo Neruda, will be read as part of the ceremony. Details yet to be discussed include: head table seating, order of speeches, how to handle the father-daughter dance; all these are avoided for now. Better to concentrate on aesthetics, on what needs to be purchased.

"What do you think of pots of daffodils as centrepieces? We could give them away as door prizes, although I suppose most of Victor's family wouldn't be able to take them back on the planes," Birendra says, twisting a five-dollar bill into the Salvation Army box for two poppies. Snow dropping in broad white waves— Birendra thinks it's cruel when the weather turns miserable like this on Remembrance Day, the veterans standing or parked in wheelchairs for hours on the concrete in their old uniforms. But Victor disagrees. "Sunny days are worse," he argued after checking the weather channel. "All the sun gives them is a better view of the schoolchildren picking their noses and rolling their eyes, dragged downtown by their schools for an 'educational experience.' These kids don't give a damn about what their grandparents or great-grandparents went through for them. They're cut off from the past." Civil servants are given time off in Victor's department to attend the ceremonies, so Birendra knows he is amid the dispersing crowd, who are more well-meaning than the selfish schoolchildren but still far removed from the suffering of the men saluting the bronze statues which through the years have become a metal neighbourhood, taking the place of their friends.

"This is your wedding, Birendra," Isobel says, Birendra catching up to her to pin the second poppy to her jacket lapel. "And I know how happy you are with the dress you've chosen, but I wanted to talk to you about something. Maybe you could consider wearing another outfit for the reception?"

"What? I thought you liked the dress."

Mother grabs onto daughter's arm to withstand the wind. "I wanted to talk to you about this before, about your father. But first I was having a hard enough time just getting you to talk when we were making plans in the kitchen, then we were having such a nice time at the bridal shop with Dorothy, and I think you should spend as much time together as possible now, before you're married. With Emile too, if you can. But I can't wait any longer. Times change, circumstances change, but people remain attached to things they once imagined. Your father imagined something for your wedding a long time ago, and you should consider it." Isobel doesn't like discussing the past in front of her children, but sometimes it's necessary. *If they want to know something, they're old enough to ask,* is what she usually thinks, but they've rarely asked anything over the years beyond *Can I have this? Can I do this? Can we afford this?* Typical for a child, she supposes, but it's time now to talk to Birendra a little bit about the past.

"He bought you a sari. A wedding sari," she tells her, as they weave through the steady stream of people freed from the war memorials, seeking shelter in the stores. "Right after you were born. Right here in the Market."

"A sari? I've never worn a sari in my life! Dad doesn't wear a turban and—"

"Look," Isobel scolds, passing an elaborate window display of coffee-table war books. "It's not about being South Asian. You know how your father feels. He's always told you, you're not half-Indian half-French, you're full Canadian. This is about something different. Hope. Hope for your future. As soon as you were born, he was hoping for good things to happen to you, and he bought you a red and gold sari. Very expensive. Very beautiful, Birendra. Handmade. He hasn't mentioned it to me in years, but I know he still has it—he's kept everything—you should consider wearing it at your reception—"

"But Mom—"

"Consider it. Your grandparents liked your father, you know, they just didn't want me to marry outside our culture. They were wrong. That's not why our marriage didn't work."

"Mom, you don't have to defend yourself," Birendra replies—then, squeezing her arm, "This is the store, I always forget its name, I love this store. Let's look. Maybe I'll find Victor the perfect wedding gift here."

"Have you been by to see him?"

"Victor?"

"No, your father," Isobel corrects, wiping her boots on the fluorescent green welcome mat of On the Tip of Your Tongue, and shaking snow off her coat. "He might need you. You should check up on him."

"Why don't *you* check up on him if you're so concerned?"

"Don't be ridiculous." Isobel follows as Birendra shuffles delicately past two display cases of art deco wineglasses and crystal figures. "Don't ignore your father right now."

Leather gloves. Wool shawls. Silver rings, turquoise earrings. Wine openers. "Mom, I won't. But a sari? That's not *my* culture."

High-end stationery. Quill pens. Personalized key chains. "It's not your father's either. Not in the way you're thinking. It's about family, Birendra. Family. When you have children one day you'll understand. Besides, I thought I saw on Fashion TV that Bollywood-inspired styles are the new rage. Think about the sari seriously. You don't respect family enough. Family means something beyond paying for things."

"Oh, Mom, you know I respect—rabbits!" Birendra coos, stopping at an entire stand of ceramic salt and pepper shakers. One white, the other black. The salt and pepper shoot out the ears.

"Clever," Isobel agrees, lightly touching the black one's nose. "But not for Victor. Cute though. I'll buy them for you if you like. They can't be that expensive, even in this place. A little present from your mother." Isobel turns to look for the salesman with the spiked hair and blue silk shirt, who has since disappeared. "I guess we don't look like criminals."

"No, that's alright. Rabbits are hard to care for." Birendra chuckles, returning the pair to their place, as her mother gives her a quizzical look. "Sorry, it's a joke. You wouldn't get it."

"Maybe your father would have some suggestions about what to get Victor," Isobel offers, though when it came to her own wedding, she needed no one's input on what to get Hardev as a gift. For six months she took private lessons in traditional Indian dance. Her ankles were strong from ballet training, but still the bangles and bells took getting used to, and she never did master the see-sawing of the chin, which, when well executed, mesmerizes the audience like a pendulum. In their bed and breakfast suite on Elgin after the ceremony, she retired to the washroom "to get into something more comfortable," and he was amazed when she emerged in silver and turquoise costume and makeup, her tape deck ready. "Dance is the most expressive language I know," she told him.

Birendra sighs, moving on to admire blown-glass table lamps.

"Just because he isn't paying for the wedding doesn't mean he shouldn't be consulted on some of the details. Keep in mind that we're *all* going to remember this day for the rest of our lives."

"The only thing that interests Father right now is the construction going on in his area. Every week I get an update. Would you like to know about the concrete foundations, the frames? How many doors and windows have been installed? How about the lock-up phase? Wiring? Ottawa plumbing policies? Zoning permits? I know so much about building houses that Victor and I could probably build our own!"

The spiky-haired young man has returned to the front of the store and begins polishing silverware. Birendra notices a hoop piercing through his bottom lip. "Be nice," Isobel admonishes, gently brushing a strand of hair off her daughter's face. "Don't forget it's his birthday tomorrow."

"I know his birthday. Dorothy's the one who needs reminding, remember?"

"People change." Hardev did. She did. After the accident, they were very different people. How could they not be? Neither of them had imagined that their marriage would end up in hospitals, doctor's offices, with round-the-clock care staff. Isobel wishes her children had more memories of them in that time before; maybe they would all feel more like a family, like a group with common goals and purposes, common understandings. Instead, they all shattered along with Hardev's spine.

"You know, Mom, you're right. Maybe I'm thinking the wrong way here," Birendra says, her eyes settling on the salesman's piercing. Even though she's seen many of them before without the least bit of interest—she even asked Dorothy to stop leaving her piercing photographs around, they were bugging her—all of a sudden, she seems to understand. "I want something that tells Victor marriage is a significant ceremony. That it means a lot more than flowers and gifts. That I'm going to be *changed* by it."

Yes, she affirms to herself, patting her mother absently on the shoulder, something to tell Victor that I'm leaving my past behind, that my future is with him. Only him. And I'm ready to go anywhere, anywhere in the world. *Foreign Affairs*. How she loves those words on her tongue. To her, they mean freedom. Her mother is wrong; it is possible to respect family while working to be free from it. Putting on her gloves, preparing to return outside, she takes a last glance at the silver half-moon punched through the man's lip, and readjusts the poppy pin more securely on the collar of her coat. They have a way of falling off.

Yearly Physical Questionnaire: To be returned to
Dr. Pittu by November 30, 2003
Do you feel better or worse than you did last year?
I feel like a man who is sinking into his bed and can't get out. I've felt like that for years though, and haven't surrendered, so I must be making progress and will continue to cheat Death and His various associates for a little longer.

Has your daily routine changed in the last year?
I think my son might have acquired a girlfriend, but I'm not exactly sure. He treats his studies like a full-time job so he's hardly ever home anyway. Homecare has finally sent me a decent, hard-working immigrant from Nicaragua named Rodriguez. He is fine company; isn't particularly interested in the news, but watches it with me; enjoys a bowl of hot oatmeal in the morning as much as I do.

I sleep and wake at the same set times as in the past; however, it's getting harder to ignore rain. Maybe it returns because I have not understood its message, or maybe my senses are getting even stronger. Construction continues in the area, and I'm able to decipher each board as it is hammered into the frame, each brick as it is fitted into place. I can smell cement and paint and even Tim Hortons coffees. With the drapes open, I can spot machinery several dozen feet away.

I can tell you who is working hard and who is slacking off. I can almost taste it.

I have abandoned the Larry King Live program. Any man with that many wives is untrustworthy. Or maybe you will argue that his wives were?

I still enjoy diluted cranberry juice although I'm not sure it helps fend off bladder infections. I've contracted a record number of four this last year, as you know. My meals are as clear-cut and predictable as items off an assembly line. Good thing I'm a fan of chicken.

Do you want to know about my inner routines too? I am praying a lot more than I used to. Not to any particular god or goddess, but to the universe as a whole, as if the universe can be spoken to inside one's head the way I compose letters or the answers to these questions before asking Rodriguez to type them out for me. I worry about the boy a lot, ask the universe to protect him, to coat him with the strength to stand tall and walk through life, to keep all accidents from his path. When you spend as much time staring at the ceiling as I do, you come to believe there are voices struggling to break through the barriers of the walls and our feeble, misguided brains, complaining we never understand what's most important. You notice ceilings are such precious things. Lovely tricks, promising not to fall upon our heads. Do you know if any poet has ever written an Ode to Ceilings?

Are you able to handle fewer or more duties on your own?
The only duties I have are to my children. I am trying my best to fulfill them. Next question, please.

Have any friends or family members increased or
decreased their involvement over the last year?
I don't know. I can't read people's hearts. What I do know
is that I spend much of my time alone and in pain and it's
not easy for people to involve themselves in these things.
Perhaps some can only do so in their hearts. But such people
do me no good in this life.

No posters or photographs or images of any kind line Mohab's
dorm room. In fact, aside from an opened box of Cheerios, a black
comb, and a bottle of Polo aftershave on the dresser, the room
looks unlived-in.

Mohab deposits his satchel on his made-up bed, unbuttons his
brown leather jacket, unwinds his scarf. Emile removes his boots,
leaving slush on a grey plastic mat by the door.

"Sorry about the mess."

"Mess? You should see my room."

"Maybe next time."

Emile senses that Mohab is not really listening. They've spent
five evenings together since Emile found him that morning in the
graduate lounge, running away from Tiffany Berdichevsky. "I've
promised myself to someone, but you know how these girls are,
they keep trying to see if they can break me. On the stairs, Tiffany
Berdichevsky hip-checked me against the handrail, then rubbed
her hand along my crotch as Professor Jenkins passed by. She even
tried to give my nuts a tug. I'm a finish line. After September 11th,
I've become catnip. There's *cachet* in fucking a Muslim now."
Mohab confessed all this in the Market over soup-and-sandwich
specials. "If I had a close friend in the program, they wouldn't keep
on me, I think. You work hard, I've seen your girlfriend bring you

lunch at the library. There are times I feel like I must have come here from the other side of the universe."

Emile interjected, not to correct him to tell him he no longer had a girlfriend, but to ask, "Speaking of which, where is home?"

Tilting the soup bowl, Mohab chuckled. "I'm from Toronto, from fucking Scarborough!"

Since then they've studied together, traded notes and ideas, enjoyed pints in the Market, taken in a movie, an exhibit at the National Gallery, and today they went to a Remembrance Day concert. Emile genuinely likes Mohab and can safely say that Mohab likes him. And their coalition has indeed made an improvement in Mohab's unwanted love life. Lisa Dobbercork, urbanist, waste management, ran into Emile at Starbucks and asked him if Mohab was seeing anyone. A friend of hers was interested. "He's got a serious girlfriend back home, and he's a loyal guy," Emile answered. "She's got zero chance." And that night Emile shared with Mohab the fact that the girlfriend he had seen bringing lunch to him in September and early October had broken up with him because of his studies, and that his father didn't respect his work either. *Is this a joke? Are you joking with me? My son is going to school to study voodoo? How is your work going to help people? Help families? What's the point of an education if you can't change people's lives?* As he explained to Mohab his father's condition, the family separation, and even a little about his father's never-ending files, Emile could not remember when he had last felt so at ease. He even admitted, "I haven't told my father she broke up with me. He never met her, and it gives me an excuse to be away from the house. Don't get me wrong, I love my father, but he's difficult to live with sometimes, and I need quiet to think."

Straddling a black desk chair, Emile wonders what Mohab

needs so that he can think as he scans the area, trying to pinpoint likes and dislikes from the objects lying about the square room with its single bed, beige dresser and desk, one black bookshelf, and a white cooler fridge. Although it means sharing washroom and kitchen facilities, Mohab told him it's easier to live in residence than to find an eight-month apartment lease. Not even a small television or a stereo, Emile registers. Perhaps he has an MP3 player or iPod, but his laptop is shut and silent on the topic. It reminds him a bit of his sisters' new bedroom that first year after they moved to Augusta Street: the cheap furniture, and much still in boxes—the few stuffed toys and dolls, hairbrushes and jewellery boxes, deliberately placed and unsure of their surroundings. And there are no books beside the bed or stacked about as in Emile's room, only course books on the bookshelf: *An Introduction to the Ethics of Anthropological Study*; *Urban Anthropology and the Photographic Impulse*; *North-American Religions: A Cross-Cultural Perspective*; *Tribes and Rituals of the South Americas*; the *MLA Guide to Research*; and two volumes of *Suicide in the Middle Ages*, all on the top shelf. Such a grab bag. No wonder Mohab can't pick an area of interest; he's interested in everything. Or nothing. Emile hopes he won't end up being one of those perpetual graduate students, PhD VII or VIII, uniformly the worst teaching assistants, filling up their time with Student Union affairs or pub night organizing instead of writing a dissertation. But he wipes the thought from his mind as premature and unfair.

"Christmas break is going to be very difficult," Mohab mumbles, cross-legged on the army green comforter on the bed.

"Christmas is always hell," Emile offers, but then worries he may have said something wrong; he doesn't know much about Mohab's family or if they celebrate Christmas.

"No, this year is really bad," Mohab explains. "My grandfather is dying. Parkinson's. It's just eating him up."

"I'm sorry." Emile doesn't know what else to say.

"Thanks. I love my grandfather. I haven't told you about him yet, but he's the bravest man I've ever met." Emile stops scanning the room and fixes his eyes on Mohab, who eagerly leans forward. "My family left Iran right before I was born. My parents were shocked by what happened when the Shah flew to Paris and Khomeini came to power. They had all learned English and my grandfather had bought a hotel that they fixed up for English and European tourists, with bathrobes and room service, lots of free soap, chocolates on the pillows. My mother handled the bookings, my father the car rentals and taxis. Tehran was thriving. Five-star restaurants, spas, casinos, and expensive, discreet brothels. My mother and father were saving up for the many children they planned on having, but my grandfather could see the tide turning, he didn't believe in the word 'revolution,' *just another name for another dirty government,* he used to say, and he was saving up for the day they would all leave. When Khomeini took over, my mother was pregnant with me. He gathered my parents, two aunts and an uncle, three nieces, and the hotel cook, and said, *It's time to read the writing on the wall or we will be left on the wrong side.* Then he asked my mother to bring him the hotel ledger."

As Mohab mimes opening the ledger, Emile suspects that this is a story the family tells often—he can picture Mohab in the role of the old man worried about the fate of his family. It reminds Emile that his father never tells him anything about life in India, or his dead grandparents, only that Emile is expected to light candles on their birthdays and the anniversaries of their deaths at St. Mary's Catholic Church, where his mother used to take him, even though these dead relatives were Hindus and would never have entered, let alone worshipped in, a Catholic church. January 5, January 28, June 1, and September 15: mute oracles; the dates reveal nothing, baffle Emile like signs in a foreign language.

"He burned it. Even now he claims he has the whole book memorized, but he doesn't dare write it down. *Our minds are vaults*, he says. *We need to be very careful who is given a key*. But it's a shame that minds can't be read after people die, the way their papers can. Anyway, in this ledger were addresses and telephone numbers. Not so strange for a hotelier—valued clients, one would suppose, and they were. But they were also contacts to the English world: the U.S., Canada, England, Australia, even New Zealand. Places my family could go. Papers were made, and promises. But not just for us. My grandfather spoke to dozens of people in Tehran and in the surrounding towns, where he had many friends and more distant family members. He promised to get them out too, if they wanted to leave. *People don't believe their own country will turn against them, so they cling like stupid spiders to their nets and get caught by their own spinning*, my grandfather says. My mother was the one who decided: *Canada. I want us to go to Canada.* An older couple who had stayed at the hotel, the Ambassador it was called, did I mention that? The Ambassador. They sent her a postcard from Niagara Falls, which she kept on her vanity; it claimed, *Canada: The Most Beautiful Country in the World*. My father said she looked longer at that postcard than she ever did at her own face, but my grandfather convinced her to burn the postcard too. My father obeyed him in everything—he had never been wrong about business or family— and so did my mother, consoling herself that she would soon see Niagara Falls for real. But the one thing she never forgave him for was that he insisted all the other people counting on him to get them out of Iran should be sent first. *Leaders should never assure their own safety before that of the people. That's the problem with this government.* But my mother was pregnant, and she wanted out. He scolded her. She waited, but vowed that if I was born in Tehran and not in Canada, she would curse him forever."

Unable to help it, Emile cocks his eyebrow at the mention of a curse.

Mohab continues: "My grandfather ignored her, sold off everything, traded in every favour, worked twenty hours a day as if nothing out of the ordinary was going on. They were the last to leave, and when they landed in Canada he'd lost twenty pounds and had developed leg spasms. But when they moved into that first apartment, only a twenty-minute walk from the falls my mother had loved all the way from Tehran, one bedroom for the four of us, my grandfather sleeping on a mattress on the floor, he purchased this cheap WELCOME TO OUR HOME plaque from a souvenir store and nailed it to the inside of the door, announcing he'd never lived anywhere more wonderful. My mother cried. It was so cold. Her baby was going to have to become an Eskimo. We all moved to Scarborough two years later. But I knew from the day I was born that my grandfather was a hero. I'd rush home after school just to peel carrots with him, or read him passages out of my schoolbooks. He didn't care what subject. *There's always learning to be done,* he'd say. *Even things we don't know we want to learn.* But my mother thinks all the anxiety she felt those months before leaving is why she could never get pregnant again, and why he's sick now. That the meanness she felt all those months caught up with her. She says to me, *Remember, Mohab, if you release hatred on the world, it will eventually hit its target.* The doctors gave him two months over three months ago. I know he hopes to see me married before his death so he can feel sure that his family line will continue. So last summer, before leaving again for school, I said, *Grandfather, this year you'll have a wedding to attend*. I don't know why I said it. I hoped he'd forget. He doesn't know I don't have a girlfriend."

"But you have a girlfriend. A fiancée," Emile interjects.

"I didn't tell you that," Mohab insists, grabbing his knees. "I told you I promised myself to someone. I know that was the implication, though, and I'm sorry. You have every reason to be mad at me, but I didn't outright lie to you."

"Not like to your grandfather, then," Emile says curtly, and mimes closing the hotel ledger.

"I wanted to tell you, but it's hard. I've never told anyone."

"Sounds to me like you know the story by heart!"

"Not that. You're right, I do know the family story by heart," Mohab replies, rubbing his eyes. "Why not? It's my story too. No, I mean the thing I need to tell you now."

Emile frowns. Even though he was raised Catholic for a time, or maybe because of it, he hates confessions. Some things are better left unsaid. Like when his mother took him aside one evening, shortly after moving to Augusta Street, and told him, *I left your father because he's the greatest man I've ever met. I don't have the strength to watch him turn into someone else.* What was the point in telling him that? *All confession is an effort to throw off a curse*, Erik Erikson wrote, and Emile quotes it often in his essays and application proposals, but what does confession solve? No matter what his mother says, she can't make his father a leader, a well-loved man, the person he was before the accident. He remains a man in a cheap wheelchair, brushing his dentures and spitting into a plastic green tub, dutifully swallowing constipants and laxatives so he can do his business when scheduled, when the government says it's time. People don't want to know these things; these are real things no one wants to talk about.

"I've promised myself to the religious life," Mohab says, lifting his head with passionate though fragile conviction.

Cheerios. Black comb. *Suicide in the Middle Ages*. Niagara Falls. Emile replays their conversations in his head, searching for a single religious inclination, but the hems of his mind keep getting caught on the room. It doesn't look as though anyone lives here. It looks staged; like his father brushing dentures in his mind, and Emile forcibly wheeling him out.

"Look. I'm not joking," Mohab states flatly.

Once again Emile is reminded of his father, who always counters his remarks with variations on the theme *Life is not a joke* or *Do not make a joke of your life*. It's funny, because Emile rarely laughs. He finds it hard to believe that this gold-skinned young man with the black hair and black-brown eyes in a Maple Leafs T-shirt, who just over a week and a half ago actually made him laugh, asking him what he liked better, blue or purple, pizza or ice cream, comedies or tragedies, as they killed time over beers after a long day at the library, is tormented by religious questing. People come to Canada to forget all that. Even his father tenses up if the remote lands on a channel where evangelists or religious figures of any kind are speaking.

"You want to become a monk?"

Mohab rises from the bed and walks to the fridge for bottled water. "I guess it's difficult to understand. I've known for some time," he says, twisting the cap. "I wanted to pretend I didn't know. I even wanted to pretend I didn't know *what* religion I was meant to follow. But I guess you can't change who you are, no matter how much you might want to."

"Only if you believe that's who you are," Emile challenges, as Mohab hands him a bottle without asking if he wants it. "So what religion won out? Christianity? Judaism? Islam? Buddhism perhaps? Scientology?"

Mohab takes a gulp of water. "The worst is, my grandfather hates talk of religion. He says it's harmed more people, killed more people, than it's ever saved. He doesn't even read fiction. After Khomeini issued the fatwa on Salman Rushdie, he gave up on religion and fiction. Non-fiction is where the real intellectuals are, he says, proud that I'm studying anthropology, that I skipped two grades to get here, but I'd rather be in religious studies, working through the Qur'an. And my grandfather hates Islam most of all. I'm ashamed of myself. I really am. I know what Islam has done. No one in my family practises, and I hide my books in the closet, sometimes one or two under my mattress. All I have is my imagination, but I imagine myself in a mosque, I really do. I want to make my imaginings real."

All of a sudden it occurs to Emile that he's never seen a Qur'an or entered a mosque, he's never been to a Muslim service—do they have services?—or festival or to a Muslim wedding. He wants to ask to see some of Mohab's books, but he's uneasy about what he might find. What does Mohab want from him, anyway? His approval? Mohab approves of his interests, is happy to discuss them. Even if it makes Emile uncomfortable, shouldn't he be willing to do the same? "So," Emile says, looking at the comforter, perhaps for bumps that might indicate hidden books, "what are you going to do?"

"I want my grandfather's last days to be happy ones. I can make up an excuse as to why my girlfriend couldn't make the trip."

"You want me to help you invent an excuse?"

Mohab sets his empty bottle on his desk. The action reminds Emile, for some reason, that his father is out of kitchen cleanser; he's supposed to bring home a new bottle and furniture wax from Home Hardware. If he stays here any longer, the store will be closed. Emile is always disappointing his father like this. *You have your head in the clouds. You don't care enough about the house. Look how you leave it.* Monique used to remind him of these things, even though she never once met his father. *Didn't he ask you to bring home chicken? Light bulbs? Crazy Glue?* She would have liked to meet him. Emile knows this. Although she would never have admitted it, Monique sought out people from other cultures. She'd dated guys whose families came from Japan, Egypt, and Cuba. Emile's mother might be French-Canadian but he looks South Asian, his skin tan, his cheeks and forehead high, hair thick, frame lanky to the point of clumsiness, like a character right out of *Gunga Din*. What would she have thought of Mohab? Would she have been one of the women hunting him down, having never read the Qur'an but secretly thrilled by the prospect of having sex with a man who had? He often wondered if such people were really interested in other people's cultures, or if they simply couldn't stand their own and were looking for a way out, without taking into account the consequences.

"No, not an excuse. I want you to help me invent a girlfriend."

The washroom door in the hallway opens and a woman's voice demands to know if her body wash will be returned to her any time soon. Emile checks his watch. His father is not going to be pleased.

SoundScape Diaries: by Roof and Key

This one named Anton: His sister was dying of leukemia, but he didn't want to visit her in the hospital.

Only when his parents forced him did he sit at a distance from the machines, playing Hot Wheels with his brother. Inside though, he had left his sister for dead and wanted no part of her. When the nurses dropped off candy, he refused to give her any of his.

This one named Wilhelm: Street performer. Beaten up so many times, one of his ribs permanently pokes out of his skin. *Touch it*, he said. *I can't feel anything.* Left home at thirteen when his father found him dancing in front of his bedroom mirror in a fairy princess costume he stole out of his sister's closet. *That's when the beatings started, and they've never stopped.* He's performed in twelve countries and was once the lover of a premier ballet dancer. *Then I beat him too, and I knew it was time to leave.*

This one named Carl: Sleepwalker. Mother used to sing lullabies to him to try to soothe his mind. The only thing that ever helped was jumping off buildings or out of airplanes. It started with swinging on trees in the front yard until the branches broke. Then hanging from roofs, balcony ledges, then hang-gliding, skydiving, bungee jumping. What a calm one he is, people used to say of him. *One day*, he said, *I'll jump off the moon!*

This one named Danny: Said, *Don't believe there is anything so sacred that it can't be betrayed and turned into bullshit.* Five years of happy marriage, then some guy at his wife's pottery class tells her she hasn't reached her full potential in this life. What's standing in her way? Her husband. After he planted that little seed it took only six months for the marriage to crumble completely. Poof! *By the end, I couldn't even touch her hand without her flinching. She said I used to be a man, but I wasn't one anymore.* She said he should see a doctor. He told her she could find one up his ass.

Text Message from Emile Dange to Dorothy Dange:
CAN I TAKE YOU TO DINNER TONIGHT? NEED TO TALK.

"I'd love to live here," Dorothy signs, after slipping her cellphone back into her pocket.

Kite files in behind her and they crunch themselves into the base of the lighthouse, the upper windows projecting light into three beams below. As visitors lift their faces, Dorothy thinks they resemble the Apostles in the paintings in her *Renaissance Masters* book, the wisdom of God as light descending on their foreheads, their hearts glowing with the unspoken message. Although Dorothy brought Kite here as per Mrs. Kotek's suggestion that *Art reveals itself in unpredictable spaces* and, as they are struggling with how to proceed with the mural, they should go to a movie or hockey game or something else unrelated, she didn't think it would be open. She's never been inside it before, assumed it was never accessible to the public, to prevent damage and vandalism. Two months ago the woman at the membership desk told her they had caught two ten-year-old boys with spray-paint cans who'd managed to write *Go Fuck Your Mother* on the rocket before security could put a stop to it. "People will destroy anything if they can," she said. "And they were members, too."

Dorothy thought maybe the lighthouse would relax them. Relax her. So she can think of something besides her SoundScape Diaries. They aren't going to help her with the mural, and she can't get out of Rousseau otherwise. *Art is messy*, Mrs. Kotek told them. *What does it want?* Dorothy asked. *For you to notice it exists, any way it can*, she'd replied. Not much help, Dorothy thought, but she is surprised by how their inability to come up with a mural idea has been bothering her. She didn't want to be involved in this project in the first place, but at any of Kite's suggestions she seizes up, as if all the imagined options are wrong and she won't put her name to them, no, she has to figure out how to represent the place accurately, and what it means, or what it *should* mean. Quitting isn't an option. Kite was right; she's spent the last three and more years here. Shouldn't she have something to say about it?

"As you can see, this is a very tight place to work," the young female guide in black rain boots and a yellow windbreaker begins, and Dorothy wonders if the guide's outfit is a costume or not. To her left is a photograph of the lighthouse on its Nova Scotia bay almost a century ago, with its red and white checkers splattered with mud, like a man crouched down in a rain slicker.

"But when you consider that a lighthouse keeper had not only to work here, but to live here for the better part of the year, rarely leaving his post, not to eat or to sleep, most of the time without anyone to talk to, you can imagine how difficult life must have been. The light was the only form of communication for the lighthouse keeper until radios. The job was not recommended for men with families."

The visitors turn their heads and nod. A toddler, braced against her father's leg, whimpers and sucks her thumb. A middle-aged man whispers to a woman something about his own workspace,

Dorothy can't make it out entirely—his lips are partly obscured as he tilts his head—only that he thinks it's just as bad as here.

"They must have been happy to see ships, hoping for landings, people to talk to, people who spoke their language," Kite signs.

The guide's attention turns to them for a moment, a familiar pause. Dorothy knows it can make hearing people nervous to realize that deaf people are in their presence and could be saying anything to each other with no one the wiser. Like being a foreigner but worse, more threatening and alien somehow. At least the Germans or Russians or Swahilis all speak with their tongues.

"You won't be able to follow me all at once," the guide instructs, slowly ascending the small spiral staircase. "Two at a time, please. As you wait your turn, please take a look at the photographs and artifacts adorning the walls. Several pertain to this specific lighthouse and the history of how it was transported here."

"It immigrated," Dorothy signs back.

The lighthouse is getting warm. Kite smiles, unzipping the top of his jacket.

"Excuse me," Dorothy voices. "Excuse me."

Noticing in his peripheral vision that Dorothy's lips are moving, Kite turns away from the lighthouse keeper's licence he's been reading and gives her a wary glance. But Dorothy isn't going to let him get to her, not after spending the last three years diligently mouthing syllables into mirrors, closet doors, and bedroom pillows, holding her hands against her lips and cheeks, carefully monitoring those who speak to her, forwarding and pausing close-up dialogues on her DVDs again and again. A cochlear implant, like a magic wand, will give him hearing and speech, plus a whole new world, whereas she's forced to create these things for herself.

The guide bends over the top railing, her brown hair falling out of her windbreaker hood, to pinpoint where the voice has come from.

"Did another lighthouse replace this one?"

"Oh, yes, yes," she responds, beaming with enthusiasm. "A new lighthouse was built. Completely mechanically and digitally run. Boats need only the light, not the person. The kind of lifestyle documented here is largely obsolete. And why did this one end up here?" she asks, pressing her stomach against the railing like a girl on monkey bars. "This museum paid for it."

Dorothy has been concentrating hard on the guide's light pink lips, since they are high up and a little far away, but is interrupted by Kite, who doesn't move his as he signs, "I hate that attitude. Just because a machine can do the job, it's better than the way things were before. Maybe people liked working in the lighthouse. Maybe they liked being shut off from others and watching the sea in peace. Maybe technology makes it too easy for us not to do what we were meant to do. This was somebody's home!"

The man scoops his toddler up in his arms to descend the stairs, and motions for Dorothy and Kite to take their place. "She's just doing her job," Dorothy signs back to him, but old lighthouse keepers do make her think of people like her father, anchored in homes with only a few communication devices to connect them to the outside world. Does that make him unimportant? Obsolete? Could a machine easily replace him as a man? She shakes the thought away, knowing his files are ways for him as a human being to chart the world, to document what might be on the horizon, steering its way to us.

It's tight, just as the guide said. The glass on the windows is thicker and far more difficult to see through than Dorothy imagined; thicker than Coke-bottle glass, nearly frosted. She figured it was the glass that enabled the lighthouse keeper to survey the area, but now she thinks she was wrong. The lighthouse keeper had to use the light to see and to speak.

"It's hot," she says to the guide.

"Yes. Can you imagine sitting in front of this all the time?"

"Yes, I can."

The guide smiles, though she seems not to have registered what Dorothy said, only that Dorothy said something and therefore she must feign supportive interest. "If you look out at the shopping centre there—" the guide adds, turning to the glass, then halts because Kite has tugged on her arm and points emphatically to his eyes, then to his lips. "Oh," she exclaims apologetically, "I understand," straightening and positioning herself directly in front on them. "If you look outside at the shopping centre over there, you can see the light reflecting off the roof and the Sears sign. You can get an idea of how bright the force of the light is, how far it can extend. If there weren't so many buildings around here, you'd be able to see for miles."

His face close to the glass, light splotches Kite's back, neck, and head like one of the strobes at the SoundScape. He has the kind of long, lean back Dorothy imagines will curve into a permanent slouch as he gets older. She doesn't like to admit it, but she's found herself thinking about him a lot, and what his future will hold. Though she is the one voicing confidently in the lighthouse, he is the one who will be countering physiognomy with technology. He may not like the technologically advanced lighthouse, she thinks, but that is what he is becoming, what she, no matter how hard she tries, can never be. This lighthouse under which she's been eating lunch for the last year is more like her father, uselessly spotlighting buildings going up around him, obscured from the people inside those buildings, who should be noticing his distress signals.

"Obstructions," Dorothy considers out loud. "Without obstructions, you could see across the city, right?" Dorothy isn't sure if she's pulled off her question. The guide waves to Kite to indicate that she will soon respond if he wants to read her lips.

"Your girlfriend here asked me if you could see across the city if there was nothing in the way." She pauses, and Dorothy, trying not to exchange glances with Kite to acknowledge the guide's mistake, focuses on her name tag, which reads "Annie," not Anne or Ann but Annie, like the little orphan girl in the musical. "It's interesting. Inside the lighthouse, the keeper was the one with the least amount of sight. The idea was that the boat or ship would spot him long before he spotted them."

They descend the metal staircase, Dorothy striding briskly ahead of Kite and past the four visitors now remaining to exit the lighthouse.

"Stop," Kite motions, managing to catch up with her after a dozen feet or so. "What's wrong?"

She looks back resentfully at the lighthouse, bolted like her father to the hard ground, and the non-orphan Annie swinging her master keys beside the door's iron lock. She loved eating her lunch underneath its swivelling eye, imagining herself as a lighthouse keeper and Roof and Key as a mini-lighthouse, collecting the stories of all sorts of travellers who'd landed in this city, this country, and the ways their ships, once ashore, were still open to shipwreck, to being violently thrown off course. It wasn't fair that the lighthouse keeper, trying to help the floundering men at sea from crashing their boats on the rocks and sinking their lives away, was the last one to know what was out there. It wasn't fair.

And it isn't fair that because of machines the lighthouse keeper has been removed from the scene altogether. Kite was right; they didn't just lose their jobs, they lost their homes.

"I don't want to be a lighthouse keeper anymore!" she yells as loud as she can, then tears across the snowy field, past the old train. "Lighthouses suck!"

She spins herself around like the useless city eye. The ground rotates seven or eight revolutions before she falls, her black hair with maroon highlights stark against the white snow. Coldness spreads across her body, from the back of her head to her heels. Kite plops down beside her, his legs extended way past her own, and she traps his left arm underneath her back.

Lifting his free hand, he half signs, half finger-spells, "Be whatever you want to be."

His fingers hovering above her, Dorothy remembers how, when she was a kid, her mother used to take her to Algonquin Park for picnics, and they'd fly this kite in the shape of a dragon, orange triangular-shaped pieces strung together as a tail. She must have been three or four, just a little older than the toddler in the lighthouse. "Dragon"—the word intrigued her; she didn't realize that a dragon wasn't a piece of flying paper but an imaginary being invented on the other side of the world. Afraid she'd let go of the string in her fascination with the object, her mother tied the string to her hand. Now Kite's hand has the same effect, keeping her close to him as thoughts of lighthouses and men drowning at sea float through her mind, as her limbs grow numb, almost unattached to her in the snow. His name really suits him, she muses as the winter light hits her eyes, so bright that she can't see anything but his hand. She closes her eyes. Next thing she knows, Kite is kissing her.

Retreating into the hole her body has made, Dorothy wriggles out from underneath him, lips wet, jacket and jeans littered with white.

"What's wrong?" he signs, his cheeks red. "You're the one who asked *me* to come here." He hits his chest on me.

When any of the men at the SoundScape tries to touch Dorothy, she writes OVER on her Palm Pilot and leaves. But no one her own age, no friend, has ever attempted to kiss her before. No deaf person has ever attempted to kiss her. She doesn't know what to do. Until this point, she's been more comfortable with the idea that lips are to be examined, interpreted, understood. Not touched with your own. The saliva on her lips tastes sweet but out of place, like sugar on vegetables.

"You don't mind having a toke with us now and then or piercing or tattooing us at your parlour, but apart from that you don't want anything to do with us, do you? You think you're better than us? You think you're better than *me*?" He hits his chest again.

"What do you want from me?" Dorothy cringes, signing back, sensing that her backside, like her lips, is awkwardly wet. "You're the one intruding on *my* life. I didn't ask to get involved in this mural project. I didn't ask you to give a shit. I choose to stay away from everyone because I *know* I don't belong!"

Kite shakes his head vigorously, slams his hand down on his jeans. "No wonder you have no ideas for the mural. You don't care to know anything about us. You can't even imagine how I feel, and you don't ask. You're ashamed of us!"

Rubbing her lips together again, strangely upset to find the taste has disappeared, Dorothy doesn't know what to say. She wishes she could tell him about the man she met last night at the SoundScape. Would he believe her if she told him that this man, who raises butterflies for weddings and anniversary celebrations, is tormented daily by a shoebox full of monarchs he sold every Friday to a couple living in a downtown duplex? Never asked questions, though once or twice he jokingly speculated that they might be eating the damn things. No, he drove to their home one Friday evening, as he had every Friday evening for eight months, and they weren't home, and there was a smell in the air, he said, a smell that was just off, like sour milk or a discarded shoe alley cats piss on, and two women and a man were standing around, just standing around with their mouths open, like people watching a building burn down. One of the women had curlers in her hair, like in the movies, he said. He opened the latch on the gate, shoe-box in his other hand, and a woman in a Blue Jays hat said, "The police came and arrested them. Sexual assault. Minors. They've been luring them into their home, promising a very pretty but-terfly collection. Who in the world has a butterfly collection?" After he drove away from the street, he threw up out his car win-dow. "I didn't let them out," he confessed. "I was too scared in case someone saw me. I thought they'd assume I was involved. Aided and abetted, something like that. So they died by morning. All thirty. I stared at those thirty pairs of useless wings, those thirty dead bodies, their bright orange markings now dull and sickly, and what I felt was satisfaction." What would Kite think about that? Or Mrs. Kotek for that matter, whose classroom has a *Make Every Day a Work of Art* banner strung across the blackboard? A shoe-box full of dead butterflies. Is that art, or a tragic accident? What would Kite think if he knew that Dorothy cares more for these people than for all the Rousseau teenagers? That she asks for one story from each man she meets there? One story each. But even with this rule, already dozens and dozens of these stories are inside Roof and Key, with hundreds, thousands, millions, just waiting to be heard. Could she ask Mrs. Kotek, *Where do all the unspoken stories go? What does art do with them?* Is her father a work of art? Who listens? Who decides?

Kite is blocking the *S* on the Sears sign in the distance, so all she can see of it is "ears." "Don't kid yourself. You're the one getting a cochlear implant so you can leave the rest of us behind!"

Eyes bulge, tongue sucks in. Dorothy recognizes the expression from Signature Tattoo and Body Piercing, has seen it often enough as clients stare at the sheets of roses and butterflies, skulls and crossbones, Grim Reapers and cougars, fairies and hearts. The Wall of Pain—they concentrate on the wall and keep absolutely still, must hold in all the pain before letting it out. She's also seen it on the face of her father, who doesn't live far from the Museum of Science and Technology; she could easily stop by before dinner for half an hour, an hour even, but she won't. She doesn't know what to say to him either, would rather keep her distance, watch from afar, as she imagined her lighthouse could—finish collecting her SoundScape stories first, stories she hopes will help her understand, help others understand how bad things happen, how important warnings are. But what if it is *he* watching her, desperate for her to notice him there, waiting for permission to come ashore? What would she say?

Though she walks away first, she feels that Kite is the one leaving, pulled back in the direction of the lighthouse. Accidents happen. Even with better tracking systems, they still happen. Can he not understand how many signals she is trying to note and answer at once?

The snow begins to fall again in a steady potpourri of white. Soon the whole valley will be a giant cup of snow, one that won't be emptied for many, many months. "I'm ashamed to *be*," she signs back, but by then he is in no position to hear her.

Dear Dor,

The day of the accident, I slept late. Work had continued until well after midnight the night before, and I'd given up my food supplies as more were due to arrive shortly and I didn't want to pull rank. I was upset at having slept in, but washed myself thoroughly to set a good example. I was a representative of the New World, after all.

The morning was a scorcher. When I arrived on site, one of the cranes had broken down and several of the men were resting in the shade and smoking. One look at me, though, and they stood at attention and returned to the irrigation system that was to be tested that day. I wanted a well-oiled machine, and through experience I had learned that workers always appreciate alcohol for a job well done, so I had brought a few bottles of whiskey to hand out once the test was complete. I was the head of this mission. If there was a problem to be solved, it was my duty to solve it. I knew they sometimes looked at me, at my skin colour, and wondered how I was so lucky, giving orders instead of taking them, but these kinds of feelings are natural, and I had also learned through experience not to take them personally.

By noon the sun was a hot tong, but the crane was fixed. I'd promised to call Isobel later that day. She was feeling fatigued, a little dizzy, and had made a doctor's appointment. I figured I would call her in the evening, after a cup of tea and a game of chess with one of the lieutenants at the embassy. I loved the Canadian embassy, the red-and-white flags lining the entrance, the white rooms with comfortable couches and tea sets and bottles of wine, the Group of Seven reproductions on the walls, and Isobel had told me it was nothing serious, nothing to worry about, the appointment was just a precaution.

Donning my hard hat, I was lowered into the irrigation system by the very crane that only hours before had been useless. Standing in the cupped hand of the machine, I felt proud. These people liked me. I made them laugh. I gave them food and drink. I spoke their languages. I was one of them. A good Indian who had returned to India to help them, who hadn't run off and forgotten where he'd come from, who didn't think he was better than the mud that formed his spine. This was my kingdom.

This was the day the west side of the irrigation system blew to pieces. The blast was quick, and I was shaken right off my feet. Mishandled dynamite. The pipes bursting above my head made such a glorious picture of sparkling white that for a moment I actually thought we were all witnessing some sort of miracle and everyone was screaming in joy. A great wave fanned over my body, the way a monarch spreads its orange wings or a tennis ball drops in for a serve out of the light, the way your mother learned to unfurl her fingers in front of her face in coy imitation of Indian dance, the way your fingers would later curl in front of your mouth and nose in one of the few dozen words of your language I know by heart: *beautiful, beautiful, beautiful . . .*

Then the next series of pipes burst. I ceased to hear any screaming, and for all I knew, before the blackness took over, I was the only one lucky enough to be alive.

Happy Birthday

Dear Dad,

Happy birthday! Here's a fax of my latest creation—a gift for Birendra. It's a Hindi henna pattern meant to bring great happiness to newlyweds. I'm practising for the wedding. I hope you approve.

Don't let Emile eat all your birthday cake.

Dor

Opening the boxes, Rodriguez spreads out the decorations on the sofa, the coffee and end tables, and the available carpet space. He extracts a dozen strings of gold and green tinsel, plastic holly and pine wreaths, a plastic glow-Santa, cut-out angels blowing trumpets, countless ball and figurine ornaments including a set of Coca-Cola polar bears and each of the Seven Dwarfs, a green and red Merry Christmas mat, a giant plastic silver bell, two books of basic carol sheet music, a festive M&M chocolate dispenser, four red stockings labelled with black marker (the original silver glitter lettering mostly faded), and a modestly sized but delicately carved oak nativity set, missing one Wise Man.

"I'm sure this stuff is worth something," he announces, hands on hips, scanning the wares.

"This junk? Oh, I don't think so!" Parked to Rodriguez's left, in the corner of the living room where the artificial six-foot Christmas tree will be assembled, Hardev yells to be heard over the sawing outside. He likes to decorate the house November 12, his birthday and, Remembrance Day past, what used to be the official start of seasonal ad campaigns on television and in the malls, before "Christmas creep" gradually made it acceptable to sell decorations and air Christmas commercials before Halloween. While Hardev does not approve of the grotesque commercialism of the holiday, he is fond of the transformation of houses, the hanging up of sparkling lights, children stringing tinsel around pine trees, overjoyed as they craft their own ornaments or play with figurines from a nativity set, alternately lively and sombre Christmas music on the radio. Isobel used to tease him that he had married her and had the children baptized Catholic just so he could celebrate Christmas, and there was truth to that. Hardev has always been fascinated by Catholic churches, their stained-glass windows, purple banners, Holy Spirit doves, organ pipes, boy choirs, and holy water reminiscent of his River Ganges. Never much of a religious man in practice, notwithstanding, he respects holy days and festivals, and he loves not only Christmas Day itself—and always makes a point of watching the Pope deliver Christmas morning Mass—but the whole buildup that comes with it. And so today Rodriguez is to forget his usual cleaning and cooking duties and turn all his energies toward decorating the house.

> *Reminders:*
> *Have the boy help with Christmas card list and postings.*
> *Order pills early so as to miss the December vacation rush.*
> *Get new window ice scraper for clearer viewing of construc-*
> *tion over the winter.*
> *Turn fifty-eight.*

"Is it worth something to you, this stuff?" Rodriguez asks, stacking three plastic Frosty the Snowman serving trays on the coffee table on top of newspapers.

"Well, of course, to me. But—"

"Then it might also be worth something to someone else, no?"

Although Hardev appreciates Rodriguez's determination to help him find a way out of his predicament, he worries that Rodriguez doesn't understand the full ramifications of the situation. Pipe dreams about starting his own soap-making business or gambling the little savings he has left in biochemical engineering stocks, no matter how many people have made money at either, are of little use to Hardev. Rodriguez shouldn't be telling him such things as when he's short of cash he sometimes collects bottles out of recycling bins. Schemes like these are not going to save his house, nor will selling his hodgepodge of ornaments. "They're not antiques. They're simply old. Like me."

Two cut-out reindeer window decorations stick to Rodriguez's sweater as he holds up a flat blow-up Mrs. Claus surrounded by penguins. "Where do want you this?"

"There's a plan taped to the inside lid of the Christmas tree box. I know every item in these boxes, Rodriguez. Our first Christmas in this house, we had only this same tree and a dozen yellow balls with thread wrapped around them, paperclips for hooks."

"Here!" Rodriguez exclaims, hanging one on the collar of his work shirt.

"Aren't you quick? Yes, those. We had one string of green tinsel. No stockings. Nothing else. We had paid for the wedding and our honeymoon ourselves and we now had a mortgage to think about. And the hope of children. My boss gave me a watch from Eaton's. The neighbours brought wine. We drove to Montreal the next day to visit my mother-in-law, but Christmas Day was ours. Oh, we had a good time, toasting the season and watching Alastair Sim in *A Christmas Carol*, and we danced beside those yellow balls imagining they were gold. Every Christmas after, I'd add a little more to the decorations, add to the plan, like to the house. Those toy soldier figurines were made by the boy and his sister. They were seven and eight years old when they painted those pink faces. I don't think the children realized that I wasn't Christian until they were teenagers!"

Laughing, Rodriguez pulls the handle on the M&M dispenser. "I bet this is a collectible."

"Oh, collectible in that it's probably been collected by everyone. Like the *Star Wars* glasses in the kitchen cupboard. Every house in the city must have a full set."

"No, no, not true, Harry." Finding the plan where Hardev said it would be, he unfolds it on top of the electric glow-Santa. "I've seen many houses in this city and no one else has those glasses.

People don't know what to keep, what to throw out. Make bad decisions all the time. Throw out what they should keep. Keep what they should throw out."

"And me, I keep everything!"

"Yes, you keep everything. So you must have things of value. You could get fifty, maybe seventy-five dollars for this M&M thing on ebay."

"Fifty? Seventy-five? I must have paid only a dollar or two at the most."

"Yes, but someone might really want this. It's worth what someone wants to pay. Isn't that what 'Free Market' means?"

"Ebay! Free Market! I thought you didn't even own a computer!"

Excitedly, Rodriguez flaps the wings of the angels before locating them on the plan. "My children use computers at school, and I go with them to the library. Free access. We buy clothes on ebay, bulk, pretty cheap. Then my wife sells what we don't want or what doesn't fit to used clothing stores. I see all kinds of things on ebay. Baseball cards, CDs, books, furniture, autographs, toys. Like an auction, but out of ordinary houses, like yours."

"You think I should put my Christmas ornaments up for auction? Then what will we hang on the Christmas tree?"

Rodriguez shakes the M&M dispenser to see if anything is left inside. "Maybe not everything. But why keep this? It's empty. Do you need it? I don't have one. I don't think I need one. It's nice, OK, my children might like it, but we don't need one."

"So I should put everything I don't absolutely need up for sale on ebay?"

"Why not? Thousands of people sell on ebay. Regular people like you and me. And even more buy on ebay. All around the world. Think of the possibilities, Harry! Think of your house!"

"But these things don't belong to me. They belong to my children. I've saved it all for them to do with as they please. Can you understand? I've been in this country a lot longer than you. It's my home. I can't just get rid of all this, or what was the point? I know those angels are worthless. I know it, but they're ours."

"Do you want a *home*, Harry?" Rodriguez says slowly, dropping to the floor to rummage through the rest of the boxes. "Or the things in it?"

"What's a home without these things? . . . I don't know."

Buzz. Buzz.

At first Hardev mistakes the sound for the stove timer, then remembers Rodriguez isn't cooking today. Front door. Intercom. Unhooking the brake on his wheelchair, he begins to back out of the living room.

Buzz. Buzz.

"You stay, I'll get it. I'm coming!" he calls, leaving Rodriguez to match the remaining decorations to the plan. "I'm moving as fast as I can!"

Manoeuvring himself into the kitchen, with his good hand he picks up the intercom box, black with orange buttons, and presses SEND. The line crackles. Though the storm died overnight, the outdoor mechanisms have suffered. He will ask Rodriguez to take a look at the intercom later, see if any snow or ice is stuck inside the speaker holes.

"Hello? Hello? I'm home. Press the orange button on the right to speak."

Hardev relieves SEND and waits.

"Mr. Dange. I am Peter Manello from Gateway Land Developers. Can I come in to speak with you, sir?"

"Rodriguez! It's a man from Gateway! Keep an eye on him."

"What do they want now?" Rodriguez yells back angrily, and within seconds Hardev hears the rings shuffling across the curtain rod. It doesn't matter if the man sees them. This is Hardev's property, after all, and he has a right to know who's at his door.

"We don't have anything to discuss, Mr. Manello. I spoke to your associates in June of 2002 and again in January of 2003 and once more in April 2003. And I'll tell you now the same thing I told them then: I'm not interested in selling my house and property. This is my home, and I am going to remain here."

"Harry, he's in a big black coat and has a briefcase. The workers aren't paying him any attention," Rodriguez reports from the dining room, then hops to the living-room window to catch another angle.

"Circumstances change, Mr. Dange. Opportunities arise. It would be better if I could come in and speak with you. I can show you—"

Hardev releases his finger from RECEIVE, bangs it on SEND.

"Your company isn't listening. I don't want to change my circumstances. This house is not for sale!"

The intercom bleats, resounding with feedback.

"Mr. Dange. Listen to reason, sir. We know you've defaulted on your mortgage payments and you can't afford this house and property taxes any longer. We know you have a son at university, and a daughter close to university age. If you let the bank take your house you'll be left with nothing. The bank will find a way, through penalties and transferral costs and other kinds of other fancy terminology that essentially translate into 'take your money,' to take everything from you. You'll end up in a nursing home or in low-income housing in some awful neighbourhood. You can't just sit there and hope for a miracle. You have to take advantage of the opportunities available to you. Sir, are you still there?"

Wavering on RECEIVE, Hardev calls to Rodriguez, "Take this for me, will you?"

Plastic icicles tied to his belt loops, Rodriguez rushes into the kitchen, replacing Hardev's hand with his own. Hardev wheels backwards, his hands throbbing with the effort. These damn Gateway people ruin everything, he thinks. *Happy birthday, let's take your house.* He will now be too tired and upset to help Rodriguez finish the holiday decorating. At least the piece of paper will guide him, he consoles himself. Isn't that what paper is for, to remember for us when we are no longer around? Not for taking ownership of things that don't belong to you.

"Mr. Dange, I'll be honest with you. The legal process of repossession is long. Gateway wants this matter settled as soon as possible and we are willing to pay. We own apartment complexes and condominiums in nice, good neighbourhoods. You and your boy could move into a two-bedroom, we could offer you a low interest rate on a loan, even waive the condo fees for a limited time. I'm sure if we work together we can come up with a deal that will make us both happy. Why do you want the trouble of a house in your condition, Mr. Dange? You can't afford it. You want to have something to leave your children, don't you?"

"Harry? Harry?" Rodriguez calls, angling his body across the doorway to the living room. "What do you want me to do?"

Lid unfolded, Hardev can see a string of lights designed to illuminate a plastic village popping up out of the tissue. He knows exactly how many pieces the box contains: eight two-storey houses, four bungalows, a general store, a post office, and a white steeple church. Isobel purchased the Christmas village the year Dorothy was born, and they laid her down in her bassinet in front of those glowing lights, captivating her for hours on end. Hardev even remembers the girl picking up the baby and pointing—*Which one is your house? This one? Do you want to live here?* and laughing when she chose the post office or the church.

"I'm going to put my card in your mailbox here, Mr. Dange. Think about this seriously. I'd be happy to return at your convenience. Just call the number on the card."

The intercom crackles again as Mr. Manello fumbles with the buttons and then with the black metal mailbox. Curtain ajar, Hardev watches him rewind his scarf across the collar of his coat, pick up his black briefcase, and walk back to his silver minivan. He entertains the idea of asking Rodriguez to take down the licence plate number, but decides against it. Mr. Manello will be back.

Dorothy is silent when Emile proposes the idea. He's borrowed their mother's Accord to take her out—Isobel pleased they are spending some time together before the wedding—and she's wiping her window with an old ankle sock so that he can see enough to switch lanes. He tries to keep one eye on the road and the other on Dorothy.

"I know this probably sounds crazy to you, but it's important to his family. Really important. You wouldn't have to do very much. Nothing, really, but have your picture taken a few times. No one will know who you are. We won't use your real name. It could even be fun."

Dorothy smirks as Emile turns on the windshield wipers in an attempt to erase the frost. "It's for a good cause," he points out. "You can make an old man happy."

"Like Dad?" Dorothy whispers as she signs, aware that Emile is out of practice and frequently needs help to follow her—one of the reasons he usually e-mails or text-messages, rather than sees her in person. The sign for their dad involves pretending to push a wheelchair forward.

"Like Dad? No," Emile replies, gripping the steering wheel and shaking his head. "This has nothing to do with Dad. Why are you bringing him up?"

Apologetically, she shoves the sock back under her car seat as Emile turns left into the Lone Star restaurant parking lot. "I don't mind the idea of lying. I've just never figured out what lie to tell Dad that would make him happy. It's his birthday. That's why I brought him up."

"Fuck, you're right. I almost forgot." Emile sighs as they circle the parking lot, searching for a space near the front. Lone Star is always busy—it's a two-floor family restaurant with big servings of toned-down Tex-Mex food, sandwiches and steaks, and a long dessert menu heavy on sugar and whipped cream. The decor features Mexican hats and piñatas mixed with hockey jerseys and baseball gloves. Emile and Dorothy haven't been out to dinner together in so long, he had no idea where to take her. At least Lone Star has lots to choose from, a fun atmosphere, and friendly staff. Emile was supposed to put up the Christmas lights tonight, but when he tells his father he went out with Dorothy instead, he'll forgive him. "We might as well keep them up all year," his father scolded him, "and then it wouldn't be such a hassle for you." Emile couldn't bear to remind him that next year he might not be in Ottawa for Christmas—it would all depend on where he ended up—he didn't have the heart to discuss it on his father's birthday as he left this morning. Those lights, which have never given Emile any great amount of joy, are important to his father, whether they have neighbours to admire them or not, and he knows he will have to find time to put them up. "Dad needs miracles, not lies. The fucking house is falling apart. We need a new furnace and we've got barely a winter left in that roof, but does he want to sell the house and move into a nursing home where he might actually be happy, talking to other people and having his lawn mowed on time? You know how hard I study, and he wants me to be a handyman on top of everything! But no, he wants to stay where he is, with our ugly ripped carpets and peeling wallpaper. Did you call him? I don't know what he thinks he's going to do when . . ."

"Is he cute?"

"Cute? Dad?"

"No, my fiancé. If I'm going to get married, I think it should be to someone cute. Is Mohab cute, at least?"

Emile realizes that he's been talking while looking out his driver's window. Dorothy hasn't taken in anything he's said about the house. Probably for the best anyway. His father never mentions any of his financial troubles to Isobel or his two daughters; it is important to pretend for them that everything is wonderful. *We only see each other on holidays. Why ruin them with discussion of sad things?* he says. Emile agrees, in principle, and he's sure they have their own problems on Augusta Street that he knows nothing about, but sometimes he does want to show Dorothy the on-its-last-legs furnace, or Birendra the stacks of medical papers they need to fill out every year, or his mother how the flower and vegetable garden she used to tend is now a haven for dandelions. "Sure, he's cute, I suppose. All the girls in the program are chasing after him," he adds, blushing a bit at discussing a man's desirability with his teenaged sister. "Wait, I've got Dad's disability sign with me. We might as well use it. There's so much ice on the ground."

Dorothy nods. *I suppose she doesn't mind lying,* Emile thinks. He inches into the reserved parking spot, jumps out of the driver's side, and opens the passenger door. Dorothy smiles, taking his hand. "Why not ask your girlfriend to do this? Do they want him to marry some young bride?"

"I don't have a girlfriend right now," he admits, locking the doors. Dorothy blinks a number of times from the force of the wind and the bits of snow flying off the car roof. "We broke up. But don't tell Mom or Birendra, OK? I haven't told Dad. They'll all worry about me for nothing. I don't need a girlfriend. The last thing I need is a girlfriend right now." To avoid explaining what went wrong, he grabs her arm and sprints to the Lone Star entrance.

"The last thing I need is a fiancé," she shouts over the wind.

It takes Emile a moment or two to understand what she's said, but when he does, he smiles warmly in her direction, pulling at the door. "Oh, I don't know. Do you want Birendra to be the only one getting married in the family?"

Despite the busy parking lot, the two long padded benches against the wall of the restaurant lobby are uncharacteristically empty. Emile takes Dorothy's white and beige shag coat—too light for the season, but who is he to butt in, especially when he wants a favour?—and is about to hang it up when she insists on doing it herself. Giving in, he offers her his navy blue winter coat, a bit beaten around the collar and ripped on the inside seams, but well padded. Waiting at the reservation station, he realizes that she probably took the coats so she wouldn't have to speak to the hostess. He is suddenly aware that, spending so little time with her, and then mostly with other family, he's not sure how she manages her life in public. Does she want him to take over? Would that offend her? To look at her, she is just like other teenagers: pretty and awkward at the same time, wearing low-rider jeans and a purple turtleneck with a silk sash across the waist, dangly silver earrings, her hair a different cut and colour every time he sees her—this time black with purple highlights—shuffling instead of walking, with an almost unshakable expression of apathetically putting up with everything around her. *I miss her*, he thinks as she returns to his side, a slight sneer on her face. *I don't really know who she is.*

"You liked having your picture taken as a kid," he jokes. "It'll just be a few photographs. He's a good friend, Mohab. I know you've probably never heard of him, but I don't know the names of your friends either. He's trying not to hurt someone he loves. It's for a good cause. If you knew the whole story, you'd understand."

"Dinner for two?"

"Yes, please," Emile answers. Dorothy nods.

The hostess, in an orange-and-white checkered cowgirl outfit, takes them past two men drinking pints of beer at a bar with a stuffed beaver in a matador's outfit on the counter and a green fairy twirling above their heads, to a table beside an electric fireplace. White bows line the mantel, and a wreath of fake pine cones and holly hangs on the fake brick above.

As they sit, adjusting their chairs and taking up their oversized plastic-covered menus, Emile is aware of Dorothy's eyes on him, and he feels exposed. As a boy he never had what others called a best friend, someone who shared the same interests, confided in him, or asked for his help. But now he knows more about Mohab's motives for faking a marriage than he does about Birendra's reasons for going through with one. Dorothy can certainly tell this means a lot to him, but she probably can't fathom why.

She taps the top of his menu to get his attention. "What if the grandfather wants to speak to me? I'm sure we can't tell him I'm deaf, and I can't have him thinking his son is going to marry some crazy person or a drunk."

Contemplating the problem, Emile nods, scrolls down the menu with his index finger. The pop music streaming out of a dozen speakers, mixed with the chatter of families and screeching of children, makes Dorothy's stilted speech and her signing less noticeable to other tables. He's glad he chose this place instead of somewhere smaller and quieter. "I know," he says, after deciding on a peppercorn steak and fries, "we'll make you a nurse. Say you're on call a lot. Up at odd hours. You can send an e-mail, a text message. Mohab can pretend he's on the phone with you. His grandfather's old. He may not even want to talk on the phone. His hearing's probably bad."

"Do you know that?"

"We'll think of something. Come on, are you in?" Emile slaps his menu on the table as the waitress returns. He can't believe how easy it is to devise this kind of plan. *A nurse is good*, he thinks, *very good. An occupation that would likely please Mohab's grandfather.* "Let's consider it your Christmas present to me."

"Have you decided?" the waitress, also in a checkered cowgirl outfit, asks warmly.

"I'll have the heart-attack special—the peppercorn steak and fries," Emile announces, chuckling as the waitress writes it down, "and my sister will have . . ."

Dorothy points to the taco salad. "This one, please," she voices, her left hand to her cheek—monitoring her speech, he guesses. She did a fine job. The waitress didn't bat an eye. He wonders if he should praise her, but instead waits for his answer.

Flipping a purple strand of hair behind her ear, Dorothy cocks an eyebrow. "None of this stuff goes together," she says, pointing to a Dalmatian in a Santa hat beside a signed and framed poster of Senators giant Zdeno Chara, "but I like it anyway."

"Me too," Emile admits, shrugging at the Dalmatian. "Maybe that's the point."

"OK, tell your friend I'll do it," she concedes, as Emile prepares to pat her on the shoulder. "But I have one condition. I want to hear the whole story from him someday. I'm a good listener. Tell him that."

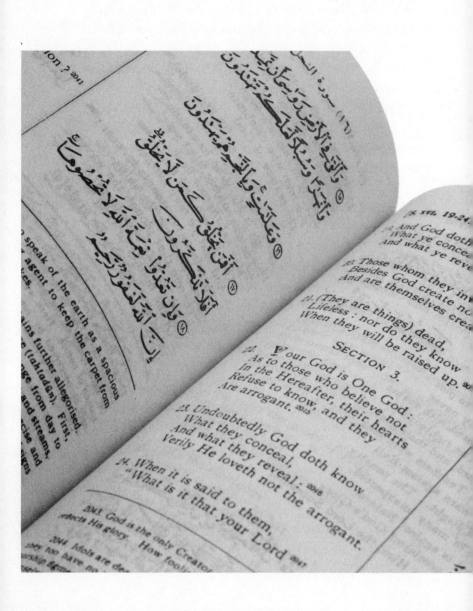

(...) speak of the earth as a spacious
(...) agent to keep the carpet from
(...)

(...)ins further allegorised. First,
(...)e (tahtadûn).
(...)ge from day to
(...) and streams,
(...)cise and
(...)ns

S. XVI. 19-24.

19. And God doth (...)
What ye concea(...)
And what ye reve(...)

20. Those whom they in(...)
Besides God create n(...)
And are themselves crea(...)

21. (They are things) dead,
Lifeless : nor do they know
When they will be raised up. 20(...)

SECTION 3.

22. Your God is One God :
As to those who believe not
In the Hereafter, their hearts
Refuse to know, and they
Are arrogant. 2015

23. Undoubtedly God doth know
What they conceal,
And what they reveal : 2016
Verily He loveth not the arrogant.

24. When it is said to them,
"What is it that your Lord 2017

2013. God is the only Creator
(...)flects His glory. How fooli(...)

2014. Idols are de(...)
(...)ney too have no(...)
(...)worship for(...)

Season's Greetings

To Whom It May Concern:

Re: Redding Electric Wheelchairs, Customer Service

My electric wheelchair model #439B was sent to pasture four months ago when it died as I was surveying the backyard with my homecare worker. There is nothing worse for a man in my position than to be stuck in an immobile chair. I've been using my backup, a 1993 manual model (I have one good arm, but it is prone to seizing up when overused) in the meantime, and while my arm muscles have, arguably, been benefiting from the exertion, my overall general health, my doctors assure me, will eventually be compromised by this "unbalanced strain." As the paperwork I've sent you already indicates, your model of electric wheelchair is no longer covered under my disability benefits through the Government of Canada or through the Province of Ontario Health Services. (Not surprising. This government keeps cutting disability services.) However, I also sent you photocopies of my warranties and the old government papers. I spoke to a Mr. Friesen on the telephone on November 2 and November 4. He has since left his position in your company and no one seems to be able to explain what has happened. Therefore, I am writing to you to help me with this matter. I am an old-fashioned sort. I prefer letters and the paper trail they leave. I am not equipped to handle e-mail without the help of my son, who is a graduate student, busy with his studies, and shouldn't be burdened by his father's problems.

Without my electric wheelchair, I am very restricted. Several of your customer service representatives have already suggested I peruse one of your elaborate colour catalogues and purchase a newer, more technologically advanced model. A Mrs. Sommerhauer informed me, *They drive like Trans Ams*.

I am an old man. I have three children. I have no need for any sports car, and I don't have the money for one. Even if the government has abandoned me in this matter, I urge you not to follow its example. My eldest daughter is getting married this May. I would like to be able to attend all the festivities without troubling anyone to push me around. I'd like to accompany her down the aisle. It is a shameful thing, sir, not to fulfill your obligation at your own daughter's wedding.

I look forward to your quick attention to this matter.

Sincerely,

Hardev Dange

E-mail message received, Kite, the period before lunch, is anxiously awaiting Dorothy in the home economics wing as she turns the basement corner to her locker.

"I thought you had class?" she signs, finding him leaning against the metal cases like a sturdy mop.

"I'm too excited!" he exclaims, eyes sparkling with enthusiasm, hands flailing. "It's a fantastic idea! Do you think it'll work? I think it will work."

As she opens the door to the photograph of her father in his tennis outfit and another now, below it, of her and Mohab in front of the giant saltwater aquarium in the waiting room of the Children's Hospital, Dorothy can't help smiling. The relief that they are back on good terms after weeks of uncomfortable exchanges in class and by e-mail is palpable for her. She was going to add to her SoundScape Diaries, but is content to put it off so they can get their project on track.

"How are we going to let people know about this? Should we get homeroom teachers involved? Does the principal have an e-mail list? And we'll need to make copies available in Braille. I love the fact that the blind kids will be able to enjoy the art too. Like that museum in Paris Mrs. Kotek told us about, for Ossip Zadkine, where the blind are encouraged to touch all the sculptures. Who's this?" he adds, pointing to the miniature Mohab in a black leather bomber jacket and dress slacks, beside her in a puffy white winter jacket and white toque and mittens, yellow, black, and bright orange fish aimlessly drifting around them.

"My cousin. I took him to the hospital to see where I spent so much time as a kid." She slaps the locker shut, concealing the photos and tattoo sketches of snakes and angels, wolves and panthers, butterflies and moons, that line the inside walls. Kite beams as a few other students, on spare or skipping class, gather up their bags and coats nearby. Now that she knows Kite is on side, she sees these others—minding their business, going about their days smoking pot or working on recycling drives, studying for term exams or waiting to lose their virginity, playing indoor soccer or watching movies on portable DVD players—as unwitting artists, people who will speak or remain silent about who they are, the choice being theirs and theirs alone. That one in her wheelchair, with the pink purse and Hello Kitty barrettes, is as worthy a subject as the Mona Lisa. That one biting her own hand affectionately as she tries to put on her gloves could be in *The Raft of the Medusa*.

"Wanna grab a smoke?" Kite reads on Boris' lips—blind, birth defect—as Boris makes his way down the hallway, tapping his cane against the row of lockers. Kite reaches out his hand for Boris to touch, his fingers extended. "Five minutes, then."

"He says he knows it's me because I have a very particular smell," Kite signs to Dorothy.

"I've heard stranger things," she signs back, protectively nudging the knapsack containing her SoundScape Diaries with her feet. "And maybe I'll share them with you someday."

"Sure," he agrees absently, waving to Hello Kitty, multiple sclerosis, and the hand-biter, Fetal Alcohol Syndrome. They both wave back. "How did you come up with this idea, anyway?"

"I like collages," Dorothy signs sheepishly. "Also, I had dinner with my brother and I was thinking about how often all kinds of different things, different people, are put together, whether they like it or not. Then I had this person come in to Signature for his seventeenth tattoo. People get addicted to tattoos, piercings too. They think, *I'll get just one at first, then two, not so bad.* Then it's a third, a fourth. Next thing you know: seventeen tattoos! But that's really only from our point of view: seventeen appointments, seventeen tattoos. Sometimes more than seventeen appointments, depending on how complicated the designs are, and on the customer's pain threshold. But when you look at the person walking on the street, it's one tattoo. One canvas. The body is a single work of art; all those scribbles, colours, shapes, are connected in some way, forming a design, but there's no clear path to interpret it all—it's a collage."

"So the Rousseau Family, though made up of so many different people over the years, is one canvas too," Kite interjects, stretching his arms out into an imaginary frame, nearly backing into a baton-twirling freshman whom neither of them knows but all notice because of her blue hair.

Kite's viewpoint is not exactly what Dorothy intended, and she frowns, but she must admit that he's probably right. She's as much a member of the Rousseau Family as anyone else, even if she's the black sheep.

"The whole point of collage is to combine disparate items, right? Force them together, if necessary. We're all forced together and we have to make some sense out of it, whether we know why we're here or not," he adds, turning his head to the side and signing less extravagantly, "and even if we don't want to be here."

"OK," Dorothy signs back, nodding, convincing his blue eyes to meet hers directly again, his lanky body to stretch. "We're all forced together. Like everyone in the world, really. When we're born, we don't get to choose where, we don't get to choose our parents or our siblings. We don't even get to choose our fucking names, so we're forced into this elaborate collage called a family, or a neighbourhood—"

"Or Ottawa—"

"—or Canada! And then we look around and ask ourselves, 'Why am I so disappointed we have so little in common?' Why should we have anything in common?"

"But we do, right? We do! Or at least we can. That's what's so cool about this," Kite elaborates, seeming about to burst out of his grey skateboarding sweatshirt with the dragon design on the arms, which Dorothy thinks looks like one of those seventeen tattoos. "In the end, you have to admit that we do have things in common. We just have to take the time to locate them before it's too late. It's hard to figure out collages at first, like you said. It's hard to figure out how everything fits. But it does fit. Or at least, it can fit, I think. Isn't that what art is about?"

Gesturing toward a group of guys in front of the cafeteria kicking a Hacky Sack around, chatting and laughing, Dorothy asks, "What if they don't agree?"

"They'll agree."

Dorothy marvels at how Kite seems so sure of everything, how he always looks as if he was sketched into the Rousseau hallways, perfectly at home. So sure of everything, except the cochlear implant. Or how she'd respond to a kiss. What bothers her now about the kiss, she has to admit, is not his boldness, or the strangeness of him kissing her, but that his anger seemed directed at her for tampering with how things should logically turn out, as if she didn't understand how their story should work.

Yet he isn't holding it against her now. And she knows a lot about stories and how they don't turn out the way you expect them to. One day, maybe, they'll talk about this, but not now.

"If we present it as this really cool thing that everyone can contribute to, that will remain at Rousseau for decades to come, wouldn't *you* want to be a part of it?" Kite points to the place where her heart should be, but where there's a pocket that reads *No Fair* in yellow lettering instead.

Dorothy leans against her locker, shrugs a little, but signs as slowly and expressively as she can: "I don't know . . . To be honest, maybe I wouldn't. To be part of Rousseau for the rest of one's life . . ."

Taking a paper out of his pocket, Kite thrusts it out for her perusal. Unfolding it, she recognizes the printout of her e-mail. In large capital letters, he's scrawled over the entire page: *YES!*

"Let's get together tonight." He gives the two-minute sign to Orca, another friend—black dreads, skiing accident, memory loss—on his way to the smoking section. "After dinner, I could pick you up, I have the car tonight—"

Dorothy tries to step back again, but she's right up against her locker. "Can't we talk now? I have time, and you've skipped class. I know you have friends waiting for you, but I can't tonight. Really, I've got to work."

Refolding the e-mail, Kite looks down at her, shaking his head in exasperation. "You work every night?"

Arguing in the hallway doesn't appeal to Dorothy; too many people know sign language or can read lips. Turning to her right, she is relieved to find that only the Hacky Sack players are in their immediate vicinity; the other students have all found their way to classes, the cafeteria, the library, or outside. "Tonight I work at

Signature. But I do other work too. I help out at home. My sister is getting married. My father's a quadriplegic. If you don't believe me, that's your problem." Although she knows she has willfully misrepresented how she spends her evenings, aside from studying for school and at Signature, she feels she has not misrepresented her allegiances. She bends down to grab her knapsack. Maybe for her spare she'll head to the library, where nobody cares what she's writing as long as she looks studious, and e-mail her brother to ask how Mohab's grandfather is doing.

"I didn't say you were lying," Kite signs back, standing in her way to prevent her from fleeing. "I'd like to think we are friends, and we can tell each other things, but you're so closed off. You're not the only one who has stuff going on. I spend every other day either with a doctor, in conversation with a doctor, or arguing with my parents about doctors. I have to make a decision about the operation. It's going to cost them an arm and a leg, ha ha, and there's no guarantee that it will work, that I'll be able to hear. I could just end up with a permanent hole in my head."

Dorothy remembers discussions with her parents about operations when she was younger, and again recently, after the cochlear information sessions at Rousseau—too dangerous with such a low chance of success—and also her father, how they tried two operations, neither of which worked, and feels her throat begin to tighten, her eyes itch. "Sometimes hope is a horrible thing," her mother told her. "I kept thinking they'd fix him. He'd be OK and we'd all go back to the way things were. At first after the accident I prayed for him to live. Then not to suffer brain damage. It wasn't enough. I had higher hopes. I wanted him to be back to normal, nothing less would do. It was devastating when we finally brought him home in a wheelchair, and I had to ask a neighbour to help me get him up the front steps and inside the house. Still, I kept thinking, an operation, they'll figure out how to fix him with an operation." Then she thinks of all her SoundScape men, desperate to change the past, to fix the present, to confess the things that distress them about who they are and what's become of their lives. "I guess risk is always involved when you're trying to change who you are. Sometimes hope is a horrible thing."

Before Kite can respond, she ducks beneath his arm and scurries down the other side of the hallway, where the smells of bread and cinnamon escaping under classroom doors assault her. She clams her mouth shut, digs her hands deep into her pockets, silencing everything.

> Subject: Season's Greetings!
> Hi Emile,
> It's been a long time since we've spoken. I've been thinking of you. I hope you're well. Just thought I'd touch base, see if you felt like having lunch or dinner over the holidays, maybe see a movie, catch up a bit. We're still friends, right?
> Later,
> Monique

The U.S. military has not unearthed any weapons of mass destruction in Iraq. The President overwhelms the television, defending his actions, trotting out his usual lexicon: *madman, terrorist, security, democracy, freedom;* words whose meanings change daily depending on context. *We must protect our families and our homes from terrorist activity. We must keep each other safe and free.* To Hardev, George Bush is like some giant head programmed to deliver the same message over and over, a machine rather than a man of flesh, though Hardev knows what that's like. Some people treat him like a head that watches lives flittering around him, or particles representing lives on television. Though he sympathizes with any mandate to protect families, he knows there are malevolent forces one will never be able to detect, let alone stop. At heart a man opposed to war, to violence of any kind (he is, after all, from the race of Gandhi, he likes to tell the boy when it suits him, as he similarly tells him he was a Trudeau man to explain his marriage to a French-Canadian woman), still, he feels sorry for the cartoonish president, the whole world knowing he never rightly earned his position. He must run for re-election, Hardev thinks, to prove that the last four years actually happened, to prove that he exists and his destiny is that of the United States.

> *Things to Consider:*
> *American soldiers have begun wrapping entire Iraqi villages*
>   *in barbed wire.*
> *Kremlin party likely to win Sunday's election.*
> *Flu vaccine demand continues to rise.*
> *Andy Roddick has finished first in the tennis rankings at 21*
>   *years of age.*

The brown plastic meal tray with his cream of chicken soup and a glass of warm cranberry juice and water enters with Rodriguez, who has a red-and-green striped apron tied around his waist and a white cotton bib folded over his arm. "For goodness' sake, Harry, turn off the television. How can you stand so much war?"

"We must keep informed about what's happening in the world," Hardev replies, though he is now distracted by his desire for food. Rodriguez heats the soup to just the right temperature, and regardless that it comes out of a can, Hardev doesn't tire of it. When Rodriguez insists that it's good to change routine once in a while, Hardev heartily disagrees. *If something's not broke, you don't fix it*, he likes to tell him. *Even if something's broke, sometimes you don't fix it either, but that's another conversation.*

Rodriguez lowers the tray squarely onto Hardev's trolley, a packet of four saltine crackers placed diligently at the side of the soup bowl. Hardev became addicted to the crackers during his rehabilitation, as patients who can't stomach anything else can frequently handle saltines. Since then it's been two packets each and every day: one at lunch with his soup, and one in the afternoon as a snack, with a box of Sun-Maid raisins. "But Harry, the world will still be at war if you turn off the television. You're not going to stop it from happening."

Taking up his spoon, Hardev stirs. "Go ahead then, turn it off. Let's not worry about anything if it's not in our own backyards," he volleys. "You've learned what it means to be Canadian!"

"I hope so," Rodriguez answers with a smile. He's been studying for his citizenship test, and Hardev knows it's making him nervous. The wife, too, wants to take the test, but only after Rodriguez passes first. Though he would prefer to remain a landed immigrant—it feels like such a betrayal, he told Hardev, to switch citizenship, even when you've abandoned your homeland—the wife insists that it isn't smart in this age of terrorism and stricter immigration laws—better to get citizenship so they can never be forced to return. "Now look, I have the list!" he exclaims, proudly extricating five pages of text and photographs off the ebay site from the front pocket of his apron. "Basement boxes numbers one through fifteen all accounted for."

Hardev knows what items are on the list, because they made the list together, but he's still excited to examine the printout. "Look at that. Just look at that!" he repeats with astonishment, fiddling with his glasses to more closely examine the first page. "The Internet knows more about what's in my house than I do!" He reads:

> Time-Life Series World War II Edition, Moonlanding, and JFK, Collector's Items. First Editions. Excellent Condition. Lowest Bid: $100 US $135 CDN

> Lunch Boxes: The Dukes of Hazzard, Scooby-Doo, Barbie, CHiPS, Collector's Items. Metal. Barbie lunch box has slight wear on the handle. Otherwise Excellent Condition. Lowest Bid: $25 US each $35 CDN each

> Antique silver spoons from India. Set of 8. Circa 1900. Imperial design. Family heirlooms. Lowest bid: $200 US $250 CDN

The accompanying photographs were taken with Emile's digital camera without his knowledge, quickly loaded by Rodriguez onto a CD, and then erased so that only the boy's pictures of his graduation and some of Dorothy with a young Middle Eastern man—probably one of her Rousseau teachers, Hardev figures—remained. He notes with satisfaction the excellent condition of the lunch boxes (except for the handle on the Barbie one), because he taught his children to be respectful of possessions. They didn't bother to photograph the Time-Life Series books, but Hardev remembers the covers, a dashing young JFK in black-and-white, World War II fighter jets with men in combat gear and helmets, and astronauts floating across the moon, the American flag coloured in so that it would stick out.

"The spoons were a wedding gift, not a family heirloom," he corrects.

"No problem. They'll be someone's family heirloom. Doesn't matter. Only to help the customer imagine, Harry," Rodriguez replies, tying Hardev's bib.

"Help the customer imagine? Are you sure? I don't want to be accused of lying. I'm in enough financial hardship without breaking the rules of Internet commerce."

Rodriguez chuckles, opens the cracker packaging, and stacks the saltines beside Hardev's soup. "There are no Internet police, Harry. On the Internet, no one knows who you are. But I can change it if you like."

"Yes, please. I'm just not comfortable with the language." Hardev pats around his bedsheets for the pencil he was using, but Rodriguez is faster, extracting a pen from his apron. The words "family heirloom" are crossed off.

"Done. Eat your soup before it gets cold."

First sipping from the warm mug with a bendable straw, then scooping a mouthful of soup, Hardev continues to read:

> *A set of three silver handcrafted elephants. Made in India. Ruby-coloured stones set in the eyes. Excellent condition. Circa 1915. Lowest bid: $150 US $200 CDN*

> *Red sari with gold embroidery. Traditional wedding colour and design. Never worn. Circa 1975. Handmade. Lowest bid: $750 US $900 CDN*

The spoon hesitates and his heart seems to drop in his chest. The sari. The one he purchased downtown in the Market shortly after Birendra was born. Her birth coinciding with his first of several promotions at CIDA; for months he walked on air, saying to Isobel, *I feel so light that I think I know what it's like to fly.* But it was conceit, Hardev now realizes, to be so certain of one's happiness. His father would have warned, *Conceit is for gods. Only they can afford it.* A South-Asian woman in her fifties with a chipped tooth, specializing in saris, shared a booth with her younger cousin, who sold Indian teas and spices and rugs. Isobel was trying her hand at cooking curries and rotis and he had promised her the finest ingredients for the finest cook of Indian food in all of Canada. She had blushed like a streetlight, Hardev joked, flicking on and off. The purchase of the sari was a whim, he told her, slightly embarrassed as he removed the delicate red fabric from the brown paper wrapping. *When our baby gets married one day, she can wear it.* That had been the plan. But since the girl's engagement announcement, he's avoided bringing it up. There are no sari-wearing brides on prime-time television or in the American movies she watches. No sari-bride customers at her flower shop. Might as well sell it to a woman who really wants it, or to another hopeful father, someone f.o.b., which Birendra recently explained to him means "fresh off the boat." And deep down, he knows he can't complain. *I'm a Trudeau man*, he has always said. He raised his children to speak English and French. To watch hockey. He bought them Golden Books and blue jeans and hung up Christmas stockings for them. Why would Birendra all of a sudden want to wear a sari at her wedding, even if it is expensive, elegant and hand-stitched with bits of gold, even if as a father he often imagined how glorious it would look on his beautiful daughter, like a fine bottle of red wine in a crystal decanter?

"Good, Harry? Many bids! You'll see! That's only a few things, and you have so much in the basement. Fifty-seven boxes! And then other things around the house you don't use. You won't miss this stuff collecting dust. After, we can close the boxes, put them back in place, and the next time you go down, you won't notice a difference, won't even know they're empty. Depends on how you look at things, no?"

"I suppose you're right," Hardev admits, though still sad to think that soon there might be all those empty boxes where before there had been his life. "It's just hard for me to believe that we're going to get so much money from out of nowhere. Out of cyberspace. It's not even a country. It's like air. I can't wrap my head around making something out of nothing."

"Harry, people make something out of nothing all the time! Let me see if we've had any bites."

Cream of chicken—Hardev savours the lingering taste. Accept daily pleasures, do not wish for much else. He has learned this lesson before. You can't control your own life. You can only come up with new ways to interpret it. Now his interpretation of his life must include ebay and a moneyed land called cyberspace.

After a few minutes in the boy's room, Rodriguez calls out, "No bids so far. But don't worry. Most of it will happen online without our help. I just posted it last night."

"But there'll be a paper trail, right?" Hardev shouts back.

"Yes, yes! Printouts of everything. We can wallpaper the house if you like."

"We might need to," Hardev laughs bitterly to himself. "Now, don't forget to take home all those things I heard you put by the door! How you manage to work so hard and still get shopping done for your family, I will never know."

Returning, Rodriguez wipes cracker crumbs from the trolley and removes the tray. "Twenty-four-hour stores were made for people like me."

"Not so different from these people on the Internet," Hardev says, sinking his shoulders contentedly into the foam mattress behind him.

"Except a lot of those people are gamblers," Rodriguez retorts, turning swiftly around at the bedroom door. "They bid on things they might not get in the end. Sometimes things sell for a lot more at the deadline. This is what we will hope! Just in time for Christmas! Rush orders overseas possible with added fee!"

"You've thought of everything!"

Shaking his head in disbelief once again, Hardev waits for Rodriguez to lower his bed and spread out his evening blanket, tucking it in at the corners and underneath his arms. Placing the remote control inside the palm of Hardev's good hand will finalize Rodriguez's leaving. Whatever hasn't sold by Christmas Eve, Hardev decides, Rodriguez can pick from for a Christmas gift. Letting him have something from the house is almost as good as keeping it in the family. Someone's family heirloom, as Rodriguez said. As he listens to Rodriguez rearrange the bags by the kitchen door, he notes on his yellow pad of foolscap: *No Pot of Gold chocolates this year!*

"I know we're not supposed to talk shop today," Emile says, sitting on a bench in front of Birks jewellers, safely out of the way of the traffic of other Rideau Centre Christmas shoppers. "But last night I finally put it together. I found the key!"

Emile has been waiting for a good opportunity to tell Mohab about this, and is relieved to have the chance to sit and eat chocolate on this bench with him, at a distance from the sounds of PA systems and cash registers and women with SUV strollers and men carrying large boxes of electronics, kids tugging on arms and squealing, *I want this, I want it*, though he knows the point of this excursion is to force him to abandon library journals and microfiche, the Internet, the photocopier; everything to do with work, all the things Monique complained about when they were together. "I've been thinking a lot about that poor guy Bartman. He's the one who caught the fly ball that cost the Chicago Cubs a chance at the World Series. The Sianis Billy Goat Curse of 1945 lives on."

Unwrapping his Kit Kat, Mohab breaks a piece in half with satisfaction. "Goat curse?"

"Yes, goat curse," Emile affirms, as an old woman carrying a large Body Shop bag turns quickly in his direction, as if overhearing and growing curious, but only momentarily, as other stores await. "The last time the Chicago Cubs played in the World Series, Bill Sianis purchased tickets for himself and for his goat— yes, his goat, I'm not making this up—as he had for *all* the games that year, but he was asked to leave because with the multitude of people in attendance his goat was considered too smelly. He tried to argue that this goat was his family, and as much a part of the Chicago Cubs family as any other fan, but nothing worked, and he was forced to take his goat home. So Bill Sianis cursed the field and all the players and the organization. He said the World Series would never come to Chicago again. And I would say believe it or not, but you really must believe it, this curse has plagued the city of Chicago for decades. Think about it. Decades of hoping and dreaming. Decades of bitter disappointment. There's no difference really between team curses and family curses like the one on the Habsburgs or the Kennedys. Family is a primitive construct. Easy to duplicate. Sports teams always refer to their organizations as families, they keep up traditions like a family, and when a team is about to be moved the fans cry like children from broken homes."

"But the stakes are higher for real families," Mohab interjects, stretching his legs out to the side of the bench. "This is life and death we're talking about."

"For them too! Just because these elaborate ties are invented doesn't mean they don't exist. It all matters how one positions oneself. There's an old saying in hockey about retirement, *First your legs go, then your wife goes*. Have you heard it? Well . . ." Tearing open his wrapper, he chuckles as he realizes he's subconsciously chosen a Baby Ruth bar.

"These guys miss their families when they're playing, but then realize they don't really have families when they get home? That's one for the highlight reel," Mohab responds flatly, taking another bite of his Kit Kat.

"No. They realize the team really *was* their family. And for fans it's just as serious. If the family is shamed, they're shamed. If the family's victorious, they're victorious. Their own fate is the fate of the team. When someone's traded, it's like trading a family member—sometimes people are outraged, scream betrayal, other times they're thrilled to be free of the black sheep, forget all about him. It's no wonder the sports world is full of superstitions and curses. A curse can cripple the family, and people want to fix this any way they can. They invent solutions, counterattacks, antidotes. They come up with explanations, invent stories and rituals.

You watch, I bet some guy is going to buy that baseball and pulverize it in the middle of Chicago to erase the curse. Why? Because it *could* work, right? The story of the goat works, so why not the story of the pulverized ball? And if you're on the other side of the curse, you have to believe it too. If you get to play the Chicago Cubs for the League pennant, like the Florida Marlins, I bet you think this isn't too bad. And they're right. It isn't—"

"Someone else benefits from the curse," Mohab interjects again, mouth half-full, catching up with Emile's argument.

Emile slaps him lightly on the shoulder for getting it right. "Yes! If no one benefited from the curse, the curse would cease to have meaning. It's changed my whole way of thinking. A curse's effect depends on which side you're on. Curses may not exist exclusively to harm, but perhaps also to help others, the people on the other side of it."

"Well, I'm jealous," Mohab says, shifting his attention to the jewellery booth to the left of their bench—less extravagant than Birks—manned by a middle-aged woman with platinum blonde hair in a tiara and blinking red earrings. "I'm having a hard enough time figuring out my own beliefs, let alone everyone else's."

"Oh, be serious," Emile responds, following as Mohab gets up and walks over to the nearest case.

"This is serious. You still haven't found Dorothy a Christmas present. And didn't you say you wanted something very small to give Monique, so when you see her over the holidays you don't appear like a total jerk? If you don't find something, a plague on both your houses!"

"Shakespeare understood the power of curses—"

"He also understood angry women," Mohab stresses, cutting him off and eliciting a smile from the platinum-haired vendor.

"What about earrings? Or a bracelet? Does Dorothy wear bracelets? I don't remember" he says, holding up one of pink stones set in silver.

Emile has always had trouble picking out Christmas gifts—decoding a person's interior wish list is a daunting prospect on the best of days, let alone when you must attempt it en masse for everyone you care about or used to care about or are forced to pretend to care about. Usually he finds himself a saleswoman at the Hudson's Bay perfume counter or in the women's clothing section to pick out gifts for his sisters, so he should be grateful that Mohab wants to help him find something nice for Dorothy, something inconsequential but kind for Monique; but instead he's annoyed, particularly that Mohab's taken such an interest in Dorothy since the photo shoot. They took pictures in front of Canal Ritz, one of the city's nicer restaurants, and Dorothy stole one of Birendra's evening dresses and a pair of high heels out of her closet, even applied full makeup to look older. And she did look older, and very striking. Her legs peeked out of the side slit on the burgundy dress, and she stood in such a way as to look curvy under the warm black woollen shawl she'd draped over her shoulders. "Make it look like you've finished dinner, like you've been celebrating good news. Your engagement even!" Emile, the photographer with his cheap digital camera, ordered them around the twinkling white lights of the exterior of the restaurant, the canal railing and dark water visible behind them. It was Dorothy who came up with the idea of changing clothes and taking a few more at the Children's Hospital. "Why there?" Emile gasped, startled that with all the time she'd spent there as a kid, all the bad memories, she'd want to return. "If I were a nurse," she replied slowly, pronouncing every syllable, "I'd want to be a nurse there.

We could take pictures in front of the aquarium. It might remind his grandfather of the sea." Afterwards, Mohab said he had really enjoyed meeting her, she was sweet, and he had always thought it would be cool to learn sign language. "I never took to it," Emile admitted. "Not to French either, unfortunately. I'm sort of a failure at languages." At the time, he hoped Mohab wasn't just saying all that to be nice because his sister is deaf; now he worries that maybe because his sister is deaf Mohab may be taking too much of an interest in her, the way the women in the program chase after him because he's Middle Eastern.

"What do I know? I'm just the brother. You're the fiancé. When's the big day?"

"It will be a May wedding." Their exchange attracts the attention of the vendor as well as two young women trying on watchbands, asking each time, *Do you like it? Do you really?*

"Great. Like my other sister's," Emile sighs. "You want me to end up broke?"

Bumped by a six-year-old running up to his mother, Emile drops the pink-stoned bracelet on top of several others on the counter. He turns and marvels at the midday hustle and bustle. Nearly every person is carrying at least three or four shopping bags, and a couple of women have packages stuffed into the bottoms and sides of strollers. *Who needs all these gifts?* he thinks. Stores are stocked to the rafters with items no one would actually buy if holidays had not been invented for the purpose. Why don't we pay each other's phone bills or life insurance premiums or car instalments instead of buying these woks or hair dryers or glass figurines or pieces of jewellery that might just sit on a dresser or in a closet, or remain in the package for years before being used or sold for a dollar or two at a garage sale? The platinum-haired vendor, removing the bracelet from the pile, gestures at Emile. "OK, I'll take it." One down, he thinks. How many more to go?

"Yes, I guess that's right. Like your other sister's. Except ours is set for the following year. How awful." Mohab frowns as the vendor's assistant, maybe her daughter or niece, also in a tiara but with her hair in pigtails, crouches inside the booth to find the right box. "I set the wedding for a year from now in case my grandfather pulls through for a few more months."

Bracelet boxed in white, Emile tucks it inside his coat pocket. "I'm sorry. I shouldn't be making such a joke out of it."

"No, it's my fault. I'm the one who instigated this whole sham," Mohab apologizes, manoeuvring around an elaborate cellular phone display as they start walking towards the Hudson's Bay tunnel. "I can't believe my family is going along with it. They're worse than we are. Now that they've seen the happiness it's given my grandfather, they're inventing more stuff. They talk to him about flower arrangements and invitations and wedding cake— they've practically started testing caterers."

How easily, Emile recalls, Dorothy adapted to the role of fiancée for those few hours. And she was happy to videotape a season's greetings message in which Mohab did all the talking and she smiled and waved with one hand, holding onto his arm with the other. It was a great idea, Mohab's, and it meant Dorothy didn't have to worry about speaking to his grandfather over the phone, risking betrayal not only by her voice but by any conflicting stories about where and how they had met, for instance, or her ignorance of Mohab's last name, which Emile thinks he never told her. Instead, in elegant handwriting, she wrote on a Christmas card: *I'm looking forward to meeting all of you, who will soon be my new family. I am sorry that I can't celebrate with you. Hospitals have no holidays. But I'll be thinking of you. Happy New Year!*

"Maybe every woman knows how to plan an imaginary wedding," Emile offers, looking out the tunnel windows at the entrance to Hudson Bay's fantasy Christmas Street. "Maybe they even prefer it that way."

Out on the real Rideau Street, more buses unload more Christmas shoppers. Emile remembers how he met Monique over the holidays, on New Year's Eve in fact, at a Tragically Hip concert. First girlfriend in two years, no real girlfriend for two years before that, just other students to go out with for coffee or to a movie, and only one in high school, who broke his heart by sleeping with her second cousin on a summer trip to Italy. Monique had lost her friends and asked him to help her. Emile didn't want some asshole taking advantage of her tipsyness, so he agreed. At midnight, they sipped champagne and the guitarist played "Auld Lang Syne" on his electric guitar amongst a pyrotechnics display. Emile found her a cab and they exchanged e-mail addresses. The very next day she wrote, *Do you think there might be fireworks?* Although their relationship didn't last until the holidays this year, he knows how events would have unfolded if it had. They would have spent the day before Christmas together, exchanging gifts, dinner at the Canal Ritz. And then he would have sprung for a taxi ride along the canal to take in the multitude of festive lights, and Monique would have snuggled up next to him and before the ride was over maybe fallen asleep from too much wine. Next she would have invited him into her apartment, Ferrero Rocher on the coffee table, Christmas cards on a tail of tinsel over the doorway to her bedroom, and they would have made love gently and languidly; and then he would have left her there in all her warmth—*Merry Christmas, Merry Christmas*—and the following day she would have wondered why she was getting all caught up when it was to be their only Christmas together, and Emile would have wondered this too, though knowing at the same time how nice it was to have someone to talk to about work, to spend the night with now and then; but here at the entrance to the transitory Hudson's Bay Christmas Street, as he watches shoppers with Mohab, and where he will probably buy Monique a Christmas decoration for a present to confirm that there are no hard feelings between them, he wonders who, if anyone, in California or New York or even Cambridge, might fall asleep beside him next year.

SoundScape Diaries: by Roof and Key

This one named Fredrick: Airport porter trying to save money to bring his first cousin from Slovenia. People complain all day to him about delays, fees, schedules, weather, bad food and service. He spends all day asking, *Why are people born in one place and not another? Why can't they choose where to live?* Says his father was born a monster. *We showed him respect, but after we buried him, we wiped our hands of him.* His mother always said, *A boy needs a father.* Has a boy. Hopes someday the boy will have no memories of his father either.

This one named Jacob: Had an affair with his grade-school teacher when he was thirteen. She taught him grammar, his times tables, and how to make her squirm in his arms. One day she left town. No one knew why. Her husband patrolled the streets day and night for three years, photograph in hand. Did she run away from her husband? Him? Both? She used to say she had a "sewing heart" but he never understood what that meant. Maybe he was never that important to her. But he still spends many nights wondering what she's thinking, who she might be thinking about. Not one letter. Not one.

This one named Stephen: Studied to be a poet: Shelley, Spenser, Tennyson, Browning, Auden. Stopped writing during the First Gulf War. *"All a poet can do today is warn." That's Wilfred Owen. World War I. What's the point? Nobody learns. I can write pages and pages of couplets, and none of them will stop the wars, the constant striking down of flesh and bone. I never learned a damn thing from a poet except how to rhyme.*

Dear Dor,

Do you know the meaning of the word *paralyzed?* The etymology is interesting. It comes via Latin from the Greek *paralusis* and means "to loose from beside." When the Toronto doctors told me I was paralyzed, I knew the dictionary definition of the word, of course, but the actual meaning, what is never included in any dictionary because it must be experienced to be known, eluded me. I understood that it meant I would never walk again. I understood I would never have the full use of my legs. *You won't be able to feel them anymore.* I understood. And my arms were also affected. Partial quadriplegia. I understood. But what they should have said was *You will never feel anything outside your-self ever again.* The word *beside* forever betrayed me. *Paralyzed.* Not the definition of an unhinged body, but of an unhinged home. I would no longer be at home inside my own body. I would now think of it as an adulterous being that deserved only mistrust. Someone should have told me this at the time, instead of explaining rehabilitation schedules, how to attach and remove a catheter. I would have resigned myself to death. But when you contemplate only the loss of your legs, your arms, those physical appendages, you say, *Yes, yes, I understand, it's not so bad. I will take this pill. And that one. Weight training doesn't look so hard. A new bed is a simple adjust-ment.* They should have said, *You don't exist anymore.*

Your mother taught me that speech can require therapy. Our most intimate and instinctual expressions can prove to be deviant or may betray us. Like everything else, speech is difficult to control, and most people do not understand *how* to say, let alone *what* to say. What *should* I say? The world is full of illusion. It's full of accidents. It's full of betrayal. Our bodies betray us and so do our minds. And so does lan-guage. *Challenged* is a word that able-bodied people invented so they don't have to open a door or help one of us in line at the grocery store. Let's look up the word *bullshit* next. The world is full of bullshit too.

Dorothy sanitizes the needle while Birendra lies with her back against the headboard in one of Victor's old Ottawa U T-shirts, angling her buttocks astride two pillows, pelvis tilted upward, a towel underneath. "Re-lax," Dorothy says, purposefully over-stressing the syllables.

"Your speaking is getting really good," Birendra tells her, avoiding looking at the needle. Although they have frequently changed in the same room—flitting in and out of bathroom towels or rubbing calamine lotion on hard-to-reach mosquito bites on tailbones or the backs of thighs—exposing her lower body to her younger sister's scrutiny makes her feel a little silly. It's almost like being at the gynecologist, except here in their shared bedroom, instead of being surrounded by diagrams of ovaries and posters urging, *Ask about birth control options*, and STD pamphlets forebodingly placed beside jars of cotton swabs and boxes of plastic gloves, Birendra is surrounded by familiar things: her oak dresser and vanity table, photographs of her trip to Cancún with Victor last summer taped to the mirror, shoe rack hanging on the closet door with scarves and potpourri sachets tied to it, the stool where she sits painting toenails or putting on nylons, Dorothy's reproduction of Edvard Munch's *The Scream* purchased at the National Gallery. Though she was the one who suggested the procedure be done at home instead of at the parlour, Birendra now finds herself thinking, *Dorothy is seventeen years old. She can't even vote, but I'm letting her pierce my vagina?*

"A clitoris ring takes about three weeks to heal, but it should only be painful for the first six days," Dorothy informs her, holding up six fingers, then threading the silver ring with its tiny silver heart onto the needle. She still breathes a bit heavily at the start of her sentences, and her cheek muscles sometimes twitch, but her voice remains relatively even in tone and pitch. Birendra sometimes hears her practising, using one of their mother's books for adolescents with speech impediments, repeating tongue twisters and vowel exercises, but only in the last couple of months has she, for the most part, chosen to speak with Birendra rather than sign.

"What's the sign for clitoris? I don't think I've ever used it," Birendra chuckles, rubbing her cold arms. "Ever been tested on that word? Health class, maybe?"

Dorothy shakes her head. Though the deaf have their own curse words and gestures, and there are no laws against obscene word usage in sign language as there are in the speaking world, this is a question only Birendra would ask; even at Signature, no one would dare. Since the first day Dorothy walked in with her typed "To Whom It May Concern" letter, announcing her desire to apprentice and explaining her disability, the tattoo and piercing artists have treated her more like a special guest than an employee. No taking out the garbage or sweeping the floor. When she tried one afternoon to clean the lunch dishes and coffee mugs, Claudia, the owner, stopped her, insisting only full-timers had to do these sorts of jobs, she could look forward to them in the future. Dorothy is aware they hold her in misplaced esteem for being deaf, as if she exists on a special plane accessible to only a few. It's romantic, but she accepts that when people know you are different, they make you either as hideous or as exotic as possible in their minds; it's better to be deemed exotic.

After Dorothy finishes threading, she curls the fingers of her right hand into an O and pokes her left index finger in and out.

"That's crude!" Birendra giggles, taking a sip of water from the tumbler she brought up with her in case of nerves. She shivers, goosebumps running up her thighs. "I'm really glad you're the one doing this. I don't know if I'd have the guts otherwise. I think Victor's going to love it. Do you think so?"

"How should I know?" Dorothy signs flippantly.

"But you must have a lot of guys come in with their girlfriends, what do they say about it? Do they say it's sexy, pretty, what?"

Relaxing her piercing arm, Dorothy brushes a light cloth over the small clamp that will hold Birendra's clitoris in place. "They say a lot of things, but you wouldn't want to hear them."

Birendra crosses her legs as another shiver runs through her. "You know a lot more than you let on. I know you do. For instance, I know you are aware when someone is calling you across the room or even up the stairs, when your back is turned, though you pretend you have no idea."

In an amused rather than annoyed fashion, Dorothy intently watches her sister's full purplish red lips, teeth so close together that she has to floss after every meal.

Birendra continues: "I know that you pretend to like chocolates because Mom likes leaving them on our pillows on holidays, but that you usually give yours to Emile when you see him. I know you read *Lady Chatterley's Lover* when you were nine and you underlined the sections of dialogue, not the dirty stuff. I know you kneel, not stand, when you shave your legs in the shower, and your period is so light you hardly ever use regular pads or Tampax. I know these things. But I don't know who your friends are. I don't know if you're in love or if you've ever been in love. I don't know what you think about same-sex marriages or the war in Iraq. I don't know if you've ever tried souvlaki or made a wish on a star or mooned someone. I don't know a lot about you."

Dorothy continues to stare at her sister unwaveringly. Forefinger up, moving straight forward from the mouth, she gives Birendra the sign for "truth."

"Okay. So before we do this thing," Birendra adds, bunching the yellow comforter under her legs, "why don't I tell you something important about myself and you tell me something important about yourself? If you're going to pierce a hole through my body, I think we can risk this at least once in our lives, don't you?"

Dorothy rolls her head from one shoulder to the other, side to side, a habit Birendra recognizes. *I let everything slip out each side*, Dorothy told her once. Then her hands strike up quickly, indicating something unexpected and dangerous. "Dare."

Birendra laughs. It's a game to her sister, but at least a game she's willing to play. Letting her eyes rest on the bright fabric of the comforter, she takes a deep breath. "Okay. I'll go first. I'm going to tell you something no one else knows. I mean no one. Not Mom. Not any of my friends. Not Victor. Wow, this is already harder than I thought. I started this, though, right? Right," she repeats, taking another deep breath. "OK. This is what happened: I made an appointment at a walk-in clinic in Nepean about ten days ago. I went there specifically not to run into anyone I know. I brought my health card. OK, no problem, I wait. So I'm finally called in to see the doctor, and you know how I hate doctors anyway, right?"

Removing a cotton ball from her fold-out workbox on the bed, dabbing it in alcohol, Dorothy begins to recleanse the needle.

"Well, the doctor is frowning, she's all wound up, and she says, 'What can I do for you?' and I just blurt out, 'I hate babies.' And she asks, 'Are you pregnant?' and I say, 'No.' And she says, 'Then what's the matter?' and I say, 'I don't want babies. Ever.' And looking at the information I filled out on her clipboard, she says, 'You're twenty-seven. You could change your mind.' And I say, 'I won't.' And Dorothy, I'm so sorry, this has nothing to do with you, I swear, I said, 'There's a history of deformity in my family.'"

Birendra wraps her ring hand around her left thigh, staring down at her bare legs. Dorothy slouches to keep her sister's lips in sight. "So the doctor says, 'I could refer you to a specialist who could go over the percentages with you regarding chances of genetic inheritance, but I have a feeling you wouldn't go, would you, Miss . . . Dange?' she says, checking my papers. And I nod. And she says, 'What would you like?' I tell her, 'A hysterectomy. As soon as possible.' She says, 'It'll take you years to convince OHIP doctors to perform a hysterectomy on a healthy woman your age. Why not just have your tubes tied?' 'Is it easier?' I ask. 'Easier. But not easy.' 'How do I make it easy?' I say. I know this sounds awful, but I've found people will generally tell you what you need to know as long as you ask direct questions, so I was really direct. Maybe that's all I know about life, so there you go. I hope it serves you at some point. 'You might want to try your luck south,' she says quickly. I never thought of that. It hadn't occurred to me to go outside Canada. 'Open up and say *Ah*.' Then, 'Your physical's over. Have a good day.'"

Eyes downcast, Birendra laughs nervously, and lowers her voice: "I *don't* want children. Victor and I haven't really talked about it yet, we have enough stuff to talk about with the wedding, so I'm hoping to get away with this one. I looked up various clinics on the Internet, made some calls. I have money saved—I don't need any for the wedding. I'm going to have the procedure done in Buffalo when Victor's away for one of his conferences. I'm going to tell Mom I'm having a weekend away with one of the girls. I don't care if Victor wants kids. *I* don't want them. I'm not having them no matter what. You can't tell anyone, Dorothy. Those are the rules here. It's my body. If he wants kids, I'll pretend I can't have them. I'll cry and act depressed and all that shit. It won't matter. He's marrying *me*, not some imaginary future children of ours. It's my responsibility to ensure I don't bring a baby into this world that I won't love, don't you think?"

Hesitantly raising her eyes, needle dangling above her in Dorothy's hand, Birendra has a sense of déjà vu, a premonition that this needle has been and will be dangling over her again and again for the rest of her life, not quite touching, but threatening all the same. *This is what family is*, she thinks, *people you barely know who have your body, your life in their hands. People you love but who also scare you.* "Your turn."

Dorothy closes her palm and the needle briefly disappears. "I can hear you. I can hear you and Emile, and Mother and Father. I hear you all. Every single day."

The game is obviously finished. Secretly, Birendra's glad. Why didn't she see this coming? Every time she learns something about her family, it's something she doesn't care to know. And here she is, naked from the waist down on a bed, convinced she's doing the right thing because of something her brother said after Thanksgiving when she phoned to tell him to relay to their father that Victor's family would be paying for the wedding and so he had nothing to worry about, no plans to make. Emile went on about his work. Typical, she thought, he can't forget about studying for even a single conversation. But he was talking about weddings, she gradually understood, as he explained tribal rituals, how they still exist in many countries of the world, and how many tribes and individual families have developed their own scarification and body modification practices, like coats of arms, to indicate who belongs to whom. *When a woman marries into a new family*, he said, *she too is branded, to indicate her change of status.* Initially, the images of hot coals and pins, irons and lip plates that immediately surfaced in her mind, remnants of *National Geographic* magazines and *The Nature of Things* television episodes, repulsed her. But when she saw the clerk with the lip ring on

Remembrance Day, something like an electric current, warm but frightening, ran through her body, and she thought of Dorothy and the piercing salon. She decided it was right, crucial, for her to be permanently changed like those tribal brides, to alter her body in some way. Moving from one family to another, it is fitting to be scarred, she thought.

Pushing the yellow comforter to the foot of the bed, Dorothy covers Birendra's knees with the palms of her hands and gently pulls them aside, parts the frizzy hairs between her legs. Carefully, between thumb and forefinger, she brings out Birendra's clitoris from the folds of skin and cleans the area. The procedure, or at least the prep work, is surprisingly sensual. Birendra can't help but wonder if Victor has ever taken such a good look at her down there, if he has ever treated the source of her pleasure with such tender care. And suddenly she is sure that she does indeed trust Dorothy, trusts her more than anyone. Nevertheless, the clamp in place, she tenses.

"Focus on something. Your engagement ring will do," Dorothy orders, looking up from between her legs. "Take a deep breath."

Birendra obeys, awaiting the pain. Dorothy was curious what Birendra was up to two weeks ago when she asked for a clitoral piercing, joking that she'd like a family discount. *What message are you sending?* Dorothy thought then. Now Birendra thinks she has an answer. Then the pain arrives like a bee sting: unexpected, as if unintentional, but once received, absolutely personal.

This one was sitting alone, left hand clutching right shoulder, bottle of Heineken on a coaster, when Dorothy spotted him on her way to the washroom. In the winter there are more older men in the SoundScape, the atmosphere is more casual, though there are those, like the one who works as a documentary filmmaker and loves to watch the young women dancing high on ecstasy or acid, who like to come on busy summer nights too. No dancing tonight, just a blues band, and this one has a baseball cap on and hasn't shaved in days. Dorothy smiled in his direction and he was startled, glancing around to check that he was indeed the intended recipient. Only when she returned and sat down at his table did she know she had made herself clear.

There are half a dozen sofas in two rooms to the left of the bar. Her favourite section once wore a "Reserved" sign on a chain, but now the chain hangs like an iron tongue to the ground and people kick it as if it was left for this purpose. Still, Dorothy appreciates the namelessness, christening the section something different each time she enters its bruised mouth into a semi-private area beside the tables or near a series of neon lamps, purple and orange bubbles gurgling up and down the glass. Though dimly lit, the area is a social rather than make-out area (making out is done in the darkest booths, on the dance floor, or in the washrooms—how people who under other circumstances can't bear to sit on a public toilet seat will rub their naked bodies up against dirty stall doors, Dorothy can't figure out). Today its name is Sandbox.

This one has not attempted any sexual advances, a good start. Even after her kiss from Kite and her feigned engagement to Mohab, she feels sexless most of the time, like the space between Roof and Key, she imagines, where things are possible but where nothing has yet taken concrete form. This one seems relieved, too, that she's only offering her company. With his watery eyes and tired face, he's probably too worn out for anything else.

TELL ME A STORY, she writes. The letters flash on the light blue screen of her Palm Pilot, the same message she sent to him at the table before tugging on his arm to follow her to Sandbox.

TELL ME THE STORY YOU CAN'T TELL YOUR WIFE

Lifting his squinting eyes from the screen, he looks like a man floating on top of a body of water, like a discarded pop can or a seagull's feather. Orange bubbles ripple over his cheeks and neck like drips of paint. "How do you know I have a wife?"

RING

"Oh." He nods with embarrassment, removing his cap. Dorothy flips a strand of dirty blonde hair extension from her wig—the fourth she owns now, and keeps in shoeboxes in the closet she shares with Birendra—behind her ear.

TELL ME THE IMPORTANT ONE

THE ONE ABOUT WHO YOU ARE

Forehead rub. Sip of beer. Chapped lips.

THIS IS WHY I'M HERE

This one closes his eyes, squinting in the glow of the lamps, puffs his cheeks, then lets out the air. Extracts a two-shot bottle of Scotch from his jacket, offers Dorothy a swig. She turns it down. "I'm on a budget. Sometimes I bring my own as a top-off." He chuckles as if it's just occurred to him that it's funny. Whoever this one is, Dorothy surmises, he is a hard-working man, a city worker but not a cop. Policemen are easy to spot and Dorothy finds it hard to be around them; the ones looking for trouble here hate themselves so mercilessly that it translates into a smell. *Turn Key*, Dorothy thinks.

"I'm a firefighter. I'm a fucking hero," this one says, laughing tremulously into his beer. "I'm sorry." He lowers his head, adjusting to a half-rising position on the sofa as a man in an overcoat talking on a cellphone saunters by. "Why do you want to know this? You have no idea . . . the things I've seen. You're young. Younger than I thought."

YOU TOO

"You don't know me. You're a perfect stranger."

This one takes another swig of Scotch and squeezes the visor of his baseball cap. Dorothy suspects this one, the fireman, would rather enter the neon lamp and turn into a bubble than be a man. She has an urge to stop his hand from crumpling his visor, but resists. Touch is tricky. Touch says too many things people misunderstand.

I'M A GOOD LISTENER

Dorothy wants to add something about the phrase "perfect stranger," how strangers are rarely perfect, how they sometimes cause disasters, accidents, misinterpretations, but how they sometimes too can be good or welcome or compassionate, without being perfect, but she knows she doesn't have time.

Left hand darts into pocket. A pack of cigarettes partially removed halts. "You can't even smoke in public anymore. No safe places to light fires, I guess." Mini-Bic flicks on and off. "I didn't go into this business to save people. I didn't go into it to be part of the brotherhood, the extended family that firemen are always bragging about. I heard it paid well and I was young and in shape and I had crazy amounts of energy, I just needed to find a place to use it . . ."

Screen goes blank.

"There was this boy . . . so badly burned . . . Oh, fuck . . . I'm sorry. I'm sorry."

Many begin this way. *I'm sorry. I'm sorry.* Many end this way too. Dorothy knows the shape of these words well, how they feel in the air, against her neck, her hair, fake or real. No need to read them on their lips. The words are part of her blood, the first messages Roof and Key ever received. Her father used to repeat these same words to her over and over again when she was a baby, when he held her tightly over his shoulder with his good hand, and she is sure the repetition marked her shoulder and her back, pressed into her permanently, in ink, deeper than where anyone can see.

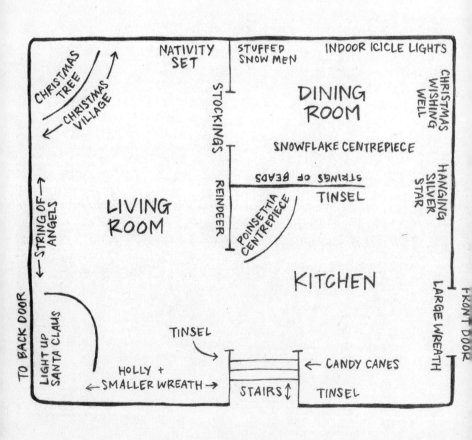

Merry Christmas

Emile wakes to the falsetto of a boys' choir. On Christmas Day, Hardev's service does not send an attendant, so Emile will be called upon to lift his father into his wheelchair, remove and reattach his condom and catheter, and dress him in his good blazer and slacks. But Emile has slept in and, hating to disturb the boy's sleep, Hardev watches Christmas Day Mass on the television.

"I'm coming, Dad! My alarm didn't go off!" Emile shouts, the door to his room flying open.

"Merry Christmas! Merry Christmas! Don't apologize. You shouldn't set your alarm Christmas Day!"

"But it's late!" Emile counters, jumping into jogging pants, loafers, and an Ottawa Senators sweatshirt, and running down the hallway. "Would you like hot oatmeal for breakfast?"

"As usual!" Hardev calls. Placed on his back the previous evening so that in the morning he could elevate himself and watch the Christmas specials, he is comfortable except for the heat of sleeping under too many blankets. Several envelopes lie stacked on the trolley. Money is his gift to his children on their birthdays and at Christmas, and the cheques are tucked inside cards. Emile is aware that his father asks his homecare workers to pick out the cards at the drugstore when they buy his toiletries and vitamins, but he knows that doesn't mean the messages inside are not sincere, and he doesn't mind getting money, prefers it actually, and his father rarely asks how he spends it. One or two hundred dollars, depending on the occasion. Not a large sum, but enough. Emile always wonders where he finds it. He must save up diligently every month.

Three rows of cherubic boys in long white gowns with red trim clutch black leather songbooks. "Where is this broadcast from?"

"England. Where else do boys look like that?"

Emile removes one of Hardev's blankets, the top blue one he's had since before Emile can remember, and raises his head to fluff the pillows. His father is in good spirits and, according to the late-night conversation that was likely responsible for Emile's sleeping in, so is Mohab's grandfather. With help from his cane, the man walked back and forth between bedroom and living room no fewer than four times on Christmas Eve, gathering around the tree with the rest of the family to participate in all their usual traditions, including the recounting of Mohab's birth. "Since they don't care about Christ's birth, they celebrate mine." Emile joked that this was why Mohab had religious complexes, but Mohab was eager to explain: "They're not really celebrating *my* birth. My birth stands in for every birth in the family, past, present, and future. The story ends with my name. My mother invented it. She wanted me to be free to invent myself. But sometimes I wish I had been given a family name, one repeated for generations, so I could be more connected to the past no one wants to talk about, but which must have made me who I am." In response, Emile told him the two things he knew about his own birth: his mother wished for him to look just like his father, and he is named after her favourite uncle, who died of pneumonia as a teenager when she was a little girl.

"They're coming at noon, right?"

"Eleven-thirty. Rodriguez laid out everything I need. This operation shouldn't take long," Hardev says calmly, pointing to the clothes on the back of the door.

The folded blanket is placed on top of Hardev's feet. "Do you feel OK today?"

"This silly infection is causing me some trouble, but no accidents so far and there's only a little pain, it won't stop me from enjoying today of all days. My favourite day of the year! Do you know that?"

Emile does. His father reminds him every year. "Where's the coat rack?" he asks, turning left, then right.

"Oh, we got rid of it. It was falling apart."

Emile slips the dress shirt from the hanger on the doorknob, smoothes out the collar with his hands. "We?"

"Rodriguez and I."

Emile forgets their names as quickly as he learns them; they have all been "the workers" to him, even the ones who over the years decided that he needed a friend, and asked about his school work, or threw a baseball or smacked an orange hockey ball around on the driveway. All these nameless people who entered and exited his home, as if the front door were a turnstile at one of those low-rent malls where the employees change as often as the stores, blur in his mind. He would forget every one if he could, but they sometimes pop up, haunting him by what they must know about him and his father and the way they've lived, what kind of family they are.

"Oh, the envelopes—put them on the tree! There's not much time. There, there. I think I hear the car!"

Hardev is right. His hearing is impeccable, Emile thinks, and rushes down the stairs, first to place the cards on the tree, then to unlock the front door.

"Merry Christmas!"

"Merry Christmas!"

"Merry Christmas!"

"Merry Christmas!"

Greetings circulate throughout the kitchen and living room, and then Emile runs back upstairs to his father's side to dress him, while his sisters wait patiently admiring the Christmas decorations Hardev puts up faithfully every year, they know, for their benefit. Fifteen minutes later, the men emerge at the top of the hallway, Emile pushing his father in his wheelchair toward the stairlift.

"It's broken," Hardev reminds him.

"Still?"

"You can do it," he assures him. "You've been working out, haven't you, for that girlfriend of yours?"

Birendra giggles and tells Dorothy what he has said, since the distance between them is too far to read lips. Dorothy giggles too.

The sisters like it when their father cracks jokes in their presence, making them feel somehow closer than they are, as if they all lived together. Careful not to dislodge the urine bag, Emile tilts the wheelchair, spins his father around. Concentrating on the task in front of him, he lowers the wheelchair down the four steps to the living room. The girls let out a sigh of relief. You never know what could go wrong; especially on a holiday, when everything matters ten times more than on any other day of the year.

Manoeuvring his father past the coffee table—his worker must have removed all the *Ottawa Citizens*—to the foot of the Christmas tree, Emile swivels him around to face his daughters sitting on the ancient paisley chesterfield.

"The stockings," Hardev tells him.

Detaching them from the hooks on the dining-room archway, Emile carries them over. Five centennial rose dishes, which usually hang to the left of the archway, are inexplicably absent. Emile vaguely recalls that his father opted for the ten-year limited-edition print, designed to celebrate the centennial of Confederation, as their family china, but gave up collecting the plates following his accident, when he could no longer afford them.

"They're heavy." Surprised, Emile secures a firmer grip on the cloth. Usually the homecare workers fill the stockings with boxes of Sun-Maid raisins and packets of saltines from the basement pantry. "What's in here?"

The girls each take their own stockings from his outstretched arms. Christmas village lights twinkle about their feet.

"Can we open them?" Birendra asks in a childlike voice, smiling widely.

Hardev laughs. Some things never change. The girl is always first to ask to open gifts. "Of course. Of course. Look inside!"

Each child shoves a hand inside a stocking, but the boy is the first to present his find. "A doorknob . . . ?" he asks, turning to his father. "Does this doorknob belong somewhere in particular?"

"Door*knobs*," Birendra corrects, displaying hers like a large piece of jewellery against her glittery silver shirt.

Giggling again, Dorothy handles the third doorknob the way one does a camera, bringing it to the level of her eyes, then adjusting position, her forehead huge and dark in the reflecting metal.

"Yes, they do!" Hardev affirms. "Can you guess where these doorknobs came from?"

"Zellers!" Birendra cries, without even checking the gold-painted knobs for identifying marks. "They were having a sale!"

"No. They don't come from Zellers! And they weren't on sale either," Hardev hints. "You can't buy these doorknobs at Zellers. Can you guess, Dorothy?"

"I-N-D-I-A?" She spells the word out slowly, as if only vaguely familiar with it. While this too is a wrong answer, Hardev admires the way her mind works, and the pattern the letters of his homeland make in the air.

"No, not India. But . . . you're on the right track. Do *you* care to guess?"

Emile rolls his doorknob back and forth on the placemat like a billiard ball. "Next door!" he replies, thumbing the air toward the construction sites.

"No! No!" though Hardev chuckles imagining a gigantic Santa Claus sack stuffed to the brim with doorknobs for all the new houses on the block, and Rodriguez jumping over the backyard fence to poach a few. "OK, OK, I'll tell you. Those doorknobs," he reveals, lifting his right hand triumphantly in the air, "are the doorknobs to your bedrooms."

"That's great, Dad!" Birendra says, polishing hers on her skirt, while Dorothy holds hers against her left ear like a seashell.

"But Dad," Emile ponders, dropping his back inside his stocking, "my bedroom isn't missing a doorknob."

"Yes, it is! It is! Rodriguez and I, we found some extra doorknobs in the basement, from when your mother and I first bought this house. We put them back on the doors so that you can each have the original doorknob to your bedroom to keep with you, no matter how many homes you live in the rest of your lives."

"Thank you," Dorothy signs warmly to her father, reading on his chin how his voice started cracking at the end. Birendra and Emile exchange glances but the messages are oblique, their eye-language a good fifteen years out of practice.

"Thank you," Hardev returns in kind. "There's more," he adds. "Under the tree. Go on."

The girls brim with excitement as Emile crouches on his knees, bending under the plastic branches to corral and distribute the presents according to their tags. While it is not out of the ordinary for the children to have a handful of gifts to open on Christmas Day, they are usually not from their father. Sometimes the various government services Hardev belongs to send them token presents: chocolates or bath beads, Santa Claus pens. Homecare workers periodically wrap up pairs of socks or bars of soap. Until his death four years ago, Hardev's old boss at CIDA sent, without fail, a bottle of wine and wine jellies by courier, and though everyone knew what the packages contained, Hardev insisted the children open the presents for him, saying, *There's not a present that's ever made me happier than having my family together in my home.*

"Open the ones from me first," he directs. "They go with your stockings."

Emile can spot them easily, as the wrapping paper is the same as on the gifts his father asked him to drop off for the druggist, for several of his doctors, for the manager of the Home Hardware, who always sets aside sale items at sale prices until Hardev can arrange to have them picked up, and finally, for the principal at Rousseau Secondary. This is the first year he has not also delivered gifts to the neighbours whose properties border their own. Not a single family remains. "At least I'm saving money," Hardev joked with the boy, and then changed the topic so as not to concern him. But Emile is aware of more than he lets on. He found a Gateway Land Developers business card taped underneath his father's telephone, and he knows it is only a matter of time—graduate school acceptance time—until his father has to make a decision about settling down in a nursing home or other facility. But Emile tells himself that Hardev will be happier there, where he can debate articles in the newspaper with other residents, watch his television and play board games, and not have to worry about leaky pipes or chipped paint or a faulty intercom or a broken stairlift.

Flat, rectangular package: Dorothy. Round, heavy one: Birendra. Square, white bow on top, very heavy: Emile.

All three playfully tear at the wrapping paper. This time Birendra is the first to finish. "A light fixture!"

"*The* light fixture!" Hardev corrects, and Birendra squints, pulling away the yellow tissue and taking a closer look at the white ceramic globe with a chain of daisies painted around the top. "You used to say you wanted one just like it for your own home. Do you remember how you'd walk around talking about 'my house,' 'in my house someday'? So now I am giving mine to you."

"I forgot all about it," Birendra embarrassedly admits, cradling the ceramic ball in her crook of her arm. "How did you remember?"

"Oh, I remember. I remember you, too," he adds, pointing to the baby blue tiles Dorothy is spreading out on the couch cushions between her and her sister, "but you are too young to remember, I think, how we used to put you in the bathtub and you'd be such a good girl as long as we left you some crayons, and you'd draw all over the tiles, those blue tiles, those very ones. I think of them as your first masterpieces. Right off the tub!"

Smiling, shaking her head in astonishment, Dorothy slides her hands gently over the shiny surfaces.

Next is Emile. He wants to look appreciative—it's the first Christmas he can remember that they've received actual gifts instead of cheques from their father—but his mind is spinning the way it does when he can't remember the name of an important critic, or where he's placed a specific article. Is the kitchen light fixture missing? Yes, it is. It is. Only a lightbulb in its place. He registered the missing object on some level, but didn't give it much thought. It's being cleaned, a crack glued, the light is hurting his father's eyes. A number of possibilities, all uninteresting, insignificant. And what about the tiles? Are they missing from the washroom? Yes. Yes, they are. His father's bathing apparatus must have knocked a few loose. Tiles crack or are dislodged over time. This is what he must have thought. But those in his sister's hands are in perfect condition. They didn't fall; they were removed.

Having overslept after not sleeping soundly for so long, Emile's brain is foggy. Shingles. Why are there shingles in his hands?

"You begged me to let you sleep on the roof. You begged me! The nonsense went on for years."

"I remember!" screeches Birendra, slapping her brother's arm across the coffee table as he holds the stack of black roof shingles tied with string. "You used to sneak out there, too. Yes, you did. What's the point denying it now? You did!"

"Well, those are from the roof. Not just to remind you of your childhood, but because you are my son. I'm sorry they're not in better condition. You will be the man of a house someday. The most important struggle a man faces is to put a roof over his head and over the heads of others. I wish I could give you a better start than this, but I hope these shingles will bring you luck."

Staring at the mass of roofing material, Emile keeps his head down, trying not to cringe. Birendra slaps him again, while Dorothy passes around the shortbread cookies their mother makes every year, but which they pretend they do. *There's no harm in it*, Isobel says. *Your father loves my shortbread cookies. He only eats them once a year. He'll be happy to think you've learned the family recipe.*

"This is great, Dad. You know what Mom got me this year? Some book about marriage. It weighs more than all these gifts put together. Russian. *Anna* something. A classic, she says. Can you believe that? When have I ever read a book like that? I love my light fixture. I'll get the hot chocolate. Do you have any?" Birendra places the ceramic globe back in the cradle of its tissue-lined box, and steps over the coffee table so as not to force her father to move his wheelchair.

"The cupboard over the stove. The kettle's fussy lately, but she still whistles."

Absently accepting a cookie and a small pack of Hershey's kisses from Dorothy, Emile pans the room. More things are missing: the silverware in the china cabinet, the painting of downtown Quebec City that should hang over the old record player, the record player itself, the portable sewing machine that usually sits on the TV unit. Yet here is his father smiling in his wheelchair at the foot of the Christmas tree, anticipating hot chocolate and indulging in shortbread cookies, as if the house isn't being dismantled outside and in. His sisters are not expected to understand, content to spend the holiday reminiscing about happier childhood moments, collecting doorknobs, tiles, and light fixtures, but Emile can clearly see that these gifts are signs.

"We are all here. I am a happy man," Hardev pronounces, tapping his armrest, as Emile leaves his shingles to help his sister with the hot chocolate.

The noon sun shines like crystal into the living room, and although the view of the street is one of abandoned machines and hardware, the shells of houses without any trimmings or ornaments to make each distinct from the rest, without any markers of the festive season, Hardev, his children home and happy, pleased with their presents, feels that he is part of a neighbourhood once again—that the fate of all those houses is also, and must be, part of his own—and a warmth, reminiscent of the surges of love he felt when he first held each of his children, runs through him, from his ever-pulsing head to his faraway toes. Not until late, late afternoon, after the girls are picked up by their mother and the boy retreats to his books in his bedroom, does he become aware of a card still hanging on the Christmas tree, addressed to him.

Dear Hardev Dange,
Merry Christmas!
I have not forgotten you. Please accept this Home Depot gift card of $100. Enjoy. Let's be in touch in the new year.
Regards,
Peter Manello
Gateway Land Developers

PART TWO

Happy New Year

The key is having trouble turning in the lock. Leaning against the recently renovated wall of the fourth-floor corridor, Birendra hiccups, giggles, then hiccups again. Cheek against the luminous grey, she can almost taste the new paint.

"Try to breathe deeply," Victor says, jiggling the handle.

"Try to breathe deeeeeeep-ly," she repeats, holding the pit of her stomach. Between hiccups, she hears Victor humming U2's "Walk On," a song played at the dance, but one he didn't dance with her, as he was busy getting them more wine. "Hurry up. I have to pee."

"Stupid fucking thing. I mean the lock. Why didn't you go before we left?" he retorts, just as the latch surrenders.

Grabbing him about the waist, Birendra kisses him abruptly on his lips and neck in jubilation, then stumbles into the apartment, lifting her bright red satin skirt and black crinoline as she rushes to the washroom. The pain from her piercing should have worn off by now, but she's still sore, although alcohol has helped take the edge off. After glass upon glass of red wine—four or five, she can't remember—and two liqueur shots, her body is thick and sugary. She wonders if Victor will honour their abstinence pact tonight, or if he'll try to start something now that they're light-headed and back at his apartment. While he didn't jump for joy when she proposed abstaining from sexual intercourse until their wedding night, not just for the purpose of keeping her piercing a secret, but to keep him away from her following her approaching medical operation, he did relent after she explained that it was extremely important to her that their wedding night be special, a night different from other nights, where she could be approached like a virgin bride, without a past, only a future. Besides, it was only a few months, she pleaded, and they could invent new fantasies in the meantime.

"Your fiancée is dead drunk!" she announces as she flushes the toilet and returns to the living room to kick off her high heels and drop her black jacket on Victor's lap. "Was she utterly charming?"

"More so than right now," he replies, hanging the jacket in the closet and removing his red tie. "Pacing, Birendra. The trick is pacing. The body can ingest almost anything as long as it's done in small amounts over time. When are you going to learn that it doesn't have to be all or nothing? I'm not tripping over everything. Just happily tipsy."

"Sometimes I like being dead drunk," she counters, sticking her wine-stained tongue out at him. "It's nice to lose control once in a while."

"But yes, earlier on you were most charming," he says warmly, leaning over the breakfast bar into the kitchen to turn on the tap and fill two glasses of water. "My mom and dad both thought so, Yolanda too. They only wondered where *your* side of the family was."

The Château Laurier engagement party was thrown by the Lanes. Birendra had been inside the luxurious building on only two other occasions—once for her high school graduation dance, when she was so high on champagne that her date took her to the hotel room early and she passed out after sloppy and quick but enthusiastic sex, and back in June, when Victor asked to meet her in the lounge bar to announce that he'd bought them tickets to Cancún. Tonight, striding past the reception desk and the high-end jewellers and art dealers to the private hall booked for the engagement party, Birendra remembered that second evening, how she thought, *Yes, let's get out of here as fast as possible, I can't wait!*, and how she spent the next two hours sipping Kir Royales in a deep armchair amid expensive china. The flowers alone must cost a fortune, she surmised, orchids and roses and tall fresh lilies perched upon every stand, on tables, at the elevators, in the lobby, at doorways. As for tonight, Victor's parents did not scrimp on the engagement party—an afternoon cocktail and hors d'oeuvres gathering for friends and family before they headed out to their New Year's Eve functions. Victor's father, a man with pure white hair, tanned skin, and good stature, held court at the cocktail bar with a goofy grin on his face as the platters of mini-crabcakes and mustard duck skewers, and the waitresses carrying bottles of red and white wine, passed back and forth. Victor's stepmother, Yolanda, whose black curly hair contrasted starkly with her husband's but whose extravagant orange-and-black patterned shawl gave her a foreign appeal, cornered Birendra in the washroom and said, "My dear, try to convince Victor to remain in a domestic position. International relations is a hideous life. You will never have anyone to talk to about anything important for the rest of your days. And you'll almost never see your family. This is the first time we've been back to Canada in years." Although Birendra nodded, looking appropriately concerned, what she really felt was excitement. *That's exactly what I want,* she thought. *To be packing bags, renewing passports, exchanging money, and boarding planes without any obligations as to when we might return.*

"Just leave it alone," Birendra says, spilling her legs over the end of Victor's black loveseat. "You don't understand my family. I told them this was a private celebration, since they don't get to see you often. It was all government people anyway. And that would have made my father sad. My family would have ruined it, made me worry the whole time. Is that what you wanted? Did I have too much fun?"

"You didn't even tell your father, did you?"

"No." Head spinning, she lowers the glass to the coffee table, and is about to take off her blouse but decides it might give him the wrong idea, so instead removes her bra only, yanking it with some difficulty out of her sleeve. "Why tell him? He'd just feel bad he couldn't give us a party like that himself. Do you want to throw your family's money in his face?"

"Birendra, you lied to me!"

"You knew I was lying, so it's not a lie," she chirps smugly, picking up yesterday's newspaper from the shelf under the coffee table. "There are bigger lies in the world. Look at the news. My father can tell you all about that,"

"Birendra," Victor sighs, pulling the newspaper from her fingers, placing it out of her reach beside his armchair. "I don't understand why you are so bent on keeping me away from your family."

"Keeping *you* away from my family? This isn't about you! This has to do with me. *Me!* I want my family kept away from *me.* In fact, it's my New Year's reso-fucking-lution! I don't want you becoming buddies with my brother or spending afternoons playing chess with my father. I don't want you planning cottage trips with Dorothy and my mom. I want to escape these people, don't you understand? I want to get out of here! Travel the world with you! Only you!"

"But it's because I love you that I want to love the other people in your family."

"Look," she says, taking a gulp of her water and staring up at the ceiling. "Don't get me wrong, I love them. You can't possibly understand how much I love them. But sometimes the past can hold you back, you know." She shrugs as if the discussion is starting to bore her, but a few hot tears emerge from the corners of her eyes. She plunks her glass back on the table. "Did I ever tell you my father was a tennis star?"

"Tennis star? No, you didn't."

"Yep, a tennis star. That's how he put himself through school." Eyes on the ceiling—she doesn't want to look at him; doesn't want him to see her lips moving. This is a side effect of living with Dorothy, since among the deaf it doesn't matter if you are trying to communicate directly with one person or not—as long as your lips can be seen, you can be overheard. As a result, Birendra dislikes people looking at her lips when she's speaking, especially when she's saying something important.

"He beat every kid they sent his way. I don't just mean other Indian kids, but British kids too, diplomats' kids, kids who'd grown up in the Third World chewing the fat at other people's expense. He could outrun, outhit, outvolley, outserve any kid his age, and sometimes the boys in higher age categories too. *Tennis is the classiest sport ever invented*, my father says. *Imagine the genius who invented the word 'Love' for the person who has no points at all.* His father, my grandfather—you know, I can't remember his name—toured him around to pay for good English schools, hoping he would eventually study at the London School of Economics. My grandmother died when he was really young, I think in childbirth, but I can't remember, it's not important. Anyway, he was supposed to do all this for her. His father would even say it: *Ace the serve for your mother. Win the game for your mother.* My father could have become a professional player, one of the first South Asians in the world to tour even the lowliest circuits, but my grandfather died the exact morning my father received notice of his acceptance to the LSE. He went, not because he wanted to study there but because his father had wanted him to. He never did anything for himself. Always for his family, for his parents, even for my mother, and for us whenever he had the chance. What's it done but bring him pain?"

Victor regards her in silence, with a nearly blank expression.

"I wish he'd gone on tour, travelled the world, forgotten about his mother and his father and just played the game he loved," she says, catching her breath, sober enough to tell the story but too drunk to stop. "That's the life I would have wanted for him. I'd give anything, Victor, anything to give him that life. I remember one of the fights he had with my mother before we left. They don't think I remember much, but I wasn't a kid and they weren't as quiet as they think they were. And they used to talk, too. Before

everything, my father used to tell us stories about his tennis days,
about his parents. I bet Emile doesn't remember, but I do; I'm the
oldest. Anyway, I knew what was coming. This fight, my father
was yelling at my mother because she didn't clean his feet properly, she was tired and did it in a hurry and my father was pissed.
She screamed back at him, 'I'm not a slave!' But he wasn't trying
to treat her like a slave. Those feet once made him a living. They
were beautiful, glorious feet, and he told her so. I'll never forget
what he said to her, he said, 'Do you know what torment it is to
see my feet turning blue? To watch them rot away like the rest of
me? Whose feet are these with the yellow nails and the chapped
skin? They aren't mine! And you know they aren't mine! You can't
even bear to touch them!' And then he started crying. He'd lived
through painful rehab and a bunch of fucking useless operations
because he was so fucking optimistic, because he still thought he
could have his Love with zero points, but now he knew. It was the
first time I'd ever heard him cry. Unfortunately, not the last."

Bowing his head, Victor says calmly, "You can't change what
happened to him. You can't make him walk."

"I'm not God, I know," she replies, kicking her feet angrily
against the loveseat. "But I can walk, Victor. I can walk. And I'm
no tennis star, either. But I've got good qualities, and I'm going to
make you happy. You'll see. Families paralyze people too. Are you
listening? Sometimes it's too much."

"We can't just ignore your family," Victor pleads, raising his
voice as he runs his hands through his hair. "I mean, when we have
kids one day—"

"Listen!" Birendra kicks again and slides a hand over her skirt,
over the piercing that's beginning to throb. Was he really talking
house and kids? *That's not my life*, she thinks. *Not what I've imagined*

for my life. "They'll be happier too. No one in my family likes to be reminded of the past!"

Hoping they won't remember this conversation in the morning, she tries to ignore the pain by focusing on her shaking hands. The light from above hits the New Year's Eve party favour glitter stuck to her fingers with just as much sparkle, she frowns, as her engagement ring.

Dear Dor,

In the winter of 1990 Emile was sent to the school counsellor. This was done with my consent after it was explained that he'd been having trouble concentrating on his lessons, and the lunch lady had noticed he was throwing out half his food. The day after the appointment, the counsellor reported that they'd spent the entire afternoon together, your brother with a sketchpad, the counsellor armed with a list of words. He'd say a word to the boy and the boy would write his response on paper, in any way he desired. It was advised that I not examine the pad, even though as his father and legal guardian I could insist on it, because the counsellor didn't want my knowledge of the answers to interfere with the counselling process. However, I was informed that Emile responded in one of two ways: either he would write a rather crude rhyming couplet using the word, or he would draw what looked like a lightning bolt, turn the page, and wait for the next word. After ninety-five words (what I was assured was a record for his age group's level of concentration), the counsellor asked him about the symbol he'd repeatedly drawn.

It strikes my head sometimes, he replied.

And then what happens?

Then it gets packed in there with all the other ones.

The counsellor agreed to send me a list of some of the words used in the game. One week later the list arrived in the mail, and I remember the envelope was red and I thought to myself, *Why, it's the colour of the boy's brain*, and then hated myself for thinking such a thing about my own son. I spent hours guessing which words struck at him and which left him alone. I still know that list off by heart:

> *Baseball. Ice cream. Monster. Rooftop. House.*
> *Telephone. Ladder. Teacher. Hospital. Balloon.*
> *Tulip. Wife. Sandbox. Bathtub. Fireworks. Purple.*
> *Elevator. Umbrella. Moon. Family. Grapefruit.*
> *Lion. Mittens. Spoon. Cavity. Door.*

It's not uncommon, the counsellor wrote, on a card with a photograph of a yellow caterpillar-like insect eating away at a plant leaf, *for young children to respond surprisingly to certain words, nor to create an elaborate fantasy in an attempt to make sense of the often strange and frightening world around them. Emile is a bright boy. He's testing his inner world against the outer one.*

Four subsequent sessions followed. Emile wrote no other poems after the first session and the counsellor was disappointed and perplexed by this, but I was relieved. He was disturbed enough without adding poetry to his list of problems. And I soon decided these meetings were a pointless departure from his regular classes. What was he going to learn that would help him defend himself from the striking inside his head? What was the point in simply naming the targeted areas?

I filed the counsellor's letter under "Report Cards" and told myself to stop worrying over which words scared him. Words are all frightening when used in a particular way. I never would have believed I'd become scared of words like *upstairs* or *physical* or *running shoes*, as I am now. We must all have words that strike our heads sometimes. You must have them too. I resurrected a copy of Plato's *Republic* from the basement and told the boy that if he read the entire thing, he would never have to see the school counsellor again. It's one of the only times he's ever hugged me.

VIA Rail has confirmed that the 4:50 PM train from Toronto did indeed arrive on schedule. Emile is watching television with his father, something they rarely do anymore, but his father saw a commercial for a two-hour Wayne and Shuster special on CBC and asked if he'd like to watch.

"Do you still like Wayne and Shuster?"

"I don't know," Emile honestly replied. "I remember I used to." And he remembered the song they sang, which he always liked, and which they are singing now, at the end of two hours of witticisms, exaggerated accents, and bad wigs—what his father calls "good clean humour," not like the filth that passes for comedy today, people using the F-word, talking about bodily functions, and humiliating people.

> Well I see by the clock on the wall
> That it's time to bid you one and all
> Goodbye . . .

And Emile has enjoyed it, perched on the stool at the foot of his father's bed, though he is slightly distracted, impatient for Mohab's call to tell him he's arrived back so they can meet, as they agreed on Christmas Eve, when Mohab phoned to describe his grandfather's reaction to the staged engagement photographs. All day he has been recalling the conversation, the play-by-play family action: how Mohab said his grandfather took a really good look at Dorothy, checking her out, and Mohab thought maybe she wasn't considered good enough—maybe because she was not Middle Eastern—but then discovered that his grandfather was checking out "her areas," as he called them, for baby purposes. "I practically burst out loud laughing. Areas? I mean, what a word. I never heard him use that word before. 'Of course, Grandpa. And she can't wait to have them, too!' I told him. The photograph in the lobby of the Children's Hospital was proof. My mother said, 'Look, she knows how to care for children.' I thought we'd all gone too far, and my father would put his foot down, but then he weighed in, 'The girl's hips are small but firm, Papa, and from what I hear, she's got quite an appetite too.'" Emile accused him of making it up, but Mohab assured him he was an accurate reporter.

Adieu mon vieux, à la prochaine
Goodbye 'til when we meet again!

He had expected Mohab to call again during the holiday break, but he hadn't, though Emile had left him a Happy New Year text message before heading out last night—a night he now regrets, but doesn't want to talk about with Mohab. Mohab's plans were to attend a charity casino; he joked that he was getting in touch with his Ambassador roots, when gambling was considered part of the family business, whereas Emile, through bad decision-making, had agreed to accompany Monique to a jazz show, where the musicians played what Emile thought was the same song for four hours. He spent much of the night certain that he would have had a better time if he'd driven to Toronto and joined Mohab. "Let's go as friends. Neither of us is seeing anyone else right now, why not?" Monique had said. "I hate being dateless on New Year's. We'll be too drunk to have sex and so nothing will get complicated," she joked. Two weeks earlier they'd had a nice time sharing a plate of nachos and a pitcher of beer at the Royal Oak, and even exchanged small Christmas presents— he giving her a blue-and-gold feathered peacock ornament, she giving him the latest issue of *The Guinness Book of World Records*— "a few superstitions must be in there," she said—and then gone back to her apartment and watched *Christmas Vacation*, laughing hard at Chevy Chase and the Griswold family blundering every aspect of the holidays, from the Christmas tree to the lights to the hysterical tobogganing scene. Nothing else happened that night; he had had no urge to kiss her pink lips or stroke her layered brown hair, no desire to slip his hand down the front of her corduroys. So Emile had agreed to New Year's Eve. But he shouldn't have. They did get drunk, but not too drunk to have sex, and now Emile feels awful for having done it, even though it seemed simple enough at the time—touch her, make her moan, enjoy being touched back—but now he feels like a liar, a betrayer, as if his body is foreign to him. He hopes that she won't call or text-message, that she'll think of it as a silly mistake, a "for old times' sake" fuck, and leave it at that. No, he doesn't want to talk to Mohab about it, about her. But he does want to talk to him; in fact, he wants to talk to him so much that he's getting impatient with his father and with the television, now that the Wayne and Shuster special is over and his father is staring blankly at a legal drama. He wants to tell Mohab about all the holiday superstitions he's read up on, how it's considered bad luck for the first New Year's visitor entering a house to be male, and maybe this explains Dange luck, because so many of his father's homecare workers have been male and the first strangers to enter the house on New Year's Day.

"I guess I can say that I outlived Wayne and Shuster," Hardev says, flipping open the top of his trolley to extract his nighttime medications, his pad of yellow foolscap slipping onto his blanket.

Picking up the pad, Emile reads:

To Whom It May Concern:

There is a date, but nothing else. Perhaps he has writer's block, Emile ponders. Or maybe he really doesn't know whom to send it to. Emile realized a long time ago that most of his father's letters go unanswered, no matter how painstakingly written. Maybe his father has come to realize it too.

"Check CNN," Hardev sighs, swallowing a mouthful of pills. "I can't stand this courtroom stuff anymore. It's all the same. Horrible people trying to take things that don't belong to them: trucks, guns, drugs, houses, lives."

Fiddling with the remote, Emile notes how haggard his father looks, how old—it's not unusual for him to get a bit depressed in January, after the holidays are over, but it usually doesn't begin until New Year's Day week is over and all the decorations are returned to their boxes in the basement. The caption across the bottom of the television reads, *Best Boxing Week of Shopping Ever*. "Not much going on in the world," Emile reports with a shrug. "I guess New Year's Day's not much of a news day. A day for hangovers and clearing out and getting ready to go back to work."

"Yes, back to work," Hardev repeats sadly, closing the trolley lid and placing the foolscap pad back on top. "But there's always something important. People keep living the tragicomedies of their lives. Nations too. Maybe they're just not reporting it. Turn it off if you like."

Emile flicks off the television, then sits back down on the stool. Apparently he hasn't been looking much better than his father lately. "You'd think you were head over heels for some girl you couldn't have," his father said last night, as Emile shuffled into the washroom to shower and shave and put on his suit. No matter how he tried to forget it, the comment weighed on him, made him uncomfortable in his clothes. It was like when he went to the gym straight from waking up, without showering; he didn't feel unclean, exactly, but stale. And the Monique situation hasn't helped. Neither did New Year's brunch with his mother. She called him "sweetheart" and presented him with a complicated alarm clock, and then they spent the rest of the frosty morning exchanging awkward staccato sentences while Birendra and Dorothy watched a video in their pyjamas. New Year's Day with his father was always much easier, especially after his sisters left, when he ate the leftover pizza and worked on the *Ottawa Citizen* crossword while his father wrote thank-you notes for the few gifts they had received; then Emile transferred his father from his wheelchair back into his bed and his father told him he was a good boy. He still loves it when his father calls him a good boy. But this wasn't his father's year to host New Year's Day.

"The world might be about to blow up and no one would tell us on New Year's Day! They'd just say, Eat more ham!" Hardev exclaims, laughing loudly but not really in Emile's direction.

"Or more pizza!" Emile offers, thinking of the empty pizza box on the kitchen counter downstairs.

"Do you want more?"

Emile's instinct is to say yes, of course, we always want more, but he doesn't want his father to think he's dissatisfied with this year's holidays, though he still doesn't know what to do with his roof shingles or, for that matter, his doorknob. But even if he doesn't know, he imagines he will take them with him wherever he ends up next year. His father is possibly on to something. Maybe the answer to all this stress about the future is just a matter of changing doorknobs. The thought struck him early yesterday, before all the business with Monique, when he was mailing off two more PhD applications and a couple in their late twenties or early thirties were standing in front of the corner Ashbrook lot, holding hands. "This is our house," the woman proudly announced as Emile neared them. "I mean when the construction's finished. But we've paid for it. Do you live in the neighbourhood?"

Emile didn't know what to answer. "My father lives here, but I don't know for how much longer," he replied. The woman lowered her gaze. Perhaps they'd heard about the man who hadn't yet sold his house, the wheelchaired man who was determined to remain the eyesore of the new neighbourhood, or perhaps they were simply embarrassed.

"We've been coming once a week or so to see the place—an empty hole at first," the man explained. "It was hard to imagine a home here, a family running around the yard. But each week they keep working, and it seems more possible."

That's all a home is, Emile wanted to tell his father. Just a hole in the ground. But he knew that he would take it badly, that he wouldn't understand the potential freedom in adopting such an attitude. And yet it's his father who's taught him not to get too attached to anything, to count only on himself, to keep on track and try to finish his work while he—

"Finally!" Emile jumps up as the phone rings. *I knew Mohab wouldn't lie to me.* Nearly tripping on his feet, he hurries down the hallway to his bedroom.

"Wait!" Hardev calls after him. "It's for me!"

MAKE YOUR MARK!

The Rousseau Mural Project is seeking material submissions to construct an enormous collage in the mural space at the Front Entrance. No submission will be turned down. You don't have to be an artist to participate. We will accept artwork, written work, mementos, photographs, posters, objects, articles of clothing, and more. Give us something of yourself. Anything we can glue, we can use! Submit anonymously at the front office or at the booth located outside the cafeteria throughout exam period. Simply write: Rousseau Mural Project on the envelope, box, or bag.

DON'T LET THE ANNALS OF HISTORY SPEAK FOR YOU!

Happy Birthday

Subject: Happy birthday!

Dear Emile,

I'm sorry you're so busy studying that you can't take time off to celebrate, but know I am thinking of you, and Birendra is too, even if it doesn't seem like she's thinking of anyone or anything but her wedding. This morning Mom asked me what I thought about light pink tablecloths. I thought, Should I have strong opinions on tablecloths? Exactly the response I imagined you would have. I like to think that every once in a while we have thoughts in unison, even if we don't recognize when. But maybe I'm wrong. If so, don't tell me.

Love,

Dorothy

P.S. How is Mohab's grandfather?

Dorothy waits anxiously for Kite by a five-foot stretch of lockers near the woodworking rooms, where the Rousseau Mural Project submissions are stored. It was Kite who had the idea to set up a booth outside the cafeteria and collect the submissions themselves—that way, no one would be intimidated by the prospect of handing in contributions to teachers and staff. The response was overwhelming. While day one submissions came mostly from art students, reminded by Mrs. Kotek to get their contributions in post-haste, by day two there was a lineup, and by day three it seemed as if every student at Rousseau was dropping something off, and some more than once. Any Excuse Jacobson provided them with the lockers for storage, though he warned them to examine all items before accepting them, as they would be held responsible for the locker contents in the event of a random search.

Although they took separate shifts to collect at as many times as possible, on Dorothy's shifts alone she accumulated three lockers of material—poems and journal pages, likely written in the dead hours of morning, drunk, stoned, or unbearably sober; music stickers, and trading cards ranging from sports and pop stars to serial killers; pressed flowers and drops of perfume on scarves and scraps of construction paper; pillboxes; the knobs from four canes; a wide-eyed blonde-haired doll, ears stuffed with cotton; eyeglasses with smashed lenses; edible condoms; a hubcap from a Volkswagen Beetle; an ice-cube container with a word inscribed inside each tiny tub: *love, hate, winter, edgy, baby, nail*; body glitter; a whoopee cushion; ten locks of hair; an eyelash curler; a swimsuit; an AeroChamber; a torn umbrella; several photocopies of the palms of hands; a locker mirror; hundred of photographs, everything from party pics to school shots to those taken at funerals and of the insides of people's mouths; a tambourine from the Cleveland Rock & Roll Hall of Fame; ticket stubs from movies and concerts; a birth certificate (copy or original, Dorothy doesn't know); a childhood report card with the words *does not respond to any verbal stimuli; has withdrawn socially*; an insert from Grand Theft Auto 2; herbal candles; three packs of cigarettes; dozens of hearing aids and batteries; rabbit salt and pepper shakers; a tourist pamphlet of the Parliament Buildings; a sheet of blotters which Dorothy concealed inside a copy of *The Diary of Anne Frank*; a papier-mâché bird; a cough syrup spoon; cases from several favourite videos, DVDs, and CDs; prints of tattoos; a gold eye mask; a Hebrew calendar; a map of Albania; rolling papers; a tin can cut and sculpted into a flower; an Ottawa Senators flag; a camera with a spent film left inside; a pink music box with a black cat in a tutu that spins as "Memory" plays; a pair of neon-green socks; pictures of dogs, cats, birds, fish, turtles, and a ferret; computer disks; a French-English pocket dictionary; seashells; a pager; a stuffed toy star that giggles when pressed; birthday cards; approximately fifty pins, from "Save the Whales" to "I Love Beer" to "Who's Your Daddy?"; a ripped T-shirt from Ozzfest; a friendship bracelet; a Canadian flag backpack patch; half-written university and college application forms; a McDonald's job application; a Young Conservatives of Canada ID card; pamphlets from doctors' offices; prescription bottles;

magazine covers; combs and a silver hairbrush; and an army recruitment poster.

Careful not to catch any hair, Dorothy slides the elastic of the gold eye mask over her head. By the time she adjusts the peek holes, Kite is peering into them.

"Hi beautiful," he signs, wiggling his eyebrows like giant caterpillars. "What's your name?"

"My name today is House," Dorothy signs back, startled but containing her laughter, thankful that the submissions bounty has translated into good feelings between them again. "Sometimes it's Door, or Hallway or Windowsill or Slide. But today it's House." Her hands remain in the triangular position over her head.

"A house made of gold? May I come in?"

"Only if you don't break anything," she cautions, and opens the first of the three lockers with her set of keys, gesturing at the mountain of plastic bags as if she's magically produced them with a flick of her fingers. "What are we going to do with all this? I got tons. We have to include everything we can. What about you?"

"Tons," Kite repeats, miming lifting such a large weight with his arms. "I've asked permission to use the gym carts that hold the basketballs to transport this stuff. Mrs. Kotek says we can store it all in the library since it's close to the mural. There's a huge backroom, and they won't be getting any new orders until next year, so it's empty. It's also locked, so everything should be safe."

Gold mask lifted to her forehead, bits of glitter fall onto her cheeks. "How are we going to do this? I made a catalogue of what I have. I can't wait to see yours."

"I'm not sure yet," Kite admits, then extricates the elastic band from her hair and swings the mask around his elbow.

Only now, handing over the yellow foolscap pad with her list of items, does she notice how different he looks today: unwashed hair, crumpled shirt, oily skin. She closes the locker, dropping the keys into her jeans pocket to show him he has her undivided attention. "Is something wrong?"

"No . . . I mean, yes . . . I mean no." Kite rolls on the balls of his feet, avoiding her eyes. "I'm excited about the project. It's great! I mean, I think it's going to be great. I'm just . . . I might have my operation sooner, my parents are looking into it. I might not be at school much longer. And I'm having nightmares. Not about the mural, but about the operation, how things will be afterwards." He makes a stabbing motion to the back of his head, then raises and lowers his arms in robotic jerks. "I figured out that I want this operation to succeed because I want to understand more than I do. I really like people. I want to communicate with them. *All* of them. I want them to be able to communicate with me. No matter who they are. Deaf. Hearing. Disabled. Abled. Black. White. Young. Old. Whatever. But I'm afraid the opposite might happen, and no one will understand me anymore. Like when I was little, before I realized I was different from the other kids, we'd be playing in the sandbox and I thought we all understood each other because we were all there in the same place, playing with sand like the box was a little home, but the other kids would build their mounds and triangles and moats away from mine. I'd be stuck either by myself or with my mother. I don't want to be stuck like that again."

As Kite talks, Dorothy is reminded of the one named Nicolas, who she met last week. "No one understands me anymore," he said. That's exactly what he said. "Not here or back in Croatia." Separated from his family for five years, he doesn't know who he is now. An all-night diner cook. "Egg sandwich, omelette, lots of coffee, hamburger, that kind of thing. People don't eat good when they're up all night. That's what I see. They feel like junk. They put junk inside." Wife and baby exiled in Slovenia. Takes ESL classes, is saving up for college. "I like your hair," he said, and Dorothy explained that she was wearing a wig. Dark brown, shoulder-length, curly. Cheap. Funny how she would have accepted the compliment for her real hair, but felt bad taking credit for picking out a nice disguise. This one named Nicolas, he came in for a beer before his shift. "I like watching people when whey are smiling, dancing. Not running, scared." So they sat together and watched a few people dance.

"The doctors, they give you these lists, names of people who've gone through with it, for you to talk to. But they're not going to give you the names and numbers of people who think they made a mistake, are they?" Tension builds up in his shoulders and arms as he signs. Frowning, Dorothy pulls on the tail of his plaid cotton shirt. "I don't want pity," he adds over her head.

Unhooking the gold mask from his elbow, she motions for Kite to bend down, and slides it over his eyes.

"Everyone has to work to communicate, whether we're perfect strangers or family," she signs. "That's what this mural's about, right? We can only present who we are at this instant, if we even know who we are, and we can't control how people will interpret it. No operation is going to make communication easier. My sister's having an operation so she doesn't have to communicate. I punch holes into people's bodies because they want to communicate with themselves. I don't understand you exactly, Kite, and you don't understand me, but at least we have imaginations and if we want to we can try. I guess the problem is that frequently people don't want to try. Or they want to harm you with their communications. Intrude. Destroy."

Slouching over her, the red of his eyes contoured in gold, Kite asks, "Why do you think that is?"

"I don't know. My father once told me that the worst invention ever created was the fence. In his village where he grew up, people didn't have fences. Neighbours ate together, their children studied together, played cricket together, prayed together. Then one family put up a fence—for privacy, to keep their garden from being trampled on, to hide their dirty sheets and underwear— and then shortly afterwards another one went up, then another. Soon, my father said, neighbours stopped talking altogether. Then they started stealing each other's stuff. I'm not sure if that's a true story or not, but it doesn't matter, I still understand it, or I think I do. When my father's neighbours all started selling their properties around him to a developer, they didn't even say goodbye. My father was devastated. He felt betrayed, like they tried to destroy his house in the process. But really, what did they know about each other? Nothing. Nothing at all. As little as I knew about you before this year, or anyone else at this school. *Your mother put up a fence between us after the accident, but I gave her the hammer to do it*, my father said to me. I was forced into this project, but I'm learning I don't want to build fences anymore, and I certainly don't want to destroy anyone's house, and you don't want to build fences either, but you can't expect people to want to eat with you and play in your yard or in your sandbox, Kite, if they're not ready to."

"But you told me I could come in?" Kite argues, hands shaking.

"Yes. But like I said, try not to break anything, if you can. That's what I'm interested in communicating. Everything's fragile. Our hearing, our legs, our families, our sense of ourselves. I collect these . . . these stories . . . like these mural items. They're not happy stories, they're fragile stories, but I collect them from these men, and I'm trying to take care of them, make use of them in a way that will eventually help me to understand other people around me. People who probably should tell me stories and don't. People I should tell stories to and don't. These other people, these strangers, men, they tell the stories to me. I write them down. That's it. Then I never speak to them again."

After a moment, flipping open an imaginary diary, Kite asks gently, "Can I read them? I'd like to read them. Maybe they'll help me. I'm not afraid of unhappiness. I think I'm afraid of fences."

Her head aches as Dorothy considers it. Although she's imagined showing him the SoundScape Diaries on a number of occasions, she's not sure she actually can. She hasn't shared them with anyone; on the contrary, she's been careful to hide any evidence of their existence. But maybe they are more like the mural items than she wants to admit. Maybe they too need to be shared, allowed to speak for themselves. Staring at the lockers, Dorothy imagines the contents tumbling out, spilling all over the hallway floors, raining from the ceiling, slithering underneath doors into classrooms and offices, sitting in auditoriums, growing in the fields, and the thought of all these objects toppling the strict structure of the school buildings, especially its fences, pleases her. Standing there with his usual slouch, Kite is so compact and skinny that he could be stored in one of the lockers himself. She decides: *I don't want that for him.*

"OK, but I need to know who to send them to. So let's start again. Hi beautiful," she mimics, leaning in close, her motions tiny and slow. "What's your name?"

Extricating the material from the three lockers, preparing for the move, Kite seems to think about it. The janitorial staff have already been text-messaged to bring one of the basketball carts down to the woodworking wing, but they are slow in arriving. After the holidays, it's difficult to return to the routines of school, to hallways devoid of decorations, to dark snow left behind by boots and tires. Dorothy and Kite work together to ensure that when the bins arrive, the heaviest and least fragile items will be placed on the bottom, delicate ones on top. "I don't know where I belong anymore," this one named Nicolas said. "Who listens to a man who speaks nobody's language?" And Dorothy told him, "I do. I do." Maybe Kite will too.

A gold-faced Kite stands by the plastic bags, boxes, and envelopes as if guarding them from some impending but unknown disaster. "House"—he turns—"sometimes I think you've already drilled a hole into the back of my head."

Dear Dor,

When the boy was fourteen I caught him hanging from the maple in the front yard, his knees wrapped around a branch about twelve feet from the ground, gently swinging. I usually take a nap after my bowel procedures, exhausted by the stress and the medication, but on this particular day I had asked the homecare worker to set me up in the living room with my writing supplies. I wanted to take inventory of the books and videos, to determine what the boy might need over the next few years to prepare him for university.

This worker was a Slovakian girl, about nineteen. Her parents had brought her here only four years earlier and she hadn't acquired much English yet, but listened to the radio and watched soap operas and had thus gathered some sort of working vocabulary. Once, she dropped a bowl of soup and cried, *This is the worst thing that's happened since my sister came back from the dead!* The thing is, the way she'd stare with those blue eyes and whitish lips, you could almost believe her. Anyway, recognizing Emile through the part in the curtains, I gasped and pointed as his upside-down chest and neck and head entered my view, then left it, then entered it again, like a pendulum.

He is like that, she said.

Like what?

He does this some afternoons, four-thirty to five o'clock.

My God, I replied. *What the hell is he doing out there?*

No, no. He knows he's not God, she said.

She shut the curtain, an out-of-sight, out-of-mind type of thing. I remember thinking, *That boy is going to be lonely for the rest of his life, even with his legs.* It was not a good thought— it was a mean thought, even. If you think about it, most people go about their daily business generally expecting things to follow their plan, to work out the way they want them to, to unfold in a logical manner, whatever logic they possess. That's why we cry when someone doesn't love us, are scared when thunder claps out of the blue, shocked when we don't get the promotion or the next-door neighbour drops dead at forty. Most people can't accept that they're not in control of their destiny, that they're actually a nobody in a story that's probably meaningless without our constant structuring of it according to our imagined rules. It's a horrible revelation. But the boy, he knew this right from the beginning. I think that's why he studies what he studies. I didn't know this then. Some nights I still feel like one day I'm going to receive back all the things taken from me, like they've been locked away in a gigantic storehouse through a massive bureaucratic error and someone is going to set the paperwork straight: *Here you are, Mr. Dange, here are your working legs. Here's your wife. Your two beautiful girls. Oh my, what a mix-up. We're very sorry. Why not take that trip back to Paris you always wanted, on us? Climb up the Arc de Triomphe (no, you won't be needing that wheelchair) and look out at what tourists say is still the most beautiful city in the world. You own it, Mr. Dange. Yes, Paris. It's all yours.* It's true. You think there's only your way of seeing things, your kind of justice. But if you simply accept that this isn't the case, that everything is out of your hands, absolutely everything, then maybe you answer no call but the wind's.

The boy hung upside down from that maple tree again the next day, and at the same time for two more years. I would turn on the outside intercom from the bedroom and hear the rustling of his clothes or the hum of a tune that took me two months to identify as a French lullaby his mother used to sing to him (*Mon petit, mon petit garçon avec les yeux doux*), but I don't know if he was conscious of that or not. Once or twice I heard a branch break, and before I knew what was happening, I was screaming. I don't think the boy ever heard. The system transmits only one side at a time. I've always liked it that way.

SoundScape Diaries: by Roof and Key

This one named Archie: Wife diagnosed with lupus. He wishes he could tell her how beautiful she is, have sex with her, but he can't. She's not a woman to him anymore. He can't stand looking at her. Every night he has a headache, blames it on rush-hour traffic. If the lupus had surfaced five years earlier, though he's ashamed to admit it, he wouldn't have married her.

This one named Felix: Car mechanic. Made a mistake while fixing the brakes on a Lincoln Town Car. His girlfriend had just told him she was pregnant, and he didn't know what to do: ask her to have an abortion, or start changing his life to revolve around a kid. A rainstorm. The owner of the Lincoln Town Car skidded off the road into a ditch. He lived. His mother, in the car on her way back from the hairdresser's, didn't. The garage had insurance. The girlfriend had the abortion.

This one named Jack: The only memory he has of his mother is of her singing him a lullaby.

This one named Patrick: Ottawa firefighter. Fifteen years' service. Saved: cats from trees (yes, people call firefighters to do this); women and children from burning buildings; men from auto wreckage. Earned a commendation from the City of Ottawa in his second year for pulling a construction worker from under a collapsed building. But his son hates him. Hates him venomously. He gives him toys, clothes, money, rides in the fire truck, anything he asks for, and this kid never says thank you or I love you if his mother doesn't force him. One night after a bedtime story, the kid

said, *You're not my real father. I know you're not. I don't care
if you die in one of those fires.* They had a paternity test
done so the boy could read the results for himself.
You're not my father, he said anyway. *You're nobody.*

Spotting Mohab pacing in the doorway of the graduate student
lounge, Emile deliberately turns in the opposite direction. The
last thing he needs in the last months of his MA is a distraction,
but Mohab, spotting him too, dashes out, grabbing his half-open
knapsack and jacket.

"Emile! Emile! Hold up!"

Figuring it's futile to pretend he hasn't heard, Emile stops but
remains where he is, blocking the front of the academic advisor's
office.

"We need to talk," Mohab says, catching up.

Emile taps his watch. "I have a meeting with Professor
Whitman. It's important."

"Oh, OK." Mohab scratches his chin apologetically. "It's my first
day back and I need to tell you some things. Can we meet later?"

"No. I'm seeing Monique tonight. It's my birthday and she
wants to buy me dinner. Then I'm going to have dessert with my
father." Although Professor Whitman's office is only a few doors
away, on the same floor as the graduate lounge, Emile heads for
the stairwell. He wishes he hadn't got himself into this mess with
Monique, but since she won't stop e-mailing, he thought maybe
they could go out again as friends, so she could see that a slight
friendship was all that was left between them, if anything. No
plans for his birthday, so why not? Better than spending it alone.

"Shit, Emile!" Mohab jams the door, where two students are
exchanging notes. "I forgot about your birthday. I'm sorry. You

must be angry at me. I should've phoned to let you know what was happening. I'm really sorry."

"I'm not angry. It doesn't matter," Emile replies, trying to sound cheerful as the stairwell fills up with between-classes traffic and someone yells, "Hey, asshole," rushing past them.

"This isn't the way I wanted to tell you this," Mohab says, lowering his voice. "After we spoke on Christmas Eve, my grandfather took a really bad turn. We had to take him to Emergency. Three days later, he died. I couldn't phone you. I couldn't phone anyone. I got back last night."

Emile remains silent but his left knee starts to twitch, as it does sometimes when he's uncomfortable and wants to get away.

"I can't believe he's gone. I mean, I knew it was coming." Mohab sniffles, covering his eyes. "But I still wasn't prepared. It's like he's just disappeared. Like he never existed. There are his things, his reading glasses or blue cardigan, or that wood pipe he quit smoking ten years ago, all over the house, but they don't belong to anyone. And I think, what am I doing? How does any of this matter? No one's going to write a paper about my grandfather. I'm not. You're not. And even if we did, what would it be about? It would be about his coming to Canada from Iran, just another fucking immigrant story to prove some point about the nation, not about him. Not about his reading glasses or that wood pipe. People say such stupid things at funerals: *He'll always be a part of the family*. That's not true. He's dead. There's no more family for him. There's no more Grandfather for me."

"I'm really sorry," Emile whispers, and he means it, though his leg is really spasming now. He'd even begun calling this man "Grandfather" in his mind, since he had never met his own, and he hopes their charade brought him peace in his final days. Did it?

Does it matter now? He's dead. And maybe, Emile supposes, there's no peace in the end, when an unused pipe lasts longer than those we love. Maybe this is what tortured my mother, why she had to get out of the house and try to start over with new things. Maybe she couldn't bear to look at the ceramic lamp fixture in the kitchen, or those blue bathroom tiles, or the damn roof shingles, and think they were surviving with more dignity than her family. And maybe that's why love is not a suitable topic for a scholar, but only for poets or playwrights or novelists. Love is not an answer to anything.

"I was wrong, too," Mohab adds, tensing his shoulders as he motions to the empty ottoman-style chairs, the academic advisor's hallway waiting room. "There's more."

"More?" Emile doesn't want to leave the stairwell or sit, but he does both, linking his leg around that of the chair to stop it from bouncing.

"My grandfather knew," Mohab says, after the hallway clears.

"He knew?"

"Oh, yes." Mohab chuckles with disbelief. He's sweating but his skin, like Emile's, doesn't turn red when he's flustered. "'You can't trick a man with a memory like mine,' he said. He knew we concocted the whole story about me having a fiancée and getting married in May, that my parents were in on it, everything."

"Oh, shit," Emile manages.

"It's OK, he wasn't angry. Knew my heart was in the right place. He wasn't even going to tell me he knew, but when he was sure he was going to die, he said he realized there was more at stake than his own happiness. There was mine as well."

"*Your* happiness?" Emile starts to sweat too, anxious over how much more he will need to take in about what's happened since Christmas Eve.

"That's right. I wasn't sure either at first. But then . . . then I was scared. Scared I did understand. My grandfather must have loved me as much as I loved him, because he knew me better than I know myself. He knew I'd been trying to outsmart myself." Shielding his face in his hands, Mohab continues to speak through his fingers. "He told me that he knew I was unhappy. That I was not following the path I wanted to follow and was *meant* to follow. He held my hand and I remember thinking, *This man has barely enough life left in him to speak, but here he is speaking to me, so I better listen.*"

"So he knew about your studies?"

"Yes," Mohab replies, but without conviction.

"But isn't that good? I mean, doesn't that free you to study Islam?"

Mohab spreads his hands a little wider, as if peering out to see that Emile is still there, then closes them. Emile barely has time to register the tears on his nose. He wishes they were at his carrel at the library instead of in the office hallways, so he could line up his HB pencils while they talked, which always helps him sort things out.

"Why not?" he asks.

"My grandfather knew about something else, too. It was the *something else* he wanted to talk to me about."

Emile remains silent, grips the chair leg even tighter with his foot.

"He told me that he's known for some time that I have no interest in women. He wanted me to know he didn't disapprove, that he thought it important for me to follow my own heart. It was a practical decision to leave Iran, he said, to bring the others too, but it was first and foremost a decision made with his heart. He didn't want his family to live a lie in Iran. No home is worth

that, he said. He didn't want me to live a lie. He knew I'm interested in . . . men. And he knew that I'm interested in you."

Emile can smell his own skin, his sweat. He can no longer feel
his legs, and the one lets go of the chair, uncurls and knocks knees
with Mohab; the contact startles him into action. Snatching his
satchel and leaving Mohab to the discretion of the hallway, he
bolts up the stairwell so fast he doesn't register the voice calling
out his name. Late for his office hours, Professor Whitman wonders why both Emile and that nice Middle Eastern boy look as if
they've just witnessed some terrible accident.

Cross-legged on the worn brown carpet, Rodriguez is surrounded
by large envelopes, packing and bubble paper, scissors and tape,
black and blue permanent markers, and every *Ottawa Citizen* from
the last two weeks. Stationed in the living room, he's been working
for two full hours when Hardev calls for help into his wheelchair.

"I can't stand it," Hardev admits a minute later, once Rodriguez
has made it to the bedroom and is hoisting him up from behind.
"You sent all the Christmas orders by yourself and now you're
going to send all these ones too. I must help somehow."

"I'm good at physical things, Harry. You're good with paper."
Dutifully staggering Hardev down the stairs and into the living
room, he hands him a stack of cheques and returns to his clear-
ing on the carpet. Hardev flips through them: Canada, Canada,
U.S., U.S., U.S., Canada, Norway, Canada, Canada, U.S. The
names are mesmerizing: Vivian Alvarez, Collingwood; Michael
Field, Penticton; Thomas Marquezee, Rhode Island; Patrick
Steven Longman, San Francisco; Sissy Beaulieu, Alabama;
Melissa Desjardins-Smollett, Halifax; Christine Heddernhoffer,
Norway; Clayton Arthur Decorte, Toronto; Amerjit Singh Uppal,

Ottawa; Halli Mortimer, Detroit. Who are these people who bid on his personal acquisitions, his souvenirs and mementos? Who didn't know until now that he existed, whom he didn't know existed as well? What are they going to do with all his things? The Christmas orders made parting with his belongings easier, like gift-giving or a yard sale, a purging of the old to make way for the new. But these new ones, in the middle of January—with the house stripped of all its colourful decorations, back to its usual tired face and achy joints—speak only to additional empty spaces in Hardev's home, each one a name in his hand. As Rodriguez wraps a Venetian teapot and serving set that Hardev and Isobel received from a distant uncle on their wedding day, Hardev can't help but feel weighed down with sadness.

Rodriguez hesitates to tape the lid shut. "Did we list the creamer *and* sugar pot? If we didn't, we can post them separately. Technically she hasn't paid for both."

"Let me see," Hardev sighs, securing his black-rimmed glasses on his nose. "Yes, you listed everything, Rodriguez. Everything."

"Damn."

"That means you did a thorough job. You should be proud."

"Listing separately is better. Must make as much money as possible," he disagrees, sealing the box, then moving on to a hand-sized silver elephant figurine bought by Sissy Beaulieu.

The living-room television is set to *The Price Is Right*. Hardev would rather be tuned to CNN but Rodriguez should be allowed to work in peace, enjoying his favourite shows. He's earned it, after all. In addition to the teapot set and silver elephant, he managed to obtain very decent offers on the antique music box that belonged to Hardev's great-aunt, a working eight-track player in near-perfect condition, a deer-leather coat lined with fake fur that he hasn't worn since his walking days and fifty pounds ago, two Tonka trucks, a ceramic table lamp, tea figurines (the silver elephant being one); and what Hardev thinks of as exorbitantly high prices for a pair of *Dukes of Hazzard* lunch boxes, Boss Hogg and Daisy, respectively.

"This lady, she asks if you have more elephants. She has a collection."

"I'm not sure, but you can check." Hardev shrugs, unable to keep track of what has left and what remains. "Even when you have so little, there's so much you can't remember you own. Go through any box in the basement you like. I'm no help to you here. Set me up near the stove. I can stir the soup at least."

"Soup's done, Harry. Why don't you help me with the citizenship questions? Here, they're in my apron," he adds, pulling a set of sheets from the front pocket. "Another thing you can get off the Internet. You can help me practise, then we can write more letters. But my oldest kid, he says people don't read letters; if you want to be heard we should e-mail, post your story on the Internet."

"My boy says the same thing! The exact same thing!" Hardev shouts over Rodriguez cutting through a sheet of bubble wrap. "'No one reads books or newspapers anymore like us, Dad! We're old-fashioned. Paper is almost obsolete, and will become so once we can sign contracts securely on the Internet.' I don't think it's good, though, if paper communication goes the way of the dinosaur. My boy agrees. Paper has permanence. You can feel it in your hands, mark it up. I hate to think of all those words sent off into space, to a place where our world doesn't even exist. Too many important messages are going to get lost that way, I'm sure of it."

Trading the citizenship questions for the manila folder with the cheques and order printouts, Hardev is reminded of his own citizenship test, how Isobel helped him learn basic French for it, and how proud he felt singing "O Canada!" in a room full of fellow fresh-faced official Canadians, waving the paper flags the volunteers gave them once they were told they had passed.

"Fancy new car, just like that!" Rodriguez exclaims, snapping his fingers, the audience on the television screaming with delight as a student in a Washington U sweatshirt wins a Subaru. "Just for knowing how much something costs!"

"Alright, let's see where you are." Hardev wants to help, knows Rodriguez has been working too hard, double-shifting with the hospital again. His fifth child was born right on New Year's Day. Four other children. Two teenagers. Two under ten. Now a baby. "Mother and baby fine, Harry. Just fine. Fifth time easy," Rodriguez told him over the phone. They named him Theodore. Teddy.

By the time Hardev has read over the first few pages of test questions, a dishwasher, a DVD player, a Panasonic stereo, and an entire oak bedroom set have been won by a hyperactive middle-aged woman clutching a Troll doll. Rodriguez stuffs the Daisy lunchbox with newspaper. If people don't read newspapers anymore, at least those *Ottawa Citizens* are good for something, he muses, and decides on an easy one to start. "When is Canada Day and what does it celebrate?"

Marking the cardboard box with an L so he doesn't forget which item he's packed, Rodriguez answers, "Canada Day is July first, and it celebrates my youngest daughter's birthday."

"You can't write that," Hardev says, shaking his head.

Rodriguez spits the marker cap into his hand. "Why not? It's true. Just because it's Canada Day doesn't mean it's not my daughter's birthday."

"But the government doesn't care about your daughter's birthday."

"Then I don't care about the government," Rodriguez counters, tapping the box. "I care more who will win the round with the wheel."

"Be serious. This test determines how much you know about *Canada*," Hardev stresses as Rodriguez checks the inside of the other lunch box, then locks it. "The idea is that the more you know about a country, the more that country becomes like family, like home, and the more likely you are to care about that country, want to celebrate it, protect it, fight for it. Now, let's see what you've learned. Where does the name 'Canada' come from?"

Stacking two Tonka trucks sold to Peter McIntyre, Bethlehem, New Jersey, Rodriguez answers, "I don't know where the name 'Nicaragua' comes from. Can't I say I'm just as ignorant about the country of my birth?"

Hardev sighs, turning the papers over on his lap. "Do you *want* to pass the test?"

"Yes. I want citizenship," Rodriguez answers hurriedly, rubbing his strained eyes. "I'm just tired, Harry. I'm sorry. Tired too much and trying to make you laugh. What does it matter if I don't know what's up with Confederation or why the Hudson's Bay began? I know about you and the other Canadians I work for, I know the hospital, people on my street, and children. I know how to pay my bills on time. Why don't they care about that?"

The giant wheel inches over to the ninety-five-cent mark and Washington U clasps Bob Barker's hand, pumping it up and down, up and down. This is Rodriguez's television show, one that immigrants have little trouble following, one that confirms their sense that North Americans have so much they can afford to give it away.

Hardev feels bad for him, for how hard he works for so little. Just three days ago, after some problems with the kitchen and bedroom lights, Rodriguez talked to the construction workers about the power lines on Hardev's behalf, to see if anyone had tampered with them. After discovering that they'd already fixed the wiring mix-up, Rodriguez returned, absolutely stunned, to the house. Innocently, he had asked them about their hourly wages. "They make five times an hour more than me. They build homes, but I help people in those homes," he told Hardev as he paced the hall-way angrily. "Why do bricks matter more than people?"

Hardev folds the citizenship notes. "You need rest. No use studying for an exam if you're not alert enough to take in the infor-mation. Lie down before you go to the hospital. You can't mail this stuff until tomorrow anyway. Take a nap in the boy's room."

"I guess I need to read more of these newspapers if I'm going to pass," Rodriguez says, collecting the unused ones, then jolting up: "Oh, no! I didn't put his cake out yet!"

"Forget it. I can do that. Or he can when he comes home. Go rest." To settle things Hardev unlocks his wheelchair, but before he can back out of the living room, the front door swings open and there is the boy, clutching his stomach, face moist with sweat.

"What's wrong? What's wrong?"

The boy runs past him and up the stairs, without removing his winter coat. "I don't feel well. It's my stomach. I'll take a pill and go to bed. I don't want to talk to anyone."

"But what about your pizza? Your cake? It's your birthday! Your sisters might call!"

"Not to anyone!"

"Oh, dear. He must have got into a fight with his girlfriend," Hardev says in a hushed voice, as he positions himself so

Rodriguez can pull his wheelchair up the stairs, step by step, from behind.

"Girlfriend? I didn't know he had a girlfriend."

"Oh yes. He doesn't think I know either, but I do. I always know. Just like his father, that boy can't lie to save his life."

Text message from Emile Dange to Monique Thériault:
I'M SICK. NEED TO CANCEL. SORRY.

LXXXIII

It is good, love, to feel you near me in the night,
invisible in your sleep, solemnly nocturnal,
while I untangle my worries
as if they were confused nets.

Absent, your heart sails through dreams,
but your body, thus abandoned, breathes
searching for me without seeing me, completing my sleep
like a plant that duplicates itself in the shadows.

Risen, you will be another who will live tomorrow,
but as for the frontiers lost in the night,
as for this being and not being in which we find ourselves

something is left bringing us closer in the light of life
as if the seal of the darkness disclosed
its secret creatures with fire.

Valentine's Day

I certainly don't need you to send me flowers, Birendra joked, as Victor apologized once again for leaving Ottawa for five days to visit his mother in Hawaii. *But Saturday is Valentine's Day*, he reminded her. *Yes, but you are going to be my husband*, she replied. *What better proof of your love do I need? Besides, considering our abstinence pact, you're making our lives much easier for this particular holiday.*

Birendra replays the airport conversation in her head in a loop. She'd already arranged for her rent-a-car and her appointment at the Buffalo Surgi-Center on the Internet, and she was actually impatient for her fiancé to get on that plane so she could be right where she is now—in this sterile waiting room attached to medical labs and four surgery spaces, a day hospital for those wanting quick, no-nonsense, pay-right-away treatments and procedures—trying to stay calm, her engagement ring buried in her purse.

After she spends nearly twenty minutes conjuring up Victor's unsuspecting face to reconvince herself that he left oblivious and happy, Dr. Rose Walker enters the room with unhurried confidence, shakes Birendra's hand, and swivels a chair over to where she is seated. Birendra is taken aback by how the doctor's grey eyes resemble her sister's, and finds herself, even in the stressful and unfamiliar surroundings, wondering for a moment what her sister might be up to on Valentine's Day, whether she has a date or is going out with friends, or if she'll end up watching a movie with their mother.

"Birendra Dange. Tubular ligation. A little young for this kind of surgery. I know you've already filled out some of this information, but I'd like to review and ask some follow-up questions."

Dr. Walker smiles in a warm yet rehearsed manner, and Birendra is immediately brought back to the room and the task at hand. Even if she is paying for the surgery, and by all rights should be able to schedule it without much trouble, she wants to present herself as a serious young woman who is making a rational and considered decision. "Of course, I understand," she replies, tucking her purse underneath the chair and gently folding her hands in her lap.

"You're twenty-seven years old, correct?"

"Yes."

"Unmarried. No children. No history of any gynecological problems. No history of serious medical conditions."

"Yes, that's right." Birendra nods cheerfully, as if she's passing an easy test.

Dr. Walker removes her glasses, wipes one of the lenses, and puts them back on. She leans back in her chair, cocks her head to one side, and gives Birendra a quick head-to-toe glance. Uneasily, Birendra smiles in response. "This is, of course, up to you, but I want to make sure that you are *very clear* about this before you make a final decision."

At the words "final decision" Birendra's heart starts to pump faster. A final decision has already been made, no counselling is going to change her mind, but she reminds herself to stay calm; Dr. Walker must do her job before sending Birendra in for surgery, or she might be answerable for it. "Yes, I know. I've thought about this for some time, and I know it's the right choice for me."

Clearing her throat in a way that acknowledges Birendra's words without accepting them, Dr. Walker continues: "You're young. You're unmarried. You're very healthy. You might change your mind. The operation is technically reversible, but it's much easier and much cheaper not to have to reverse it. Of course, if you were married and you and your spouse decided not to have children, I would recommend a vasectomy over tubal ligation. Why do you want this operation?"

Although Birendra has coached herself over the six-hour drive to answer this very question, imagining even the customs officials demanding an explanation, now—asked point-blank by a woman not that much older than herself, with such distressed and disappointed grey eyes just like her sister's—she feels small and helpless. Her mind flashes back to her baby dreams, how not once has she ever hoped the baby belongs to her, and how she wakes up time and time again in a sweat, aching to erase the image from her mind, the heaviness from her belly, stumbling, upset and afraid, to the washroom to check her face in the mirror, startled to detect no change but the dawning comfort that comes from reminding herself that dreams are only dreams. The vividness of the dreams sometimes haunts her days at strange times—while she is tying bridal bouquets, or on the bus, when one of the Catholic girls in their blue-and-grey uniforms hops on, or while cuddling with Victor. She doesn't want to jinx or curse herself, her brother would probably say, by these dream memories. Unless she can eradicate the chance of such a dream coming true, it will remain a possibility.

"I've *never* wanted children. I don't want to bring an unwanted child into this world. I don't want to have an abortion. I want to make sure it never happens. If I get married someday, that person will have to accept that he can't convince me to have children. I don't think people should compromise about children. I've thought about this very carefully, Dr. Walker, and I want the operation."

Dr. Walker frowns but Birendra's heart stops racing, as if by voicing her reasons for the operation she has relieved it of anything to fear. "I would still advise against it, but again, this is your decision," concedes the doctor. "At least wait a few weeks before phoning to schedule the operation, OK?"

Sighing in part relief, part surrender, Birendra agrees.

Dr. Walker continues to frown as she makes her notes, and Birendra suspects that this woman in her mid- to late thirties, quite attractive with her slight build, her blonde hair tied back in a ponytail, and those piercing grey eyes, must have children, or at least beloved nieces or nephews, to be staring at her between scribbles with this mixture of pity and incomprehension. She assumes she will have to accustom herself to this look as she gets older and women her age are having kids or desperately fumbling through fertility treatments or adoption papers, while she remains happily childless. Without being able to pinpoint why, she knows that most people are uncomfortable with chosen childlessness, as if it represents a rejection of the future, a rejection of hope. But Birendra doesn't see it that way. She *is* thinking of the future, and she *does* have hope. In fact, the surgery is all about hope. The only rejection is of herself in the role of mother, a role too many people take on without thinking, without being equipped to handle it. *I'm being responsible*, she wants to say to Dr. Walker, but refrains.

"There are risks. With any surgery that requires anaesthetic, there is a one-in-ten-thousand chance of death. There is also the possibility of bleeding or hemorrhage, bowel or bladder . . ."

Birendra keeps nodding in the right places, but is no longer paying attention to the doctor's warnings. She has read pamphlets and online information about the surgery and potential complications and side effects, and her heart begins to race once again, beating high in the back of her throat and her ears—just one heartbeat, yes, just one, no matter how fast—in anticipation of settling everything permanently, securing her future.

Several minutes later, Dr. Walker rises. Birendra follows, directed back to the reception desk. But just before she extracts money from her purse to pay for today's visit, the doctor, tapping her lightly on the shoulder, adds one more thing:

"Just so you know, if you do meet someone and decide to get married, you have to tell him about your operation. If you don't, it's grounds for annulment."

A woman named Roxanne has cancelled her appointment to have her septum pierced. Crossed out in blue, her name has been replaced with "Corey: Nipples."

As Dorothy waits for Corey: Nipples to show up, she sterilizes the chairs by wiping them down and covering them with plastic wrap, trying to steady herself after the incident with that one at the SoundScape. Was his name Edgar? Edmund? He said Ed, that she is sure of, but her mind is a whirlwind, a hurricane of the conversation and her anger and panic, her need to bolt out of there. Although Claudia, the owner of Signature Tattoo and Body Piercing, was surprised to see her tonight, she was also relieved because Heidi, their piercing specialist, had called in sick. Dorothy could pierce her first clients on her own. Corey: Nipples had called and asked for her. "Probably another one of your school chums," Claudia said.

This one named Ed—, he was about thirty, Dorothy thought, as he willfully approached her while she nursed a rye and Coke at the booth farthest from the empty stage, scanning the area for potential stories. A man in a wrinkled suit writing in a leather-bound notebook caught her eye, and another forlornly watching a group of young women laugh and giggle on the dance floor, one of them sporting wild red hair and a handmade *I don't need a man to be happy* sign on her back. But this one, this Ed—, he came to *her*, wearing blue jeans and a red plaid shirt, his dark brown, wavy hair slightly too long for his thin, pinched face. Lips: purplish, rounded, mole on the left. Scraggly but cute, she might have thought, if he hadn't introduced himself this way:

"I've heard about you," he told her, in a whisper, clasping his hands. "I've seen you here before, talking to men. I think your name is Dor, right?"

"Why not?" she voiced, confident that she could get away with such a simple phrase, as she pulled her Palm Pilot out of her sweater pocket, turning it on.

"I hear you don't mind listening, that you *like* listening. I need to talk to you, to someone. I think you'll understand if you hear me out. Can I sit with you? Can we talk? My name is . . . Ed—"
What was it?

About to slide into the opposite side of the booth, he hesitated as Dorothy wrote furiously:

I'M NOT A PRIEST OR A SHRINK. IF YOU'RE LOOKING FOR HELP, I'M AFRAID YOU NEED TO GO ELSEWHERE. I COLLECT STORIES. ONE STORY FROM EACH, THAT'S ALL.

"That's fine. Please," he replied, clutching the edge of the table, his brown eyes intent on hers. "I don't need therapy, and I'm not religious. I don't even drink. I want to tell this story to someone. I *need* to tell this story to someone."

Turning away from his lips, Dorothy looked about her. The man with the forlorn look was chatting with one of the ladies from the dance floor, who was teasing him with her blue feather boa, and the one in the suit was counting money to pay his bill. Still, Dorothy felt Roof and Key tingle like a fire alarm alert to the smell of smoke.

"I did something . . . eighteen years ago now. I was a kid. A stupid kid. It still haunts me . . . like a curse."

She flashed her original Palm Pilot message to him again and he waved her off. "I don't need to confess for some sort of absolution. I don't expect forgiveness. And no shrink is going to make me forget or help me feel different about what I did. I want to tell you because . . . well, because you're here and you've listened to the others, so why—?"

"Corey?" Claudia chimes from behind the desk as the door swings open.

"No. No," Dorothy signs, but Kite nods at Claudia, hip at forty in her high-heeled boots and angora sweater, her black dye job cut like a razor across her eyebrows, with two pencils criss-crossed through her hair bun.

"Dorothy will be your piercer," she tells him, as he proceeds to unzip his ski jacket and wipe his boots on the "Blondes Might Have More Fun, But Brunettes Can Read" mat. He tilts his head at Dorothy, ignoring her confused expression, as if contemplating her suitability. He nods again.

Not knowing what game he's playing, she decides to play along, at least for now, and offers her hand as if meeting him for the first time. *Today is not the day I imagined it would be,* she realizes. Valentine's Day—she thought she'd head to the SoundScape for an hour or two, collect a story, go home and watch a movie with her mother, who was always a little sad this day, as it was when her father had proposed. "I wish our lives weren't so dictated by occasions and dates," she said as Dorothy left the house this morning. "They only tell us how much time has passed." Instead, she was faced with Ed— and his story. A story she just didn't want to hear.

"I was excited because I just got my licence," Ed— told her. "I didn't even ask permission to take the car—with that licence in my wallet it was as if I'd been given the *right* to the car. I did some doughnuts around the shopping mall parking lot. Nothing crazy, just enough to make me feel like I owned the universe, that it was all open to me. I drove by a couple of my friends' houses, honked and blared my music as I idled outside. I swear I was getting so wound up it was like I was going to spend every waking moment in that car—eat in it, sleep in it, do my homework in it, have sex in it—like I would have complete freedom from my family and take up residence in the car. I'm not sure why I thought this, since it wasn't even my car, but I did. I really did."

She listened attentively. He wasn't a bad storyteller. His face had relaxed a little and his lips were easy to read—he was intent on communication. She did not interrupt.

"The Blue Room," Claudia instructs. "I'm still waiting for Boris to come and fix the lighting in the Yellow Room. Two years after the divorce, you know it's funny, he doesn't care what I screw as long as it's not the light bulbs in this place."

Not entirely sure what Kite managed to catch of Claudia's speech, Dorothy slips the roll of plastic wrap under her arm and is about to grab her Palm Pilot, then remembers and leads Kite to the Blue Room, the largest of the four, which boasts the most light and has a long blue desk in the corner to sketch upon, and two deep shelves filled with photo albums of past clients, the tattoos and piercings recorded like addresses in a phone book.

Closing the door behind her, she drops the pretense of anonymity. "What are you doing here?"

"I phoned to see if you were here. I came two days ago for a consultation and you weren't. I want to have my nipples pierced," he signs back.

She is struck by how strung out he looks. Is he high? Hair dull and oily, skin broken out in red and pink splotches over his nose and neck. He may have shed a few pounds too, she surmises, and he didn't have any to lose. "One hypoallergenic sterling silver ring on each nipple," she voices, reading the order. "Is that correct?"

"That's right."

"Are you thinking of any other piercings?"

"Maybe a cock ring." She tries not to laugh at the sign as Kite gestures quickly at his crotch, then slides thumb and forefinger back and forth along his ring finger. "But I don't think I can brave the pain of one right now. I know it's only supposed to last for a couple of weeks—"

"How long pain lasts always depends on the person," Dorothy whips back before he finishes, signing in harsh, quick strokes. "Why me?"

Kite shrugs, rubs at his irritated face, then signs, "Isn't this what you do?"

And Dorothy remembers something Mrs. Kotek said to them once, frustrated by all the doctor and counsellor notes she was receiving from students who wanted to hand in their assignments late or not at all, but without penalty. "Life is difficult," she scolded. "You teenagers are going to have to realize that the whole world doesn't stop because you have problems. Do you think your teachers don't have problems? But we show up to work. That's what life is about, showing up to work anyway." Dorothy showed up to work at the SoundScape, but she left her assignment unfinished. Instead, she bolted, unable to bear the end of this particular story.

The ring selection is preconfirmed; Kite hands her a white box with COREY written on masking tape on the side. Seeking the clamp, Dorothy motions for him to take off his black sweater, and he drapes it over the back of the piercing chair, unbuttoning the first hole of the grey skateboarding shirt underneath. Before he can free his hands to say anything, Dorothy adds, "This *is* going to hurt."

At the third button, mid-chest level, he stops. "I'm sorry I've been avoiding our work lately," he signs. "I know we need to get the mural done. I've been putting off everything. My parents aren't happy with me. They think I'm ungrateful. The only thing I seem to want to do is read your SoundScape Diaries. Over and over. Those stories, I mean . . . those are *real* people."

"They're strangers. They probably lie a lot. Why should it matter if they're real? You shouldn't care so much about them," Dorothy responds, as casually as possible, afraid that if she voiced this her voice might break or quiver and she might cry—an advantage over hearing people she's never appreciated before. "Think about yourself, and when you need to leave. We all need to leave sometime. At the end of this year we won't know each other anymore. We'll both leave. You'll even forget that I pierced your nipples."

"I won't forget you!" Kite signs emphatically. "I hope you won't forget me."

"Does it matter?" she retorts, flipping open the box, extracting the two silver hoops and slipping them on her right hand. "I can't stop anything from happening to you. You can't stop anything from happening to me. You're putting off the operation because then you think you won't be responsible if you make the wrong decision. You can hold it against everyone, your parents especially. All they want is for you to be able to hear so they can finally feel like one big happy family!"

"You're no different!" he volleys, his finger practically hitting her face. "You'd reject them all if you could: your sister, your mother, even your father, I bet."

Dorothy lifts the clamp and drops it onto the desk, which she knows makes a thud, though neither can hear it. "You don't understand. My family isn't a normal family. Now take off your shirt."

"Whose is?"

The two rings, like matching wedding bands, slide off her fingers and into Kite's palm. Dorothy starts shaking, her chest spasming as she holds in tears. That one named Ed—, she wouldn't listen to him. And now she won't listen to Kite. She's hurting him. Just as she hurt that Ed—.

"I turned a corner," this one told her. "I was going really fast. I know it. Not racing fast, but fast, and the corner was a blind one. I hit this man. I hit him on the passenger side and it crushed him into the concrete median. At first, I stopped the car. I hit the brakes. I couldn't believe what had happened. And then I bolted. I fled the scene. I turned myself in later—I just couldn't live with myself. I wanted to know how the man was, if he was alright. I found out he had a wife and two kids, another on the way. A good man. Government. An immigrant. I had just ruined his life. It was so hard to imagine, but I knew this. I had just ruined his life, and the lives of his family, because I wanted to eat and sleep and fuck in my car. So I . . ."

"SHUT UP YOU FUCK!" Dorothy screamed across the table, Roof and Key burning, her head bubbling as if it were going to— a sound, was this a sound? "SHUT UP YOU LIAR! I WON'T LISTEN! YOU FUCKING LIAR!" And, her head full of something she couldn't name, she left him there, stunned, alone with his story—*let him tell it to someone else,* she raged, *someone else, not me, I don't want to hear it*—and she ran out of the SoundScape, bumping into a couple out for a fun, romantic evening, and she dropped her Palm Pilot, it fell to the floor but she didn't want to take even a second to scoop it up, and she sought refuge at Signature, where no one knew about her story collecting, where they always tried to make her feel comfortable and at home, even though she doesn't have any piercings or tattoos—she tells them she prefers to think of her own body not as a canvas but as a chalkboard—where they let her practise on fruit and vegetables before graduating to people. A place where she somewhat belonged. But now Kite is here, where he somewhat doesn't belong.

Staring down at the two silver rings, he shivers.

"I'm sorry. I'm sorry," she signs, her eyes brimming with tears. "I can't do this. This isn't you."

She folds her hands gently over his. The silence isn't deafening.

For the life of him, Emile can't explain what he is doing riding around on his bicycle through the University of Ottawa campus at eleven PM on a Saturday. Valentine's Day, no less. Luckily, no one has asked him to explain yet, though he worries that a woman in one of the residences may spot him through a window and alert authorities to a potential lurker, an ex-boyfriend no doubt, the holiday bringing out the worst in some people.

It brought out the worst in Monique when he told her that this weekend wouldn't be a good one to get together either. *My stomach*, he e-mailed. *This attack has been bad. It's taking all my energy not to get behind at school. Maybe it's best if we just say we'll try to meet up again once the term's over.* Monique was obviously upset: *I still have a birthday present for you and you're brushing me off? Is this how you treat your friends?* No, Emile wanted to write back, I lie for my friends, I have my deaf sister pretend to be my friends' fiancées, I lie to my friends, and when they love me I don't know what to do. Instead he wrote, *Happy Valentine's Day, Monique. Take care, OK?* What else could he write? Was there anything else to say?

He pedals aggressively through the maze of streets, the February weather not conducive to bicycle riding, and wishes, not for the first time, that he had enough money to fund both his education and a car. Passing the drama building, the sciences building, the library of medicine and then the bus terminal, he feels sweat pouring down his forehead into his eyes. The moon sheltered by clouds, he is glad that at least he's not spotlighted under the sky. Deliberately he avoids the graduate residence, ignoring the street sign, quickly turning back, swerving to miss puddles of slush and snow. He can turn back; he *will* turn back, any time now, and go home, lock his bicycle in the garage and tip-toe to his bedroom so as not to disturb his father watching the late-night news; he'll forget about the e-mails and phone messages Mohab kept sending until a week ago, asking to talk to him, to say anything, to meet at his convenience wherever he wanted, under any circumstances.

The third time he skips Mohab's street, two headlights glow from the nearby parking lot as if scolding him. The car hugs the curb, and he struggles to maintain his balance. *I'm not guilty of anything, I haven't done anything,* he repeats to himself. But it's a lie. He isn't home where he's supposed to be, studying or helping his father by clearing the buildup of snow on the emergency ramp at the side door. The night has fingerprinted him, taken his mug shot.

Sweating almost through his winter jacket, a minute later Emile is indeed in front of the graduate residence. Though he has approached the steel gates at the front entrance dozens of times before, he only now appreciates how impersonal they are, how anonymous the university is to its residents. No trees or bushes line the walkways, no wreaths or ornamental plaques hang on the main doors. In the dark, from his angle, not a single poster can be spotted in the windows above. *The perfect place to pretend you don't exist,* he thinks; *that's why Mohab's comfortable here. If he's comfortable anywhere.*

Finger punching the square knob of the intercom, Emile has the sudden feeling of being watched, or tested, as if he is pressing the button of a lie detector.

"Who is it?"

"It's . . . Emile," he says. Not hearing an answer, he repeats a little louder, "Emile . . . Dange?"

"I'll buzz you in."

Is that *his* voice? It doesn't sound like him. Is he in the right place? But voices always sound off over scratchy technology.

Buzz. Buzz.

Once inside, he takes inventory in the elevator mirror: skin a bit pocked on the chin, and his eyebrows look hairier than he wishes they did. Next, he closes his eyes and tries to imagine what Mohab looks like, but he can't exactly, the way he has trouble conjuring up the faces of people who move away, like the neighbours to the left and right, who didn't leave all that long ago, but also his mother and sisters sometimes, all the faces he has known losing distinctiveness and merging together, loved and unloved, friend and stranger, into one giant goodbye. "I can turn back," he says out loud. "But I won't." And his stomach cramps.

Mohab, black hair ruffled, is waiting for him in the open doorway in a grey track suit. Techno music escapes from one of the other rooms.

"Did I wake you?" Emile asks, remaining in the hallway.

"No. I've been reading. The girls are having a party. Come in."

Mohab closes the door after him. Emile paces around the bed, the largest object in the room, in a horseshoe pattern. The place looks just as unlived-in as it did the first time he entered its walls: same brand of cereal on the counter, same books on the shelves, no dirty dishes or languishing laundry or disorganized papers, only a book on the bed in the hull of Mohab's bunched-up comforter. Mohab remains near the door, as if he's the guest and might rush out at any second, instead of Emile.

"I don't know what I'm doing here," Emile confesses, pacing

faster. "I don't know why I've spent the last hour circling this campus, sick to my stomach, on my bicycle. I don't know why I'm here, or why I've been thinking about coming here for weeks. Or why I'm pissed that you sent me e-mails and messages and pissed that you stopped. This is fucking crazy. This isn't *me*. This isn't who I am—" He stops short, identifying the book on the bed. It's the Qur'an; a bilingual edition, Arabic on the right, English translation on the left. In pencil, in Mohab's meticulous handwriting, are notes on the meanings of Arabic words: "messenger," "home," "victory," "companions." He's learning the language? Emile is shocked; he assumed Mohab could read and write Arabic.

"What if it is?" Mohab replies.

Emile turns to look at him, now doubly baffled. "What?"

"What if it is who you are?"

"Then I'm fucking cursed, like you!" Emile tries to laugh, but what comes out is a hollow groan. "That's not fair. I just don't know what to say."

"I'm not a good judge of what's fair. There's this passage that's been sticking with me lately, that I looked up again." He points to the Qur'an on the bed, then sits with it holding it in his lap in the same way as the imagined ledger. "*And had we commanded them: 'Slay yourself or go forth from your homes,' they would not have done it, except for a few of them; but had they done what they were exhorted to do, it would have been far better for them and more reinforcing.* I don't know why I keep coming back to this. It's an upsetting passage. I don't know anything about fairness. I don't know anything about the world, about faith, about the true meaning of home. I'm just learning."

Seized by another stomach cramp, Emile tries to ignore the pain by concentrating on the book, but it's too strong, he must balance himself by placing his hand on the end of the mattress, wait for a moment, and stretch up again. The bed creaks.

Lowering his head, he whispers, "Am I . . . am I staying?"

"Only if you want to."

The Qur'an remains between Mohab's legs, and Emile recalls the phone book Mohab showed him months earlier, all the churches and synagogues, temples and mosques he had visited crossed off, as he hoped to convert his religious leanings into architectural or ritual curiosity. But it didn't work. He looks out the window to his solitary bicycle chained to frozen steel, and feels suddenly unknown to himself, like a man with amnesia. "I can't go home. Not now. Not after coming here. I'm *not* going home."

Midnight is approaching. He takes a seat on the bed and waits, like the obedient student he has always tried to be, even if they both have a lot to learn.

YOUR HEARING AID AND **YOU**

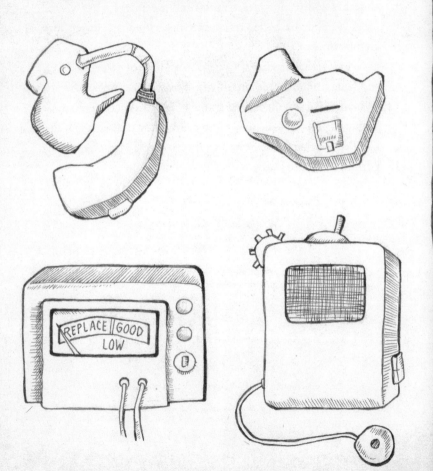

Happy Birthday

Dear Dor,

Happy eighteenth birthday!

I checked my files, and on your first birthday I wrote you this note:

> *A little girl is a father's most precious jewel.*
> *I wear you on my shirt, in my lapel, on my finger.*
> *I place you against the light of the window and you shine like*
> *   a promise.*
> *When you fall, where do you land, little girl?*
> *You land on your father's smile.*

To you it's silly, I imagine. The translation is bad, but it's a nursery rhyme my father told me my mother sang when she was pregnant. There is a rhyme for a boy child too, and she sang it to me before she died, but I forget it, something about stones in a boy's pockets being the wishes his mother has for him so he must not throw them away. It's a warning really, not a wish, and I suppose boys need warnings, but it isn't as nice as the one for girls. I thought you might sense your grandmother in you if I gave it to you. I didn't know you were deaf then, so in retrospect I'm glad I wrote it out instead of just singing it.

If I sang it to you now, though, do you think together we could remember how it goes?

The hallways smell different on a weekend. Kite mentions it too. The cleaning staff scrub the place top to bottom so that it reeks like an open jar of acne medication. The drama club usually practise in the auditorium on Sundays, but this week rehearsal is cancelled because Mr. Potter has a funeral to attend in Montreal. The gym, however, is in use for a volleyball tournament. The players are warming up. Dorothy can sense the balls slamming against the walls and gym floor from where she and Kite are stationed, just right of the main entrance, in the foyer. The impact reverberates like a pinball machine.

Dozens of submissions are laid out on the newly disinfected floor in preparation for their permanent placement on the mural. Yesterday they finished checking them off against the master list, and spent the rest of the afternoon and evening sorting through everything, pairing pieces up according to shape or colour or any other common characteristics they could determine. Next they assembled the items into three tiers, like the floors of a house: a foundational level (consisting mostly of textual submissions or flat visual art: poems, diary entries, song lyrics, tattoo designs, posters, photographs, which will be used to create a backdrop); a secondary level (small or medium-sized three-dimensional submissions); and a top level (large objects requiring pins or brackets to mount). While it was difficult at first, with the foundational level, to decide how to lay out the individual sheets of paper (right side up, diagonally, upside down), once they decided on a handful of pieces, the others became less individual and more like lines or drops of paint, and they started scattering them instinctively, until the entire square area of the mural was covered. While they were pleased with the initial results, they left utterly exhausted, barely saying goodbye as Dorothy shuffled into her mother's car and Kite trudged to the parking lot to start his own. Now, Sunday morning, they are sorting through the second tier, Dorothy a bit faint from skipping breakfast and from the fumes of the astringent floor cleaners.

"You can get high off this stuff," she signs, inhaling an invisible roach between her lips.

From her perspective, bent over and scurrying on all fours, Dorothy must concentrate to ascertain where Kite's hands are positioned as he circles around her. "Hash cookies—to have with our coffee, should you be so inclined," she translates, his SUM 41 concert T-shirt upside down like a barcode as he pairs up the tambourine and the AeroChamber. Even if they can't hear the music, many deaf students at Rousseau love going to concerts; the vibrations, the lightshows, and the performances are still incredible sensory experiences. She reasons that Kite's paired up the two objects because they are both musical in a way, one relying on tapping, the other on breath. "I also have a few hits of acid," he adds.

"I don't like acid," she signs back, then pulls her yellow plastic gloves up to her elbows and plugs in her glue gun. "I can't stand seeing things that aren't really there. It's hard enough to see those that are."

Nodding casually without the least hint of rejection, Kite has perhaps heard the argument before. Or maybe he's already high, she thinks, and he's not listening anyway. Why not? They're creating a mural, not performing brain surgery. Getting out of their normal way of perceiving things is part of the point. She'll happily partake of a hash cookie, but after she eats something a little more substantial. Right now, as she waits for the glue gun to heat up, she picks up the tambourine and bangs it against the heel of her palm. The tiny cymbals flutter against her hip bone.

Joining in, Kite snatches a pair of drumsticks she has grouped with a pack of cigarettes and a peacock feather, and kneels with her on the floor. Dorothy raises the tambourine above her head, clapping forcefully. With the sticks, he raps the other objects. They begin mimicking each other. *Bang. Bang. Bang. Chuck-a-chuck-a. Bang. Bang.* Tambourine close to her chest, she pulses her wrists. *Ching. Ching.* Then slower. *Ping. Ping.* He softens his movements down to a hum. *Tap. Tap.*

They continue this way, each contentedly responding to the other, until four knee pads appear at eye-level. Dorothy and Kite freeze, instruments halting in their hands. "Be quiet!" the two girls in volleyball uniforms yell, and run back inside the gym.

Kite laughs. "Can you remember the last time someone told you to be quiet?"

Dorothy pretends to be dumbfounded, shakes her head, but

she does remember. It was that one, that Ed—, once she started screaming. People turned around. They were listening to her, and she didn't want to be listened to by them. She wanted it all to stop, Ed— to disappear, vanish, get blown up. "Maybe this is what Mrs. Kotek meant when she said art announces it exists any way it can."

Placing the tambourine back beside the AeroChamber as Kite returns the drumsticks to their pile, Dorothy tries to forget Ed— again, to think about the one named Peter she wrote about before him. "I'm afraid I don't exist, that I only exist on paper," this man who weighed at least two hundred and fifty pounds, completely overwhelming his chair with his bulk, had said to her. "Credit card statements, bills, birth certificate, light them on fire or throw them in the nearest trash can, and I disappear. None of my life ever happened. Sometimes I think I'm trapped in a novel where I'm not the main character. I'm just some guy who gets mentioned because he's crossing the street at the intersection when two lovers meet, and maybe the reader is told about the bowler hat he's wearing or the umbrella he's shaking because it's just stopped raining, but by the next paragraph no one gives him a second thought. In answer to your request," he said, pointing at her Palm Pilot with a look of disgust, "I don't have one." She let him leave. But why won't Ed— leave her alone? Last week he sent her an e-mail, from her Palm Pilot. *I'm sorry I upset you. I just wanted to talk. I still want to talk, but if not, I want to return this to you. It's yours.*

Kite hammers in brackets to secure a red music box at a height where someone walking underneath can reach the winder. "I wish sometimes I could be a musician," he confesses, making a mishmash of signs, from piano player to guitarist to saxophonist.

"How many people do you think actually get to be what they want to be?"

"How many people get to go where they want to go? Get to meet people they want to meet? Get to say what they want to say?" Dorothy dabs hot glue onto one side of the peacock feather, then presses the blue and gold silkiness against the wall. Excess glue bleeds out near the bottom, and she wipes it off quickly with Q-tips and a rag. Unlike Saturday, Sunday is messy.

"I want to be able to do that."

"So do I," she admits. "I want . . ." She pauses, glancing again at the array of eclectic objects on the floor: buttons and swatches of fabric, cellphone cases and Pez dispensers, retainers and screwdrivers, hearing aids and Tensor bandages; all these mouthpieces that will be imprinted on the school's bold face, the first place visitors pass on their way through the halls. In the past, Dorothy thought of herself as just a visitor here, but now she wonders if they are all visitors here, visiting each other's lives for a select amount of time, then leaving, and in her case leaving soon, and isn't this in itself a reason not to dismiss everyone around you, but to try to take something of them all in? "I want . . . to collect as much as I can. But I have to choose, don't I? I mean, we have to choose, right?"

"Art?"

"Yes. No. Everything."

"You're going to need a pretty big house." Kite spreads his thin long arms out and Dorothy stifles a laugh, struck by how much his pose resembles the tattoo of an ostrich a woman in her sixties had inked just last week. Left shoulder. Dorothy drew the template, a skinny, skinny bird, feathers like arms bent at the elbow, eyes the same as those typically drawn on swans—a more common tattoo, and one she was comfortable drawing. "It's a reminder," the woman said, "to stop burying my head in the sand." Only now does Dorothy realize that she drew Kite. Kite as a bird, on this woman who's never met him but will carry part of him in her skin for the rest of her life. The thought genuinely pleases her as they continue to work.

Music box mounted, Kite hands her a silver heart-shaped photograph frame with a key inside it, and a plastic purple children's wrench. "Aren't you going to say anything about me leaving?"

Dorothy pretends for a moment that she hasn't caught his question. Eyes on the mural, hands on her glue gun, there is a lot she hasn't said. For instance, she wants to tell him that it's her birthday today, her eighteenth birthday, but she knows he'll make a big deal about it. She doesn't want a big deal made about it. What she really wants is to say, *Here, Kite, take my wish.* But sometimes it's so hard to communicate, just to communicate, even when they've been working for a day and a half in a state of near perfect synchronicity, even though he read all the SoundScape Diaries she gave him and never judged her or her men, said only, "Thank you for sharing them with me. They're up here now," pointing to his brain, to the place they'll drill for his implant.

Five, then ten minutes go by. Dorothy adds a friendship bracelet and a closed Swiss Army knife to the wall. A kaleidoscope of disparate signs, all of which she wants, like letters in the alphabet, to eventually spell something important, momentous. To translate their needs, dreams, stories; like those of the SoundScape men, all those things they can't usually say to each other. But what if the mural ends up a giant letter to some equally giant recipient of unknown name? *God can't see through walls*, she remembers Emile saying in the hospital waiting room two years ago, when their father was admitted again for bladder infection complications, *or else he'd take pity on Dad.* God can't *hear* through walls either, she thinks now. How do we tell him we're here? *We're here! And we have so much to say, but you didn't give us the right words!*

Resting her glue gun in its holder, she meets Kite's gaze. "My father writes letters," she signs, halting her imaginary pen in mid-air. "All the time, even when he doesn't know who to send them to. *Dear Doctor, Dear Canadian Paraplegic Association, Dear Prime Minister of Canada, To Whom It May Concern . . .* Most people think it's futile, a total waste of time and energy, but isn't it important to keep sending the letters, even if no one responds?"

"Maybe your father isn't sending his letters to the right people," Kite signs back, sizing up the next group of items, a Senators hockey puck and dolphin key ring. "Maybe we choose the wrong recipients. Like that guy who came to see you at SoundScape you told me about. He shouldn't have done that. You weren't the right person for him to talk to."

She was the *wrong* person for Ed— to talk to, but maybe that's why she should have listened. She didn't. And she knows she won't now. Will he eventually find someone to listen to him? She thought she could take them all in, with Roof and Key and her diaries, she thought she could. But Ed— proved her wrong. She chose not to. And she hasn't returned to the SoundScape since, not even to retrieve her old Palm Pilot. Is that what God did, choose not to acknowledge her father's constant pain? Was it not worth His time? Did it hurt *Him* too much to listen to his story? Considering all this, she loses her concentration, staring into the air, glue gun in hand.

Tap on her shoulder. "*To Whom It May Concern.*"

"What?"

"The title of the mural: *To Whom It May Concern*."

It's a phrase that, until today, she's not sure she's ever signed. "*To Whom It May Concern*." It feels awkward on her hands and lips, but appropriately so. He's given her an idea. "Yes!"

Jumping over the collection of submissions, Dorothy flips open her knapsack, removing her brand new Palm Pilot and a stack of papers in a manila folder. She eagerly trades the Palm Pilot for a swim flipper in Kite's hand. She will miss him, but she doesn't want to show it, doesn't want him to feel guilty for doing what he must do. "Type your first word!" she proudly signs. "The first word you will speak once your operation is over."

Kite hesitates but complies, keeping the screen turned away from her as he decides what his first word will be. Dorothy glues her folder of Dear Dor letters to the wall, then outlines the back of the Palm Pilot with glue. The device is then pressed against the mural, smack in the middle, onto the folder like a seal. It's true that the electronic message will disappear when the battery wears out, but it doesn't matter. She decides it doesn't matter. The message itself still exists. Sometime in the future, Kite will be learning to speak—as she is, as so many others are—first words, important words, uncomfortable words, and this message on her Palm Pilot will be here, invisible to future viewers but still here, waiting for its recipient, as do so many other exchanges that go unnoticed, unheeded, unanswered, in even the simplest of forms, even the simplest of salutations:

HELLO

For the better part of the afternoon, Rodriguez has been cleaning the stove and fridge, which cry out for mercy as he curses incessantly in Spanish and English, trying to remove the grime and guck from the crisper drawers and oven racks.

"It's been almost two years since someone cleaned that stove," Hardev admits, as Rodriguez empties a pail of dirty water in the adjoining bathroom while the old television rests for the moment, recovering from a blinking spell.

"Two years?" Rodriguez repeats incredulously.

"There was this one they sent from homecare, dumped all the cleaners together, those for the stove, the floors, for rust, carpet cleaners, silver polish, everything, into one bucket. When she washed the stove, the potion she'd concocted was so toxic it erased the paint. That's why our stove has no numbers! This woman had two kids. I kept imagining them without faces! Her scrubbing their faces right off!"

Refilling the pail, Rodriguez calls over the flow and splash of the water, "Some people! They just don't have respect for other people's houses!"

"That reminds me—next time you talk to the workers, ask about the water systems. I'd really like to know what kind of pipes they're installing, and if the sinks will all be equipped with purification systems. Please don't forget to ask them about that. I'll send a pot of coffee with you."

Pots of coffee have been useful tools for getting information from "our new next door neighbours," as Hardev calls them, and he anticipates the reports with keen interest to see if the construction plans match his predictions. He was correct that all the houses were being built with walk-in closets and finished basements. He was also correct about central vacuum and air conditioning and two hundred amps of electricity. Yet Rodriguez frequently returned with all kinds of information Hardev had not foreseen.

Homeowners today want elaborate steel-appliance kitchens with island counters and hanging racks, two sinks and two ovens, even though they are cooking less at home than ever. Equally perplexing to Hardev is the desirability of open-concept living. While his own home was altered into an open concept format to make it easier for him to navigate the ground floor, he sometimes misses the old doors that would keep the smells of the kitchen separate from the sounds of play or work in the living room. "Every single one, open concept," Rodriguez reported. "I guess parents want to see what their kids are doing at all times."

"Purification systems! You're living in a relic, Harry, compared to what they have going up! Those kitchen tiles might as well be one hundred years old, not twenty-five. You need a fireplace, skylights, a sola . . . solarium? Yes? If these men could get their hands on your house I bet in a month we wouldn't be able to recognize it!" Rodriguez exits the washroom, sits on the footstool at the end of Hardev's bed, placing the newly filled pail beside him, and sighs. He's losing hair, Hardev notes. His scalp is flaking and white chalklike dust gathers on the collar of his smock.

"Are you alright, my man? Are you still working double shifts?"

Rodriguez scratches his forehead with his yellow-gloved hand. "I don't know what to do, Harry. The wife had the baby and everything was fine. Fine. Then two days ago, the baby won't stop crying. He gets red in the face and there's blood in his diaper."

"My God!" Hardev cries, slamming his good hand on the bed trolley. "Why didn't you tell me? Did you take him to the hospital?"

"Yes, Harry. Yes. My wife took him to the Children's Hospital. Emergency. They tied him up to tubes. Gave him all kinds of medicine, more than in your trolley, I think. We don't know how long he'll be there. The doctors speak so fast, and we don't understand so well. My wife stays at the hospital now, and I ask my neighbour to keep an eye on the other children because I work so much. They let me use a bed at Riverside and I sleep between shifts, one or two hours, depends on the bus schedule, but all I can think of is my little boy and how I can't be with him and he's suffering."

"No. No. I'm very sorry to hear this. You should have told me." Hardev shakes his head. *The man is in pain, his child hurt, and here he is cleaning my ancient stove.*

"I didn't want to worry you, with all your problems," Rodriguez replies, leaning forward, grasping his knees. "But now I'm not sure if the baby is going to make it. And life might be easier for him, yes, easier, if he doesn't. What a world we live in! You see it on the news every day. Those things you write down. All terrible. Tragedies. Families torn apart. Blown up. Murdered. Erased. What a world!"

Bile wells in Hardev's throat. Even if he may sometimes agree with Rodriguez's line of thinking, it sickens him to hear him speak this way about his new little boy. "It's not your decision . . . not *your* decision, if the baby lives or dies. Even my boy would tell you that. You must leave it up to God," he says firmly, swallowing hard, not wanting to invoke God but knowing no better word for those forces out of any man's control. "And don't worry about me. You've done so much already. I got a letter just this morning, I was going to read it to you later, over tea, but I'll tell you about it now. Because of the lump-sum payment we sent from the ebay sales, the bank is giving me a three-month extension. And Dorothy, my little girl, she turned eighteen today. She'll be going to university or college next year. There's only so much we can do. If I didn't call Mr. Manello to ask about his offer, I would be irresponsible. Still, I have hope. If we give up hope, we are also being irresponsible. Your boy needs you to hope for him!"

With a clean sock rag, Rodriguez wipes his forehead and his nose, and returns the cloth to his pants pocket. Hardev turns over the yellow pad, on which he has been drafting a letter to the Canada Pension Plan protesting the proposed changes to cut disability pensions by half. *You are placing heavier burdens on families and forcing people into nursing homes*, he's written. Although sometimes he wonders if people like Rodriguez and him have ceased to exist in the world, still, he means what he says about hope, and he will write his letter, even if it's true that people don't reply to paper or to people like him. If no one listens, he has still written the letter, and that has to matter.

"Listen to me," he offers, his thoughts running more quickly than his tongue. "I have something in the basement, in the red trunk under the stairs—tucked behind the stairs, you know where I mean?"

Rodriguez looks up from his gloves, eyes red, and Hardev wonders if he has harmed them with toxins from all the cleaners. "Yes."

"Good, good." Hardev conjures up the basement arrangement of boxes and filing cabinets. "Go into that red trunk. There's a long box, like those that carry musical instruments, long and thin. I used to carry my tennis racquet in that case. I got rid of that racquet before leaving for England, never mind about it, but what I have there now is very special: the vials of water from the sacred River Ganges. It's an Indian tradition, but I don't see why it wouldn't work on non-Indians. There are two vials left. One is for my daughter for her wedding day, like we discussed. You take the other one. Take it and sprinkle it on the head of your child."

"But . . . but that's yours. The one for when you—"

"I won't need the good fortune when I'm dead," Hardev replies, waving him off. "How silly of me to think of taking it to the grave. Death houses souls forever, with no fear of eviction. You need the luck now. Your boy needs it. You may not think the Dange family has amounted to very much, we're not Kennedys or Trudeaus by any means, but we've survived, and we continue to survive, and if the water from the sacred River Ganges hasn't helped, it certainly hasn't hurt. There's no life without water, Rodriguez."

> *Things to Consider:*
> *Bush maintains support on the re-election trail.*
> *Japan seeks robotic help in caring for the aged.*
> *More North American independent bookstores close.*
> *New Chairman of Walt Disney Corporation appointed.*

Rodriguez fiddles with the pail handle. "But what's it all for? You still have to phone Mr. Manello about your house. All those notes you make about the news—so horrible. How is it you just don't check out, Harry? What keeps you here?"

"I can't walk, my man. I have nowhere else to go." He does not intend it as a joke, but Rodriguez laughs nonetheless.

Emile is not a fast skater, and lags behind Mohab and Dorothy. Although he can stay on his feet, he has trouble gaining momentum with any control, while Dorothy, even hindered by the puffiness of her coat, executes crossovers and spins with ease. A hockey player in high school, and sporting his old Sharks jersey, now tight at the armpits, over a thick red turtleneck, Mohab sprints back to check on him.

"Stop!" screeches Dorothy, skating backwards to keep an eye on where her companions are. "Get away from my fiancé!"

Emile laughs but is amazed at how well she has been speaking, how comfortable she is among them, almost as if she actually is Mohab's fiancée and Emile is enjoying a day out with her and his soon-to-be brother-in-law. He has certainly never had an outing like this with Birendra and Victor. And, admittedly, an outing with Dorothy is also very rare. Throughout his university years, they've really only seen each other on holidays. The Winterlude festival almost over for another year, Mohab was the one to suggest they skate along the Rideau Canal to celebrate Dorothy's eighteenth birthday. He even suggested they eat at Canal Ritz, the restaurant where they'd taken the engagement photographs for Mohab's grandfather, but Dorothy text-messaged that she couldn't yet, she was with a school friend and they were finishing their mural project, but an evening skate would be wonderful. Dorothy has always been an adept figure skater, having taken lessons when she was younger, and loves to spin, her hands spread out like a bird's. *How many talents my sister has*, Emile sometimes thinks. *I wonder if she knows how lucky she is.*

Dorothy gives him a push and he tries to steer as he glides toward a boy with a string of mittens behind him. "You'd better not do anything to jinx my wedding," Mohab says, circling him. "It's only a few months away."

"Not jinx, curse!" Dorothy chimes in, making the sign, her hands sending out invisible lightning bolts of doom.

"Only a parent has the power to curse a wedding," Emile insists, slightly embarrassed by his need to set the joke straight.

"I think your parents ought to be thrilled to have me in the family," Mohab replies, ignoring his academic point and gesturing at him for comparison. "Better than him, right? What kind of weird kids would he have?"

The three of them weave through the crowd to the kiosks selling hot chocolate and Beaver Tails. Having trouble keeping his blades steady, Emile leans against Mohab, but quickly straightens and separates himself, digging into his winter jacket for his wallet. He knows that the other graduate students are already talking. They quiet down to whispers when he takes his seat in class, avoiding his eyes, and he doesn't have the guts to drink coffee in the lounge anymore. "Birendra doesn't want children," Dorothy voices, with more difficulty than her previous speech.

"Really?" Emile produces a twenty-dollar bill and orders three Beaver Tails and three hot chocolates with extra marshmallows. "I always pictured her with children someday."

As the clerk hands them their paper plates and steaming paper cups, she shrugs. "Will you have them?"

Emile's stomach tenses at the very words, and his left leg starts to shake. He tries not to look at Mohab. "I'm beginning to think they're not in the cards for me. Life of the lonely, eccentric professor. Bachelor. Unlike Mohab here, I'm not really popular with the ladies." He sips his hot chocolate and tries to enjoy the comforting taste of melting marshmallows on his tongue, but finds his thoughts turn again to curses. It is the curse of families, he thinks, that everyone has a role, and if you challenge that role or, as in his father's case, that role gets taken away from you, then the family breaks down. Or else you imagine a new family, new roles—but it is easier in the end, perhaps, to be alone. Is this what Birendra thinks? Why is it that Emile shows them so little of his imagination? Why is it that they seem, instead, to rob him of it, through no fault of their own?

"She doesn't want a family. She thinks marriage is some sort of permanent vacation. No work. Endless holiday. She'll send us postcards."

Mohab and Emile exchange bemused glances as Mohab bites into his warm, sugary pastry. Is Dorothy kidding? Emile isn't sure. He knows Birendra is not always the most responsible of the bunch, believing for the longest time that she wouldn't need anything but her florist certificate from college for her livelihood, predicting a good marriage for herself—and right about that, in the end—but Dorothy's verdict seems rather cold.

"I still have a lot to learn about this family I'm going to join," Mohab offers, trying to inject a little levity, "but don't you think she's going to miss all of you when she leaves home? And isn't there the possibility that her husband's job will move them to another country? At least, that's what I understood from Emile."

"Birendra will move them away," Dorothy replies, wiping cinnamon off her mouth, trying her best to monitor her voice but making a couple of accent errors; a few other people standing near the kiosk catch her voice and stare uneasily. "She used to run around pretending she had no parents. That she was adopted. I remember."

Emile wants to keep his eyes on his feet but he can't. Dorothy needs to read his lips as he asks, "Do you think they'll survive?"

She takes another bite of her Beaver Tail and swallows before answering. "I suppose that depends on what kinds of lies they tell each other. I don't think lying is wrong. It just depends on what the purpose is."

"A means to an end?" Mohab interjects, taking the opportunity to sit on the nearby bench and retie one of his skates.

"Lying to your grandfather wasn't wrong. Even he said so," Emile agrees. "It made me know him a little, and I won't forget him or his story. I won't, my . . . friend."

The two men exchange glances again, this time sad ones. *What will our story be? Can it even be a story? Or is it a prologue to nothing? To disaster?* Finishing his food, Emile changes the subject. "I wanted to ask you, Dorothy, has Dad been, uh, giving stuff to Birendra that you know of?"

"Like what?" Throwing away the cups and dirty paper, they glide off down the ice again. The sides of the frozen water are lined with bright lights, white and red and blue and purple, all aglow with the promise of happy trips, happy evenings and endings. Dorothy feels as though she's been plopped down inside a lit birthday cake. Only a hundred or so feet more and they'll arrive at the Crystal Garden ice sculptures, one of her favourite Winterlude traditions, where they will marvel at ice castles and ice Trans Ams, ice elephants and ice CN Towers, ice volleyball matches and ice wedding feasts— hardy and tough in the deep cold, but so fragile that, the second the temperature rises, they melt away.

"Like furniture, figurines, paintings?" Emile continues.

"The light fixture."

"No, more than that," he insists. "There's a lot that's gone missing from the house."

"Why not ask Dad?"

No matter how much Dorothy and Mohab try to keep pace with Emile, inevitably they get ahead. They stop. "I'm afraid of the answer," he tells them, and as he says it, he knows it's true. There is simply too much going on this year. Too much that he's attempting to keep together, to control, to experience, to hide. Something is up with his father, with his house, but Emile doesn't want to know what it is, just as he really doesn't want to know that Birendra will not be having any children.

Sharing Dorothy's hands between them, Mohab pulls brother and sister along, and Emile finds himself pining for the days when they were young, when he and the birthday girl had their own language. He had a box of Crayola crayons and they would talk to each other through them, picking colours out of the box to indicate their desires: blue, *go outside and play*; green, *let's eat*; purple, *watch television*; black, *nap time*; orange just meant they were pleased with each other. He can't recall exactly when they stopped using the system, but he thinks that moment must have marked the start of his gradual estrangement from everyone in the family—more than the distance between Ashbrook Crescent and Augusta Street—the differing trajectories of their lives. And here he is now, developing a language with Mohab, devoid of colouring crayons but elemental all the same, and he is aware that whether he wants it to or not, this may come to an end before he is ready, before he even knows how to read and interpret all the signs. He takes a stronger grip on Dorothy's hand, but as he does so his skate catches a groove in the ice. Like a chain, Mohab and Dorothy snap around, following him into the snowbank.

Emile can't help it, he hates himself for falling. Wiping the snow off his stunned face, he is reminded of his father, how he once fell right out of his wheelchair and spent an entire afternoon struggling just to get up again, only to pass out from dehydration. "It's not even easy to fail," his father said to him.

Dorothy starts laughing, throwing up snow this way and that, and Mohab finds her glee contagious. He throws a snowball at Emile, hitting him smack on the left side of his chest. "The tin soldier has been given a heart!" Dorothy shouts, slapping her mittens together to release more bits of snow into the air.

"Your sister is amazing! I wish I had a sister like her. Or any sister," Mohab says.

"Well, since you really don't need a fiancée anymore, who knows?" Emile states with forced cheer, trying to shake off his melancholy. "Maybe I can convince her to be your sister too."

Now it is Mohab and Dorothy's turn to exchange glances. "What about you, then? Will you have kids someday, carry on the Dange name? Doesn't someone have to?" Mohab asks her.

The loud rumble of the snowplow sweeping the canal bothers Emile's and Mohab's ears. Dorothy barely notices the giant creature creeping by as she helps pull her brother out of the bank.

"I suppose I will," she tells him. "I like naming things."

April Fool's Day

In a black oriental-style dress and fake white pearls, Dorothy stands in front of the tarp with three-piece-suited Any Excuse Jacobson, who is about to unveil *To Whom It May Concern.*

"*To Whom It May Concern,*" he reads, from a short text Kite and Dorothy prepared before Kite left for the U.S. for his operation, "we envision as an infinite collaborative project. It is constructed by the current student body, but reaches out to past and future student bodies as well. While this mural might be encased in glass (and it took a while for that glass to get here!), the life of the mural should not remain within these borders.

May both past and future generations reimagine themselves here. This mural is only one incarnation of our common spirit. May there be others. May each of us take the spirit of the mural into other lives."

Excited to see their creation, students from grades nine to twelve are jammed into the front entrance and adjoining hallways. Several in wheelchairs are parked behind a long red velvet rope that the drama club lent for the occasion, others clamour for a view of the tarp, while another group smokes outside, waiting for the first rush of onlookers to dissipate.

Any Excuse Jacobson offers Dorothy his hand and they shake a number of times, Dorothy careful to keep her balance in Birendra's black high heels. The student council and the yearbook committee take photographs. Amid the flashes and immediate sharing of digital images, Dorothy thinks about Kite, over a thousand miles away—already in his paper gown in a hospital bed, being monitored and hooked up to monitors, undergoing his own renovations, a new receptacle of sounds. Like other students, she's heard horror stories about those who are overwhelmed, like blown-out stereo speakers, and choose to turn off their implants, unable to get used to those distracting, disruptive, disturbing noises the hearing population accepts and ignores: toilets flushing, cars honking, cellphones ringing, cash registers reeling, police sirens wailing, lawnmowers buzzing, dogs barking, balloons bursting, faucets dripping, vacuums screeching, crows cawing, snowplows beeping, sprinklers sputtering, winds howling, airplanes zooming, engines rumbling, cameras clicking . . . the endless onslaught of sound. But oh, how she hopes he will hear his mother's voice, his brother's laughter, a nurse's comforting sighs, robins at sunrise, a cat's purr, and music—his favourite rock bands, but also Mozart, which Mrs. Kotek says makes her believe that God exists. She is aware that if Kite hears only pleasant things, he won't truly understand what sound is. Nevertheless, why is it that, according to what she has been led to believe, the most hostile sounds are also the loudest?

The pewter placard that will accompany the mural reads:

TO WHOM IT MAY CONCERN
From the students of Rousseau Secondary
past, present, and future.

Presented with the placard, Dorothy admires the Book Antiqua lettering as she would a fine tattoo, and imagines the mural as a collective signature she is pressing into the school's skin. She shakes Any Excuse Jacobson's hand again, steadies herself, and each of them takes an end of the tarp. On the tap and count of three, they yank the canvas down.

The response to *To Whom It May Concern* is immediate and enthusiastic—a fierce rattle of hands clapping and feet stomping, then pointing, talking, laughing, shrieking, as students identify submissions, their own or those of friends, some reading bits of poems and writings out loud, others exclaiming about the pro-truding objects. While it was eventually agreed that in order to protect the mural a glass covering was necessary, Any Excuse Jacobson ordered a case with removable glass so that, under super-vision, blind students could also experience the art. Encouraged by Mrs. Kotek, a group of blind and visually-impaired freshmen and sophomores duck underneath the velvet rope, and Dorothy takes pleasure in watching them tentatively, then more confidently, lay their hands upon the mural.

Maybe the school is like a lighthouse, she thinks. *Maybe I've just had trouble interpreting its message, always concentrating on the rocks instead of on the light.* For the first time since she entered its doors four years ago, the L-shaped hallways and C-shaped entrance, the gymnasium with its trophy cases, the long domino-row of lockers, the library that has more movies than books, the crappy cafeteria whose special is always meatloaf or spaghetti, those damn prized rose bushes—every floor and lab and cheap plastic school desk, through this unveiling, has suddenly become hers. She can almost *hear* them all, students and objects alike, hoping, fearing, growing together. Wishing Kite were here to hear her say it, Dorothy turns to Any Excuse Jacobson and announces proudly, "I do," accepting her place, whatever that may be, in the Rousseau Family.

Dizzy from the Tylenol 3s and lack of food, Birendra has a hard time concentrating on much of anything as she wanders through the Happy Village shopping mall, but she doesn't want to spend the whole day cooped up in her Holiday Inn room with nothing to do but watch television. Better to stroll around aimlessly and distract oneself with perfume bottles and handbags, then order room service and a movie and turn in early, anticipating an uncomfortable drive back home in her post-surgery condition.

It is difficult for her to believe that she is now physically altered. Unlike her clitoris ring, which can be removed and has little effect on her future place in the world, her new biological reality makes her a very different person today than she was yesterday morning. Browsing through the mall, gently fingering sweaters and scarves, digital cameras and martini shakers, almost afraid to touch anything for too long, unsure of what her imprint on her environment means, in her fog and with a dull ache in her pelvis, she thinks back to her mother seeing her off, wishing her a fun time in Buffalo with her work friend Tracy, shopping for a few wedding things while Victor is in Toronto for a conference—thank-you cards and nail polish, a raincoat and new luggage for their Parisian honeymoon.

"Buy more underwear," her mother advised. "You'll need a couple of pairs to keep you fresh under your dress for your wedding night. Buy three or four exactly the same and he'll never know the difference." The thought that Victor would be concerned about her underwear made Birendra laugh, but as she spots Good Evenings, a hosiery and lingerie shop beside a dollar store and a deli-style lunch counter, she thinks her mother was on to something. New underwear. To match the internal changes in her body. Nothing cotton or girlish. Seamless underwear, the sort women wear under slinky dresses to pretend they're wearing no underwear at all. Sexy. Mistresslike. No hint of domesticity. No man thinks of kids when his wife is wearing that kind of underwear. Or a thong, like those in the pink box at the front of the store. Dozens of thongs with small messages written on them: *Diva, Drama Queen, Foxy, Love Kitten, Bad Girl, Bitch*. The company called Smart Ass. *Bride-to-Be*. Birendra grabs one, remembers her mother's instructions and, chuckling, takes two more out of the box, then stops: *Desperate Housewife*. It's funny, and she sometimes watches the trashy television show—manipulative women living on the same street, having affairs, destroying lives—but it gives her a chill. The sort of lives the women lead on Wisteria Lane are the kind she hopes to avoid by going through with the operation. She will never end up as a pill-popping soccer mom, or a single mother without a date in nearly a decade, or an unhappy trophy wife impregnated by her young gardener. No children to worry about, to work schedules around, to keep in contact with a father or stepfather or siblings or half-siblings or step-siblings. The modern family is simply too large, too sprawling. Too complicated. There are days, like today, when she can barely keep track of herself. Of course, the drugs aren't helping.

Last night, in her room at the Surgi-Center, she wove in and out of drugged dreams. After several of bizarre surgical equipment and malevolent nurses, she passed once more into the baby dream, as if it were pushing its way in—the familiar sirenlike crying, the awful stairs and narrow hallway. Deeply annoyed as she felt her way, in her dream, to the bedroom, she spat out, *I took care of you. You shouldn't exist anymore.* But this time, when she approached the bed, prepared through endless repetition for the baby's grey eyes and limp mouth, the accusing glance, she encountered instead grey fur and black beady eyes, a twitching nose, large padded feet. *A rabbit?* she asked incredulously, as if the creature would answer her. And then she laughed hard and loud, remembering childhood books—*Peter Rabbit, Runaway Rabbit, Watership Down*—and how much she had loved them at the time and wished she had a rabbit of her own to feed carrots to and brush and pet. She was about to pick up the fuzzy grey rabbit and caress it when it opened its mouth, hissing like a snake. Alarmed, she jumped back. The rabbit spoke with the same tone of voice as Dr. Walker during the consultation: *You don't want babies to live, but what about rabbits? Are you pregnant, Birendra? Are you?*

The dream ended and she woke up with white fluorescent lights in her eyes, and a fat nurse at the other end of the room clanging something on the other patient's bed, and she could smell disinfectant and lavender and urine assaulting her nose, so she groaned. "Am I pregnant?" she called to the nurse, who turned her bulk slowly around, looking at her quizzically, some metal contraption in her hand, and walked over, but by then Birendra was wafting back into her dream, to her bedroom and the rabbit, the grey fuzzy rabbit she knew was waiting in the tub in the washroom. She remembered that in health class in high school her teacher had told them that rabbits used to be employed in pregnancy tests. The rabbit was injected with the woman's urine. But did the rabbit die if she was pregnant? Or if she wasn't? She couldn't remember. Sitting in that cold and dusty classroom, the slide projector flashing endless drawings of ovaries and umbilical cords, Birendra had been horrified by the fate of these rabbits. Though she thought she'd forgotten all about it, her mind must have been storing the information away until now, her brain perhaps like her father's totem of files in the basement, waiting to be consulted when the time was right. But to what purpose?

The young woman at the register, with ring piercings in her nose and eyebrow, wraps up her purchase with tissue paper like a firecracker, and Birendra congratulates herself on her good thinking; she needs to bring back at least a few packages on this shopping trip so that her mother doesn't get suspicious and think something's wrong, that she's perhaps having second thoughts about the wedding. Her next stop should be a stationery store for those thank-you cards, and then she should get something to eat. But as she shuffles along, catching her soft, numb face reflected in the glass of the storefronts, she finds herself at what appears to be a photo booth. Dorothy used to love it when Birendra dug into her pockets for a couple of dollars in change and they charged in and made funny faces at each other and at the camera. At least fifteen or twenty of these strips of photographs are in albums in Birendra's closet, their early years told in a series of mall shots.

She is filled with a sudden nostalgia, a desire to go back in time with her sister, to be twelve years old, her only concern whether she'll pass a math test or whether she has enough money for candy and a magazine after the photographs. Pulling on Dorothy's pony-tail. Dorothy sticking out her tongue and licking her cheek. Yuck! Giggles and pushes. How different times are, she thinks, her tubes tied, worried not so much about her decision but about whether Victor will ever find out. The surgeon scolded her before releas-ing her. "You need a family doctor. You can't keep relying on clinics for yearly checkups. You're too old for that." And Birendra knows it's true, but since she turned eighteen and left her childhood doc-tor, she's avoided getting herself a family doctor. In fact, she hates the title "family doctor." No one in her family goes to the same doctors. Her father has more doctors than she's had physicals. Her sister's school is riddled with all kinds of doctors, and she can remember that when they were young Emile was sent to head doctors. She wants to avoid them, avoid knowing them, them knowing her. Why does she need to cultivate a familial relation-ship with the person whose responsibility it is to prick her skin and scrape her insides once a year?

There's a lineup for the booth. Either that or a dark-haired man and blonde woman in their thirties are patiently waiting for their photographs to shoot out the side of the box. How cute. Birendra hangs around, wondering if she should dig through her purse for change, go inside the booth to commemorate this day, analyze the picture back in her hotel room to see if there's any indication of what she's done on her face, on her person. A minute later a large sheet prints out the side, and the couple huddle together, pointing and laughing. The man wraps his arms around his companion's neck, holds up her puckered chin and showers her pink lips with quick kisses. Birendra is about to retreat, to leave the booth for the stationery store, when the man turns to her, letting out a joyous yelp: "It's a boy! It's a boy! My wife and I are having a boy!"

Startled, Birendra claps, along with a few other shoppers passing by. The blonde woman bounces up and down on her toes and hugs the man, who must be her husband. Only then does Birendra figure out that this is no regular photo booth but a self-serve ultrasound. A stop in a couple's shopping day. She didn't know such a thing existed. If she went into the booth, would her photograph come out black and empty? Would it be worth checking, just to be sure? No. No. What's wrong with everyone? Surprisingly close to tears, she clutches her firecracker and runs out to the rent-a-car in the parking lot, determined to push away all thoughts of babies, babies, and more babies; to stop the constant multiplying.

Hardev is stationed at the kitchen table in his red-and-white striped sweater, Mr. Manello directly across from him and Rodriguez on his right. Both Hardev and Rodriguez are equipped with yellow foolscap pads, Mr. Manello with a black portfolio containing laminated sheets, Gateway Land Developers' logo embossed in silver on the cover. Rodriguez sips a Coke, Hardev a cranberry juice and water. A pot of brewed coffee placed on a faded red tea towel at his side, Mr. Manello helps himself. He has brought a box of Russell Stover chocolates, and it remains open but untouched on top of the stack of Crown Bank files to the left of Hardev.

"A one-bedroom condominium in one of our buildings is worth quite a lot. Starting at $160,000. With what you've already paid off on this house and what we are willing to offer, you could own this condominium and live debt-free, or borrow against it at a low rate." Hands folded over the Gateway Land Developers' logo, a patient smile on his lips, Mr. Manello waits as Hardev examines the four-page pamphlet and dictates key bits of information—square footage, washroom and kitchen appliance descriptions—to Rodriguez to copy down. "You can keep the pamphlet, Mr. Dange."

"Yes, thank you. I like to make notes all the same," Hardev replies, giving Mr. Manello a quick, stern glance. A young man in his prime, Hardev might say: cuff links, silk paisley tie, quality wool suit, penny loafers, sharp haircut; the accoutrements of a professional, not a shyster. Nevertheless, Hardev has met licensed shysters before, and reminds himself that Mr. Manello is not a business associate and he's not here to do him any favours. "One-bedroom apartment," he mulls, taking stock of the series of photographs, all presenting clean, tasteful, beige-decor rooms with tiny terraces, adorned with silver platters, silk comforters, and crystal vases, as in a Hudson's Bay or Ikea catalogue. Mentally, he tries to peel these objects from the pages, so he can focus on the structure of the rooms rather than the extraneous content.

"Not apartment. Condominium. A few of our other condominiums have built-in electric fireplaces in each unit. Not this one, but if that's something you'd like to consider, I'd be happy to show you another pamphlet." Mr. Manello flips open the black portfolio and selects another crisp white envelope with silver embossing. "Those are less centrally located than where you are currently living. I thought you might like to remain relatively near the same area."

"Ottawa is my home," Hardev agrees, but then wonders, as Mr. Manello slides the envelope over to him, whether this is only an illusion. What does he really gain by living in Ottawa as opposed to any other place? Para Transpo? Government services? The health services are province-wide, and he uses Para Transpo so rarely, compared to the time he spends in his home. The *Ottawa Citizen*? The paper can be purchased easily in other townships, is perhaps even online by now, like everything else, like half his possessions. Perhaps Ottawa isn't so much a place as it is a marker: he landed in Ottawa; he worked for the federal government; every one of his children was born here; therefore Ottawa matters. Yet he is aware that if he were pressed to describe Ottawa to an outsider, in terms of its distinctive urban features, its exceptional opportunities, its potential drawbacks, he would end up describing the Ottawa of eighteen years ago, not the Ottawa of today. What does he know of today's Ottawa except for what he sees outside his window? What does he know besides construction workers and tarps, central air and open-concept living-dining rooms, double ovens, minivans parked outside and businessmen making real estate deals?

"A large one-bedroom, open-concept condominium in a building equipped with spacious elevators, permanent ramps, a swimming pool and sauna, a high-tech security system with cameras and twenty-four-hour doorman service, and its own convenience store plus video rental. For someone in your condition, Mr. Dange, delivery service of all basic necessities would be available at no charge. Your property taxes and condo fees," Mr. Manello continues excitedly, extracting a silver pen with matching Gateway logo from his inner suit pocket, "will be your only expenses, totalling approximately one-third to one-half of what you are paying now, easily affordable on your disability pension and later on your old-age pension. We have several seniors living in this particular complex, which is why I think it would be very suitable for you. The building is less than three years old and the property value is already rising. It's a great investment opportunity. The washrooms, which I understand are a concern for you, are spacious, include bathtubs, and can be easily equipped with safety handles and railings."

"What do I need a doorman for?" Hardev asks, turning to Rodriguez.

"What do you need a doorman for?" Mr. Manello chuckles before Rodriguez can answer. "Mr. Dange, living isn't just about necessity, it's also about *luxury*. Think of the luxuries you'll be able to enjoy. Your homecare worker can help you into the swimming pool. Grocery shopping can be conducted over the phone. You won't have to worry about theft or home security. And in case of an emergency, all kinds of people are available to you *right on the premises*. You don't have any of these benefits now."

"That's true," Hardev admits soberly, sipping his cranberry juice. "But those are things I can imagine living without. I find it hard to imagine living without these walls, Mr. Manello, without the *memories* they contain."

Mr. Manello places his pen between them on the kitchen table like a bread knife. "I hope you won't mind me saying so, Mr. Dange, but aren't there also *bad* memories here? You've not led an easy life. Why make life harder on yourself? Why not see this as your opportunity to shed certain burdens you've accumulated and can do without?"

Rising from his chair, Rodriguez offers everyone truffles from the Russell Stover box, but with little enthusiasm. Hardev and Mr. Manello both rest theirs on napkins while Rodriguez munches on his with a frown.

Hardev taps his yellow foolscap pad thoughtfully with his good hand. Though there is a part of him that wants to take up Mr. Manello's pen and stab him with it, there is also another part that knows that the decision to ask him over was a practical one, and he must obtain as much information as possible. "What will happen to my house? You're just going to demolish it, aren't you?"

The patient smile returns to Mr. Manello's face as he withdraws the pen from Hardev's reach and uses it as a pointer on an imaginary chart. "Our usual procedure is to make an assessment of the house and costs of renovating or developing upon existing structures and properties versus costs of starting anew. In this area we did demolish a number of the houses that were in terrible condition. But we moved several others."

"*Moved* them?" Hardev again turns to Rodriguez, who looks equally perplexed.

"Yes, we moved the houses, transporting them to surrounding areas where we own some cheaper properties: Cornwall, Curran, other places you've probably never heard of. We drive them out of town, right on the highways, with professional house movers and a police escort. This way the houses don't go to waste, other communities benefit from them. That's if the cost ratio ends in a profit, of course."

"And mine?" Hardev ponders out loud, imagining his house raised off the ground by a giant forklift and slid onto a rig like a piece of pie onto a plate. "If my family can't live in this house, I'd like to think that another family could. If I make a deal with you, can you guarantee that this house will be moved, not destroyed?"

"I'll look into that, Mr. Dange," Mr. Manello replies, clicking his pen and closing the portfolio. "But keep in mind how much we are already offering. My boss might not be willing to make many other concessions. We are dealing quite fairly with you as it is."

"Quite fairly?" Hardev snorts and slams his good hand on the table, disturbing the coffee pot. He's had it with this Mr. Manello. Had it. But Mr. Manello's a guest, still a guest at the moment, he reminds himself, and tries to gain control over the volume of his voice. "One bedroom for a man with three children is a strange definition of fair. It means my children will never be able to visit me properly in my home again. You tell me to put a price on that. How much is that worth? I'm not a greedy man, sir, just a family man. My friend here"—he gestures to Rodriguez, who refills Mr. Manello's coffee mug to the brim—"his newborn has been in the hospital one month now. Would I ever say to him, a new condominium will make everything better? No. This isn't about investments and taxes and debts; it's about the fact that we have fewer options in this life than we'd like. You probably already know I've managed to secure a three-month extension from Crown Bank," he adds, indicating the papers underneath the Russell Stover chocolates. "I know that this extension won't last forever, and it isn't likely I'll be able to get another one. My friend here, he knows that too. These homes you're building, they're not any better than mine, just bigger, and there's just more of them. The families who live there aren't any better than mine, they just have more options. And you'll probably end up adding this house to the end of your very long list, but not yet. Not quite yet. My eldest daughter is getting married in May. I want her to have her home until that time, in case she needs it, for whatever reason. After the wedding, I will be in touch. Until then, this is still *my* house!"

"Companies have their own timelines, Mr. Dange," Mr. Manello says without a smile, extending his hand, which Hardev takes grudgingly although it pains him to do so. "We're listening to you now, but we may not be in a few months." After collecting his portfolio, he exits the front door.

Hardev closes the box of chocolates and stares at his foolscap pad. Rodriguez peers through the curtains at Mr. Manello talking on his cellphone in the front seat of his minivan. "I can take you out today to see the houses, if you want. The snow has melted. Good for both of us to get fresh air."

Hardev nods, but his heart isn't in it. With barely an hour left in Rodriguez's shift, it will mean an awful lot of trouble for fifteen minutes of fresh air, and it took so much energy to talk a good game today, so much energy, and in the end he knows that's what it will be, just a game, and one he can't win—one people like him, families like his, with few options, can't win. The last letter he sent to CIDA, to the head of the division, who was once under his supervision, even that plea has gone unanswered. One of mine, he thinks. Even my own have turned against me, or at least turned away. About to call Rodriguez back, to tell him not to bother to retrieve his scarf, his jacket and shoes, a short tour will be more feasible later in the week, he notices that on Rodriguez's foolscap pad, under Gateway Land Developers, he's written only one thing: *Russell Stover chocolates. Goddamn.* Nothing else. He must know it's a game too, an unwinnable game. He's only pretending to play along with the possibilities in Hardev's imagination.

Depleted, Hardev decides to surrender, let Rodriguez dress him and wrap him and wheel him to end of the street that might as well be the end of the universe. Half a minute later, Rodriguez reappears with a slice of dark cake with white icing, a lit blue-and-white candle on top.

> *Happy birthday to you!*
> *Happy birthday to you!*

Confused, Hardev glances at the free Lorenzo's Pizza wall calendar beside the front door, then at the window. April. Not November. Driveway clear, no snow. So why is Rodriguez smiling ear to ear and singing, presenting him with cake on the day the man from Gateway Land Developers has come to discuss the business of selling the house?

> *Happy birthday dear Harry!*
> *Hap-py birth-day toooo you!*

"I checked at the agency. That's how I know!"

Beginning to comprehend, Hardev claps his good hand against the armrest. The agency has April 1, 1945, listed as his birthday, the date decreed by the authorities when he landed in London, England, from his small village in India. As he was unable to produce an official birth certificate, the officers assigned him a birthday: April Fool's Day. It was a joke played on numerous landed immigrants. All over the world, men like him have the wrong birthdays on birth certificates and driver's licences, health cards and passports; paper fictions that allow them to exist, to buy things and sell things, to have a medical test done or to vote. Hardev doesn't have the heart to tell Rodriguez that it's just a clerical mistake. "When did you find time to get a slice of cake?"

"Two slices," Rodriguez corrects, still smiling broadly. "The other is in the fridge. I asked one of the workers to pick them up for me at Tim Hortons when they went for a coffee break, so they would be fresh."

"You shouldn't have spent any of your money on me." Though Hardev intended his words to be teasing, as he gazes down at the thin blue-and-white candle pressed into white icing he has a sudden and overwhelming urge to weep. He can't remember the last time anyone presented him with birthday cake. It will be an effort to eat it, not because of his dietary restrictions but because he knows Rodriguez will have to leave when he finishes. He wishes they could go outside and watch the construction workers until they quit for the day, contentedly eating slice after slice of sweet cake. To fend off the tears, he surveys the kitchen, rests his tired eyes on Rodriguez's usual array of plastic bags at the door—he's always running around, bringing things home for his children or wife, extra clothes for his hospital rounds, delivering goods to clients for a bit of extra money. Today Hardev catches a glimpse: Green Giant peas, frozen cranberry juice cans, milk powder. A package of chicken legs, and Shake'n Bake barbecue powder.

"Make a wish!" Rodriguez commands, the cake at Hardev's chin level so he can blow out the candle, and Hardev remembers months ago Rodriguez trying to convince him to sell his things, saying that it would be easy to pretend all the basement boxes were still full, that there would be no difference in how he went about his day after all his things were gone. Turning wearily away from the plastic bags and the new knowledge of how Rodriguez manages to do his shopping amid all his other duties, swallowing hard, he tells himself: *Forget what's leaving the pantry. He's a good worker, the best I've ever had. I must listen, close my eyes, use a little imagination. It's my birthday, after all.*

Dear Dor,

Your health is your wealth! A frequent toast of my father's. I could now understand what he meant. Dr. Ekhart at rehab was still flushing my system of toxins from the accident. *You'd be surprised how much the body will hold onto even when it's doing harm. We think the body wants to rid itself of poisons and disease, but it doesn't really. We have to find ways of tricking our bodies into doing what's best for us. Our bodies never grow up.*

Meanwhile all my children were growing up, and did they understand that I was still their father? That they were siblings of the same two parents? I doubted this. Your mother and I, do you remember, instituted Brother-Sisters Night, twice a month get-togethers where you'd all go to a shopping plaza or movie or play board games. How long did that last? Two years? Three? We didn't think we should force it on you, but I wonder. Would you feel differently about each other now if we had? The boy can't seem to imagine your sister's wedding, doesn't know what to buy, what to say. I ask him if he's bringing a date and he just changes the subject.

Once, in her frustration over my depression at being at home, your mother accused me of loving my work more than my family. *Think of all the time you'll get to spend now watching your kids grow.* I know why she said this; I wasn't just paralyzed, I had all kinds of medical problems, pains, conditions, ripple effects, and no one knew where to build a dam to make it stop, least of all me. It was hard on her too. She wanted to make it stop by pretending it wasn't so bad. But she was wrong. And wrong about what she said. It was the other way around. I couldn't believe I'd be enough for all of you without my work. I still don't. People stopped visiting to see how I was. Eventually, you kids stopped visiting each other except on holidays. I'd lost more than my legs and my work. I'd lost my name. What does *Dange* mean to me if not my family? My one named Dorothy, what does *Dange* mean to you?

Text message from Birendra Dange to Victor Lane:
THINKING OF YOU. BOUGHT SOME-
THING SEXY.
WILL SHOW YOU ON OUR WEDDING
NIGHT.

Sample Question

Answer this question. Draw a circle around the letter beside the answer.

What are the colours of the Canadian flag?

a) red, white and blue

b) red and white

c) blue and white

d) red, orange and green

The answer to this question is (b). You should have put a circle (b) like this:

a) red, white and blue

(b)) red and white

c) blue and white

d) red, orange and green

There is only one correct answer to each question.

Good Friday

"I feel at home here," whispers Emile, head resting like a favourite book on Mohab's chest. They should be up and studying, but those plans were disposed of quickly upon Emile's return from the shower this morning, Emile surrendering willingly to the comfort of Mohab's bed, unable to believe how much of a servant he's become, as it were, to his own desires. Five months ago he would have been horrified at the thought of lying in this residence room naked, wrapped around a man's body—so different from a woman's—solid and hairy and pungent. While he's experienced sexual longing, lust, and affection with girlfriends in the past, only now does he realize that he never experienced the intensity of really wanting to take them in, connect with them in a secret language that only the two of them understood, that only the two of them could create with their hands, lips, clutches, releases. It's like the excitement that overwhelms him when he is deep in study and all the dots are about to connect, the brain's electricity at its most potent and flexible, flying here and there, securing knowledge into a body larger than the self. But after the dizzying excitement there was an anxiety-ridden intellectual hangover, when thoughts of insecurity, irrelevance, and helplessness overtook him and the only cure was to start the whole process over again, hopeful that his work would be understood, deemed helpful and useful. He feels something similar when he is away from Mohab; the universe they've created doesn't make sense under the harsh lights of the Morriset Library or the sagging roof of Ashbrook Crescent. Squeezing his right hand under Mohab's left armpit, he registers only a slight difference in skin tone, like that in layers of sand on the same beach. "I know you want to meet my father, but it's just not possible. I've spent so long wanting my dad to say he's proud of me. He won't understand this. He's not a well man, you know. I can't tell him."

"You could introduce me as your sister's fiancé," Mohab proposes.

Emile snorts, squeezing harder. "That's all he needs, another wedding. Ahh, the joys of family. Did I ever tell you that only a parent has the power to curse a wedding? Forget the 'speak now or forever hold your peace' nonsense. And some curses are more binding than others. When a parent curses a child, the curse is almost certain to come true. Especially if it's uttered on a deathbed."

"What about a regular twin bed?" Mohab teases, licking Emile's ear. "So we won't tell your father about us. I won't meet him. I understand. It's none of his concern."

But to Emile, the agreement seems worse than the lie. He pulls the white sheet up to his face. He can smell their sweat on it, a mix of scents like malt and pine. Never before has he smelled a man's sweat that wasn't his or his father's on a sheet. "It's the occasion that heightens the intention," he continues, inhaling more deeply. "Under certain circumstances your words have more power, more weight. People need to be careful. Jokes at weddings, for instance, can, by the ritual of the ceremony itself, turn into prophecies. But that's why speeches are part of the celebration. They're important. Families gather to hear people on their deathbeds. We put a great deal of stock in someone's last words."

"Like the last words of a letter," Mohab offers. "Or a prayer."

"Yes," Emile concedes, sighing a little. "I've never been good at writing letters. That's my father's specialty."

"But if someone puts a curse on you," Mohab asks, stretching his legs out past the end of the bed, "can't you fight it?"

"I don't know. If you're from a certain family and that family's cursed, I don't think there's much you can do. You can change your name, maybe, but it doesn't matter. You can invent all kinds of other destinies for yourself, and sometimes these take shape and sometimes not, but you're still who you are."

"But what if I refuse to believe the curse?"

Rolling over, commandeering the sheet, Emile now wishes they weren't having this conversation lying naked in the half-light, even though he started it. Better to imagine they exist alone in this room, without others to worry about, without any consequences to their actions in the outside world. The room should be safe, he thinks, like a book, where no one can intrude and change the text on him, where his thoughts are free to explore and roam—not an intersection with other people wanting something from him that he doesn't know how to give. "From what I've read, I'd have to say the answer is still probably no. It's the *lex talionis* principle: we lie, so we will be lied to. Look, I'm sorry, I'm still thinking about my father. I wish I didn't have to lie to him."

"What's the big deal? It's not like we're getting married, right?" Lifting his chest, Mohab turns on the bedside lamp and grabs his crumpled shirt and socks from the floor. "You know, I wasn't lying to you. I didn't expect to want to be with anyone except my God. I knew I was gay, but I didn't think it would matter." He laughs, pulling the grey T-shirt over his head. "I really thought it wouldn't matter. That I wouldn't be distracted."

Emile shakes his head. Though he knows how hard it can be sometimes to focus, to concentrate on graduate work, he's surprised by the idea that *he* is a distraction. "I thought I wanted to be with Monique. I mean, not forever, but until I went away. I was just passing the time, though," he admits, drawing the sheet even closer to his chin and clenching his stomach, which has started to cramp again, as it does whenever he starts to think about where this affair with Mohab will lead, what he's supposed to do about it. He knows he should get up, put his clothes back on, and get to work, but leaving the bed means entering the regular world again, where what he's doing doesn't make sense—not just to people like his father, but to himself too. "I'm not sure I'm . . . you know, like you. I don't know what this means."

The alarm—the complicated clock radio that Emile's mother gave him for New Year's, which they set so they wouldn't lose the whole morning by giving in to each other's warmth and the pull of contented sleep—interrupts to inform them that more hostages have been taken in Iraq, and that commentary on the fallout of Condoleezza Rice's testimony on the 9/11 Commission is to follow. With a hint of exasperation, Mohab shuts off the twenty-four-hour news station. "It means you want to be with me until you go away. You never brought Monique to meet your father, or any other friend, I bet. You don't have to bring me."

No. I want to be with you. You. Period, Emile wants to say, astonished by the strength of his feelings, as he watches Mohab jump into a pair of jogging pants, the body once exposed to him now tucked away, but he won't. He can't make promises. Promises are in themselves a type of curse. Once they're uttered, people can't be free from them, either. "Thanks," he says instead, as his stomach cramps again. The last month and a half have been too much for his brain, let alone his body, to fully accept. Whenever he tries to make sense of it all, his conflicting feelings surround and overwhelm him like a heavy fog, where nothing exists, not Emile, not anyone else. This scares him, so he tries not to let the thoughts take shape in his mind. "I can't tell you how many times after my father's accident I've wished for a normal family life, and how often I've promised myself that I will create one someday. I . . . I just need some time to figure out how to explain this."

"You need time to figure out what story you're going to tell. Or are comfortable telling. I understand that. Religion is a story. You pick the one you're most comfortable with, where you can find yourself a place. I know that since I'm gay I shouldn't be comfortable believing in Islam, but for me it's like you and your father. You love him, I know that. Even though he doesn't understand you and can't accept you the way you are—even what you study, let alone who you might choose to be with. You're still his son and you respect that, so you're able to sleep under the same roof, and eat together and watch television together, and you wouldn't let anyone tell you that you have to stop loving him. My parents left Iran, but I still feel like I have a home there. Not in the physical place, but in its history. I don't have to agree with everything in the religion to have my room in that house. My grandfather taught me that, I think, before he died. He worried that I was going to try to kill off the parts of myself that I didn't know how to recognize, that I would want to drown out those voices inside me rather than listen to them."

Emile rolls toward the light. On the end table is Mohab's *Suicide in the Middle Ages*, a book they discussed last night, Mohab explaining that the word "suicide" was only coined in the seventeenth century, and never used in Shakespeare. "And not a scene goes by in Shakespeare's tragedies without the possibility of some character going off and killing himself. For centuries and centuries we haven't let people decide this most basic thing, whether they want to live or not."

Normally interested in such a topic, Emile was surprised that he cringed every time the word "suicide" crossed Mohab's lips or his own. It made his leg twitch, his stomach clench. "Deep down, we don't believe we control our lives," he replied, voicing something he'd thought about often in his curse studies. "It goes against our very nature to tamper with fate, even if we'd give anything to change the lives we actually have."

Mohab accused him of being a doomsayer. "You'd make a great preacher, not me," he joked. It was an exchange that led them into this bed.

"We don't have much time," Mohab announces, opening the blinds. "You don't want to hurt your father. I understand. Like I didn't want to hurt my grandfather. I know it's not about me.

You're not me. You live with your father. You can't just make up stories the way I did."

"You're right. I'm not . . . you." But Emile knows that this thing with his father *is* about Mohab, just as all their previous efforts to create an imaginary fiancée out of Dorothy were about Mohab's grandfather. Emile's stomach cramps again. He will need to get up soon, use the washroom, take some medicine, but he doesn't want to. He wants to keep watching Mohab comb his hair. "Why are you so interested in suicide?" he asks finally, opening the book to where Mohab has marked with yellow highlighter a section titled "The Sick and the Melancholic."

Resting on the edge of the bed, his backside against Emile's knees, Mohab shrugs. "Great thinkers always have something to say about suicide. The history of it is as interesting as the history of religion, and tied up in it, too. Most people commit suicide when they can no longer stand the discrepancy between who they wish to be and who they are. It's the ultimate offence against God because God made you this way."

"Because God made you this way . . . ," Emile repeats thoughtfully, closing the book and feeling a pang almost like jealousy for what is contained inside it, that Mohab already knows but he doesn't.

"Another interesting thing about suicide," Mohab adds, taking the book from him, "is that if someone is trying to kill you, you're less likely to kill yourself. Especially if it's a family member. Shakespeare used this all the time. Your basic instincts for survival kick in and you want to spite everyone by living. Including the gods. As Gloucester says in *King Lear: As flies to wanton boys are we to the gods. They kill us for their sport.* Suicide rates among active soldiers are surprising low."

Maybe that's the trick, Emile thinks, as Mohab gently tickles his feet. Spite everyone and live, whatever way you want to live. Could it be that easy? Of course it couldn't, but maybe for brief moments it's important, necessary even, to imagine so. "I'm not sure these books are good for your health," he says, lunging forward and swatting the book out of Mohab's hands, its pages tenting as it falls to the floor.

Pouncing, Mohab easily pins him on the bed. "I'm not sure this is either, but I know this is who I am and I'm willing to take the risk. How about you?" he asks, lowering his lips to Emile's.

For the second time this morning Emile surrenders, although in the attic of his mind a flag—red, not white—reminds him of acceptance letters from UBC and Berkeley. They arrived on Wednesday, the same day he told his father that he had gotten back together with Monique to explain all the time he was spending away from home, the same day he came back to Mohab's with a toothbrush and his clock radio, no longer pretending he wasn't staying the night. Until now, all those university applications he laboured over and fretted about had been sent to almost imaginary places; they hadn't yet materialized into a reality of his leaving here, leaving his father, Ashbrook Crescent, his siblings, his mother, and now Mohab too. "Soon I won't be living here," he mumbles into Mohab's warm chest. University of British Columbia: full scholarship. Berkeley: tuition scholarship with added teaching assistantship to make up the difference. Both promising to work with him *to achieve professional and personal goals*, and assuring *successful graduates of the highest rank*. Both giving him two to three weeks to accept or decline.

Dear Dor,

The week your mother moved me back into the house, she had Birendra and the boy paste up a *WELCOME HOME DAD* sign they had printed with permanent markers, with potato wedges dipped in green and purple paint providing colourful geometric shapes around the letters. Birendra wore her pink princess Halloween costume, and she waved her silver star wand through the air and jumped up and down in the driveway as your mother wheeled me up to the front porch. One of the neighbours had offered to build a wooden ramp until more permanent construction could begin on the house, and there it was, varnished and shiny, in front of me, and I should have felt grateful but I felt pitiful instead. The boy was in a bow tie and his best black shoes. He waited inside, afraid, your mother said, that he might scuff them.

Daddy's home! Daddy's home! Birendra screamed, while the boy watched my arrival through the heavy curtains in the dining room.

Don't overdo it, I told your mother. *You're in no condition for it.*

I've carried babies before, she said. *It's a walk in the park.* And then she cringed at her choice of phrasing, and I could feel her grip tighten on the wheelchair.

Your mother used to say that travelling was a kind of homelessness, and she never liked it when I was away so long. Well, I'd never been separated from my family this long, and I felt as if I had ceased to know them. She was eight months pregnant when they finally let me out of rehab. I'd been transferred from Toronto General, where it was decided no more surgery would be attempted, to the Ottawa Rehabilitation Centre, and they wanted to keep me for two or three months more but your mother begged them to release me. I was on so much medication there were times I could barely speak, but she said the children were developing bad habits without me and she was afraid of them becoming permanently scarred. Your mother was optimistic then, she had to be, and believed that once we all accepted the new condition of our lives, we could go back to carefree games of Monopoly on rainy afternoons, backyard picnic summer days, long intimate nights cuddling and watching television, just the two of us, while the kids slept over with friends or at Boy Scouts or Girl Guides. My paralysis could be like one of the lisps she cured in her speech therapy practice. We'd work around it, learn to control it, not allow it to interfere with our quality of life. I'm sure you already realize this, but a man in my condition is not capable of real intimacy. Your mother refused to talk about what we could do to make things easier on her, what I might be able to do if we tried, if we made an appointment with one of the marriage counsellors at rehab. *Don't think of me right now,* she said, shooing my objections away. But I knew it would get to her sooner or later. How could it not? She's a woman, after all. I had been a man until then.

Yet the amazing thing is losing that part of my life was not quite the end of the world I would have imagined it to be. If you had asked me as a young man if I could live for twenty years and more without sex, I wouldn't have been able to imagine it. *I'd wish I were dead,* I'd probably have said, and laughed at the ridiculousness of the question. But here I've been, in a situation I never imagined, and I could tell you it's the worst part of being stuck in this chair, but it's not. Don't get me wrong, I miss it. Terribly sometimes, especially when it rains and I hear the windows rattle, and though I can't actually feel my body I can feel something press inside me and ache to burst out if only for a second, if only to convince me such a thing can still exist. Then I watch the lightning flash and remember what Emile said to that counsellor, *It strikes my head sometimes*, and I know what he meant, how there is a place inside us that gets hit and hit again and again and you can't believe it hasn't been destroyed yet, but you still haven't figured out how to protect it.

That place is what I've become. Where I live. And I know it. Your mother knew it too. You're not meant to see or hear or put down bearings in such a place. It's like a void left by a god's last breath. But it doesn't make me wish I were dead. That's the worst part. I've lived with pain the likes of which I never thought possible, but there's nothing that could make me wish I were dead. When you realize that, you have the most exquisite pity for yourself and everyone around you. It might seem like anger or ruthlessness or sometimes even love, but it's pity.

When your mother brought me back to Ashbrook Crescent, to Birendra dancing around in her princess costume eating sugar cookies and sipping soda, and your brother pacing the room like some old English butler in his goddamn bow tie and polished shoes, and her in all her radiant pregnant beauty, kissing me on the mouth and saying, *We're all so happy you're home*, it was her greatest performance, her greatest dance, because she didn't look scared. All I kept thinking was, *What does God expect from me for saving my life?* And I treated everyone with love, but I felt nothing but pity. Nothing but pity for you all.

Lying on his right, Hardev can't reach the button to raise the bed. Rodriguez is now four hours late and the television remote control batteries have died, so he is stuck with CBC children's programming, and the high-pitched voices and singalongs are bothering his ears. How infants and young children are able to withstand the constant blinking and beeping of the TV shows designed for them is beyond him. He suspects their brains are fried before they even reach high school. *Their brains are paralyzed,* he thinks. Like those people on reality shows, flinging their bodies around, competing to prostitute themselves, eating bugs, whipping obscenities at their parents and each other. How did shows like *The Partridge Family* or *Eight Is Enough* get replaced by *The Osbournes?*

But he doesn't mind waiting for Rodriguez today, as he doesn't want to tell him the results of their latest attempts to save the house. "You should phone that guy there, see if he can get your story on the news, raise—what do they call it—awareness?" Rodriguez said, pointing to the *Your Ottawa, Your Voice* man. "Maybe they can even set up a fund, like for charity." Although Hardev tried not to imagine himself with a Salvation Army bell around his neck and a plastic ball or box of donations in front of him, he had to admit that maybe at this point the only people who would help him were those dedicated to fighting for underdogs. "It's about time the news did something for you, Harry." Hardev agreed. "And don't waste time writing letters. Phone. Phone this station, phone all of them. Local, national. Why not? Someone's bound to call back." And he was right; someone did call back: the *Your Ottawa, Your Voice* assistant to the producer, a girlish-sounding woman with an Asian accent, named Jennifer. Hardev had five minutes to explain his situation. *Huh,* she responded. *I'm not sure that's really a story. I mean, nowadays a man losing his home to a good economy is sad, I suppose, but not dramatic enough, global enough. The rest of your neighbours made money. Have you considered selling?*

The phone rings. On his right, Hardev is able to answer it. Anxious to hear from Rodriguez, find out what's been keeping him, he stretches out his left arm, more on the numb side than the pins-and-needles side of the scale this morning, and presses SPEAKER. Through the static he shouts, "Rodriguez? Rodriguez, is that you?"

"Hello, Hardev Dange?" A woman's voice. A tad gruff. Not Birendra. Not Isobel.

"Yes. Is this the pharmacy? Is there something wrong with my order? Dr. Pittu said he put lots of repeats on the last set of prescriptions. My condition is permanent."

More static. "No, Hardev Dange, this isn't the pharmacy. It's your homecare service calling. It's Penny Goustapoulos. Do you remember me?"

Pausing to search his memory like one of his files in the basement, Hardev halts at the letter G. "Oh yes, Penny Goustapoulos. You're director now, aren't you?"

"Yes, Mr. Dange. That's right."

"Congratulations. Your family must be very proud." He continues his calculations, figures it must be almost ten years since he's spoken to Penny Goustapoulos, who used to coordinate his homecare workers before her promotion.

"That's very kind of you, Mr. Dange."

"Call me Harry, like you used to. Is there a problem?"

"I'm afraid so, Mr. Dange. I wanted to call you myself."

Hardev clenches his teeth, his neck stiffening. "Are those suits on the hill making more cuts? Trying to get us to roll over and die, or what?"

"No. Not this time, Mr. Dange," she replies, without a hint of her old smoker's voice. Ten years ago she puffed away while talking to him. "It's about Rodriguez Santiago."

"Rodriguez? Oh, he's not here yet. He's late. Rarely late, though. Sometimes just a half-hour if he worked the midnight shift at Riverside—he's a janitor there, I'm not sure if you know that, I hope it's allowed. He needs the money. He has a large family to support, a newborn baby. He always finishes his work here. But four hours? I'm worried about him. He's never, ever been this—"

"Rodriguez Santiago will not be returning to work."

"Not returning to work?" *You will not be returning to work*, the doctor had told him. *You are permanently paralyzed from your chest down.* Hardev had felt his head spinning at those words, as if he were a comet hurtling toward the earth. *Do you mean this is who I am now? I'm this person?* he had whispered, so his wife wouldn't hear. *Yes*, the doctor had replied. "Is it his little boy? He's been sick, can't put on weight. My God, did something happen?"

"He's been arrested for fraud. Internet fraud."

Discarding the image of Rodriguez carrying the tiny child in a hospital towel, Hardev tries to orient himself around the phrase. "Internet . . . fraud?"

"Hardev, I mean Mr. Dange, I know this is difficult to understand. Internet fraud is a new sort of crime, maybe you've seen something about it on the news?"

"On the news . . . sure . . ." And Hardev can't help it; he thinks back to Jennifer. *Is it an issue of discrimination, prejudice against the disabled?* her voice rising with mild excitement again. *No, no.* Then *Are they threatening you with bodily harm?* Hardev was shocked: *No, of course not.* Jennifer sighed, a long sigh, and Hardev could hear her ripping a page from a notebook. *If we did a piece on it, all you'd get would be people phoning your place to give you an offer on your house. Look, there's no story here for us. Sorry. Maybe another time. Remember, Your Ottawa, Your Voice is interested in hearing from you . . .*

"Please take a breath and listen." Penny Goustapoulos speaks slowly, enunciating every word, and Hardev abandons his thoughts of Jennifer, who is probably phoning someone else, hoping for exciting bodily threats and other atrocities more dramatic and ratings-grabbing than his situation. *Would Internet fraud qualify?* he wonders. *Is Internet fraud a story worth telling?* "The staff know how fond you are of Rodriguez, we have that detailed letter you wrote recommending him for a raise a little while ago, so I know this is going to be hard for you to believe. I didn't want you to hear it from anyone else. This is the truth."

"The truth," Hardev repeats.

"Yes."

Trying to turn his stiff neck closer to the intercom, he notes with disgust that the yellow wallpaper he had installed three years ago is already peeling. The boy picked it out for him from a selection of discontinued samples, all over eighty percent off. The weekend the boy rolled it onto the walls, Hardev was unduly hard on him. Used to working with his brain rather than his hands, the boy made mistakes. Hardev wishes he could take it all back. Since then, the boy has done little around the house. Hardev has had to rely on people like Rodriguez. And now Rodriguez is not coming back to work? "OK. Tell me what I need to know."

"Rodriguez Santiago has been arrested for Internet fraud. We got a call this morning, but it appears he was arrested almost thirty hours ago."

"Thirty hours ago? Yes, OK, he was with me Wednesday and then he had his day off, to work at Riverside, like I said. The other one, that little one, what's his name, Sebastian, part-time, short guy—he can barely lift me, you know—he was here yesterday. He's the one who put me on my side before leaving."

"Rodriguez was arrested soon after leaving your address on Wednesday. He's accused of setting up a business selling vials of tap water over the Internet to unsuspecting and naive South Asians, claiming the water is from the River Ganges. He charges a hundred dollars Canadian per bottle, and it seems he sold to over a hundred buyers in the last month alone, here and in the United States. That's a significant amount. According to the police, he has no immediate family in the area, and few friends who might put up bail, but they probably won't consider him a flight risk. He's had a few minor charges before for shoplifting but nothing like this, and until this is worked out, we must, for the safety and protection of our clients, release him."

Penny Goustapoulos catches her breath, giving Hardev a moment to take in what she's said. Little bottles of tap water. River Ganges. Internet. "By 'release,' you mean 'fire,' don't you?" he asks.

"Yes, Mr. Dange."

"Please, call me Harry. It's so difficult . . . God, it's so difficult to raise a family. Poor Rodriguez. Four kids . . . I mean five kids, and a wife. Refugees from Nicaragua—"

"Mr. Dange!" she loudly interrupts, nearly scolding him. "Rodriguez Santiago was born in Canada. He's a Canadian citizen. Single. As far as the government is aware, he has no children.

Mother deceased. Father alive, but whereabouts unknown. Grew up in foster care. We hired him in . . ."

Having little desire to listen any longer, Hardev turns the speaker off in his mind. As Penny Goustapoulos recounts Rodriguez's history with homecare services, Hardev pictures him in a lifeboat, a boy of twelve with the promise of North American shores and safety and opportunity in front of him, hugging a few family photographs and the clip of money his father and uncles gave him to help get him out of trouble should they become separated to his chest. Rodriguez of the wide nose and darting eyes, muscular, strong body, shrinks down to a skinny ostrich-legged boy, fuzzy black outline of a moustache on his upper lip, salt water on his skin. Boy Rodriguez hums an American tune, something like "Home on the Range," trembling with fear and excitement, remembering his parents' instructions: *Do what you must to survive. We are going to live in paradise, but it will not come cheap,* kissing his mother's fat cheeks, bowing to his father's mud-stained feet, replying, *I will do my best. I will grow up and raise a family and I—*

"Mr. Dange, are you still there?"

—will make you proud. Waves lap up against the boat in the darkness, at times like a large cat's tongue, at others with the violent pressure of a car crusher. *Father, is this what it is to be a man, to be scared but to keep on going?* Boy Rodriguez red and burned on his nose from the scorching, unforgiving sun—

"Hardev, are you listening?"

*—the sharp light from the moon reflecting off his father's buttons, he breathes the night air deep into his lungs, wants to stop himself from being scared, from fearing all there might be to fear in the world, things he hasn't been able to fathom, worse than the beggars he's seen without hands or feet, the women with children

clamped to their breasts, vomiting with disease, the unspeakable
acts of women's bare buttocks and men ramming into them in the
alleyways in exchange for a bag of potato chips, as he—

"Harry, we are sending someone to you right away. You won't
be left without a worker today, so please don't worry. I know
Friday is your commode day."

"Penny," he answers finally, "I don't like this story."

"I'm sorry, Harry. We had no knowledge of any criminal activity. He had no previous record of fraud, only minor shoplifting
charges. We've had to be a bit more flexible in recent years.
Homecare is not a lucrative profession. We try to give people a
second chance, benefit of the doubt. I hope you didn't lend him
any money," she adds, genuine concern evident in her voice.

"No. He never asked me for any money. He worked hard.
Every day. We were going to have fish tonight for Good Friday. I
never have fish. It's a shame. He probably thought he was helping
them."

"He was helping himself, Harry."

The puppets on the television are singing a song about team-
work: *Let's help each other. Let's work together. And the work will get
done twice as much faster. And then there'll be plenty, plenty, plenty, then
there'll be plenty, plenty, plenty of time to play.* Hardev is sure Penny
can hear their high-pitched voices too. So Rodriguez does not
have a wife or kids. Neither will he, soon. They will all be married or studying elsewhere, and he'll be in some goddamn
condominium, watching a world that doesn't care about him from
on high. Only a single family complained and laid charges. Maybe
the others were satisfied. Maybe Rodriguez actually sold them
some form of hope. Dishonestly, sure, but people are often dis-
honest with themselves. Did they really expect to get holy water

from the River Ganges on the Internet from some Canadian named Rodriguez Santiago? Did they really expect that water to make any difference in their lives? They must have realized it was only an illusion. The way ebay or *Your Ottawa, Your Voice* saving his home was only an illusion. A necessary illusion, maybe, but still an illusion.

"Thank you. I appreciate your call. Who are you sending me this time?"

Happy Easter

The boy lays out Hardev's pinstriped navy and white dress shirt and his navy blue blazer with the gold buttons, placing them on the blanketless bed and pressing down the collars. The shirt and blazer were last worn at the boy's undergraduate convocation, although the heat wave made it impossible for Hardev to sport the blazer for long. The boy resembled a thin bird in his gown, and the chair of the Anthropology Department pronounced their last name incorrectly during roll call. The shortbread cookies were soggy and the champagne tasted like flat ginger ale. "This is a happy day for the family," Hardev announced regardless, as they filed out into separate vehicles, the boy's mother and sisters in their car, the boy with him in the Para Transpo van. And he meant it. The boy had accomplished what he had set out to do.

"I suppose your sister will provide us with boutonnieres," Hardev ponders aloud, also concerned about the gold buttons, whether they will clash with anything on her dress as he accompanies her down the aisle. She keeps promising to bring over a picture of it from the catalogue when she has a spare minute, but apparently spare minutes aren't easy to come by these days.

The boy says nothing. Hardev thinks he looks thinner lately. Yellow skin, bags under eyes. He has cramps, sometimes locks himself in the bathroom for twenty, thirty minutes. Studying too hard. The books are killing him. And for what? How is his work on curses going to help people? If he believes in curses, then there's nothing that can save people from one; if he doesn't, he isn't going to convince others not to believe in them. What's the point? Though he imagines that his son has inherited his father's work ethic, he wonders why he hasn't inherited his practicality.

"Aren't you the best man? A groomsman? Has she asked you?"

"No."

"You're not the best man?"

"I don't think so."

"Who is?"

"I don't know."

"Who's the maid of honour?"

"I don't know."

"Who's Victor, then?"

"I don't know."

"Boy! Pull yourself together. Filling your head all day with magic, no wonder you can't concentrate! You're living in the clouds!" With his good hand, he gives the boy a smack on the back and gestures to the shirt. The boy turns it over, his leg twitching, inspecting for stains, loose threads, or holes. Bought five years ago to accommodate Hardev's larger waist, it seems to be in good condition, and the blazer has lasted for twenty-five years, the shoulders an inch too wide when purchased. About to travel back to India, Hardev had spotted the blazer on a mannequin in a window in the Market and stopped, struck by the regality of the buttons, buying it with only a glance at the price, pleasing the saleswoman, who enticed him to add a matching handkerchief and socks to his tally. He wore the blazer with a starched white dress shirt and black slacks and shoes on the plane, for the entire length of the journey, even when they stopped overseas for fuel. He was so proud of it, he couldn't wait for the men at the embassy to see him.

"Why haven't we been given all the details? Details are important. Then I can picture what we're supposed to do. When you're there tonight for dinner, you find out. I need to prepare. Phone people, make arrangements. May is . . . well, it's going to be busy. I can't adjust to things as quickly as you all can. You need to plan too. Maybe your girlfriend can help you. Women are better with weddings than men. Make sure you take her with you to pick out a tuxedo."

The boy turns away from his father, bending his head and shoulders sluggishly, and slides the closet door on its track: one more blazer, black, for funerals and nondescript events like parent-teacher interviews; four dress shirts, three plain white, one white and green pinstripe; one mustard-yellow Polo shirt Birendra gave him for his fiftieth birthday; three pairs of slacks, all black. All of his pyjama pants, which he wears most days to make it easier to transfer him in and out of bed, are in his dresser drawers, along with undershirts, T-shirts, socks, and underwear purchased one size larger to account for his urine bag.

"No, this is the shirt. Let's see how this all looks with a few ties."

Dutifully, the boy finds the first of two tie racks at the other side of the closet, withdraws three ties, and places them in ascending order according to length: navy blue with a gold airplane that Hardev bought ten years after purchasing his blazer (together they make him look like a pilot); yellow with a white diamond pattern in diagonal lines like snowflakes stuck to a window; and stark burgundy silk acquired at the Toronto airport. He is superstitious about his ties, about anything wrapped around his neck, and it will take him time to choose, but he doesn't want to tell the boy this, worried it will only encourage him. Years ago Isobel jokingly accused him of vanity, catching him in front of the mirror trying to decide among seven or eight for an evening out together. "I'm not vain," he replied, "I'm just in love. I want to make sure I send you that message." She always took well to declarations, and since they did not speak each other's native languages, Hardev tried to be expressive with clothes and moods, and in other ways too.

What would he declare at this wedding—that by the end of the summer he would be living in a one-bedroom condominium with the boy? Without the boy? Among a bunch of strangers? That Rodriguez will be out of jail but unemployable? Burgundy tie on top of the navy and white pinstriped dress shirt—Hardev shakes his head. Nothing looks right. "Have you heard from any schools yet?"

"Not yet." Emile inspects Hardev's sock drawer for the best pair. At least all his father's clothes are still here, unlike some of the furniture. Where did it go? He never asked. Probably better not to ask. Maybe he sold the stuff to his worker to buy Birendra a wedding present? He will probably find out soon enough. "The application process takes time. I might not hear back for another month. Also, I don't think I'm going to bring a date to the wedding."

"I thought I saw an envelope from Berkeley."

"Residence information."

Hardev strokes the tongue of the blue tie, flattening the gold airplane, and Emile stacks three pairs of underwear on the trolley. "Why aren't you going to bring your girlfriend? Women love weddings, son. She'll have a good time. I could meet her."

"There's no point. We're not serious," he says, placing a pair of black socks beside the dress shirt on the bed. "I can't get attached to people right now. I have to think about my work and where it might take me. I know we haven't talked a lot lately, but—"

"You don't want to live here anymore." Hardev hears his own voice tremble, and looks away to the mirror. An old man with tanned skin and salt-and-pepper hair stares back at him. *Are you me?* the face seems to ask. *Was that boy once you?*

"I have to go wherever I'm accepted. You know that."

"Yes. Yes," Hardev concedes, wiping his brow and turning his attention back to the clothing on the bed. "And whoever offers the most money. I guess U.S. universities have more money for these curses of yours. Canada won't do."

"It's not that, it's—"

"Three more, please. There must be one tie worthy of my eldest daughter's wedding. Your girlfriend must be waiting to hear too, I bet. You don't want to burn any bridges. I know I've told you not to get too involved while you're finishing university, but that was before the PhD. You need someone to take care of you, to help you with things. You should be thinking of settling down someday, buying a house, having kids. These are goals to aim for in life. These are dreams worth having. Why are you filling your head with curses all the time, instead of happy dreams?"

Emile hangs three new ties around his father's neck: green paisley; checkered red and black; and light orange with a thick navy stripe down the middle. "Listen," he says, lifting the red and black to his father's cheek. "I would never choose to leave you and this house if I didn't have to. Please know that. I'm not ungrateful. I'm ... I'm trying to figure out what I want. Maybe I'm a late bloomer. I ... want to tell you something, but I can't. In school we learn how to write in the third person, not the first person. In fact, we're discouraged from it, from telling personal stories. I ... don't know how to say what I want to say."

Hardev surveys his son; the boy appears taller, skinnier than before. He's inherited Hardev's large feet and thick dark hair, and probably has lots of hair on his legs and chest that maybe his girlfriend finds attractive. "What is it?"

"I ... I've never wanted to be more like you, Dad, than now. I'm beginning to understand how hard it is just to ... just to ..."

"Exist?"

"Yes, just to exist. To be a man. I guess I'm studying too hard. You're right. Curses are not always good for the brain. They're not good for girlfriends either. Let's order the pizza soon, OK? Wear what you want to the wedding," he adds, arranging the green paisley tie with the blue blazer, and seeming to snap out of his funk a little. "You know Birendra, she won't notice."

It's true. Birendra won't notice his tie on her wedding day. She's never been perceptive, Hardev admits to himself. But the boy, *my* boy is. He will miss him for it. And for the first time, Hardev realizes that he is a bit afraid of the boy, and for him. Afraid of what he thinks and will think, what he'll see, what he'll say. Afraid of what will become of him, especially after there is no longer a home to run back to. Afraid he'll end up like his father: alone. Maybe it's better to live in the clouds.

Dear Kite,

To Whom It May Concern's unveiling was a great success!!! Any Excuse Jacobson mentioned you and all your hard work. I did too. I could have added that you also contributed some pretty delicious hash cookies and that if you play the mural backwards it will spell out "Down with Capitalism," but it didn't seem like the right time for such revelations.

Anyway, I hope you're feeling alright. I have a bunch of photographs waiting for you and a clipping from the school paper. CBC Ottawa even interviewed a number of us and yes, we were on the news for about twenty seconds near the end of the six o'clock broadcast, a feel-good story to uplift hearts after an hour's worth of floods and bombings. Just kidding. It was pretty cool actually. The mural showed up well. My mom taped it. My brother e-mailed to say that he and his friend Mohab watched it online.

I phoned your place to find out how the operation went. Your brother is nice, a fast typer too. He wrote it's too early to tell, but I think sometimes patients know better than doctors. Please let me know how you are. I know you don't have e-mail access there, probably the last place on earth you can't get e-mail, and you'd think it would be one of the most important. I'm keeping my fingers crossed, which means that now even deaf people can't understand me. Ha. Ha. If you're feeling low, just remember how lucky you are not to have to write final exams this year!!!

I haven't been going to the SoundScape lately, so I don't have any new diaries for you, but you might be interested in some of my letters. Something in me has changed since we finished the mural. And after that incident with Ed—. It's not that I think what I was doing was wrong or anything, I don't. I guess I just want to know more about the people around me now. I have a list of questions for you about five pages long! Maybe friendship isn't such a scary thing. Until now I've only really dealt with strangers or family. What's funny is that sometimes strangers have seemed more like family members and family members more like strangers. I guess the categories don't need to be strict ones all the time. It's amazing to me how often I've listened to strangers and forgotten to listen to my family. I'm trying to change that. And I like this idea of listening to friends. Why can't friends be family too?

One last thing: Forget about piercings. You're going to have a pretty unique one as it is. Think about tattoos. I've started designing one already. Of course, it's a kite (how inventive, right?), but in my mind the kite is not composed of four triangles, but of four dimensions. And there's an ostrich holding it. It's hard to explain, and I don't want to send you any early sketches in case you think they're crap, so I'll just wait for you to return. I've been accepted to Ottawa University. I also applied to Gallaudet in Washington, but I don't want to leave my family right now. I'm looking into deferring for one year and working at Signature full-time to save money. They have many bursaries and scholarships for students like us, but they don't cover all expenses, and I'd hate to go into debt. I'm told I'll have two interpreters in every lecture and one in each tutorial plus a notetaker. I'll be a moving broadcast system!

My mom's making a ham for Easter tonight. Although she says we're not going to do anything fancy (wedding plans are draining her energy), she wants me to go to Mass with her. I don't think she's gone for years, but she used to say, *Once a Catholic, always a Catholic*, so maybe it's true. I had this weird feeling about Easter this year, like my mom was going to bring home a rabbit or something because Birendra will be leaving, but I guess we're just going to become religious. I'd rather go to the Landing Pad and wait for your Mystery Girl to return for her clothes! My sister doesn't want to go either, but she's trying not to rock the boat. I think even Victor, that's her fiancé, might make an appearance. Sooner the son-in-law starts sucking up, the better, right? I can't believe I'm going to have another brother soon. It feels weird. I barely know the one I have.

I miss you. My sister named me after the character in *The Wizard of Oz*. Did I ever tell you that? *There's no place like home. There's no place like home.* I'll keep repeating this until you return. Then you can tell me what I sound like. Today my name is Dorothy.

Dorothy

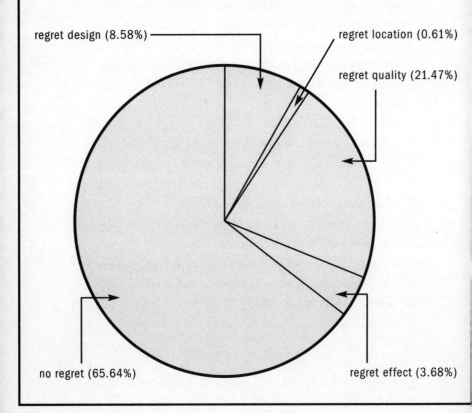

COCHLEAR REGRET CHART

regret design (8.58%)

regret location (0.61%)

regret quality (21.47%)

no regret (65.64%)

regret effect (3.68%)

Easter Monday

Because there are three police cars parked at the front entrance of Rousseau Secondary, Dorothy reroutes to the smoking section. The smokers usually have the lowdown on locker searches and any petty theft that has warranted police intrusion. The only difference between Rousseau and other high schools in Ottawa is that here the police generally require the assistance of interpreters. According to Dorothy's calculations, the police were called three times during the fall for gang-related violence (parents phoned in shock—it had never occurred to them that disabled kids would form gangs), and once after Valentine's Day, when a bad wave of LSD infiltrated the school dance, ending with six students in the Children's Hospital Emergency. Kite was nervous about the searches then, Dorothy recalls, although it wasn't his stuff the students had taken, and with the help of the boys' basketball team he quickly transferred his stash of hash and ecstasy to the gymnasium weight bins.

Rounding the east side of the building, she can sense that something is really off. A number of other almost-late students run down the path, but the smoking section is empty. Several cars are parked around back, including Any Excuse Jacobson's Mazda convertible, which the students like to call his mid-life-crisis-mobile, but the grounds are devoid of students practising sports or trading homework papers or friendship bracelets or making out. Dorothy decides to head to the cafeteria when Mrs. Kotek's pinched face emerges from behind the door.

"I found you!" she calls, too wound up to even attempt to sign. Then, eyes glassy, crumpled wet Kleenex in her other hand, "Oh, dear." The word "accident" crosses Dorothy's mind. Has there been an accident? "I don't know why people do these things. We need to talk to the police."

Dorothy makes the sign for "dare."

Mrs. Kotek is either too upset to decipher the message or doesn't care to. Keeping to Dorothy's right, she grabs her hand and squeezes. Hand in hand they stride down the hallway, Mrs. Kotek's grip loosening a little as they go, and Dorothy feels silly, as if she's a little girl who needs help finding her classroom. She can't remember the last time she held a woman's hand. Her mother's, on the way to a doctor's appointment?

Students step out of their way to let them through. Many are swearing both out loud and in sign. No one reprimands them. The front entrance now visible, Dorothy spots multicoloured debris all over the floor, and lockers sprayed with red and blue paint. Two janitors fill trash bins with sharp wedges of glass. Mrs. Kotek drops her hand.

No one touches her. No one pats her back. No one speaks to her as Dorothy halts in front of her mural, or rather, what's left of it. It is difficult to know where to focus. The protective glass has been shattered. Only the pine frame and short, jagged triangles teetering on the casing corners testify to its earlier existence. The layers of carefully arranged poems, journal excerpts, stickers, trading cards, calendars, dictionary entries, photographs of beloved friends, relatives, and pets, university application forms, are torn, as if by giant hands; segments of half-phrases bleed down the wall, alphabet letters shake like dandruff to the floor. Objects have not fared any better: pressed flowers disintegrated, scarves cut with scissors, locks of hair and seashells dumped into the trash bin, Buddha's head smashed; the papier-mâché bird's beak trampled, its eyes poked out.

"What's that smell?" Dorothy signs absently, then spots the baseball jersey near her feet, its blue discoloured into a yellow-green. "It's urine, isn't it?" And for some reason she thinks back to last week, how because of a flash rain she ran into the Museum of Science and Technology and spent an entire hour playing with the Great Moments of Communication display. It was divided into three sections: *Sender*, *Medium*, and *Receiver*, and she felt pleased and excited by the telegraph and two-way radio broadcast in particular, even though she didn't have anyone on the receiving end—inspired by the idea of messages being sent and duly received throughout the ages in all kinds of different ways, and how systems would continue to evolve. But now here she is trying to make sense of smashed glass and urine—what the message might be, to whom, for what purpose—her throat burning while two officers speak to Principal Jacobson, who for once seems not to want to accept just any excuse.

She reads: Policeman #1: "Likely students from the tech side. Rarely do shared school arrangements work. It's the same with the English-French schools. Maybe they think it's unfair they didn't get their own mural, or they couldn't contribute to this one. Maybe they were jealous the kids were on TV. Or maybe the mural wasn't the target, only the school, and they would have vandalized the gymnasium if it wasn't locked. Who knows?"

Principal Jacobson: "Only a week. It was unveiled a little over a week ago."

Policeman #1: "Didn't take them long, did it?"

Principal Jacobson: "I guess not."

Policeman #2: "The glass case was a good preventative measure. You can only do so much. You can't stop these things from happening."

Policeman #1: "We'll ask around if anyone saw or heard anything. You'll need to tell us who was in the school this weekend for games or club meetings."

Adjusting his tie, pulling at it as if it's hurting his neck, Principal Jacobson turns to find Dorothy watching their lips like tickertape headlines.

"She built the mural," he says and signs. "This was her project."

"*Our* project," she signs back, encompassing as large an area as possible with her arm motions. Principal Jacobson interprets for Policeman #1. Policeman #2 takes photos of the wall with a digital camera. Janitor Poppyfield, whose grandson attends the school, stands by his pail, awaiting permission to scrub the floors and walls.

Only when she takes a step back from the case does Dorothy notice that the red paint splashed along the massacred mural, extended onto the band of lockers to the right, spells something.

Dorothy receives: YOU'RE NOT SO FUCKING SPECIAL!

Satchel bumping on his shoulder, Emile runs to his room and shuts the door before Hardev can call him. He does not ask about the new woman, named Yvonne, who has taken over light household duties, or the broad-shouldered and arguably fat man named Reickel who transfers Hardev in and out of bed. Cheques from ebay listings still coming in, Hardev fears he will need the boy's help to package the goods and send them off before he can wash his hands of the whole business. Though he's made some money—a few thousand dollars, in fact—it isn't enough, and Mr. Karkiev has started phoning again on Mondays, like clockwork, insisting that if no new funds are secured, legal proceedings will be initiated by the end of May. *We have been very lenient and patient with you, Mr. Danke,* he said—Hardev no longer correcting his mispronunciations—but explained that legally the house could not be sold until the proceedings were fully completed and the keys changed hands. Until then, Hardev could conceivably repurchase the house, although the option was highly unlikely without new income—moreover Hardev's income as a disabled pensioner is set to decline in the coming years. He knows he has to come clean to the boy about all this, but every time Emile shuts himself up in his room Hardev thinks, *after* the wedding, *after* the wedding, let my children at least enjoy the wedding. And yet he doesn't know if he can stand it any longer. The whole affair has been making him feverish and faint.

Yesterday Yvonne did a load of laundry, dusted the living room, sewed two buttons back on to a shirt, and left without baking any chicken. Today Reickel switched his commode and bathing routines. Last Thursday, no one showed up. *My household is in disarray*, Hardev despairs, *like me, but what can I do?* He doesn't bother to ask about the neighbourhood construction, now as far away as France or India; what does it matter if he keeps up or not? The writing is on the wall. Reickel won't go next door with coffee and ply the workers with questions about the plumbing or wiring or interior decorating. Reickel doesn't care. He's a lifter; performs one action repetitively, performs it well, but can do little else, so Hardev surrenders when Reickel staggers him up the stairs at four-thirty in the afternoon, wheels him to his bedroom, and quickly and forcibly hoists him back into bed before the light of day has disappeared. And the one-bedroom condominium floats in and out of his line of vision as he eats, watches TV, performs his various medical rituals, like a *fait accompli*. He might as well start memorizing his new postal code.

"OK, chief," Reickel says, roughly tucking the blankets in at the corners, dislodging the bedside trolley from its place to the left of the bed.

"Water King," Hardev mutters, guessing that Reickel calls all his male clients "chief" and likely has a standard nickname for all his female clients too, "doll" or "hon."

"What, chief?"

"Nothing. Thank you. I'll see you in the morning."

"Sure thing, chief." Reickel turns on the television and presses the remote control into Hardev's hand before tearing down the stairs and out the door.

CNN reports are steady, unrelenting. The heat is on the U.S. and Britain to prove that their war is legitimate and to uncover

some weapons of mass destruction, and Hardev is sad to see
Tony Blair, a man he previously admired, and Britain—a country he once thought the most civilized and wonderful nation in
the world, before coming to Canada—kowtowing to American
interests. Body counts are not as high in this war as in numerous others, as the figures written on Hardev's yellow pads filed
away in the basement attest, but still he is sure this war will cause
a long-term rift between the U.S. and Europe and the Middle
East, if not Asia, like some giant messy global divorce. Once like
brothers and sisters, a large family with similar aims, they will
turn back into themselves, insist they are dealing with strangers,
and either wash their hands of each other or attempt to crush
each other. Distressingly, he recalls his own naivety when performing his missions in the Third World, bringing water and
resources and work and education programs to areas where none
were available, where villagers were starving, where parents were
so ignorant they were feeding contaminated food to their children, trying to keep them alive; he thought then, *I am going to be
part of the solution. I am going to help these families survive, bring them
hope.* But the word "solution" is used now as an excuse for bombings and terrorism, for killing people and asking others to clean
up the mess. Peter Mansbridge doesn't have an answer. Neither
does Lloyd Robertson, much less Lisa LaFlamme. The news
anchors on CNN don't even try. All mouthpieces, like speakers
on a stereo. Some are clearer than others, but they don't choose
the music.

Thinking he's heard a noise on the stairs, Hardev turns down
the volume. As far as he knows, the boy hasn't left his bedroom;
the button on his phone indicates that the line is in use.

"Reickel? Did you forget something?"

No answer; Hardev mutes the television and listens. A few seconds later, finger to his lips, a man crouches at the foot of his bed.

"Harry," he whispers.

"Rodriguez?" mouths Hardev, recognizing the figure before him, though his hair is cut within a sliver of his scalp, and he's wearing jeans and a baggy black T-shirt instead of jogging pants and a smock.

"Something wrong, Dad?" It's the boy. He must have heard the noise too.

"My homecare worker!" Hardev shouts. "He forgot to bring me a form to sign!"

Hardev listens. The boy's bedroom door remains shut. Rodriguez motions to Hardev's left hand, and Hardev presses MUTE again. Wolf Blitzer's face settles into an expression of mock concern.

Silent for a minute, the men watch the screen. More looting in Iraq. Locals steal anything they can get their hands on: sofas and chairs, food supplies and clothes, toys and lampshades, and specialized objects the regular public can't possibly have any use for, like sophisticated medical equipment—all hauled into basements and fifteen-person shacks. Women scream for their sons to drop canisters full of coffee, sugar, and flour off buildings, while daughters scrounge alleys for wayward cans of tuna and beans, wristwatches, knives. Men break into cars and stores, trying to outrun and outgrab their neighbours, while prosperous nations send reporters to videotape the disaster for consumption back home. No one can protect the museums from the thieving—never mind sacred objects, they're not oil, are they? *These people need so much*, Hardev thinks. *They can't leave even a crumb behind.*

Rodriguez's eyes are bloodshot. There appears to be bruising around his neck, but it might be the light, as Reickel left Hardev with only a small lamp by his bedside, and the glow of the television. Rodriguez looks old, older than Hardev ever suspected, not in his early thirties; possibly forty or forty-five. Hardev has never registered the wrinkles on his neck and around his eyes. Those large hands that carried him with ease up and down stairs, in and out of bed, the bath, and pushed his wheelchair over grass and mud, utterly baffle him; they are thin and weak and shaking.

"You shouldn't be here," he says. He knows he needs to be firm. He can't afford to get involved.

Rodriguez reduces the bedroom door opening to a crack. "I wanted to see you, Harry. I am going away for some time."

"Jail?" Hardev asks softly. "Are they putting you in jail?"

"You could say that," Rodriguez chuckles humourlessly.

Something in Hardev's mind clicks like the remote control. "You're not running away, are you?"

No answer. Instead, Rodriguez scratches his head and peeks into the corridor.

Trying to control the volume of his voice so as not to alarm the boy, Hardev insists, "You must not run away. Think of those who need you. I'm sure there are people counting on you to accept your punishment and resume life when this is over."

"I have no life. No one's counting on me. They must have told you."

"You mustn't give up," Hardev pleads. "What you did isn't so bad. The way the court system works nowadays, even murderers get early parole—I keep lists, I can show you. You'll be out of jail in no time."

"I don't want to spend one day in jail. I can't imagine spending *one day* in jail," Rodriguez counters, scratching his head more furiously. "It will be just like the foster home the bastards threw me in. Made out to be like some great holiday away from my original family, right? Sure they mistreated me, but the foster home was worse. It was a jail. No one gave a shit about me, Harry. And the people who threw me in there, they never once asked about my home life or checked up on me. They signed a piece of paper and I lived somewhere else. My foster family just fed me on time and made me work for nothing. That's jail. I've had enough of jail."

"But at times we all face what we can't imagine. Remember you told me that people make something out of nothing all the time. This isn't the end of your life. You will survive. You'll serve your time and then they'll let you go. You could be out by Canada Day!"

Rodriguez steps closer to the bed, and the cuts on his scalp and arms are more visible. With a swift motion, he rearranges Hardev's toothbrush and denture case the way Hardev likes them. "I don't think it's fraud when people want to believe. That's what I keep telling my lawyer. People wanted to believe, they wanted their relatives to feel good and safe and happy so they wouldn't curse themselves for not bringing any of the river with them when they left. Only one family complained. The children tried to heal their father dying of prostate cancer. It's a horrible death, Harry, I've seen it at the hospital. They became so enraged when he died, they blamed the water, thought it might have been polluted. Can you believe they paid to have the water tested? Of course, the test came back that it was regular Ottawa tap water. But what would show up if the water was sacred? I'd like them to answer that."

Rodriguez doesn't look well. There's no point arguing, Hardev realizes, as this will certainly be the last time they ever see each other, so he nods.

"I didn't take your vial of sacred water, Harry. I left it in the tennis racquet case." He stands at attention as he says this, and his manner reminds Hardev of his old hydro workers, the ones who called him The Water King when he gathered them together and repeated the mantra he had created for the missions: *The work you do here every day benefits your own families. You are helping your own community grow. Think about that when the sun gets too hot or you feel too tired or you get in a scuffle over who was last to use a machine. This isn't about any one of you. It's about all of you.*

"I have . . . some food in the basement," says Hardev. "The pantry, the stockpiles. Take some plastic bags from under the sink and fill them with canned food and juice and rice and anything else you need, as many bags as you can possibly carry." Rodriguez stares at the denture case, not acknowledging the offer in any way, yet Hardev is sure he will take him up on it. He has done so in the past, and at least this time he has Hardev's blessing.

"I came back to tell you that I really liked working for you." Fingernails filmed with dirt, knuckles red, Rodriguez reaches out his hand. "I like you, Harry. I really do."

Firmly, Hardev grasps the man's hand, though the action sends pins and needles up his arm and through his upper chest and neck. Holding on, he shakes with determination three times, the way he used to greet other civil servants when he was first introduced to them, in hopes they would remember him. But now Rodriguez is leaving, and Hardev knows that this man has forever altered the way he looks at his sink, his trolley, the dresser, the television, the living room, the stove, the coffee pot, the stairs—this man, immigrant or not, lying about his story or not, changed the house for the better. Hardev adds, "Open that tennis racquet case and take the vial of water. It *is* sacred water, Rodriguez. From the River Ganges. If you believe in it, I want you to have it."

Rodriguez scratches again, lowering his head. "I'm sorry I lied to you. I always wanted a big family. A real family. When I spoke to you, I believed I had one. A wife and four kids and one on the way. Then five. And he was sick. He got sick. In my head he was so fragile, Harry. He almost didn't make it. I wasn't lying, Harry."

Hardev feels his chest constrict, his throat get warm. He wants to say, *Me too, me too, my boy. I always wanted a large family, and every child is so fragile, every family is so fragile,* but he can't, he can't, and there won't be another opportunity.

"Goodbye."

"Goodbye."

The news is wrapping up for the hour. The lead anchor musters up a last smile for a day of human atrocity, forest fires, and disease, and the next hour's anchor will do the same, and then all over again tomorrow. Hardev turns off the television, then the bed lamp. The light on the telephone indicates that the boy is still talking. He listens. "New Year's was New Year's, Monique," Hardev makes out, "a mistake. We're practically strangers now. Let's move on." Lovers' quarrel? Good; at least the boy won't hear a thing. Long after Rodriguez has left for wherever he is going, Hardev will lie awake contemplating the darkness. For in the darkness anything, absolutely anything, seems possible.

"This place is my sister's second home!" Birendra gushes to Victor's mother, Emily, as they enter Memories and peruse the three glass cases loaded with cakes, tarts, pies, and mousses before sitting down at a table for two near the front of the café. "She treats herself here after a hard day of studying. I'm glad those days are over for me."

"Me too," Emily agrees, removing her grey wool overcoat with matching hat, hanging the overcoat on the back of the chair, and revealing a mauve dress suit with a gold tulip pin. Although Birendra is wearing an attractive scarlet gypsy-style blouse and black dress pants, she now feels underdressed, even childish. "Will Dorothy be going to university? College? Is she able to?"

"Oh yes, sure," she replies, looking up at the perky teenaged waitress with her bra straps peeking out of her thin cotton top, and ordering water for both of them. As she speaks, though, she realizes that, with everything happening in her life this year, she hasn't asked Dorothy what her plans are after graduation. No wonder Dorothy's been so distant lately, she figures, so uncommunicative. "She likes art—painting, drawing. She's really good." Birendra doesn't mention that her sister works at a piercing and tattoo parlour. Let Dorothy tell Emily herself, at the wedding or afterwards. It isn't her job to explain her family.

"I'm glad you had time to see me today before I leave again. We don't know each other well, although I know my son is very happy, which is my first concern, and you are very pretty and seem quite nice." She smiles, and her face, though powdered whiter, lights up a lot like Victor's. They also share small but penetrating blue eyes, dimples on right cheeks, thin but expressive lips. "But I don't live in Canada, so we probably won't have many opportunities to talk like this."

Nervous, Birendra can barely make out the lettering on the Parisian-themed menu. This is only the second time the two women have met, the first being at the engagement party, and she doesn't know what to expect, how to act in front of this woman, and she keeps locking her feet around the black iron legs of the chair. Victor picked his mother up at the airport only last night, and Birendra was busy with inventory all day at Wall Flower.

When Emily phoned, she was filling up the pamphlet racks with "How to Best Care for Your Beloved Plants and Fresh-Cut Flowers" and "Ten Mistakes People Make When Choosing Plants," favourites with women desperate to care for something, anything, who come in once a week with photographs of their budding gardens and window or table displays, times, dates, and ages noted on the back in pencil. Birendra has even started selling overpriced "Plant and Flower Diaries," available right at the cash counter, and they've become a quick bestseller though a comparable journal can be purchased at the bookstore in the mall for half the price.

"I'm looking forward to getting to know you," Birendra says, as convincingly as she can, and points on her menu to selection #11, Bailey's Cheesecake, because it is the first cake she saw on the way in, while Emily orders a strawberry and kiwi trifle.

"It's not the chit-chat that's important," Emily replies dismissively, diligently unfolding her red paper napkin and catching Birendra off guard, "it's the big decisions. I have two things to talk to you about. And I have a gift for you. No need to be nervous, dear, have some water."

"Oh, thank you." Birendra is unsure, complies by drinking her ice water, though she's impatient for her cake to arrive so she can comfort herself with sweets. All she really knows about this woman in front of her is that Victor's father left her eight or nine years ago and, according to Victor, the split was amicable, Emily receiving a large sum of money and no divorce, though it was clear that Victor's father would now live with a woman ten years younger than Emily, in essentially a second marriage.

"I'm not against the church wedding service. I think it will be nice. I like Catholic churches, all the beautiful stained glass, the organ and all, I'm sure your father likes it too, which is probably why he agreed to this . . ." Birendra does not interrupt, does not want to admit her father wasn't consulted. "You were baptized Catholic and so you should have a Catholic service, though Victor tells me you're not religious in any way, that you're basically secular and this is about pleasing your mother."

The desserts arrive just as Emily finishes saying "your mother," and Birendra takes up her fork right away. "It's probably a lack of imagination on our part," Birendra says, chuckling in embarrassment, annoyed that Victor didn't prepare her for this meeting, leaving her vulnerable to this stranger who will soon be her mother-in-law.

"I raised Victor in the United Church, but not thoroughly. He even refers to it as Church for Dummies. Short service, then barbecue. I'm sure you've heard him." Bailey's Irish Cream melts in Birendra's mouth as she nods. Emily's trifle remains as perfectly presented as in the display case, like a flower in Birendra's store.

"What I'm getting at is, this is alright by us, and I mean Victor's father too—we've consulted—for the wedding. But when you two have children, we would be very strongly, *very strongly* against you raising them Catholic."

Birendra coughs, covering her lips with her napkin to catch any cake. "When we have children? I haven't really thought . . ."

"We're not fans of the Catholic Church or that Pope John Paul, who refuses to die. And all those scandals on the news! As bad as a mob family, Catholics. No. This would be very upsetting to us. We don't want our grandchildren to grow up Catholic."

"OK, I understand," Birendra affirms, although she's bewildered by the sudden talk of Catholics and children and the United Church. Victor never mentions God except in a vague

"Thank God" or "Oh, God, how stupid" kind of way. Why was God now another place setting to account for in their upcoming marriage?

"You look pale. Don't be upset. Enjoy your cake. Here, I'll start mine." Emily smiles again and Birendra is struck once more by the strong family resemblance. Victor is also patient with his food, and can be coolly businesslike about important things like this, and then gentle with her.

"I'm not upset. I'm just ... surprised, I guess. I haven't really thought about these things, but I don't have any real desire to bring up children ... Catholic. Or Hindu, for that matter." The cake feels heavy on her fork now, too sugary, too rich before a proper dinner.

"Good, good. Hindu? I hadn't even thought of that. Why confuse the children with so many religions? I think it's important for us to be honest with each other about these things early on, before it's too late. These things can strain family relations. You say your sister paints and draws? ... Good. Teach them art. Religion is false hope, darling. It's good to know a few of the stories for culture's sake, but in the end all churches are Churches for Dummies. Join the yacht club." A piece of kiwi and strawberry and a lump of vanilla pudding disappear into her thin, efficient mouth. The teenaged waitress returns with a swagger to ask how they are, and of course they are fine and don't need anything. "I'm glad that's settled. No religion for the children. Now to the second thing. A gift!"

Normally the mention of gifts is enough to make Birendra clap and giggle with anticipation, but this time, without knowing why, she dreads Emily's gift, wants to leave it unopened, refuse to sign for it, send it back. "You don't have to give me anything. I mean, how can I ever thank you for paying for the whole wedding? My family would never be able to afford such an event. Really. You've done too much already." She means it. She doesn't want Victor's family to do any more, doesn't want to end up in debt to them beyond them paying for the wedding, which she easily accepted as common in many family traditions, not as a bribe designed to keep her and Victor under their power. Aside from providing a detailed guest list, which Victor and Birendra requested, up until this point Victor's parents have maintained a hands-off approach, and it has eased her nerves. She has even pointed out to her mother how non-interfering they've been. She figured his parents were going to leave them to make their own decisions about everything. Especially about kids. Why is marriage automatically paired up with children in people's minds? Many married people have no children. Many married people with children should never have had them. Divorce rates have never been worse, so why are people so determined to bring more children into the world, into broken, unhappy marriages? *It was devastating when my parents separated,* she admits to herself. *I no longer know my own father or my brother.* However, she doesn't really know her mother or her sister well either. *A family should just be who you want to live with. I want to live with Victor. He's my family. That's it.*

"Victor is our only son . . ." And why do people always qualify things this way, Birendra wants to know, staring at the bits of kiwi smothered in the white pudding of Emily's trifle. Would they care less about one if they had many? Did her mother or father care less about her because they had two daughters? Just this morning, Tracy was saying that as her parents' only child, she wished they would take more of an interest in her love life. "I would totally consider an arranged marriage," she announced. "My friends and I, we all pick assholes to go out with. I can't even decide what to wear half the time, let alone who to choose for a life partner. How did you know Victor was the one?" The first thing that came to Birendra's mind was that Victor had few family attachments and a well-paying job that would take them away from here. Instead, she made a joke of it. "He asked, and I wanted a new dress."

Emily leans in conspiratorially, fluttering her eyelashes. "We want your marriage to start off on the best footing, and to us this means a better place to live than Victor's apartment."

"Oh, we've already talked about getting a bigger place. Victor is—"

"Our gift to you is that we are going to give you enough money for a significant down payment on a nice three- or four-bedroom house. What do you think of *that?*"

Smudges of white and off-white are all that remain on Emily's plate, and droplets of brown on Birendra's. Emily takes a deep gulp of water. Nothing has altered the brightness of her rose lipstick. "I don't know what to say."

"Just say thank you."

"Thank you," Birendra practically whispers. "We're just not sure where Victor will be next year. His boss keeps hinting that there's a position opening up in the Caribbean and . . . I'm not sure it's the right time to buy a house."

"My dear, Victor knows all about this. I spoke to him about it when he visited me in February. He's all for it. He just wanted to keep it a surprise until I could tell you in person. Don't you worry," she adds, tapping Birendra's hand excitedly, causing her to drop her napkin on the table, "you don't have to live there forever. Think of all the houses I lived in with Victor's father, and all the properties I own in Hawaii. A house is always a sound investment, especially in this city—real estate prices keep going up, there's such a low vacancy rate. Surely you can see the sense in this."

"An investment . . . OK, I understand," and Birendra thinks of that man her father told her about, the head worker on his street who's overseeing all the houses rising up from holes in the ground as if out of nowhere, like cement and brick trees and flowers, and she is filled with apprehension at the vision of these house gardens with stairways and sunrooms and several bedrooms (for who?), and she wants it to dissolve like a mirage in her mind, but Emily is dusting the vision off, polishing it, holding it up in front of her like a lollipop to a baby, no, not baby, not baby, like valued stock to an investor."I don't think I'll have the energy after the wedding for a housewarming."

Casually tilting her head back and licking the last of the pudding off her spoon, Emily laughs. "You haven't even bought the house and you're worried about the housewarming . . . Well, at least you're a planner. That's a good sign."

The perky waitress drops the bill in the middle of the table and Emily quickly scoops it up with another rosy smile, before Birendra can argue about it. Two seniors in matching "We Survived the Ice Storm" sweatshirts shuffle in and wait for them to vacate their table. *What's coming next?* Birendra thinks to herself, and Emily, as she grabs her coat and purse and steps aside to let the older women sit, leans close to Birendra and whispers, "The great thing about mixed marriages is that they produce the most beautiful children. Have more than one. Don't make the same mistake we made, thinking it was better to concentrate on one rather than have a brood. We should have had five, ten. We could afford it. How many do you want?"

After spending most of the day with the janitors, trying to salvage as many items from the mural as possible—not in hopes of reconstruction but to at least return them to their owners—Dorothy is so tired she can barely think. Head pounding, she walks home in a daze, takes a two-hour nap, then wakes with the strongest urge to go to the SoundScape, not to collect any stories (she'll demand Roof and Key take their own rest this evening) but to sit like a regular patron, just existing in her own skin, without a mission, without ends.

At the bar Iris recognizes her, holds up an Export and, when Dorothy nods, brings it over. No one at the SoundScape checks her fake ID anymore, though tonight she would welcome being asked, forced to present herself in public as the fraud she is, an eighteen-year-old who pretends to know about all kinds of people and the unvoiced messages they carry, who sees herself as the keeper of these messages, a collector and protector, a listener but no judge. Yet as she dumped the unsalvageable bits of paper and pieces of plastic into a row of three trash cans, including bits of writing she recognized as her own from the folder behind Kite's obliterated Palm Pilot message: *Why not take that trip back to Paris you always wanted, on us? . . . I wondered who would hide the chocolate eggs for you kids, who would go to the store and buy them . . .* , she heartily wished for the destruction of the entire school, for the pulverization of them all under a massive bomb, every student— on her side, on the tech side, whether deaf, blind, dumb, brain-damaged, mentally ill, or healthy—everyone she's ever met and those she hasn't. For they all seemed to her potential enemies, as senseless as the sounds she will never hear. She can learn how to speak, how to negotiate her way through the world, convincingly even, but it's all a form of false protection and false presentation, like her ID, like her stories. You can go ahead, send out a call, like her father and his useless letters, but there's no guarantee of a welcoming answer. *YOU'RE NOT SO FUCKING SPECIAL!* I can't be a good listener, she concludes, if I can't accept what is said.

It's Retro Eighties Night, and Iris is apparently reliving her teenage years, traipsing around the back of the bar, twirling swizzle sticks, jiggling to entice the bartender, Yorie or Borie, Dorothy has trouble distinguishing which, to dance with her. Dorothy never dances at the SoundScape, and has attended only one Rousseau dance in her four years there, in grade nine, when if you didn't go the teachers phoned your parents to discuss your low self-esteem or unsociability. She spent the evening handing out drink tickets for pop and water with the young science teacher, Mr. Ambrosier, who talked about his own high school days. He told her about his love of tennis, how he nearly won provincials, and how he ended up in chemistry and physics because he had a huge crush on his neighbour and decided to enroll in all the same classes she did, and then how when he was a junior, on the way home from a camping trip, a Jeep carrying a group of his friends rolled on the highway and two of them died. "I was in the other car, that's the reason I didn't die," he said. "There was a memorial at the school and they played 'Wish You Were Here' and the girls were all crying, and lots of the boys were crying too, but I wasn't crying. I was dumbstruck. What did it mean? I couldn't understand. I thought, *What does God expect from me for saving my life?*" Why he confided in her, Dorothy couldn't guess; perhaps he was bored, perhaps he'd had a little to drink, perhaps Pink Floyd reminded him of his old friends, she didn't know; but he did, and he was the first of the men whose pain reminds her of her father's, the first to make her ache for understanding, for conversations she's never had with him, which she will likely never have.

Sipping her beer, she realizes she forgot her newest Palm Pilot. She also forgot to recharge her cellphone. If anyone wants to talk to her tonight, she will have little recourse except her voice. Before she has time to panic, Iris speaks.

"Can I ask you something?" she calls into Roof.

Tilting her head quizzically to better read her lips, Dorothy waits until Iris repeats her question, then turns the palms of her hands up in a "why not?" gesture.

Iris starts scrubbing the counter with a blue dishcloth. "Yorie and I are having an argument. Do you think it's possible to change your life, I mean one hundred and eighty degrees, a complete turn-around, or are we just kidding ourselves if we think we can construct our own destiny or change who we are?" As Iris replaces Dorothy's paper coaster with another one, Dorothy grabs her arm and gently extracts a pen from her right shirt pocket. Pausing as Iris leaves to take a couple of orders, she watches a young woman with long black hair pull teasingly at her boyfriend's black suspenders while a man at the bar with a scraggly beard stares vacantly at the shelves of liquor bottles.

Then she sees him: Ed—. He's not drinking. He's just standing at the other end of the bar, hands in his pockets, staring at her. But she recognizes him, and he recognizes her. As he makes his way over to her, she starts shaking. She doesn't know what she's going to say until she mouths, "Who are you?"

"Nobody," he replies.

"Me too," Dorothy says, as he keeps walking past her and out the SoundScape door.

She writes furiously:

WE SEE AND HEAR WHAT WE WANT
Then on the back: WE ARE ALL ACCIDENTS OF GOD
THE REAL QUESTION IS WHETHER WE FLEE
THE SCENE

I'm not going to flee the scene, she decides. *No matter what I hear.*

When Iris returns, she plops both elbows on the counter and reads the coaster, front and back, gives Dorothy a wary look, then reads the coaster again. Although she seems to be concentrating, Dorothy can't tell if Iris is actually thinking about what she's written or simply attempting not to be rude. In the meantime Dorothy spots a new man, apparently in his early forties, sidling up to the bar where Ed— was. His clothes are baggy, possibly dirty, and he looks out of place at the SoundScape, assessing his surroundings as he surrenders to them. Close-cropped hair black as the countertop, skin orange-brown—Dorothy figures he's of Spanish or Mexican descent.

Chuckling a little, as if she finally gets the joke, Iris twirls the coaster between her fingers, then hands it back to Dorothy. Before Kite left, she came close to bringing him here for a drink—with his height she didn't expect he'd have much trouble getting in— but she decided against it. After the incident with Ed— on Valentine's Day, it didn't seem like *her* place anymore. But now, even if she doesn't know how to belong here again, she does feel justified to be here.

"Most people aren't deaf but don't know how to listen. I'm deaf but I'm a wonderful listener." Dorothy both speaks and signs these words as she slips off her stool. Iris stops cold, holding her blue dishrag. Yorie, or Borie, who has also heard her and seen her sign, spills tonic on the counter. *Maybe today will be a new unveiling, or the end of a second apprenticeship*, Dorothy thinks.

She does not intend to alarm the man, but appears to when she hops on the stool beside him. His dark brown eyes meet hers with panic and he almost spills his yellow-orange drink, barely catching the round of the glass.

"I'm deaf," Dorothy says and signs, "but I'm a wonderful listener."

The man squints as if trying to place her, opens his mouth and shuts it again. Iris puts his change on the counter. He keeps staring at Dorothy as though she's someone he vaguely knows but didn't expect to see.

"What's your name?" he asks.

"Accident. What's yours?"

"I've never met an Accident before," he replies, collecting his change. "My name is Rodriguez."

"I have never met a Rodriguez before," she signs and speaks. "So, Rodriguez, tell me a story. Don't worry, I can read very well," she adds, pointing to his lips, which are swollen, the top one bruising like the patches around his squinty eyes. She offers him her hand, and he accepts it and presses. *That's my mouth*, she thinks. *He doesn't realize that he's kissed me*. And she thinks of that other one, of Ed—, who was just here, nobody special, whom she refused to listen to, and she hopes she's making it up, not to him but to her father, who she knows would have wanted her to hear his story. To hear it so she could understand, no matter how difficult. He has been able to forgive. Why not her?

"I don't know where to begin," Rodriguez says, his leg catching a plastic handle from the mound of bags he's placed against the bar. "I guess I should tell you first that I'm the worst kind of man. I'm a man without a family."

Dear Dor,

I suppose you already know the end of this story, but the details will likely help fill whatever gaps you may have unwittingly been carrying with you. I don't know what events you'd like to hear about, what interests you most about my life, so I am forced to choose, select what I think would appeal to you. I ask myself: *Would she like to know what hospital I ended up in? How I took the news that her mother was pregnant? Would she like to know more about her brother?*

I can only assume that you would, and face the consequences of satisfying your curiosity. So here we go again: *In a previous episode, the hero was left unconscious after a great explosion.*

Three weeks later, bandaged like a mummy in Toronto General Hospital, I thought I was a ghost haunting irreverent scientists who had broken into my tomb. I couldn't feel my own body; whatever flesh could still experience pain had been numbed by shots of morphine. I truly did not think that I existed, that I was present in any bodily sense. But your mother cried, screamed for nurses, who ran in and rushed about pulling the blankets from my torso and poking things inside me. I felt none of it. Absolutely nothing, except how parched my mouth was. I tried to speak but nothing came out. I wanted to ask about my men, the workers, where were they? Were they hurt too? Whose fault was it? What was CIDA doing about it? Your mother was like a puppet. She bobbed up and down, her arms and legs waving and dangling, and I couldn't stop her, get her to focus long enough on my face to transmit any of my thoughts.

Later, she brought in your sister and brother—I still can't believe they allowed it—who hid behind her. They didn't recognize me all wrapped up and attached to tubes. Your mother also looked strange. She was wearing clothes I recognized, but it was as if another woman was inside them. Did she always have such thin lips? Was her voice always so high-pitched? Her face this white? Nothing looked like what I remembered. And my children, well, they were even worse. Though they had been given more of my features than your mother's (as you were too), their dark hair and thick eyebrows did nothing to connect them to me lying on that hospital bed. I remember thinking, *What are they looking at? Who are they looking at with such fear in their eyes?* I tried to reach out, to touch their little hands or stroke their hair, not for the sake of comforting them, but to make sure they were real.

Your mother was pregnant. She told me later that evening, after they removed one of the drips from my arms. And when she mentioned it, I could see she was. Her breasts were larger than when I'd left. As she poured water directly into my mouth and down my throat, I could see those breasts strained against her starched blouse, burgeoning. *I'm wearing a bib,* I thought. *I'm a grown man and I'm wearing a bib, and my wife is feeding me.* I couldn't feel my arms or my legs. Your mother talked about the accident, but I wanted to know who was in India overseeing the work, who had taken my place. I couldn't speak and she didn't mention it. Instead, she spoke of surgeries and drug therapy and X-rays. The children played in the corner with little Hot Wheels cars but were otherwise silent, crashing them against each other without making any noise. It made me angry with them, and with your mother, holding her stomach and adjusting my bib while I was barely able to turn my head. I was not in India taking care of the hydraulics project entrusted to me. My men were waiting for me and I needed to set them straight, keep them on track. I wasn't responsible for what had happened. I wasn't! CIDA had told Isobel this. It was an accident. But all I could see were white boxes upon white boxes with dozens of dead bodies in them, like suffocated butterflies. And at that moment I hated you. I hated you for being inside your mother's body, for touching her when I could not, for being where you should be when I was where I shouldn't be. I hated you for all kinds of reasons I can't even begin to list. And though I need your forgiveness for this, this is also part of the story.

I'm sorry. I'm sorry.

Mother's Day

With the wedding less than a week away, Birendra can't believe how many things are still left to do. Not only is she behind on constructing the table centrepieces, but the list of favourite songs the DJ asked for is three days late, she needs to find nail polish to match the ribbon on her bouquet, e-mails keep pouring in from Victor's family with special requests (don't seat Aunt Claire with Uncle David; remind the caterers about cousin Peter's nut allergy), and the Château Laurier concierge needs her to confirm details for the honeymoon suite. Now she can sympathize with the stressed-out mothers and maids of honour who frequently pace the floors of Wall Flower Florist and Gifts, biting their nails and bitching about late limousine drivers and catty hairdressers. *Do we really need all this stuff to justify living with someone for the rest of our lives?* she thinks, tearing her hair out in her mind. It is at this point that, feeling the answer moot, the machinery of weddings and all the stuff that comes with them already in motion, she leaves Victor in the kitchen with her mother to work out the changes to the seating arrangements, and ends up, as if unable to stop herself, at her father's address.

"Did you change something? The place seems different," she says, looking around with a vague sense of disorientation as she wheels her father from the kitchen to the living room. "Was the furniture rearranged?"

"No. You just don't visit so often ... Understandably, with the wedding and everything. Looking for a house, too," Hardev replies as he is parked beside the mahogany coffee table with its stack of *Ottawa Citizen*s. "You came alone."

Sighing, she flops on the couch and surveys the room again, unable to put her finger on what's different but pretty sure that at least a painting or two are missing—why can't she remember what they look like? Scenes of Quebec City?—but she shrugs it off. "It's enough trouble planning this wedding. I don't want a house. All that work! I'm trying to convince Victor to get a nice condo. Two or three bedrooms so it's still a good investment, but where a superintendent can deal with leaky faucets and cracked tiles. Victor's no handyman and I'm no housekeeper. I don't need a garden. I've had enough flowers to last a lifetime at the store. And condos are less hassle when you move."

Locking his wheelchair, Hardev gazes at his daughter on the couch—tired but womanly, not a child any longer, worrying about investments and houses—with some sadness. "Is Victor being transferred? Has he heard anything yet?"

"No, not yet. I'm just babbling. I've got a lot on my mind." Her mother was always fearful, she recalls, that her father would be transferred. Bad enough he was constantly travelling, taking off to one foreign land or another for weeks, sometimes months at a time, leaving her to deal with the house and raising them on her own, let alone they should be forced to uproot for two or three years or longer if he was promoted again. She didn't want to end up somewhere without four distinct seasons, where she'd have to learn to cook new dishes and grow exotic plants, where she'd need to learn another language. "I'm sorry I came without calling. I guess I wanted to surprise you."

"You look so beautiful," he replies, nodding wistfully, whereas Birendra is struck by how weak he appears, hairline receded halfway across his scalp, a dullness in his dark eyes, deep wrinkles on his neck, as if she hasn't visited in years, not months. And she's certain there's something different about the living room beyond a couple of missing paintings. The kitchen, the whole house, something is off—is it a smell?—although she can't figure it out. "If you want anything out of the fridge, help yourself. This is still your home. You don't have to call. You are welcome any time. It's just for your convenience that I ask you to call, so I won't be held up by homecare."

"I know, Dad. Don't worry. I don't need anything," she says, straightening up. What happened to the curtains? The orange curtains, the heavy ones she used to hide in as a child, teasing her brother. They're gone. *Yes, they're gone,* she thinks, satisfied at least that her sense of things being altered wasn't just in her head. "I already ate and we'll be having a big dinner tonight—"

"Yes. Wish your mother a happy birthday for me."

"Uh, OK." Birendra can't remember the last time her father asked her to wish her mother a happy birthday. And before she headed over, her mother asked her to tell him that she was looking forward to seeing him walk, no, *escort*, that was the word she used, *escort* their daughter down the aisle. Not sure how to relay this message, she doesn't.

"I've come for something else," Birendra says, folding her hands politely together over her long white knit skirt. "Can you guess?"

"Guess?" Hardev turns over a stack of papers on his tray, then winces. The motion is so quick that she can only discern a column of numbers, like an account. "No. I can't."

"I'm . . . I'm getting married next weekend. Isn't there something you want to give me? Something you've been waiting to give me for a long time?" Smiling exaggeratedly at her father, she points to herself as a clue.

"I don't understand," he says, obviously perplexed, his hands acting as paperweights. "Your mother said Victor's family was paying . . . I want to help, but . . ."

"No." She pinches the hem of her skirt as if modelling the apparel. "Hmm?"

Forehead furrowed, Hardev shakes his head. "I'm sorry. I'm old, I guess. I don't know what you're talking about." His good arm goes into a spasm, shaking the tray.

"Dad?" Birendra frowns and crosses her legs. "Haven't you been saving a sari for me since I was a little girl? A *red* sari? Mom told me. She said you've been saving it all these years for my wedding. I would have come earlier, but I've been so busy it slipped my mind."

Hardev smacks the papers with his uncontrollable hand, and

his eyes widen. "But . . . but I thought you had a wedding dress. Dorothy phoned months ago. November, I think. Yes, November. She said you picked out a wedding dress. The one you wanted. I thought—"

"Dad," Birendra interrupts, leaning across the newspapers on the coffee table, almost whispering, "Did something happen to it? Did you . . . did you give it away?"

"Give it away? No. No. I . . ." Then his left leg begins.

"But I was planning to wear it to the wedding reception! Mom said. She said . . ." She races back and forth in her mind over the details she has planned with Victor and her mother. Wedding reception: red sari, red shoes, red rose in her hair. It's true she wasn't excited by the idea at first, and kept putting off dealing with it, pretending she wasn't getting the hint as her mother left magazine photos of South Asian brides on the kitchen table, but when she mentioned it to Victor, he argued in its favour. He teased that he would love to have two brides instead of one—his French Catholic bride at the church, and his Indian one at the reception. And after dessert at Memories with his mother, she wanted to wear the damn thing just to unnerve her, keep this woman, who she hoped would leave them alone once the vows were spoken, at a distance. "How could you get rid of it?"

Wanting to turn away from her pleading, angry eyes but trapped in his wheelchair, he slaps his forehead instead. "You never cared before! Why are you asking for these things now? You thought they'd just be here when you wanted them, didn't you? Well, sometimes these things can't wait!"

Stunned, Birendra feels her throat start to throb. This isn't how she imagined things would go today. In fact, she expected gratitude, an expression of her father's pleasure that she would be wearing this important piece of clothing. What happened to all the "family pride" he liked to talk about so often? Where was her sari? Was it somewhere with the Quebec City paintings and the heavy orange curtains? "Can we get it back? Did you lend it to someone? One of your workers?"

"No. No," Hardev repeats, slapping his forehead again. "I don't know where it is. I mean, I know where it is, but I can't get it back. If you had told me . . . You never cared about anything Indian before! Not one thing. You never asked me to tell you any stories about India. Not one, ever! You never asked me one question about it! You kids! I tried, I tried so hard to give you all everything, everything I could! You never wanted a sari before. How was I to know you wanted to wear a sari at your wedding? Now you want it. Next you'll want a father! A house! You'll tell me you've always wanted to live in this house with your father!"

She tries to catch his eyes but he's crying now, and he won't look up from his tray, where his papers are edging closer to falling. "It doesn't matter. It's OK, Dad," she whimpers, wishing she could go back to her car and return to the kitchen with Victor and her mother, make a different decision than the one she made barely an hour ago. She hates when her father cries, and before she can force herself to look away, she too is sobbing. *I'll just tell Mom and Victor I don't like the red sari, it doesn't fit right or there's a moth hole in it or something*, she thinks, tears rolling down her cheeks onto the top headline: "Property Taxes to Rise Again." Besides, it could be true. She's never worn a sari. It might have looked strange on her, and then she'd have upset her father more by having to leave it behind. But she's not crying for his sake, she knows this, and she doesn't want to think about what he just said to her—it's too much to deal with, just too much right before her wedding. She

PRISCILA UPPAL 343

can't believe it, but she's crying because it never occurred to her that her father would give up on her, give up on who he imagined her becoming all those years ago. No matter who that woman was, she now wishes she were more like her, more connected to the family, notwithstanding her desire to disown them. The sari is gone. Could it be that her father's imagination disowned *her*? "I better get back, Dad. I'm sorry. I don't know what I was thinking. I didn't want to upset you. I'm glad you're going to walk me down the aisle," she adds, wiping her eyelashes on her hand.

"I'm not *walking* you down the aisle, Birendra."

"Escorting. *Escorting* me down the aisle. I mean, that's the important thing, that you'll be there."

"No," Hardev says firmly, without emotion, though his face is wet with tears, unlocking his wheelchair just as the papers tumble to the floor. "No. And don't pick those up. Forget about them. They're not important either. The important thing is to give you something, something you can *use* in your new life. I don't have anything of material value to give you. All that stuff is gone. It's junk—"

The heavy orange curtains, the Quebec City paintings, the red sari. Gone. It's true. The china cabinet. The ivory elephant. The gold-plated candleholders. And more. More is gone. Perhaps even more than what remains. And though her father is speaking directly to her—indeed he's blocking her way as she tries to rise from the couch to leave—Birendra can't stop turning her head and raiding her mind to fill in the shapes and colours of objects that ought to be here, *that have always been here*, in the living room. "I don't . . . I don't understand . . ."

"Dresses. Flowers. The church. Even the house. None of it's important, Birendra. Those are just things. *Things!* Think about the *promises* you are making. No one should break a promise. You're right to be upset with me. I was wrong to get angry with you. I broke a promise. That red sari was a promise to you, and I broke it, and I was wrong. It doesn't matter that I didn't think you would care about the promise. I made it, and I should have honoured it. You're right. But there are bigger promises, and you need to really think about them before you make them. Most people don't."

"I want to marry," Birendra says, dropping back down on the couch, although her voice wavers. "I love Victor."

"Yes." Leg and arm spasms having run their course, Hardev wheels closer, offering his daughter his good hand. "I know you love him the way he is right now. And the way you imagine he will be in the future. That's what marriage is. Something imagined. A shared imagination between two people. Marriages end because people can't imagine certain things."

His hand is weak, the fingers cramped. "Does it hurt?" she asks, lightly massaging the rough skin. The wedding ring. Where is his wedding ring? She can't recall a single occasion, a single moment, when it has not been on his finger. She looks away. The sewing machine. The crystal water pitcher. The World War II figurines. "Dad?"

"For richer or poorer. Through good times and bad. Think about it, Birendra. Marriage is a contract. You should read that book your mother gave you for Christmas: *Anna Karenina*. You could learn from it. Marriage is a written contract, but also a contract of the imagination."

"Dad, are you moving?" Moths, yes, she will tell her mother and Victor that moths destroyed the red sari—too many years in storage in the basement. It's a good lie. Everyone will be happy with it.

"In sickness and in health."

"Answer me, Dad. Are you moving?"

"Who can imagine this? Really imagine it? Very few—"

"I can't listen to this anymore," Birendra cries, pulling her hand out from under his. "I have to go. I have to go home!"

Stepping over her father's papers on her way out, she keeps her eyes to the floor so she won't have to notice anything else that might be missing.

Dear Dor,

When I was a young man, I made a promise to myself the day I landed at the Toronto airport and took a bus downtown before boarding the train to Ottawa to start my new job and my new life. Waiting for my track number to be called at Union Station, I imagined I too was connected to the land, like a vein in this country's body. I could already feel its lifeblood inside me, the lifeblood of immigrants, pumping in and out of its heart.

So what was this promise I made? Well, I took a look around at all the bright lights, the baggage stands and porters, the hundreds of men with briefcases flying this way and that, taking notes, pouring change into pay phones, waving tickets in the air. I thought about my father, and the mother I never knew, and the aunts who barely spoke to me, and the many things we all miss out on because of death and time. And I promised this: *I will make a good home here.*

Within hours of arriving in Ottawa, I found your mother. Did I ever tell you this? No, I don't think so. And your mother could never have told you, because she doesn't know. The government was putting me up for the night in a hotel not far from the Ottawa train station, but who could sleep? I was so excited I couldn't sit still. If I'd had my tennis racquet with me I might have tried to find someone to play against, but I didn't. I'd given it away to a local club before leaving. I was going to build a new life. I took a taxi to the Market. Oh, those words, *the Market*, reminded me of home, but this place looked nothing like home, and nothing like London either, with its maple syrup stands and leather and fur hats and dark flowers your sister would grow up to arrange, and I asked the taxi driver to follow the square's perimeter two, three times, and then, then I spotted her: your mother standing at a corner holding a bouquet of daffodils. I tried to keep her in my sight as long as possible. I remember thinking how there are always so many things competing for your attention when you first arrive somewhere new, how difficult it is to concentrate, but there I was, my gaze locked on this young woman whose name I couldn't even guess. The taxi drove the route once more, and she was gone.

When we met ten months later in the lobby of the National Theatre (a co-worker had given me a free ticket to the ballet—*Swan Lake*, oh *Swan Lake*), I knew I had found the same woman. She explained that she was a dancer but was studying to become a bilingual speech therapist because, she said, the body was so unpredictable.

I want to make you my wife, I said to her over coffee and two slices of strawberry cheesecake. I cut quite the figure then, dark, tall, with a hint of a London accent, so I could get away with saying things like that.

Your mother said, *What's the rush?*

I made a promise, I told her. *Our children are waiting for us. And their children. And their children. They're saying, Stop all this nonsense. Make this woman your bride so we can leave your imagination and live, truly live!*

And you're listening to them? I see, she replied, pretending to look worried. *What are they saying now?*

I said, *They're saying the worst kind of man is a man without a family.*

Your mother laughed. I had succeeded. She gave me her phone number, and when we did finally get married and she lay down beside me as my wife, she never looked so beautiful and so nervous all at the same time. She was happy. We were both very happy. She had danced for me that night. In our suite. Not *Swan Lake*. An Indian dance it had taken her months to learn. How exhausted she was! Head on my chest, almost asleep after dancing her little heart out, she whispered, *Promise me you'll keep listening to our children. And our children's children. And we'll always be together, a real family.* And I did.

So if I hand this promise over to you, and you keep it in your heart as I have kept it in mine for all these years, do you think maybe, just maybe, it will come true?

Text message from Monique Thériault to Emile Dange:
NOW I KNOW WHY YOU DON'T RETURN
ANY OF MY MESSAGES.
I SAW YOU. LIAR.
YOU'RE GOING TO PAY.

Love fills a lifetime
and a lifetime begins this hour
when the two of us

Birendra Angelique Dange
&
Victor Michael Lane

begin a new life together.
We invite you to share
this day of happiness
on Saturday the fifteenth of May, 2004
at 6 p.m. at the Château Laurier
in Ottawa, Ontario,
Canada

Wedding Day

Guests are greeted at the hall entrance by the happy couple. The Château Laurier's marble and stone fireplaces provide an elegant backdrop for photos of the wedding party and individual guests, while others admire the high ceilings and Edwardian window dressings. Waitresses hoist platters of hors d'oeuvres: cucumber sandwiches, salmon, curried lamb, samosas, and a selection of French cheeses. Red and white wine, vodka and gin martinis are served at two semicircular bar stands. For nearly an hour, the tuxedoed attendants have been guiding the two hundred guests to their tables and place cards. As the head table settles in on the stage at the back of the hall, Victor insists on being the one to wheel Hardev, still without an electric wheelchair, up the short ramp to the one place setting without a corresponding chair.

Train caught on the leg of her chair, Birendra dramatically sweeps it up. The water glasses on the tables are already filled, and Birendra, in an eggshell dress with sweetheart neckline, beaded pearls along the corset and her eight-foot removable bunched train, raises hers and giggles; "Hey, where's my champagne? I didn't agree to *water* in this marriage!" Assuming his spot beside her and caressing her shoulders, Victor plays along; "You're absolutely right! Waiter, please keep my wife as tipsy as possible, so she doesn't change her mind!" Hardev laughs, but Isobel, staring at her daughter, experiences a kind of disorientation. Her child has grown beyond her imagination, into this glorious, smiling young married woman. Victor's three parents—as Birendra refers to them—smile warmly to each other as they check the place cards. Emile fiddles with the microphone and the knobs on the speakers. He didn't want to be the MC, but Birendra insisted. "Shit, brother, you're the only one in the family who won't attract more attention than I will!" Amused by her honesty, he agreed.

Wedding Menu
Cream of Asparagus Soup
Penne in Tomato Sauce with Goat Cheese
or
Spinach and Mushroom-Stuffed Chicken with
Yukon Roasted Potatoes and Carrots
Tea and Coffee
Chocolate Mousse Cake

or

Crème Caramel

plus vanilla wedding cake

"Is my veil still on straight?" Birendra asks her sister, fluffing the white netting around her shoulders. "I don't want to look lop-sided in the photos."

Laughing as she adjusts the comb, Dorothy notes that Birendra has never seemed so comfortable to be Birendra as she does today. It isn't that the exquisite makeup job or the talents of the hair-dressers have turned her into a dark-skinned princess; it's that she looks truly at ease in her new place in the world as Victor's wife.

"Dorothy!" Hardev gets her attention by waving his good hand. "Find out if he needs help with the microphone. You know he won't speak up if something is wrong."

"Not like the rest of us, right, Dad?" Birendra calls out, placing the bridal bouquet of daffodils she arranged herself between the bride's and groom's plates.

Although Hardev does not recognize most of the people in the hall, he shook every hand on the way in, withstanding the pain. Most are from Victor's side of the family, extremely well-dressed, articulate business types, making a good first impression; they asked about his health and wished him the best on this joy-ous occasion, confirming to Hardev that even though he wished she had checked with him first, Birendra had indeed picked an excellent match for herself. *Lucky girl,* he thinks, *to join a family of such distinction.*

Microphone in working order, Emile returns to the head table and the waiters pass out bread rolls and butter, wafting fresh yeasty smells into the air. Isobel understands why the traditional places for the mothers have been switched, and while she was initially grateful to be spared sitting next to Hardev, she now stares at her son—a man she barely knows and only remotely understands— at the other end of the table, and wishes she were seated between him and her husband.

Dorothy slips a wicker basket filled with disposable cameras over her arm and weaves between the tables like a matchstick girl, slinking to one side, then the next, her slim figure accentuated by the yellow mermaid dress with the open back that she and her sister chose way back on Halloween. Seated next to the two fathers is Emile, and Victor's father, Stuart, immediately takes to him. Hardev is happy to see it. The boy will get a professorship with the University of Ottawa, he decides, and his children will live only blocks apart, the best way to live in the world. *You siblings need to realize you have only each other*, he has said often to the boy, feeling it needed to be said.

"Who are all these people?" Emile asks Stuart, as he vacates his seat to begin the dinner ceremonies. "I think I recognize about ten in total."

"That's your new family!" he shouts back, playfully punching the young man on the shoulder in what Hardev would call a London School of Economics way.

If it were not such a special occasion, Emile would contradict him. The strangers removing folded napkins out of water glasses, fiddling with purses and cufflinks, dropping off gifts in silver and gold and white wrapping paper onto silver carts decorated with yellow and white balloons and more of Birendra's daffodils, are *not* his family. While Emile is certain that he loves his father, his sisters, and his mother, he can't even say for sure whether they are his family, or if family is essentially a good thing, something to be celebrated in and of itself. Besides a last name, they share very lit-tle common vocabulary. *What is a family*, he thinks, *but a series of lies and misunderstandings, of broken promises, unfulfilled expectations, of pretending to belong when you don't?* He told Birendra he wasn't seeing anyone important enough to bring to the wedding. He doesn't tell his father about the horrible nightmares or the bouts of panic that grip his chest and stomach at all hours. How can he tell his mother or Dorothy that he's in love with Mohab and Mohab loves him back, but that the whole situation fills him with tremendous aching shame? And who can he talk to about Monique's text message? When he bought the newlyweds the sushi dish set from Bowrings, Mohab helped him pick it out, and he wanted him to sign his name to the card too but of course it was impossible. Emile was able to admit to himself that he might be gay, but he was not ready to admit it to the world. *May you enjoy a lifetime of marvellous dinners together!* he wrote instead, stealing Mohab's suggested message. But what are the odds that Birendra and Victor will stay married when their own parents couldn't? And if they do, what are the odds they won't be miserable? Promises can't save you from misery. And neither can family.

To gain the crowd's attention, Emile clinks his water glass with a spoon into the microphone. Between their seats, Birendra's feet tapping with excitement, Victor affectionately holds her hand.

Clink, clink, clink.

"Kiss!"

"Kiss!"

"Kiss!"

Voices rise in chorus with the spoon, and bride and groom gra-ciously comply. Birendra thinks how sweet it is to kiss in front of so many people this one day of your life; how people invite it, demanding public demonstrations of love they would normally deem inappropriate. Lips puckered in a glossy pale pink, she offers her mouth to him, careful not to spread lipstick over his cheeks. Then, crossing her legs, she feels the small ring that Dorothy pierced into her body rub against her thigh, and smiles at the thought that this ring, like her new white-gold wedding ring, will connect them, that the whole world likewise is connected by rings, some we can see and some we can't. In those few seconds, the tingling sensation moving all the way up to her shoulders and down to her toes, Birendra closes her eyes and vows not only to love and cherish her husband from this day forward but, no matter how far she ends up from them, to also try to think of each sibling and parent as a loved and cherished ring pierced into her heart, even if some of the wounds take a long time to heal.

"Dinner before the honeymoon!" a bombastic male voice yells. A gush of laughter follows.

Clink. Clink. Clink.

"Kiss. Kiss. Kiss."

Gazing dizzily at all these unknown, laughing people yelling a single order, Dorothy wishes she could hear the reverberation of the glass when Emile hits it with the spoon, so she could understand the connection. *It strikes my head sometimes*, she thinks, as Emile continues tapping.

After a few more kisses, the natural cycle of sound subdues and everyone, including the bride and groom, is satisfied with the display, and ready for dinner. Dorothy rises from her seat at Birendra's side on cue, and Emile leans into the microphone: "At this time we'd like to ask our father, Hardev Dange, to say grace."

Dorothy unhooks the brake on Hardev's wheelchair and pulls him from the table. As Hardev concentrates on extracting something from his blazer pocket, she steers him over to the microphone stand. Emile lowers the microphone to Hardev's height while Dorothy adjusts his reading glasses, even though he will not be reading a text; he is simply more comfortable this way. Hardev Dange, father of the bride. His first-born child. *Little flower*, he used to call her. *Our little flower.*

After a smattering of coughs and chair-creaking, Hardev speaks: "Thank you, God or gods, all gods of different names, you are welcome here. Thank you for this opulent feast we are about to receive. Thank you for these beautiful children, who will one day have beautiful children of their own. Bless those children too. And here, Birendra," he says, holding up the small vial, which until a moment ago was wrapped carefully in tissue and hidden underneath the yellow handkerchief in his blazer pocket, "is holy water from the sacred River Ganges, for you to bless them with when they are born. Amen."

"Amen."

"Amen."

"Amen."

The head waiter pops opens a bottle of champagne and the loud burst takes everyone by surprise except Hardev, who sits grinning widely, triumphantly raising the vial of water for everyone to admire as the bubbly is served. Victor's father jokingly grabs his heart. The hall catches its breath and joins in the chuckling. The microphone gives off feedback. A wave of clapping ensues.

"To the bride and groom!"

"To their children!"

"To their children!"

The hall bellows as waiters and waitresses pop open more bottles and bottles of champagne, and guests eagerly push forward crystal flutes. The only one who does not lift a glass is the bride herself. *How wonderful,* people in the crowd tell each other. *She is too overwhelmed with happiness to respond!* And lifting the vial even higher, as high as his good hand will let him, Hardev welcomes all the happiness and joy, wishes the world itself to be on fire with it. Comets flash and implode before his eyes and, breath suddenly short, he surrenders as the boy tries to catch him slumping forward and unconscious off his wheelchair, the last vial of water from the holy River Ganges smashing, as if fated for such a purpose, on the floor.

Emile Dange's Toast for the Night of Birendra Dange's Wedding:
I am pleased to celebrate my sister's wedding with you all. It's no surprise to anyone who knows her that she is the first among us siblings to get married. Not just because she's older than we are (did I mention she's the oldest? Birendra, your secret is out!), but because when we were little and watched commercials together, she'd always point to the screen (this is why she has contacts, I keep telling her, and I don't)—"I'm going to wear that at my wedding, but with a veil," or "I want that as a wedding present"; so if somewhere in that pile there's a pink satin duvet or a Black and Decker rice cooker, I assure whoever brought it that you are going to receive one very sincere thank-you card a month from now—or, knowing my sister, a year from now. But seriously, on behalf of my father and me, it is my job today to officially welcome Victor to the family. Please treat my sister well. A toast to your future happiness. Imagine only the most beautiful life for yourselves!

Three days after his daughter's wedding, as the heavy-set hare-lipped nurse finishes administering a new regimen of insulin injections, Hardev hits the SPEAKER button on his bedside hospital phone—which, as arranged with the phone company, receives calls made to his home number—ending his conversation about his daughter's honeymoon. It would be very difficult for Birendra to cancel the trip at such a late date, he told her, and even if it was possible, he didn't want her to. "Just send lots of postcards," he insisted. Bad enough that an ambulance had to be summoned in the middle of her wedding reception. Bad enough that the boy had to leave before delivering his welcoming toast. Although Birendra maintains that they all had a lovely time, that people danced until two AM after receiving word that Hardev was going to be fine, he's still distressed that his health interfered, once again, and played havoc with a happy occasion. The only comforting thoughts he's had since the wedding have been of his daughter and her new husband roaming the cobblestone streets of Paris arm and arm, stopping for crêpes on the way to the Louvre or the Musée d'Orsay, buying up dozens of Eiffel Tower postcards to mail home.

"Hello?" he hears, as the nurse exits quietly with her swabs and syringes. Then static. "Birendra? Is that you?"

"Um, no. My name is Monique. Emile's . . . friend?"

"The boy's not here right now. He's at the library. I'll tell him you called."

"No, he's not. I called to speak with you, Mr. Dange."

About to hit SPEAKER again, Hardev hesitates. "With *me?*" Did the boy tell his girlfriend that his father was in the hospital and might be feeling lonely, might like to chat? Is this his way of finally introducing them?

"I was your son's girlfriend a little while ago, Mr. Dange, but we are no longer together," she says with exactitude, like a doctor. *Yes, just like a doctor,* he thinks, *and I would know.*

"I'm sorry, young lady, but I don't see what this has—"

"He's with a man. Right now. He's not at the library. He's lying to you, the way he lied to me," she continues, her voice gradually rising. "I thought you should know he's gay, Mr. Dange. I'm sorry to be the one to tell you, but it's true. He's queer."

For a brief moment Hardev thinks this young woman has phoned the wrong room. She's looking for Mr. Ferguson, the man recovering from bypass surgery, right? Or possibly Mr. Yi, who has had a cyst removed and will be discharged later this evening. Or maybe the man on the other side of the curtain, who breathes through a tube and has to call for a nurse every hour or so to drain it. Not Hardev Dange, father of Emile Dange, who studies hard and barely has time for romance in his life, who has never, ever given him any indication to believe, to think . . . Why were strangers always intruding on their family, rearranging things? Bringing their terrible news in all kinds of different forms?

"Are you there? Are you there, Mr. Dange? This is the tru—"

Before she can finish, Hardev presses SPEAKER and cuts her off. Who is she to send him this message? Who does she think she is?

Class | Classe
HOSPITALITY

Flight & Date | Vol et date   Gate | Porte   Seat | Place

9500   18 MAY 2004   5C   35A

▶ 9:20   0174096025

From | De   To | Destination

OTTAWA   PARIS

Name | Nom   Airline use | À usage interne

Boarding Pass | Carte d'accès à bord

Happy Anniversary

Left on the boy's bed, the note is not discovered for several days. The Crown Bank manager is through fooling around. Legal papers arrived the day Hardev returned from hospital. Spring afoot, Mr. Manello has lost interest in negotiating. As Gateway Land Developers cannot build and sell a home on Hardev's property to coincide with the others, it no longer matters if they wait a few months more. The offer for an open-concept large one-bedroom condominium has been revoked. "You must understand that first and foremost we are a business," Mr. Manello said over the phone, not bothering to stop by for coffee or with another box of chocolates. "I'm sorry for your circumstances, but my hands are tied." *What a ridiculous expression*, Hardev thought, *your hands work perfectly well!*

There is no getting around it; he needs to speak to the boy, who Hardev thinks has been flying under his radar since his return home, sneaking in and out with his usual unobtrusiveness or staying at his friend's place, the friend Hardev is not supposed to know about, the one who shattered that girl's ego.

Roccina—a frumpy fifty-year-old Italian housewife whose husband left her two years ago and whose grown sons call her "Rocky," who is now his government-funded housekeeper—enters the boy's bedroom. Air stale, she opens a window to dust and vacuum but sees the note, which has flown off the bed onto the carpet. Speckled glasses on the tip of her nose, she presents the paper to Hardev, who is soaking in a tub of lukewarm water. He must simply accept his nudity in front of any Tom, Dick, or Rocky they send his way. Once he is in a nursing home, it will only get worse. There will be days, he projects, when he won't even be told their names.

"Your son has left?" she asks with mild interest, offering him a towel from the rack. He dries his hands so he can take hold of the note without making a mess of it. She's interrupted his daydream, a daydream he's been having more and more lately, trying to take comfort in the past and ignore the dreary future. Rocky's question forces him to abandon his hydraulics site at a crucial juncture: his workers gathered around him, tools hanging on belts, machines parked on the next road, anticipating Hardev's signal to set the entire apparatus in motion. Instead of the job-well-done speeches, the acknowledgment of all the hard work and thankless repetitiveness it takes to develop a structure that will soon be taken for granted—for once not a bad thought, as they will be released to their homes, their wives and children, to other jobs—he's faced with the boy's stick-like handwriting.

"He used yellow paper," he mumbles, glancing down, his penis floating in the water, his purple nipples drooping. If he doesn't immerse his hands or sink to his chest, he can't even feel the water temperature. *I'm shrivelling,* he thinks. *Gravity defeats me.* And today, today would have been his thirty-second wedding anniversary. Time keeps moving, but I keep sinking. Placing the paper momentarily on the toilet lid, he grips the steel harness to raise himself out of the tub.

"No, no, no." Roccina waves her finger at him. "You get a full half an hour in the tub twice a week. You still have eleven minutes."

Roccina refusing to set his machinery in position to hoist him out, the yellow paper waiting for him, Hardev grabs the ends of the steel apparatus with all his strength. She looks on smugly as he eventually concedes defeat, lowering himself back down into the lukewarm water.

For the first time in years, he wants to hit someone, actually punch another human being—why not this Roccina? This stupid stranger who cares nothing for him or his family?—to revel in the impact of his fist meeting another's flesh and bone.

He dislikes her; he dislikes the way she peels potatoes and the way she spices his chicken; how she opens his bedroom curtains in one aggressive gesture and how she folds his sock toes to the left rather than the right; the slow manner in which she globs on her lipstick before taking out the garbage and the hoglike posture she assumes when she bends over to pick up the pencil she's always dropping; her bizarre appearance in yellow rubber gloves and her pink frilly cooking apron; her thin brown pencilled-in eyebrows; the kettle-whistle pitch of her voice; the way she jams the remote control into his hand; the fact that it takes her more than one try to dial any telephone number properly; the satisfaction on her face when the news reports the capture of Muslims; the Italian songs she sings to herself while washing the floors; and more. This piece of paper is not this frumpy middle-aged woman's message to deliver, just as it was not that young woman's job to deliver the other message about his son. And yet this has been his life. Strangers intruding, delivering messages, indifferently, passionately, angrily, unconcerned how fragile a man already is, or a family, dropping words like bombs. Rodriguez would understand this, and his frustration. He would not let him wallow in a tub of water like a useless washboard. He would get him dressed, ready for action, for defence. The boy is fleeing, surely, to protect himself, not from his friend that Hardev isn't supposed to know about, he suspects, but from other strangers, like this girlfriend, who will not understand. He just hopes his son's fleeing won't result in the boy denying who he is, a form of suicide. Hardev is capable of understanding—love is easy to understand in his view, and to accept; the hard and maddening part for him is the proof that he has known his own son so little that he could not help him accept his new place in the world, that he could not even sense that he'd left. But maybe he left a long time ago, as his mother had, before renting her van and packing up the girls.

"I can't get out myself, you have to help me," Hardev says firmly to Roccina, who has removed her glasses and sits like a fat toad on the fuzzy toilet lid cover, having placed the note on the edge of the sink. "Take the pad of paper off my trolley and go into the boy's room, open each of his drawers and take stock of what he's left behind, if anything."

"That's not part of my job description."

"Are you going to do this for me or not?" Hardev shouts, splashing the tub water in his frustration. "Or do I have to fight my way out of this room? My own fucking bathroom!"

Shuffling to the edge of the toilet, Roccina calmly stores the Windex bottle back in the box of cleaners kept underneath the sink. "It's not part of my job description, Mr. Dange. Nor is it part of my job description to listen to cursing."

"Then will you *please*," Hardev says with forced civility, his urge to strike her even greater now, "check if on the top shelf of the boy's desk, inside his thesaurus, the photograph of his mother holding him in the hospital just after he was born is still there? And check his drawers for a doorknob? Yes, his doorknob! If it's not there, I know he'll be gone for a long time. Are you listening? For God's sake, are you just going to sit there?"

"I don't think I should," she replies, massaging her foot. "I don't want to disturb anyone's privacy."

Maybe she's used to old men having tantrums, Hardev thinks, splashing more water out of the tub in a fury. If she won't hoist him out, at least he can try to get rid of the water that now seems to weigh on him like concrete. "I've lived without privacy for twenty years! Do you hear me, Rocky? This is still *my* house! I deserve to know what is in it and what isn't!"

Not caring if he breaks ribs or causes internal injuries in the process, he throws himself against the tub. What does it matter? He can't feel anything. And there's always something tearing inside him that he can't see. There's something tearing inside the boy, too. He did see it; if he asks himself the right questions, he did see it those many weeks leading up to the wedding. He did, but he could not enter the boy's head or heart to see what was there, what was frightening him, eating him up and paralyzing him. He must have packed while Hardev was in the hospital, must have seen the opportunity to flee, and taken it. And how can Hardev blame him? What does he have to offer? Daydreams? And those daydreams are so fragile; Hardev knows they too are set for demolition, like the houses deemed not nice enough to move elsewhere. Never will he be able to go back to them now. This is the end of a lot of things. The boy left just in time. He is right to study curses, Hardev finally concludes. At least he won't be surprised by all of life's humiliations. People are already moving into the neighbourhood, the vans a regular fixture outside the living-room windows these last weeks. New families—couples whose incomes are comparable to his own before the accident and their children with name-brand clothing and twelve-speed bicycles—eyeing gardens and buying patio furniture, preparing sandwiches and celery sticks for a picnic in one of the many nearby parks, are scurrying around everywhere. The Danges have no place among them. This is their daydream now.

"I'm going to call the agency. I will tell them your son has left. Maybe they can help you," Roccina says matter-of-factly as Hardev, losing his balance, slips back down into the tub. Already halfway down the stairs, Roccina leaves him there as the note from his son floats off the sink, over the toilet, toward him into the spilled water.

Dear Father,
I'm sorry if my leaving upsets you. I can't explain to you exactly why I have decided to leave this way, but I hope

you will understand that it's important for me to be on my own right now and figure out how I will make my way in the world. I hope you will believe me when I say that it is when I think of you and how you persevere despite everything that I know I must do this. I have always avoided knowing myself. Studying is good for this. I've never been strong, but I've been persistent. I'm not ready to face who I am, but I need to start somewhere. You are a real man. I realize that now. I am still a boy. But I want to be a man. I want to be a man someday, Father. I promise you that once I figure things out, I will be. At least I'll try. I don't lack imagination. But doors are such scary things. They really are. Sometimes, I lack courage. Please try not to worry. I'll write soon.

Your son,

Emile

Welcome to the Ambassador
We hope you will enjoy your stay in Tehran
and join us again in the near future

Begrüßen Sie zum Botschafter, wir hoffen, daß Sie Ihren
Aufenthalt in Teheran genießen werden und sich wieder
uns in nächster Zeit anschließen,

Bienvenu à l'Ambassadeur Nous espérons que vous
aimerez votre séjour à Téhéran et nous joindre encore
dans le futur proche

Benvenuto all'Ambasciatore Noi speriamo che Lei godrà il
Suo soggiorno in Tehran e ci congiungerà di nuovo nel
vicino a futuro

Bem-vindo ao Embaixador esperamos Nós que você
desfrutará sua permanência no Teerã e nos unirá
novamente no próximo futuro

Bienvenido al Embajador Nosotros esperamos que usted
disfrutará su estancia en Teherán y nos unirá de nuevo
en el futuro cercano

Father's Day

At exactly two o'clock, after an hour and two large cups of coffee at Tim Hortons debating whether or not this is a good idea, Mohab approaches the asphalt driveway of 90 Ashbrook Crescent.

The post-war bungalow has seen better times: the oak door frame, paint peeling, cracked in spots; the red bricks facing the street discoloured orange and grey; window ledges damaged; several screens torn; deteriorating roof shingles; rusty eavestroughs. The lawn, splattered with splotches of yellow, leads to a rotting wheelchair ramp at the side entrance, the red wood practically white. The black tar on the driveway is the only feature of the property that looks new, like the other much larger houses on the street.

"Please come in, come in," the intercom announces almost instantaneously as Mohab presses the buzzer. *He must be waiting for me*, he concludes.

The screen door sticks a bit before opening. Hardev is seated at a half-circle kitchen table, the straight edge against the wall, a pad of foolscap in front of him. The wooden cupboards and off-yellow diamond tile floor remind Mohab of his parents' home in Scarborough, before his mother pushed for a series of renovations.

"Mr. Dange, thank you." Mohab slips off his shoes on the brown WELCOME mat, each with the other foot so as not to dirty his hands, but unsure whether to extend one to Hardev to shake; he offers a tight-lipped smile instead. Standing in the cramped, stuffy kitchen, the smell of cooked chicken and the heat of the stove lingering in the already humid summer air, he searches his memory for Emile's voice telling him how his father became paralyzed, but is fairly certain that Emile never explained the specific circumstances, only that there was an accident and his father was not at fault but the culprit fled the scene. Mohab never probed any further because it was obvious Emile didn't want to talk about it, but now he wishes he'd asked more questions. With a few more stories about him, maybe the man in front of him wouldn't seem like such a stranger.

With his right arm, Hardev extends his left. His grip is firm but sweaty. Like Emile's, Mohab thinks. A warm face, too. Wide, tired, but warm. And skin just a shade darker, providing a stark contrast to the grey at his temples. "May I sit down?"

"Yes, yes, sit." Hardev indicates the folding chair to his left.

Resting his hands on his lap, Mohab scans the room, imagines

Emile sitting in the very chair he now occupies, eating breakfast with his father (did they eat breakfast together? Cereal? Porridge? Scrambled eggs?) or playing a round of cards (Crazy Eights or Old Maid?) on the semicircle table, or loading the boxy brown dishwasher. But just as quickly, as his eyes dart from the microwave to the stove with the missing numbers to the stack of *Ottawa Citizen*s on the other folding chair, tucked in the corner, the many Emiles he has conjured disappear, wiped away in a bold streak like chalk off a blackboard.

"Are you doing alright without him?" Mohab asks finally.

"Yes," Hardev replies, looking the young man in the eyes. "I am."

"Well . . . Mr. Dange," Mohab admits, trying to keep his own gaze straight, "I'm not. I'm not at all."

Hardev flips over his pad of paper on the table. "In the fridge there's a pitcher of cranberry juice. Why don't you pour us each a glass?"

Mohab rises from his chair, walks toward the white two-door fridge with freezer on top but stops before opening it, recognizing Emile's handwriting on a piece of paper like the paper on Hardev's pad, although blurred in spots, possibly water-damaged, pinned to the freezer with a twenty-four-hour-pharmacy magnet. He reads the goodbye note two, then three times. The phrase *I'm not ready to face who I am* rings like the tune of a song he once loved but now denies he listened to. No note was left for him.

"He lied to you too, I see," he says, searching the top shelf of the fridge for the pitcher of juice.

"Oh, no. My son doesn't lie well. Never could. Too much like me." Two glasses of cranberry juice are filled almost to the rim as Hardev extracts two bendable straws from a blue mug of pencils with a hand imprint on the side—the same mug Emile used to keep at the graduate lounge. "The boy, my son, he used bendy straws in his drinks too, after the accident. At first I scolded him, saying it was wasteful and lazy. But then one of the homecare ladies I had, a woman named Nina—she drank a single Blue Light every afternoon—said it was his way of putting himself in my shoes, pretending to be me."

They both dip straws into the juice and sip. The room remains like this for a good two minutes, no one speaking or making any significant motions, two still men with their private thoughts.

Eventually Mohab speaks: "My grandfather ran a hotel in Iran. The Ambassador, it was called. One of his favourite sayings was, *Because each man must carry his own burdens, once in a while he must let someone else take care of his luggage.*"

"Your grandfather is a smart man."

"He's dead now," Mohab blurts, then raises his hand. "I mean . . . let me start again. My name is Mohab. I'm not sure if I told you on the phone."

"No, you didn't." Hardev takes another good look at the young man, from his shoeless feet up his beige corduroy pants, his light blue Polo shirt, to his thick black, well-combed hair. "You told me you were a good friend of my son's and you wanted to speak with me. How do you spell *Mohab?*"

"M-O-H-A-B," he says, as Hardev turns his pad of paper over again and with evident effort, his hand shaking all the while, writes it down. Each then goes back to his drink.

Glass almost empty, Hardev asks, "What can I do for you?"

"I'm a good cook and gardener, Mr. Dange. I'm also pretty handy at fixing things. I noticed your roof could use some work, and that ramp on the side, you must have a hard time getting around. I doubt Emile told you much about me, if anything, but

I was his friend. His . . . close friend. I'm a PhD student at Ottawa University, the same department as Emile, anthropology, but I think I'm going to move to religious studies. I want to move to religious studies to study Islam—my family never taught me much about it, I've learned on my own, and I'm curious, I want to know more than I know. My mother taught me how to sew. My grandfather taught me how to build a radio in an emergency. He died. I'm living week by week at the residence right now, but I don't want to live there anymore and I don't want to go home. I can't go home yet. Or I guess I'm trying to figure out where home is."

Bright summer light from the sink window streaks into the kitchen and onto Hardev's face. He squints while staring at Mohab. "Are you asking to work for me?" he asks. "I don't have money . . ."

"No. Yes. I know you have a spare room now. I want to help you. I can pay rent. The same rent I pay at the residence. But here is a house and company. I know this sounds strange, but you must miss your son. I miss him. I miss my grandfather." Mohab sighs, wipes his hands on his pants, and looks up again. "I'm not so much asking to *work* for you as to *live* with you."

Straightening the wheels on his chair, locking them into place, Hardev watches as the young man wipes his hands once more on his pant legs. "Why would you want to live with me?"

"As I said, Mr. Dange, I'm not doing very well. I'd like to be of use to you. I wanted to visit before, help out with the house, the stuff Emile told me needs fixing, but I could never convince him that I . . . I need to use my hands. Be close . . . to where he used to be. I'm sure you observed your son. You must know a little about what I'm talking about. I just started to understand where I belonged and then he left and I can't think what do to. I lost my

grandfather in December. I lost Emile the same time you did. But
I'm the one who's lost. I would have followed him if he had wanted
me to. I can't go home. I want to make another home."

Worried he's babbling and confusing the man, Mohab opts to
shut his mouth, refrain from drinking any more cranberry juice,
and wait for Hardev's pronouncement—even if he calls him crazy
or tells him never, ever to get in touch with him or his son again.
He's risked it, and now there's nothing left to do but see the
dealer's hand. His grandfather had a saying about that, too: *The
smartest gamblers have already reconciled themselves to losing. It's the only
way to place an honest bet.* As Mohab stares at Hardev—his oval
brown eyes and bushy eyebrows, the square cheeks so much like
his son's—he knows he has placed an honest, if not necessarily
winning, bet.

"It's not good to wait for someone who will likely not return.
Trust me, son," Hardev replies, still squinting as he removes the
cloth bib from his lap and wipes his mouth.

As the light changes direction, the warm beam shifts from
Hardev's face to the refrigerator, the yellow note with Emile's
blurred handwriting on it aglow as if in a fluorescent frame. "It
must be worse to live without hope, though, don't you think?"

If someone should know the answer to Mohab's question, it's
Hardev. He has to admit on that score the young man is right.

Dear Hardev,
I am writing you because I know that sometimes our telephone conversations are difficult, and the diabetes affects
your energy levels. I don't want to add to your stresses, but
I'm sure Rousseau Secondary must have already contacted you
to discuss Dorothy's communication studies assignments,

those "Dear Dor" letters she wrote as her final project over the last school year under the pretense that they were written by you. She handed them in to her teacher, Mr. Scobie, in May, and the school psychologist showed them all to me, the whole stack. I can't quite figure out what the order is, or if there is one, but what is clear is that she has a very large imagination. I know she didn't get that from me. You were always the one who could imagine anything. Have you read them yet? Of course, she's wrong about an awful lot, but some of her errors, at least, seem to be deliberate. She certainly knows that you became paralyzed in a car accident outside Kanata. She knows it was a reckless kid who hit you, not even drunk, just reckless, who then fled the scene. I've told her so many times, and she's heard me telling Birendra not to trust anyone out on the road, to always be as careful as possible. Not that you weren't. Of course you were, but sometimes there's nothing else to say to your children except *Be careful.* So I'm not sure why she insists on pretending you were paralyzed in India in a hydraulics accident, but she must have her reasons. On the other hand, she sometimes imagines details correctly that she couldn't possibly know! One thing's for certain—I am in agreement with the psychologist on this one—she needs to spend more time with you and get to know who you are. I'm sure you don't need me to tell you that she loves you, that all your children love you, that never stopped—whether you want to believe it or not, I still love you—but I know it has been hard over the years to get everyone together in the same place to just talk and enjoy each other's company. I should have forced the children to spend more time together. You've always been right about this. I thought it was better if they came to it on their own, but we both know everything in life is hard work. I'm sorry. Dorothy has told me that she wants to move in with you for a while if that's alright with you. I thought it best to wait until you settled in again after the wedding and your time in the hospital before broaching the subject. What do you think?

Also, she's determined to defer her acceptance to Ottawa University no matter what I say, insisting she needs a year off and wants to work full-time at the tattoo parlour. The place is nice actually, friendly and clean, and the henna work she's added to their services is quite lovely. Plus, she's with hearing people all the time, and drawing. If you take her in, she'll pay you rent. I think it's important for her to learn how to budget and keep accounts and see what it's like to earn a living. Birendra paid me rent once she finished school. And it came in handy. The townhouse is small, but the utilities and property taxes keep going up. Plus girls—how much they always need! I think with Birendra married and moved out, I will sell the place. Dorothy knows you are going to keep a tenant too (a friend of Emile's, right?) and she's fine with the arrangement. I'm glad you decided to get a boarder. I'm sure you can use the help around the house, and the money. It must not be easy to keep that house running. I admire you for it. I really do.

And I'm sorry about Emile. You must miss him terribly. I'm worried about him, but I think he's more like you than he knows. He's strong, mentally. Still, I can't imagine why he chose to leave this way. He didn't bother to tell me at all, you know, though Dorothy didn't look surprised when I relayed your message. She just made some joke about run-away brides, but she looked sad. All my years as a speech therapist, and I am no closer to understanding why we communicate the way we do than when I was a toddler banging soup cans together to get my father's attention.

I know you've always said your door is open night and day to your family, and so I'm hoping Dorothy can stop by this week to work out the details. Have pity on her if she makes mistakes. She's young, and a bit troubled too, I think. She needs you, Hardev. I wish I had noticed her banging those soup cans earlier.

Je souviens,

Isobel Dange

Subject: Rebirth

Dear My Mystery Girl,

I see you've finally returned to earth to find your clothes and to claim me! Thanks for the letters. I'm well. It's taking a little while to adjust to all the new things running through my head—the *sounds*—I still can't believe I'm hearing sounds—little blips and bleeps and flits and zips and ahhs and ughs and all kinds of things—not that I actually understand all of them—but I'm keeping my spirits up when things get hard to figure out or to bear. They call this period *rehabilitation*, but I call it *rebirth*. I feel like I have to learn how to do everything all over again, like I'm a stranger to myself with this new added sense to take into consideration. My mother is really pleased, of course, as is my father, though he's quieter about it, literally leaves bells and whistles around for me to try out. I get tired pretty fast though, and sometimes I turn the cochlear implant down so I don't have to take any more in. I don't think that's cheating really. It's like when I need to put a book down to think for a little bit about what I just read. I'm trying to figure out who I am now, I suppose. I hope I'm still your Kite though. I hope you're still House, or Mystery Girl, or Dorothy, or whoever you want to be. Just be there when I return, OK? And tell me a story. I'm sure you'll have a few more by then.

Peace and love,

Kite

Dear Dor,

My mother died shortly after childbirth and my father refused to look at me for an entire year. Two spinster aunts from my mother's side told me this—they moved in hoping for the chance to marry my father themselves. They fed and bathed me, and changed my diapers. They were women with "sewing hearts," my father said, meaning women with hearts that could be tailor-made to suit the situation. Though they possessed decent dowries, they had both contracted small-pox as children, and the money was little compensation for faces and bodies with deep pincushion scars.

I thought childhood was a waste of time, and I wanted to grow up more than anything in the world. Leave the village, my father, India, the mother I had barely known, the aunts who followed me around with flour on their hands—take my white sneakers and wooden racquet and go somewhere else where my name was not yet recorded or even imagined. My aunts would say, *No one can thwart his own path.* And I used to think, *Why not go around?* I was young and full of dreams.

It's not unique to suffer disappointment. I think it's an important lesson, as ordinary as tea and coffee and plastic. Every time I flick on the television or flip through the *Ottawa Citizen* or brush my teeth or stir soup or answer the telephone, I witness people experiencing the limitations of their own existence. We can't even conquer the common cold. What chance do we have to overturn life? Think of Adam and Eve. God said, *Go take a walk. And while you're at it, take a walk across the entire earth and have babies and then have more babies and then maybe you'll forget that you're mortal and the earth has no use for you.*

This doesn't mean that I don't believe in you or think you will have a wonderful life. I do. Just accept that it won't be on the terms you've laid out for yourself. I am telling you this because when the promises you made to yourself either as a child or as a young woman are eventually broken, I want you to forgive yourself.

My father used to say that my mother died so her child could live. I used to think, *Is there not enough room for us all?* But the truth is, Dor, there isn't. You have to make a home where you can, with whom you can. If the door is locked, use your imagination. Perhaps a window will open. Perhaps somewhere in the house is your father, waiting to hear you breathe your new name over the intercom.

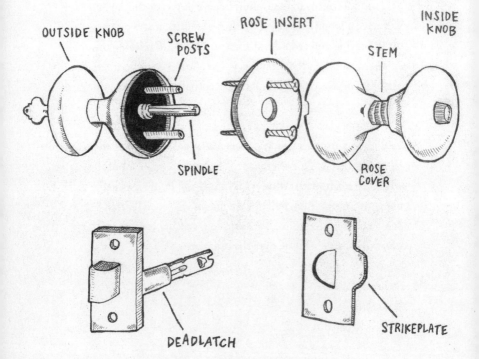

OUTSIDE KNOB

SCREW POSTS

ROSE INSERT

INSIDE KNOB

STEM

SPINDLE

ROSE COVER

DEADLATCH

STRIKEPLATE

Canada Day

The green moving van is not much wider or taller than an SUV. Hardev locks his wheelchair just outside his bedroom door so the Slavic mover can obtain easy access to both the stairs and the stairlift Mohab has managed to fix. The tall, wiry man sprints past Mohab, who has just arrived back from the library, with two cardboard boxes.

"I'm not late, I hope!" Mohab calls.

"No, no. The mover's early. It's alright," Hardev replies.

"I bought clam chowder and the Nutri-Grain bars Harry says you like," Mohab tells Dorothy in the doorway between the kitchen and the living room. He takes a clear garbage bag filled with sweaters and jeans out of her hands.

"Thank you," she voices, and adds the sign, pressing her fingertips to her lips and then lowering her hand outward.

Mohab mirrors the gesture.

"Not bad," she voices, handing him a hat box.

"I'm learning sign language," he says sheepishly.

"It's a difficult language," she signs and says. "But we'll learn together." Noticing her father's feet in the metal wheelchair, stirrups peeking out from his bedroom into the upstairs hallway, Dorothy asks loudly, "What's your name?"

He finger-spells: "M-O-H-A-B."

"Nice to finally meet you, Mohab," she signs and says with a wink. "But you can choose another name if you like. Today my name is Kite. Tomorrow it might be Collage, or Accident, or Neighbour, but today it's Kite. Today I can fly anywhere in the world as long as I have a little wind at my back."

"OK, Kite, nice to meet you," he replies, a bit tentatively but with amusement, winking back. He flings the garbage bag across one shoulder, transfers the hat box to his other hand, and heads up the stairs and down the hallway. Dorothy follows, a stack of four shoeboxes filled with her letters and diaries in her arms.

Hardev keeps his eyes on the scurrying mover, the duct-taped cardboard boxes and small pieces of bedroom furniture he's carrying in his arms and on his back: a computer desk, electronic equipment, a vanity table, apprenticeship tools, books and magazines. On his fourth trip, with a swivel chair—its front legs on either side of his neck, the bottom ones along his waist—he halts abruptly at the top of stairs, gesturing toward Hardev's wheelchair.

"My father is the same back home," he says, producing the bill from his front pocket and placing it on the plastic tray on Hardev's knees. "It's not easy."

Not contradicting him, Hardev asks, "What were you back home? A chemist? An architect?" He's grown accustomed over the years to immigrant tales of bankrupt businesses, unhonoured BAs and master's degrees, doctors without Canadian or American certification who are painting houses, mixing gravel, delivering pizza, or turning him over on his side at night.

"I moved furniture," he shrugs. "Same as here. People are always leaving places. Evictions, new jobs, just sick and tired of the same place, the same people. Moving is a steady business, steady line of work."

"I suppose it would be," Hardev defers, never having considered it before.

The mover points through the small hallway window to the workers already repainting a neighbour's house another colour, and building a patio deck. Hammering has been steady all day, and sanding too. "Some people want bigger houses, others smaller. Some want lots of stairs, others no stairs. Some people love the place they're moving into, others hate it but can't afford any better, or need to stay in the city or take care of some dying relative or kid whose mother can't put food on the table. Some you can tell everything's going to stay in boxes, it's temporary. Others, once they put down their things, you'll need a crowbar to separate them from their stuff. But happy or not, everybody's got to live somewhere."

"They said on the news this morning that today is the busiest moving day of the year. Even though it's a holiday, tens of thousands of people spend it unloading boxes and hauling furniture.

Like us, I guess," Hardev adds, raising his voice at the end to speak over the buzzing of lawnmowers.

Mohab and Dorothy exit her room, one right after the other, and stop beside the mover, who has put down the swivel chair for a moment. "I came to this country in 1990 and at the immigration office they gave me an address for an apartment complex in the west end. The elevator was down, I had to drag up my three heavy bags, all the stuff I owned in the world, but the whole time I was thinking, I'm now in Canada, Canada, where I wanted to go to get away from all the craziness back home—I'm from Russia—it didn't matter that things might get better, I wanted a new place, a better place. Truth be told, I wanted to get away from my family, find a woman, put together a new family here. And this lady, she's running down the hallway, now *my* hallway, cigarette hanging out of her mouth, holding a baby to her chest, a small baby, and she's got this pot of rice and she's flinging the rice at a little boy who's screaming back at her, big wet tears on his face. I think then: *This country is bullshit, like any other. People need better imaginations than this.* I go into my new apartment and shut the door. Next morning, I find a junk shop and buy myself a television." Snorting as he laughs, he points to the bill. "I just need you to sign there. Bottom of the page. I can make an X for you. Do it all the time. You'd be surprised how many people can't write. You have a good excuse, though."

"No, no. I can sign for it. I can sign," Hardev assures him, as the mover pulls a pen out of the same pocket as the bill. He has witnessed such quick retreats into the past by immigrants before, and finds it rather comforting, as if one's memories were on some endless escalator that rises often and then disappears, leading nowhere, but nonetheless in motion. Does it matter if some are embellished here and there, added to, subtracted from, or perhaps untrue? They are good stories, and serve a purpose. Today, the mover's story makes Hardev appreciate even more the fact that his daughter and this new boy, Mohab, are moving in with him.

"You can postdate the cheque for up to a week if you want."

"I'd rather pay today. I always try to stay on top of my bills."

"Yes, yes." The mover pulls out a calculator the size of a credit card from his jeans pocket. "It's the best way."

Hardev ignores the mover's pen, using instead one attached to a string under his shirt, a black pen left in his mailbox almost two years ago by Gateway Land Developers, the first time they contacted him—logo in white on green, the G in the company name made to look like the handle of a gate—and he thinks about his decision to keep it, to not throw out a perfectly useful pen, and how pleased he is that he can use it today. It doesn't hurt to sign his name, only to remove the cap.

"What else can I do?" asks Mohab, his forehead and underarms sweating heavily from the heat as well as the strain of carrying his own luggage into Emile's old bedroom.

"Just get settled in, then you can help hook up Dorothy's communication devices. We might live in the oldest house on the block, but we'll be the most technologically advanced!" Hardev laughs, the Gateway Land Developers' pen bobbing on the upper half of his belly, as Dorothy heads down to the kitchen to check if the cranberry concentrate is thawed.

Two minutes later, she serves up a tray of glasses for them all, the mover included, although he is outside on the phone, working out his next pickup and drop-off.

"We have a present for you, don't we, Dad?" Dorothy voices after handing out the glasses, tugging Mohab's sleeve. Her hand is cold from the frozen can, and her touch makes him shiver.

"What? You didn't have to get me a present!"

Hardev throws his hands up in a gesture of mock surrender. "It was her idea."

"Women!" the mover pipes up, turning at the stairwell with two pillows and a yellow comforter. "Every day is a day for presents!"

Having missed his comment, Dorothy grabs her canvas backpack from the corridor and pulls apart the strings at the top. The mover, hands empty again, grabs his glass of cranberry juice and gulps it on his way down the stairs. "Don't close your eyes," Dorothy says to Mohab.

She places a new gold-painted doorknob, the same as the ones Hardev hid in his children's Christmas stockings, into Mohab's open palm. He wraps his hand around it and squeezes. Does he understand? Hardev wonders. Did the boy tell him about Christmas? When Hardev realized that the boy had left, his only comfort was that he had indeed taken his doorknob with him. "Tell him," Dorothy urges.

"This is yours, for your room. But you're to take it with you wherever you go," Hardev explains, as Dorothy extracts her own doorknob, and a pencil case with a screwdriver and a number of tiny gold screws, from her backpack.

"Doors are the most important features of a house!" Hardev exclaims, patting Mohab on the shoulder. "Emile left a feng shui book behind. I've been reading all about it. We have to be careful how things are arranged. We don't want money or good fortune leaking out of the house."

"I don't know how to install mine," Dorothy voices, dropping the screwdriver into Mohab's shirt pocket.

He turns the screwdriver this way and that, pretending not to know which end is which. "We'll have to learn this together too, I guess."

Aware all of a sudden that the lawnmowers, sanders, and hammers have ceased, Hardev checks his watch. "Dinnertime."

"Pizza!" Dorothy signs, flipping imaginary dough in the air.

"Good. Then ... fireworks?" Mohab makes the sign, his hands dancing, opening up like bursts of flowers. "Maybe that will be my name today: Fireworks. Is that OK?"

"Fireworks!" Dorothy repeats.

"Pizza it is," Hardev decides. "Then go downtown for the celebrations, and I'll look for you on TV."

Dorothy and Mohab head to their adjacent rooms at the other end of the hall to set up furniture, unpack clothes and books, hook up equipment, and, Hardev anticipates, install their doorknobs. Both are obviously excited, and are being very kind and conscientious to each other, though the politeness has a formal quality to it. That will soon change, though, he assumes. They'll be arguing like brother and sister in no time. And Hardev, sitting in his wheelchair at the top of four stairs in his post-war bungalow home, looks forward to it. All those years, he and Emile on their own, he almost forgot how comforting the sounds of siblings teasing, bickering, even arguing, can be. Isobel is wrong, he thinks. It isn't language that's the issue. Language can only do so much for people. Then we all end up banging cans to be heard. The most important thing is imagination. While this isn't the way he originally imagined saving the house, the arrangement is fair and, he has to admit, suits them all rather well. Even Mr. Karkiev is satisfied: *It's a practical solution, Mr. Dange. It might just work.* And why not believe that this time a stranger intruding into their lives is not going to leave him paralyzed, make the boy flee, cause his house to be taken from under him? No—as when Rodriguez joined the fold, this boy may bring them some needed comfort and joy, understanding and compassion.

The front door of 90 Ashbrook Crescent swings open again just as Hardev hears Mohab close the one to the boy's bedroom. *Mohab's* bedroom now. Or *for now*, he reminds himself. Mohab's bedroom. Dorothy's bedroom. But others are welcome. Others can return. They can return any time.

The mover swipes his copy of the receipt off the tray on Hardev's lap and exits once again, the door shutting behind him.

Three postcards:
Dear Dad and Emile,
Victor and I are enjoying Paris immensely, although the euro is killing us! Yesterday: the Mona Lisa and the Eiffel Tower. Today: we picnicked at the Luxembourg Gardens. Tonight: a boat tour on the Seine. The boats leave every hour, so if it rains (as it is prone to do) we will munch on crêpes until the sky clears and redeem our ticket later. How lucky we are! Everyone is in love here! No children anywhere. This is a place for lovers, not families . . .

Dear Dorothy,
Everything is a work of art here. I think you would enjoy it. I'm glad too that Mom taught us French, as they don't like to communicate much with you if you can't speak their language. Then they really look at you with tourist disdain. Who knows? Maybe someday Victor and I will live here. I've been pushing him to find out whether there might be any openings in France. I think I can convince him. He loved his

wedding gift, by the way. He said he was surprised by both my courage to go through with the procedure and how imaginatively I hid it from him for months. He said it with pride. I love him, Dorothy. I really do.

Your Sis

Dear Dad and Emile,

... We're going to see this stunning city from every point of view if we can! I am also going to try to keep up with the Oprah Book Club summer reading chart for *Anna Karenina*, though why Anna hasn't appeared yet and I'm already fifty pages into the book is beyond me. (Victor says these postcards might not arrive for a month due to a postal strike here. Parisians are always on strike. It's what makes them a "civilized society," people joke. That and the fact that they know when to leave their children with a babysitter. By the time you both get this, maybe we'll already be home!)

Love,

Mrs. Dange-Lane

house—house—house = many houses

P. S.

Dear Reader,

> *Well I see by the clock on the wall*
> *That it's time to bid you one and all*
> *Goodbye . . .*

You have reached that point in the novel when we all must bid you adieu.

Tolstoy was wrong. No family is the same. And who says happiness is what families need? What about doors, windows, staircases? Ears and mouths? Shakespeare was right: *A man may see how this world goes with no eyes. Look with thine ears! Nothing can be made out of nothing.*

Please feel free to construct your own fictional family and rearrange over time as you see fit.

> *Adieu mon vieux, à la prochaine*
> *Goodbye 'til when we meet again . . .*

THE AUTHOR

Acknowledgments

Imaginary people, like real people, need protection, inspiration, and transformation now and then. I would like to thank everyone who has supported this novel throughout the writing and publishing process. Thank you to Hilary McMahon, for believing in this book from the beginning, and fighting for it. Thank you as well to Nicole Winstanley, Natasha Daneman, and the Westwood Artists team for your tireless efforts. Thank you to the people at Doubleday Canada, particularly publisher and editor Maya Mavjee, editors Martha Kanya-Forstner and Lara Hinchberger, and copyeditor Gena K. Gorrell, who all contributed to this book in important ways. I am very grateful for the hard work, the sensitivity, and the warmth with which you've carried these characters with you. Thank you to Barry Callaghan, Claire Weissman Wilks, and the entire Exile Editions gang, for supporting my endeavours, and for publishing an excerpt from this novel in the 120th anniversary issue of *Exile: The Literary Quarterly*. Thank you to Richard Teleky, for being one of the most intelligent readers in the world, and one of the greatest friends too. Thank you to Dr. Iris Gorfinkel for explaining medical procedures and other logistics after hours. Thank you to York University, the Humanities Division, the English Department, the Creative Writing Program, and Graduate Studies, for supporting my work. Thank you to Winona McMorrow and Matt Carrington for research assistance. I would like to acknowledge financial support from the Ontario Arts Council Writers' Reserve program (several grants were awarded to me from this program, and I am most grateful for them). Also, thank you to the Women Writers Salon of Toronto; our little group of wine-drinking, book-debating ladies has been a great comfort on many occasions. Many thanks to Tim Hanna and Tracy Carbert, for being such wonderful friends, and for going out of their way to assist in any way possible, and particularly for helping put together the book's images. Thank you to Tara Bursey for your amazing drawings. Thank you to Avtar Uppal, Jit Uppal, Jen Hacking, and other family members, for teaching me an awful lot about family that went into this book. Thank you to all friends for your ears, and most of all for your laughter.

Lastly, thank you to Christopher Doda, for loving each version of this novel, just as you've continued to love each version of me.

HOLIDAY, VACATION, IDLE
Tap the thumbs of the "5" hands, palms facing, to the armpits with a double motion.
Hint: Sitting back with your thumbs under your suspenders with nothing to do.

VALENTINE'S DAY
Use both "v" hands, palms toward body, to trace the outline of a heart on the chest.
Hint: Initialized sign indicating the location of the heart.

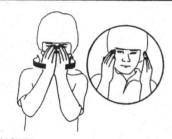

HALLOWEEN
Move open hands from together, palms toward face, outward to side of face.
Hint: Removing a mask.

THANKSGIVING
Starting with the open right hand, palm facing mouth, and the open left hand slightly forward, palm facing face, move both hands outward and upward drawing up and extending fingers as they move.
Hint: "Thank you" and "give" directed toward God.

CHRISTMAS
Flip the "c" hand, palm down and knuckles forward, to the right, ending with palm up. Note: Can be done with two hands.
Hint: Opening a present.

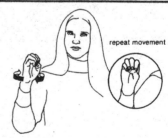

EASTER
Twist the "e" hand back and forth.
Hint: Initialized sign.

PERMISSIONS CREDITS

Grateful acknowledgement is made to reprint the following:

Page 76: John F. Kennedy stamp © Snem | Dreamstime.com

Page 108: Lighthouse. Reprinted by permission of the Canada Science and Technology Museum, Ottawa, Canada.

Page 124: The Noble Qur'an © Paulcowan | Dreamstime.com

Page 162: "Floorplan;" Page 194: "Make Your Mark;" Page 236: "Your Hearing Aid and You;" Page 298: "Ostrich and Kite;" and Page 380: "Doorknob" by Tara Bursey. Reprinted by kind permission of the artist. All illustrations copyright © 2008 Tara Bursey.

Page 218: "Sonnet LXXXIII" from *100 Love Sonnets by Pablo Neruda*, translator Gustavo Escobedo. Reprinted by permission of Exile Editions, Toronto, Canada, and the translator. Copyright © 2004.

Page 258: Half box of chocolates © Zeneece | Dreamstime.com

Page 336: Henna tattoo on hands © Stockshoot | Dreamstime.com

A NOTE ABOUT THE AUTHOR

PRISCILA UPPAL is a Canadian poet and fiction writer born in
Ottawa in 1974. Among her publications are five collections of
poetry: *How to Draw Blood From a Stone* (1998), *Confessions of a
Fertility Expert* (1999), *Pretending to Die* (2001), *Live Coverage* (2003)
and *Ontological Necessities* (2006); and the novel *The Divine Economy
of Salvation* (2002), published to critical acclaim in five countries.
Her work has been translated into numerous languages, and
Ontological Necessities was short-listed for the prestigious Griffin
Prize for Excellence in Poetry. She has a PhD in English Literature
and is a professor of English at York University in Toronto. For
more information please visit priscilauppal.ca.

A NOTE ABOUT THE TYPE

To Whom It May Concern has been set in Adobe Jenson (aka "antique" Jenson), a modern face which captures the essence of Nicolas Jenson's roman and Ludovico degli Arrighi's italic typeface designs. The combined strength and beauty of these two icons of Renaissance type result in an elegant typeface suited to a broad spectrum of applications.